The Royal Sorceress

TO PAULINE AND KATE,
WITH LOVE
CHRIS

JAN 2014

The Royal Sorceress

Christopher Nuttall

Elsewhen Press

The Royal Sorceress
First published in Great Britain by Elsewhen Press, 2012
An imprint of Alnpete Limited

The use of the typeface Goudy Initialen was
graciously permitted by the designer Dieter Steffmann.

Elsewhen Press, PO Box 757, Dartford, Kent DA2 7TQ
www.elsewhen.co.uk
British Library Cataloguing in Publication Data.
A catalogue record for this book is available from the British Library.
ISBN 978-1-908168-08-5 Print edition
ISBN 978-1-908168-18-4 eBook edition

Printed and bound by CPI Group (UK) Ltd, Croydon, CR0 4YY

This book is a work of fiction. All names, characters, places, colleges,
and events are either a product of the author's fertile imagination or are
used fictitiously. Any resemblance to actual events, organisations,
places or people (living, dead or undead) is purely coincidental.

Dedication

There are a great many people who have followed my writing from when I started to the present day, too many to name for fear of missing someone out. But one person deserves to be mentioned because she was there at the start.

It was my grandmother, Ellen Nuttall, who gave me my first books and encouraged me to read and – later – write for myself. I therefore dedicate this book to a wonderful person I miss dreadfully.

Christopher Nuttall
Kota Kinabalu, 2012

Chapter One

re you paying attention to me?"

Lady Gwendolyn Crichton looked up at her tutor, deliberately allowing a languid expression to cross her face. Henry Morrison was the latest of the tutors her mother had selected for her, a pimply-faced youth who had won a scholarship to Oxford – a scholarship that had paid for lessons and lodging, but very little else. His desperation to make ends meet – and to afford to match the lifestyle of his richer contemporaries – had ensured that he'd accepted the position without asking too many questions. He was the seventeenth tutor Gwen had endured since coming into her powers and, if she had anything to say about it, he wouldn't be the last.

"I am listening carefully," she assured him, in the airy voice that irritated her father and drove her mother into fits of rage. Poor Morrison was no match for her. "Pray, continue. I am agog."

Morrison gave her a long look and then turned back to his book. Gwen sighed inwardly. It was a shame he wasn't more handsome, or she would have flirted with him in the certain knowledge that it would have impelled her mother to dismiss him at once. But there were some things she couldn't bring herself to do, even if the rewards seemed likely to be vast. She would just have to find another way of convincing her mother to find another tutor. It wouldn't be the first time, after all.

"As we covered yesterday," Morrison said, "the American rebels made a serious tactical error when they allowed their ragtag army to be cornered near New York. They were unaware of the Talkers assigned to General Howe's army, which allowed him to coordinate his activities on a scale the

Americans could not begin to comprehend. The traitor Washington's army was trapped and forced to surrender, bringing the period of outright warfare in the Americas to an end."

Gwen smiled and pretended to listen. There was only one subject she wanted to study and Morrison, whatever his other qualities, was not permitted to teach it. Indeed, as far as she could tell, he had no magic whatsoever. He certainly didn't know much about the history of magic, or how it had flourished since it was put to work in the service of George III. Women, as a general rule, were not expected to study magic, let alone apply it. As the eldest daughter of Lord Rudolph, Undersecretary of State for Foreign Affairs, Gwen's course had been set a long time before she'd grown into maturity. She would learn how to be a respectable aristocratic housewife, marry a man her parents chose for her and bear his children. No one had anticipated that Gwen would develop magic, or that the rumours surrounding her would make it impossible to find a proper suitor. At seventeen years old, she knew that she should already be married.

She ran a hand through her long golden hair, her lips thinning into a frown. She didn't want a husband, or a family; she wanted to learn about magic. But it was not a career path for a respectable young woman, or so she had been told. There was no way that her parents would allow her to set out on her own path. They wanted her to serve them by marrying someone who could help her father's career, or – failing that – to die an old maid. Gwen couldn't expect anything better from life, magic or no magic. For a highly intelligent young woman, it promised to be a fate worse than death.

Morrison cleared his throat again. "Please pay attention to me, Lady Gwen," he said. "I still have to cover the aftermath of the rebellion in the colonies."

"I am paying attention to you," Gwen said. She gave him a smile that should have chilled his blood. "You're very…interesting to watch."

"I just said that you had a leg growing out of your chest," Morrison said, with some irritation.

"I thought you were being metaphorical," Gwen said. Her smile widened, to the point where Morrison looked away, unable to meet her gaze. There was a reason Gwen hadn't been allowed to go to school, even the expensive finishing schools that turned young ladies brains into mush. Her father knew better than to turn her loose on other young ladies, or tutors who couldn't devote all of their time to her. "It was an interesting parable to the case of the Americans…"

"It was not," Morrison said, hotly. He was only a year or two older than her, but he was already schooled in not allowing his betters to irritate him. It was just a shame that he hadn't met anyone like Gwen before. "You're not paying attention to me."

Gwen sighed inwardly and drew on her powers. Her skin seemed to glow with bright light, before flames appeared around her, illuminating her body. Morrison stumbled backwards in shock, one hand reaching for the decanter of water before he caught himself. To someone utterly unfamiliar with magic, it would have looked if Gwen had spontaneously burst into flames. The heat would scorch the chair, the table and Morrison himself if he got too close.

He stared at her for a long moment, and then almost ran out of the door. Gwen watched him go, slowly pulling the magic back inside herself. It wasn't his fault, she told herself, even though part of her felt a guilty thrill at how she'd scared him half to death. He was just her mother's tool in the endless battle to turn Gwen into a proper young lady, one who could make her mother proud. But a life spent as the wife and helpmeet of a suitably aristocratic young man was Gwen's worst nightmare.

She pulled herself to her feet and headed over to the desk. Morrison had left his books behind him and she opened one of them at random. At least he hadn't been *that* bad a history teacher. History was also not a subject for young ladies, but her mother had reluctantly agreed to allow her to study it in exchange for an hour's practice with the harp every day. Music was *the* thing in High Society these days and a young woman who could play was assured of finding a husband, or so Lady Mary believed. Gwen doubted that anyone could play the harp well enough for a prospective husband to overlook her other failings.

The book was written in dull tones, somehow sucking the excitement out of the Anglo-Spanish War of 1799, yet Gwen was midway through a description of the Battle of Cuba when the door burst open and Lady Mary stormed into the room. Gwen's mother had the same blonde hair as her daughter but, where Gwen was slim, her mother was alarmingly fat and energetic. Lady Mary had always said that she'd married beneath herself, even if Lord Rudolph had been an up and coming politician in government. The Undersecretary of State for Foreign Affairs wasn't exactly a powerless post.

"Gwen," her mother snapped. "What did you do to poor Henry?"

Gwen sighed inwardly. Her mother always brought out the worst in her. "I was bored, mother," she said, sardonically. "His lessons were driving me insane."

"And you will drive *me* insane," her mother snapped back at her. "How do you think you will get a good husband if you keep doing...*that*?"

"Most of the men you have introduced me to are cads of the first order," Gwen said, imitating the tone her brother had used during his teenage years. Like most aristocratic men, he'd spent them gambling, drinking and whoring – although Gwen wasn't supposed to know about the whoring. At least her brother knew better than to try to lord it over her, no matter what the Church said about the duties of a sister to a brother. "I would sooner marry a muckraker than any of those weak-chinned vagabonds with titles."

Her mother purpled. "And you'd be lucky if you married anyone," she said, tartly. "It is not *right*, in a respectable society, for a woman to practice magic."

Gwen's eyes flashed and she felt the familiar pain behind her eyes, the sense that her magic was flaring up and demanding an outlet. She clamped down on it hard. Her father might be able to tolerate her scaring the staff, but losing control and harming – or killing – her mother would be disastrous. His reputation would be utterly destroyed. If she'd had proper training, perhaps it would be easier to control her magic. Young male magicians didn't burn down houses by accident; they learned how to do it on purpose.

"I have no wish, my darling mother, to marry anyone," she said, flatly. "You may as well stop trying to shove me into the arms of any passing nobleman. I will not marry him."

Lady Mary glared down at her daughter. "You seem to be unaware of your place in society," she said. "You were born into great wealth and power. Your position means..."

"That I have to do what I am told," Gwen said, dryly. Her mother had said the same thing almost every day, ever since the day Gwen's magic had first flared to life. She'd been nine years old at the time, verging on womanhood. Her life had turned upside down that day and would never be the same again. "You would prefer me to be like Lady Cecelia?"

"She does do honour to her parents," Lady Mary pointed out.

"Cecelia is the most boring person in the world," Gwen said. "All she talks about are horses and men, mainly the horses. Her parents have bought her over a hundred horses and a small staff to take care of them. And she can talk about nothing else!"

Her mother scowled. "It is more womanlike to care about horses than…"

There was a knock on the door and Lady Mary stopped in mid-sentence. The door opened, revealing a maid, one of the younger ones. Like most of the servants in Crichton House, she had nowhere else to go. Gwen's reputation drove away servants who found employment elsewhere – but then, what could one expect from the lower classes? They expected her to wear black and cackle to herself while drowning eggshells in a caldron, or having midnight orgies with the devil and his servants. In some ways, Gwen envied the servants. They might face Lady Mary's temper or the back of her hand, if they displeased her, but at least they weren't suffocated under her towering ambitions.

"Begging your pardon, Lady Mary, Lady Gwen, but Lord Randolph requests the pleasure of Lady Gwen's company in his study," the maid said. She was short, with curly brown hair and eyes that refused to look up from the ground. Gwen terrified her. "He said it was urgent."

"You've probably upset Henry so much he's given in his notice," Lady Mary said. Her voice could have cut through glass. "Go and see what your father wants, child. I'll start looking for a new tutor."

Gwen nodded and left the room, heading down the long corridor to her father's side of the house. She rarely entered his study, if only because he flew into a rage at the slightest hint that anyone had tampered with his papers. Gwen had spent many happy hours in the library as a child, but now that she wanted more advanced books to read – particularly books on magic – her father had refused to buy them for her. And, as a woman, she wasn't allowed any resources of her own. Whatever she inherited from her parents would go to her husband.

She stopped outside her father's door and hesitated. Her father was a gentle man, outside his work, but she knew that he was growing increasingly exasperated with her. God alone knew what he would say; he might even decide to marry her off to someone, with or without her consent. Or perhaps he would do worse, if there *was* anything worse. Shaking her head, she lifted her hand and knocked twice on the hard wooden door. A moment later, her father's voice bellowed for her to come in.

Her father's study was a cosy room with a roaring fire, several shelves of books and a number of comfortable chairs. He wasn't alone, she realised in shock, as she recognised Lord Mycroft, one of her father's peers at work. He was an immensely fat man with sharp, intelligent eyes, wearing a suit that failed to conceal his spectacular bulk. Beside him, another man sat, wearing a black cape that covered his suit and holding a top hat in one hand. He looked up at her as Gwen hastily bobbled a curtsey and his blue eyes seemed to peer right into her very soul. His pinched face and greying hair suggested that he was old enough to be her grandfather; for a moment, Gwen wondered if she was about to be introduced to her new husband. The thought was absurd, she told herself firmly. Her father wouldn't have invited Lord Mycroft to anything that wasn't strictly government-related. It was strange enough seeing him outside his normal routine of office, his club and home.

Lord Randolph was as thin as his wife was fat, a hard-worker who had made himself rich and earned a peerage through careful speculation in the British shipping industry. He had pioneered the use of airships to connect Britain with Europe, Russia and even the Ottoman Empire, a trade that had brought the British Empire closer together. Lady Mary had the blood to ensure that her son rose to the very highest levels of society. It had been a match made in heaven.

"Gwen," her father said. He didn't seem annoyed with her, which suggested that Morrison hadn't managed to complain to her father or hand in his notice. Perhaps he was just having a cup of tea with the cook. Tea was good to settle one's nerves. "You know Lord Mycroft, of course" – Gwen nodded – "and this is Master Thomas, the Royal Sorcerer."

Gwen stared at him. She had had no formal training in magic, and she'd had to learn by herself, but even she had heard of the Royal Sorcerer. The post belonged to the strongest magician of unimpeachable loyalty to the Crown and the British Empire. Only two magicians had ever held the post, if she recalled correctly. They'd both been men, of course.

"Charmed," Master Thomas said. He took Gwen's hand – Gwen fancied there was a tingle of magic as his hand touched hers – and raised it to his lips, kissing the air just above her bare skin. "I have wanted to meet you for quite some time."

"Thank you, sir," Gwen stumbled. She rarely met anyone who had impressed her on first glance, even King George IV. The Royal Sorcerer had wanted to meet *her*? He could have visited at any time and Lady Mary would have been more than happy to play chaperone. "The pleasure is mine."

Lord Mycroft cleared his throat loudly. "The Empire has something of a problem, Lady Gwen," he said. His voice was sharp, as penetrating as his blue eyes. Lord Mycroft was a genius, a man who had made his own place in government. He had no discernible vices, or indeed any interests at all outside making the government run smoothly. "Our monopoly on magic has slipped over the past two decades."

Gwen nodded, without speaking. The French and Spanish had originally persecuted the magicians who had appeared within their borders, even though magic had given the British Empire some of its most stunning victories. It was too much to hope that the Kings and Emperors of Europe – or Russia, or the Ottomans – would not eventually accept and even condone magic practiced in their name. Britain might have ruled a vast empire, but magicians seemed to appear almost at random. A slip in the magical monopoly would be disastrous. At the very least, any war with the French or Spanish would then be fought on even terms.

"It was originally hoped that a new Master Magician would appear who could take Master Thomas's place when he retired," Lord Mycroft continued. "At first, we had high hopes for one young magician who entered the service of the Crown, but matters came to a bad end. Finding people with the required…qualifications is not easy, and of course not all of them are suitable for the most sensitive post in the country. Master Thomas has convinced us that we must look outside the traditional boundaries for recruitment."

"Lady Gwen," Master Thomas said. "We first became aware of your magic during that...unfortunate incident when you were barely nine years old. Your parents were contacted by the Royal College and asked to keep an eye on any further development of magical potential. It was seriously considered to offer you a chance to train with us, but various other events prevented us from making a formal offer until now."

His sharp eyes met hers. "I need an apprentice," he said, flatly. "Would you be interested in serving your country as the next Royal Sorcerer?"

"Royal Sorceress," Lord Mycroft corrected.

"I..." Gwen broke off, astonished. She hadn't dared hope that they would make an offer of training, let alone offer her a post in government. If she succeeded Master Thomas, she would be the most powerful woman in Britain since Elizabeth I. And there had been people who had whispered that Queen Elizabeth had been a witch, although they hadn't dared whisper it very loudly. "I would be honoured."

Automatically, she glanced over at her father. Lord Rudolph wouldn't like the idea, she was sure, but if Lord Mycroft was involved then the Prime Minister, Lord Liverpool, would have a hand in it somewhere. If he refused to allow Gwen to apprentice herself to the Royal Sorcerer, his career would hit a brick wall and he knew it. Lady Mary would not be charmed with the idea of her daughter leaving home as an apprentice, rather than a wife, but what could she do?

"I have provisionally granted my consent," her father said. His voice was under tight control, but Gwen was sure that she detected a hint of...concern. Lady Mary was *not* going to like it, not even slightly. On the other hand, Gwen *would* be mixing with blue-blooded aristocratic magicians. She might find a much better match among their set. "Should you refuse, of course...?"

Gwen smiled. Her father loved her, despite everything. He hadn't even taken a cane or his belt to her when she sent tutor after tutor fleeing in horror. And he wouldn't have allowed Lady Mary to marry her off to a man she detested.

"I won't lie to you, Lady Gwen," Master Thomas said, quietly. "The position is difficult and very dangerous. You will be pressed to the limit; you'll have to learn magic quicker than anyone else your age. We wouldn't offer you the chance to learn if we didn't think that you were capable of it, but we will understand if you reject the offer."

Gwen didn't hesitate. "I would be honoured," she repeated. It was everything she had ever dared to dream of, when she allowed herself to consider a life without her social obligations. "Thank you, sir, thank you!"

She found herself dancing out of the room, leaving the adults behind to talk through the details of her apprenticeship. Her mother was waiting outside, looking angry enough to curdle milk. Perhaps she had some way of listening to her father's meetings, or perhaps the Butler had told her who had come to visit.

Gwen jumped in before her mother could say anything. "Guess what, mother," she said. "I'm going to be the Royal Sorceress!"

Her mother fainted dead away.

Chapter Two

avendish Hall," Master Thomas said, quietly.

Gwen peered through the window as the carriage came to a halt. She saw iron railings, surrounding a small garden – and a massive black building, sitting only a short distance from the Houses of Parliament. The statue positioned neatly in front of the building was of an elderly man, staring down at her with an expression of quiet amusement at the world. She didn't need Master Thomas to identify him as Professor Cavendish, the man who had first put the study of magic on a scientific footing. The British Empire owed its current supremacy to one man, and his disciples had never let anyone forget it.

The coachman opened the door and Gwen slipped through the hatch, jumping neatly down to the pavement. Her mother had tried to convince her to wear one of her formal dresses, but Gwen had ignored her and donned a light blue dress that clung to her body in a faintly scandalous manner. It also didn't billow up or hamper her when she tried to run. She would have preferred the trousers she'd worn out in the country estate, where she'd learned to ride with her cousins, but that would have been a step too far. Everyone knew what kind of woman wore trousers in civilised company, particularly the people who weren't supposed to know anything of the sort.

Outside, the air around the building seemed pregnant with possibility. She turned her head from side to side as Master Thomas strode up to the gate, holding a silver-tipped cane in one hand. The gate slid open without any visible means of locomotion, suggesting magic to her eyes. He beckoned her to follow him up the path to the house and she did, pausing long enough to take a closer look at the statue as they reached it. Professor Cavendish seemed to be smiling at her personally.

The doors in front of the building swung open as they approached, revealing a surprisingly ordinary lobby. A handful of men wearing black suits were on guard, but apart from a handful of surprised looks at Gwen they showed no visible reaction to the new arrivals. Gwen realised that they had to be trained magicians, ready to react at once to any hint of magical attack – or waiting for instructions from Master Thomas. They all looked tough and capable, although she knew that that might be an act. High Society taught the nobly born how to conceal their real feelings.

They passed through an archway into a long, gilded corridor. It was lined with portraits, starting with the latest official portrait of King George. A copy hung within every patriotic house in the land. Another showed Field Marshal Arthur Wellesley, the first Duke of India, who was currently Commander-in-Chief of the British Army. His many conquests in India – painting the subcontinent pink – had earned him far more than just a comfortable position in the very heart of Britain. Gwen knew – from her mother's gossip – that the Duke of India was tipped as a possible Prime Minster when Lord Liverpool finally shuffled off the mortal coil.

"David Kendrick," Master Thomas said. He pointed at one of the portraits with his cane. "The very first magician to enter the service of the British Empire."

Gwen halted in front of the picture, studying it. Kendrick had been thin, almost painfully so; his eyes seemed sharp as knives within a pinched, almost unhealthy face. And he'd been a magician...judging from what she knew, Kendrick would have seen service at New York, helping to coordinate the attack on the city that had destroyed the American rebels. She wondered, just for a second, what he would have made of her. Who knew what sort of man Kendrick had really been?

A thought struck her. "I thought that Professor Cavendish was the first magician."

"The Professor had no magical talents of his own," Master Thomas said. He seemed content to wait for her to finish studying the portrait before leading her onwards. "He was merely the person who discovered the first magicians and outlined their powers in terms...that would be accepted by the King and the Church. There may well have been others before Kendrick, but they passed unnoticed."

"Or were burned at the stake," Gwen said, remembering some of the horror stories from Spain. The Inquisition had developed a nasty habit of burning witches, who were often lonely old ladies whom no one liked very much. It was impossible to defend oneself against a charge of witchcraft – and anyone could denounce a person and be believed. Even the worst excesses of Bloody Mary's reign had never come close to matching the horror birthed in Spain.

"True," Master Thomas agreed. "One thing you will learn as you study magic is that most of what the common herd knows about magic is actually untrue."

Gwen wanted him to expound upon that, but instead he strode off down the corridor and she had to move swiftly to keep up with him. They walked past hundreds of paintings, ranging from the surrender of George Washington to a group portrait of the first magicians, until they reached a flight of stairs heading down into the basement. Master Thomas strode down the stairs, which narrowed until they were barely wide enough for two people walking abreast. The door at the bottom was locked, yet there was no keyhole. Master Thomas placed his hand on the handle, closed his eyes for a long moment and the door clicked open. Inside, there was a dark tunnel leading into the distance.

Master Thomas grinned at her, held one hand in the air and generated a ball of light. Gwen watched, entranced. She'd had some success generating light herself, but it had never been as steady as the light he produced from nowhere. A silvery glow illuminated the bare walls of a passageway that seemed to lead on for miles, deep under London. She looked up at him and saw him smiling. It struck her that he loved showing off – and as Royal Sorcerer, he was not supposed to show off his powers. Gwen wanted to tell him that she didn't mind, but she couldn't find the words. Instead, she watched as the ball of light wandered away from his hand and led them down the corridor. It was, she realised, a simple defence against intruders. Only a magician could light his path down the passageway.

"Or someone with a lantern," Master Thomas pointed out, when she asked him. Gwen flushed. She ought to know that magic wasn't everything. "But no ordinary locksmith could get through the door."

He looked at her for a long moment. "I want you to concentrate here," he said, as they left Cavendish Hall behind. "Tell me what you feel."

Gwen screwed up her face in concentration. There was nothing, beyond a slightly musty atmosphere and a tingle in the air from the ball of light. She kept walking...and felt it, suddenly. An urge to turn and run, a sense that something was badly wrong, a sense that she could barely take another step forward...she pushed forward, gritting her teeth, but she slowly came to a halt. An invisible field hung in the air, mocking her. She couldn't go any further forward.

"I can't go any further," she said. Her emotions seemed to be spinning out of control. She couldn't tell if there was something blocking her way, or if she was suddenly too terrified to go any further forward. Only sheer bloody-mindedness kept her from running – that, and her reluctance to show weakness in front of Master Thomas. She didn't want to convince him that she was just another weak female, someone who needed a man to hold her hand at all times. "What is it?"

"A complex zone of emotional repulsion, infused into the tunnel," Master Thomas said. He took her hand and the sensation vanished instantly. "Only twenty people have permission to enter the tunnel network. Anyone who broke in without permission would find himself frozen and held until we discovered him. Someone with powerful magic – like you – might be able to escape, but they wouldn't be able to actually break into the network."

Gwen looked up at him. "Are you sure?"

"There's enough magic infused into this part of the network to repel almost anyone," Master Thomas said. "Even I would have great difficulty in escaping."

They walked onwards, into the network. The walls were no longer bare; they were lined with different paintings, some explicit enough to make Gwen blush. Master Thomas ignored them magnificently as they reached a door set into the walls . He tapped it with his cane. A long moment passed and then the door slid open, revealing another flight of stairs. Gwen rolled her eyes behind Master Thomas as he led the way up and through another door. This one opened into a richly decorated living room. A set of gold-edged chairs dominated the room, along with the inevitable portrait of the King. This one looked to have been painted during the period when he'd been the Prince Regent, wearing a blonde wig and looking surprisingly thin. The opposite wall held a painting of a rosebush. Gwen wondered absently if it was the rosebush George III had attempted to put on the Privy Council. It hadn't been long after that that his son had effectively assumed his powers.

She looked up at Master Thomas. "Where are we?"

He smiled. "Haven't you guessed?"

The double doors at the far end of the room opened, revealing a dark-haired butler with a faintly contemptuous sneer on his face. His brown eyes were surprisingly intelligent; they glanced once over Gwen, and then met Master Thomas's eyes. They exchanged a long look of wordless communication, and then the butler beckoned for them to follow him into the next room. It was even more richly decorated than the last room, but it wasn't the decorations that caught her eye. The man climbing to his feet was King George IV.

Gwen gaped at him, and then remembered her manners and went down on one knee. She knew she wasn't supposed to look directly at the King – it had only been a few years since her coming out at the Palace, where she'd been introduced to High Society – but she couldn't help it. King George was alarmingly fat, his hair – half-concealed by yet another wig – was thinning out, and his eyes lingered for several seconds too long on Gwen's bodice. His relationship with Queen Caroline hadn't been good before the Queen had died, Gwen recalled; Lady Mary had happily shared rumours about the King's many illegitimate children and affairs, even though properly brought up young women weren't supposed to know anything about such matters.

"You may rise," the King said. His voice was surprisingly deep; Gwen recalled hearing that George IV was clever and could be remarkably well-informed on any subject, but he preferred to leave politics to his ministers and spend his time enjoying himself. His ministers, many of whom would remember George's father, probably preferred it that way. "We welcome you into Our presence."

He returned to his seat as Gwen rose, feeling oddly

flustered. The last time she'd seen the King had been when she'd been presented at Court. There had been an entire ritual to learn, one that marked both her entry into High Society and her position as a potential bride. Nothing had ever come of it, not when Gwen's magic had been the subject of rumours long before she'd grown into a young woman. She had never been taught how one should address the King in private. The thought of a private interview with him would have sent her mother into hysterics. Gwen wouldn't have been able to leave the house until her mother had briefed her on all aspects of Royal Protocol.

"Thank you, Your Majesty," Master Thomas said, gravely. Behind him, Gwen was suddenly aware of the butler's presence, ready to advise his master if necessary. "I am happy to report that Lady Gwen has accepted the offer we made to her."

The King studied Gwen for a long moment. Gwen almost flushed under his steady gaze. "It is necessary that We have a Royal Sorcerer to handle the affairs of magic," he said. "The post requires qualifications and abilities beyond that of any normal magician. Master Thomas has served Us well in this post for the last ten years and it is Our dearest wish that he should continue to serve Us in that manner for many years to come."

Gwen said nothing. She honestly didn't know what to say.

Master Thomas stepped forward. "Your Majesty, I have no intention of dying in the very near future," he said. "However, Lady Gwen's education in matters magical is sadly deficient and she will have to study hard to make up for lost time. And then there is the danger of the French or Spanish raising their own corps of magicians. They have not forgiven us for the sound thrashing we gave them over the last century."

"Very true," the King agreed. "Lady Gwen – are you prepared to accept the responsibilities that go with the position of Royal Sorcerer? You may find that you assume the position far sooner than anyone expected."

Gwen swallowed, hard. "Yes, Your Majesty," she said. She couldn't help feeling that she was in over her head, but it was too late to back out now. "I am."

The King rose to his feet. "Then kneel," he commanded, "and give me your hand."

Gwen held out her hand and the King took it in a surprisingly strong grip. "Do you, Lady Gwendolyn Crichton swear to serve Us all your days, to uphold the laws of Our Kingdom and defend it against Our enemies, whoever they may be? Do you accept the position of Apprentice to the Royal Sorcerer, to do him honour and obey him in all matters, to learn from him and eventually take his place when God calls him home?"

"I do," Gwen said. It struck her suddenly that it reassembled a marriage ceremony and she had to fight down an insane urge to giggle. "I swear before God."

The King held her eyes for a long moment, and then he stepped back, releasing Gwen's hand. Gwen, unsure of what to do, remained on her knees. There was a long pause and then Master Thomas stepped forward. His large hand took Gwen's and shook it, firmly.

"I accept you as my apprentice," he said. "I vow before God the Father, God the Son and God the Holy Ghost that I will educate you, clothe you and prepare you for the day when you take my place."

He released Gwen and motioned her to her feet. "Thank you, Your Majesty," he said. "We will begin training tomorrow."

The King motioned Gwen forward and removed a ring from his finger. "We hereby invest you with Our ring," he said. Gwen took the ring and held it. It was too large to fit on her fingers. "Should any question your fitness for the position, you may show them Our ring as an expression of the confidence We place in you."

Gwen found herself unable to move until Master Thomas nudged her, gently. "Thank you, Your Majesty," she said. "I will do you honour."

"See that you do," the King said. "You are dismissed."

Outside, Gwen found herself almost dizzy on her feet. She had been rushed forward, without any time to think. Master Thomas caught her and steadied her before she could fall over. "If you wish some refreshments," he said, "we can find something to drink in the Palace before we return to Cavendish Hall..."

"No, thank you," Gwen said. What she really wanted was a chance to sit down and reflect on the day's events, but she had no idea how she could say that out loud. The butler's constant presence behind them was a reminder that anything they said would be reported back to the King. Her mind caught up with him and she stopped. "The Palace is connected to Cavendish Hall through the tunnels?"

"There are always broadsheet writers outside the gates," Master Thomas said. He sounded vaguely disgusted. "We bring people in through the tunnel network if we don't want them noticed and written up in the newspapers."

He looked up as the butler passed him a sheaf of papers. "Thank you, Edmund," he said. He led Gwen back to the stairwell and paused at the edge of the steps. "Please advise your master that we will keep him informed of progress."

Gwen said nothing until they were back in Cavendish Hall. The magical barrier seemed to have vanished, or perhaps it only affected people who were trying to break *into* the Palace. Master Thomas led her up four flights of stairs and into a large set of rooms. One of them was dominated by a four-poster bed; the others with empty bookshelves, empty tables and one of the largest bathtubs Gwen had ever seen. A maid who was busy cleaning was unceremoniously invited to leave the room. Gwen stopped dead as she saw a set of familiar suitcases. Her mother had already packed for her – or, more accurately, she'd ordered the family's maids to pack for her.

"These are your rooms, Lady Gwen," Master Thomas said. "I suggest you spend some time resting and preparing yourself, then you can join us for dinner at six and then catch an early night. Tomorrow is going to be a very busy day."

"Yes, Master," Gwen said. It struck her suddenly that she'd sworn to obey him in all matters. He had effectively taken her father's authority over her for himself, simply by taking her as his apprentice. It was far from uncommon among the lower orders, but for a nobly-born woman? "Are we going to start learning about magic?"

"You have a great deal to learn," Master Thomas said. "But you're very bright. I'm sure you will pick it up in no time."

Gwen could only hope that he was right.

Chapter Three

wen's first lesson on magic began early the next morning.

She hadn't been sure of what to expect, so she'd dressed herself as simply as she could, wearing the dress she'd worn when running outside in the country. Breakfast had been a subdued affair, with a handful of magicians staring at her and wondering – clearly – what she'd done to deserve the position of apprentice to Master Thomas. They'd all been male, she'd noted, all young. She was going to be more isolated than she had thought.

Master Thomas had escorted her into the classroom personally. It was somewhat disappointing to her eyes, a stone room with a set of tables, rough wooden chairs and a handful of maps hanging on the walls. A bowl of water dominated one corner of the room, reminding her of the bowls they'd used to dunk for apples during one of her birthday parties, before she'd come into her magic. The teacher, who had been introduced as Doctor Norwell, had looked equally unprepossessing. He was a grey man wearing a grey suit and wig; one of those men who had been born old. Master Thomas identified him as a theoretical magician, a person who studied magic, but without any actual talent of his own. If his subject hadn't been so fascinating, Gwen knew that she would have started playing tricks on him within seconds.

"The first important thing to remember about magic," Doctor Norwell started, in a fussily precise voice, "is that most of what the common folk know about magic is wrong. More nonsense has been written about the subject of magic than any other subject, even though magic has only been seen as a subject of...ah, *legitimate* study since Professor Cavendish first documented its existence. A popular book of magic, distributed despite the ban, states that one can summon demons by dancing naked in the forest at night. That is, quite simply, untrue. Many magicians come to study with us and wind up having to unlearn a great deal before they can proceed."

He paused, long enough to fix Gwen with a pale stare, before continuing. "The *second* important thing to remember about magic," he said, "is that the study of magic is only in its infancy and there are a great many things that even the Royal College of Sorcerers doesn't know about how it works. We have isolated a number of magical talents and attempted to put them to use serving the Crown. There may be other talents as yet undiscovered. There may be facets of the known talents that are poorly understood. Every year, scientists attempt to find a unifying theory that would link all the talents together. None of them have even come close to success. Some talents seem simple and easy to understand. Others make little sense.

"What we do know is that magical talents breed true. The children of a magician or a person with an undeveloped magical talent will generally have magical talents of their own. However, this seemed to follow no logical rules. Theoretically, the child of a Mover and a Charmer should share both talents. In practice, they tend to get one."

Gwen frowned. "Talents?"

Doctor Norwell scowled at her, clearly resenting the interruption. "We have isolated ten different talents so far," he said. "There are persistent rumours of an eleventh talent, but despite careful research we have not been able to isolate it. With only a handful of exceptions, each magician will have just one of the talents. Their precise power level and skill will depend upon training. Some people with magical potential simply never bother to develop their talents."

"And a number," Master Thomas put in, "may never discover that they *have* a talent."

Doctor Norwell nodded. "I shall begin with Blazers," he said. "Master Thomas, if you would..."

Master Thomas held up his hand. A flame started to flicker over his skin, eventually becoming a pillar of light that danced over the ceiling before fading back into nothingness.

Gwen felt a tingle as she stared at the light, remembering how she'd summoned light and heat herself. Master Thomas had far more skill than she'd ever been allowed to develop.

"Blazers manipulate energy," Doctor Norwell said, flatly. "All of their powers revolve around their particular talent."

He nodded to Master Thomas. "Infusers push magic into an inanimate object," he said. "The magic can be keyed to perform certain tasks, such as not permitting anyone to open a particular lock without the correct key. Again, the magician needs extensive training in using his power before he can amount to anything. Changers also push magic into an object, but instead of infusing the object with power they alter it at a molecular level. As you can see..."

Master Thomas picked up a small block of wood from one of the tables and held it in front of Gwen's face. Before her eyes, the block of wood slowly transformed into a bar of gold. He put it down in front of her and it started to resume its original shape and colour. Gwen was almost disappointed. A Changer could presumably create enough gold to keep himself in luxury for the rest of his life.

"Making it stable takes years of practice," Master Thomas said. Perhaps he'd had the same thought when he'd been trained himself. "Which is lucky; we have too many problems with forged coins already."

Doctor Norwell cleared his throat. "Movers, as the name implies, move things," he said. Master Thomas gestured and the block of wood flew out of Gwen's hands, circled the room twice and then dropped into the bowl of water with a splash. "A Mover with enough power can literally fly, although only a handful have enough power to do it without losing control and falling to their deaths. Do *not* try to practice without having someone in place to catch you."

Gwen had to smile. She'd often dreamed of riding on an airship and staring down at London below, but her father had never permitted her to fly on one of his craft. Now, if she mastered the talent, she could fly on her own. The thought was tantalising. Whatever it took, she vowed silently, she would learn to fly.

"A Talker can send messages from his mind to another person's mind," Doctor Norwell continued. If he was aware of her thoughts, he showed no sign of it. "The more powerful ones can actually read thoughts, although they can be delayed by someone with the mental discipline to shield their thoughts. Talker Kendrick was the first proper magician and, as you will have heard, he and his fellow Talkers were the key to the great victory in the Americas. There are now Talkers scattered around the globe, linking the British Empire together."

As you can hear, Master Thomas said, directly into Gwen's mind. She jumped as if she had been stuck with a pin. Just for a second, she felt helplessly naked and vulnerable, wondering if he could read her mind. And then she realised that she could form a barrier with her thoughts and keep him out. He tipped his hat to her by way of acknowledgement.

"Charmers can influence other people through their voices," Doctor Norwell said. "Master Thomas..."

"Gwen," Master Thomas said, *"why don't you put both hands on your head?"*

Gwen's hands were already in motion before her mind had realised what was going on. She fought to slow her treacherous hands, yet it was impossible. Her hands rested against her head for a long moment and then the effect abruptly vanished. She stared at him, honestly shocked. A man with that kind of power could rule the world.

"Charm has its limits," Doctor Norwell said, by way of explanation. "You will discover that you can block the Charm, once you develop sufficient mental discipline. The more complex the Charm, the more likely it is that someone will realise that something is wrong and start acting against the Charm. A very powerful and subtle Charmer will be able to alter someone's mind slowly, over the course of a few months, until their victim has no idea what has happened to him. It may well be the most dangerous of the talents."

"That's a manner of opinion," Master Thomas said. "They can all be very dangerous in the wrong hands."

"Seers and Sensors seem to go together, although we don't fully understand the nature of their powers," Doctor Norwell admitted. "Seers can see any point on the planet through their mind's eye, but the talent has limitations we have been unable to understand. Sensors pick up flashes of information from people and objects they touch, sometimes including visions of the future. We do know that such visions are often misleading, with a single exception. It is said that each Sensor sees their own death perfectly – and that there is no way of avoiding the end."

"That has never been confirmed," Master Thomas said.

Doctor Norwell nodded. "Weres can change their form from human to a specific animal," he continued. "A werewolf would move between human and wolf forms, sometimes with perfect control, sometimes with no control at all. They can be incredibly dangerous as they combine wild animal ferocity with human intelligence."

There was a long pause. "I see," Gwen said, finally. There was really too much information, but she had been listening raptly. The little demonstrations helped. "And what is the tenth talent?"

Doctor Norwell looked at her, sharply. "Necromancy is the darkest of the talents," he concluded. "Necromancers have the ability to manipulate the dead. Some can reanimate dead bodies and send them out as revenants, others can summon up ghosts and ask them questions. For once, the Vatican and the Church of England are in full agreement. Necromancers are to be killed on sight. They are simply too dangerous to be allowed to live."

"Ten talents," Gwen said, slowly. She'd never thought of her magic as falling into separate talents. And Master Thomas... "What talents do you possess?"

"There are a very few individuals who possess all of the talents," Master Thomas said. "They're the ones who can combine the talents into a single whole far more than the sum of their parts. We call those magicians Masters and there have only ever been five of them in existence. Two are dead, one is missing and presumed dead – and the last two are you and I."

Gwen stared. "I have all the talents?"

Doctor Norwell cleared his throat. "Surely a person as intelligent as yourself would have noted that you were drawing on several different talents," he said, sardonically. "Your powers are not restricted to a single category."

Gwen flushed. Hardly anyone had called her intelligent before – or even expected her to be intelligent. A succession of tutors had resented trying to teach a girl, particularly one who was expected to look pretty, attract a good husband and spend the rest of her life raising children. Gwen knew that she was smarter than her brother, but she'd been warned never to make an issue of it. It hardly mattered. The rumours that had swirled around her had ensured that she would never find a husband her mother would consider acceptable.

"Very few people outside the Royal College know about the talents," Master Thomas reminded him, gently. "Like you said, most of what people know about magic is simply untrue – and Gwen was never even given the overview provided to government ministers without any actual talent themselves."

He smiled at her. "You and I will be spending many hours developing your talents," he said. "You will discover that people with a single talent are often better at using it than myself, even though I am a master. When restricted to one talent, I often lose practice duels and tests against my opponent. You will probably also discover that you are better with some talents than others. I myself am capable with Blazing, Moving and Charming, but my talents for Changing and Infusing are far more limited."

Gwen leaned forward. "And what about Necromancy?"

Master Thomas stopped smiling. "You will not be permitted to practice Necromancy," he said, flatly. "If you are caught using Necromancy – or even suspected of using Necromancy – you will be hauled in front of a Court and Charmed until you can hide nothing. If the charges are sustained, you will be executed. Necromancy is simply too dangerous to be used."

Doctor Norwell cleared his throat. "Only two years ago," he said, "there was a revenant outbreak in Manchester. The military had to be called in and the whole area had to be burned to the ground. We believe the outbreak started by accident; a small child who had lost her grandmother accidentally came into her powers and reanimated the grandmother's corpse. And everything just spiralled out of control."

"I understand," Gwen said. She winced, inwardly. Had she ever come close to practicing Necromancy? She might have stumbled into it through sheer ignorance. "What happened to her?"

"Dead," Master Thomas said, flatly. "We do not suffer Necromancers to live."

"But she didn't mean to raise a zombie horde," Gwen protested.

"That doesn't matter," Doctor Norwell said, sharply. "The

use of such powers is forbidden under the Demonic Powers Act. Anyone with proven Necromantic talents is to be executed."

There was a long, uncomfortable pause. "And she might have vanished into the underground," Master Thomas added. "They certainly took some interest in the whole affair."

Gwen looked up. "The underground?"

"Officially, the only magicians permitted to practice are licensed by the Crown, either as part of the Royal Sorcerers Corps or the Royal College," Master Thomas explained. "Unofficially, there is a small underground of magicians who work for criminal interests or merely struggle to stay alive. They tend to blur into the social liberal underground and its political wings, although so far they have never developed a coherent political philosophy or a strong leader. We scattered the rabble during the Year of Unrest and taught them a sharp lesson in knowing their place – and sticking to it."

He looked up at her. "One of the prime responsibilities of the Royal Sorcerer is upholding the laws of the land, created by the King and the Houses of Parliament. When the established ordered is threatened, it is my – our – job to defend it. You will find yourself having to make many hard choices in the course of your duty."

Doctor Norwell nodded. "With your consent, Lady Gwen, I will leave you with your Master," he said. "I cannot assist you with practical magic."

Gwen watched him go and then looked back at Master Thomas, who had taken a chair opposite her. "I heard about how you came into your magic," he said. "Have you practiced since then?"

"Yes," Gwen said. She didn't want to talk about what had happened that day. "Sometimes it worked and sometimes it didn't."

"Magic is often that way," Master Thomas said. "But you slipped into multiple talents, which would have confused anyone who didn't know how magic worked. I want you to try and summon fire. Be careful you don't burn your clothes."

Gwen held out one hand and summoned a blaze of fire. It roared upwards towards the ceiling, but the air was cool. Master Thomas reached forward and pushed his bare hand through the flames. Gwen scowled as she concentrated. The flames weren't real. They were just illusions she'd summoned.

"Close your eyes," Master Thomas instructed. "Concentrate on the flames. You want them to be hot and warm and hot and warm and..."

Gwen flinched backwards. For a long moment, she had *felt* the flames burning in her mind. A second later, a wave of heat had struck her and sent her tumbling backwards. She opened her eyes and saw a roaring pillar of flame, so bright that she could barely look at it. Her hand wasn't burning, but her arm seemed to be on fire...

She closed her hand and the flame vanished. Her dress was smouldering; quickly, heedless of what her mother would say, she tore at her sleeves until they were bare. The skin below was red, burned by the heat. Her hand seemed as pale and perfect as ever.

"Blazers don't burn themselves," Master Thomas said, softly. "Doctor Norwell thinks that it is caused by something in their minds, something that tells them not to harm themselves. But they can set their clothes on fire and that *does* burn their skin." He nodded towards the bowl of water. "You might want to cool yourself, and then we will try again."

Two hours passed slowly. Gwen's dress was almost totally ruined, but she had managed to master the talent, at least to some degree. Creating illusions was possible, Master Thomas assured her, yet it took years to become really skilful at creating ones that would fool an outside observer. It was easier to summon fire, or beams of energy that could burn through wood and even metal. The classroom's lack of decoration was explained. Young magicians, according to Master Thomas, frequently destroyed the room back to bare stone.

"Your Blazing will probably never be as good as a pure Blazer's," Master Thomas admitted. "However, by combining Blazing and Moving, you will be able to shield yourself in a manner that no pure Blazer could match. However, learning to combine both talents without actually *thinking* about it requires *years* of practice. You'll be working with some of the younger apprentices to develop your powers over the next few weeks. I may also make you work with some of the more qualified magicians. They, however, are likely to be more jealous of your position."

Gwen nodded, soberly. Some of the looks she had received from a few of the apprentices made sense, all of a sudden. Of course none of them would be able to reach the highest position in the magical world, not when they could only master one talent. And if a male Master arrived, Gwen was certain that she would be sent back home and told to marry well.

"Tell me something," she said, suddenly. "What happened to the other Masters?"

"I'll tell you when you are ready to hear," Master Thomas said. He made a show of checking the pocket watch he wore in his waistcoat. "For the moment, we will go for lunch. Eat well, Lady Gwen. There is an entire afternoon of hard work up ahead."

Chapter Four

ould all passengers please return to their seats," the stewardess requested. "The airship is about to land."

Jack leaned back in his chair as the airship began to descend over London. From high above, the Thames was nothing more than a silver band running through the darkened city. London had been sprawling out ever since the Romans had arrived and nothing, not war, famine or even death, would ever slow the city. It had expanded out until the green fields of England were facing the risk of being turned into housing blocks or factories to feed the country's endless appetite for manufactured goods.

He smiled at the stewardess as she paused in front of his chair. The stewardess, no doubt used to far crasser behaviour from junior scions of the aristocracy – both English and French – ignored the smile, checked his belt and then strode on to the next passenger. There was no better way to travel, if one had the money, than via airship. Jack took another sip of his gin and tonic and allowed his eyes to rest on the stewardess's behind as she swayed through the cabin. There were times when playing the part of a junior aristocrat was far too easy.

A dull rumble ran through the craft as the engines pushed it down towards the landing field, far below. Jack had to smile at the nervous expressions on some of his fellow passengers, the ones who had never flown by airship, but preferred the thought of flying to spending hours on a leaky boat and then a railway trip to London. The direct flight from Paris to London only took around three hours and the food was extremely good. It should have been, given what he'd paid for his ticket. The vast majority of London's inhabitants would be lucky if they could have afforded a trip to Blackpool or Dover, let alone a visit to France.

London grew closer as the airship settled to the ground. Darkened blurs became buildings, the new high-rise tenements built by the city corporation to house the influx of labourers from the country. The development of farming technology might have made it easier to raise crops and feed the animals, but it had pushed many thousands of farmers off the land. They ended up travelling to London or one of the other cities, looking for employment and a better life. Others went to the Americas, or Australia, or even the growing settlement in South Africa. Few found a better life.

The hatch opened, allowing the air of London to slip into the airship. After Paris, it was always a shock to smell London. The stench of industry hung in the air, mocking the puny humans who had to breathe the stuff every day. People got used to it quickly, Jack knew, but it was yet another reminder of how the world had changed over the last three decades. Airships, railways and farming machinery had changed Britain forever. And, as always, it was the poor who bore the brunt of the suffering imposed by the changes, for was there not pain in birth? The price of the brave new world was paid by its people.

He followed the other passengers out of the airship and onto the landing field. It had expanded since the last time he'd visited London, with several new airship hangers and more hackney cabs waiting for the wealthier passengers. There was no security worthy of the name, but that wasn't a surprise. Anyone who could afford the price of an airship ticket, the secret service had reasoned, wouldn't be interested in overthrowing the established order. There was far more security on the docks, where poorer folk from Europe came in hopes of finding a land of milk and honey. They had been sadly deceived.

Jack waved to a cabbie and the man brought his horses over to meet him. "The Bainbridge Hotel," Jack said, as he pulled himself into the cab. The horses neighed as their owner cracked the whip. London's cabbies competed ruthlessly for passengers, knowing that a wealthy passenger might tip them enough to allow them to feed their families better food. "And don't spare the whip."

He settled back into his seat as the carriage cantered away from the airship field, into Greater London. London had changed in some ways since he'd last visited; the glowing streetlight network had expanded and a handful of automobiles could be seen on the streets. They said that one day everyone in England would own an automobile, but Jack had his doubts. The best the industrial geniuses had been able to produce were cranky, prone to breaking down and incredibly expensive to run. Horses were far more reliable, even if they did have a habit of leaving their waste on the cobblestones. It was easier to pay the poor to clean the streets than it was to iron the bugs out of the automobiles.

London had its rich areas and its poorer areas, just like any other city in Europe. The Bainbridge Hotel was right on the verge of the middle-class area, rich enough to be respectable, but too poor to be taken entirely seriously. Jack had made the booking through the services of the telegraph, trusting that the Bainbridge Hotel wouldn't ask too many questions. They thought he was a poor nobleman, with a name, a title and little else. There were hundreds of second sons who had the right to be called noblemen, but stood to inherit little or nothing from their fathers. And there were plenty of little accidents who had been given a proper education by their fathers, even if they were never acknowledged as noble-born children.

Jack slipped out of the cab, tipped the cabbie just enough to be sure that the man wouldn't remember him, and strode into the hotel as if he owned the place. As he had expected, the manager was more than happy to take his money without asking too many questions; the Bainbridge had a reputation for discretion that would have done credit to a nun. Jack suspected that some of the wealthier segments of London society used it as a base for activities that would draw the disapproval of their wives and the Church. The last thing they would want would be a scandal that would call their discretion into question. In the unlikely event of the Bow Street Runners coming around to ask questions, the manager would have seen nothing and heard less.

The room was as he had expected; a simple bed, a small washbasin and a tiny mirror hanging on one wall. He glanced out of the window and smiled to himself; the manager had given him the room that stared towards one of the poorest sections of the city. The haze of smog that hung over London seemed to be heavier over the East End. It was probably an optical illusion, Jack told himself firmly. Even the worst of the industrialists wouldn't deliberately set out to poison the poor and helpless. It was merely a by-product of their industries.

Shaking his head, he lay back on the bed and concentrated. A capable magician could detect when a Seer was looking at him, even though the Seer might be on the other side of the world. Jack had a profound respect for the Seers in the Royal Sorcerers Corps and knew that if they believed him to be still alive they would have been monitoring him almost constantly. There was no tingle suggesting an invisible presence, no sense that he wasn't quite alone. Out of habit, he checked the room for knotholes and other ways he could be watched, before he placed his case on the bed and opened it with great care. If anyone else had tried to open it without his permission it would have been the last thing they ever did. There were items in his case that would have aroused suspicions in even the stupidest Bow Street Runner.

The two fine suits of clothes would have passed without comment. Under them, Jack had hidden a far less reputable outfit, one that would only be worn by someone who had no money to buy something better. He donned it quickly and glanced in the mirror, smiling at his appearance. Anyone who looked at him on the streets would see a common labourer, perhaps one of the Irishmen who had fled to England to escape the famine and seek daily work as builders and carriers. The Irish were often hated by the poorer Englishmen, who believed that the Irish took their jobs and money. They had a point, Jack knew; the only thing that motivated the rich was cheap labour.

Outside, the night was slowly falling over London. Jack donned a walking cape that would hide his outfit and then stepped outside into the corridor. As he had expected, it ended with yet another window, staring down into the courtyard behind the hotel. Jack opened the window, pulled his magic around him, and jumped down to the cobblestones. Anyone watching would have seen him fall several meters without being hurt. It was astonishing what magic could do.

He walked into an alleyway a gentleman, wearing his cloak, and walked out of the other end a labourer, carrying the cloak under one arm. It wouldn't arouse suspicion; anyone who saw it would think that it was a blanket, like the one carried by many homeless men who had found themselves trapped in London. Jack's lips twitched as he smelt the stench of alcohol and tobacco smoke outside a pub. The working men would be inside, having a few pints before they returned home to their wives. Their pay packets, meagre as they were, would be depleted quite a bit before they left the pub. Jack knew that their children would be lucky to survive the coming winter. It had only been last year that London had suffered an outbreak of cholera and hundreds of the urban poor had died.

The streets were still alive with people, although many of the shops were closing before the drunkards started pouring out of the pubs. He saw a little girl selling matches and another girl selling flowers and felt his heart break, just before he saw what had to be their older sister, who was selling herself. The poor often had no recourse but to sell their children into slavery, or worse. Few of them could be proud when they lived permanently on the edge of starvation. He caught sight of a black-clad preacher and scowled inwardly. The Church railed against the desperate straits of the poor, but it rarely did anything effective to help. And its preachers claimed tithes from those who could scarcely afford to pay.

He wandered down the darkest streets, waiting for what he knew would happen. There was no point in going to any of the addresses he'd known last time he'd been in London. His friends would be long gone. The Bow Street Runners turned a blind eye to prostitution, gambling and drinking – at least when the Church wasn't breathing down their necks – but they broke up socialist meetings with great energy. His old friends would be well hidden. It didn't matter that much. He would find someone who would know where they were, or knew someone who would know. It was very difficult to hide in London if one wanted to run a criminal or underground enterprise.

The touch, when it came, was so light that he would have missed it altogether if he hadn't been waiting for it. His hand snapped down and caught the hand of a grubby little street urchin who had been trying to pick his pocket – and the wallet Jack had placed inside, knowing that it would tempt someone to try his luck. The child struggled against his grip, but couldn't break free as Jack hauled him into the alleyway. No one would notice, or care if they did. There were hundreds of children running wild on London's streets. The lucky ones died early, before they matured.

He used a touch of magic as he gripped the boy's shirt and lifted him into the air. It would seem an impressive demonstration of strength to anyone without the ability to sense magic. The child kicked and struggled, but it was useless. Up close, he stank of the streets, a stench that would put the hardiest of souls to flight. It was self-protection as much as anything else, but it still disgusted him. How could anyone live like that?

The boy – no; he looked at the face and realised that he was holding a girl, dressed as a boy – stopped struggling and stared at him. Jack read hopelessness in her gaze, the awareness that her luck had run out. If he handed her over to the Bow Street Runners, she would be condemned to transportation as convict labour, if she were lucky. And there were people who had far darker ideas about what to do with a young girl. She couldn't be older than eight, perhaps nine, but her eyes were already old. Jack knew she would be lucky to survive into her teens.

"You tried to steal from me," he said, evenly.

"I didn't mean to, master," the girl pleaded. Her attempt at producing a masculine voice wasn't perfect, but it would probably fool someone in the dark. It had been a long time since Jack had visited the places where the street children slept, but he knew that they could be a very nasty place for a young girl. No one could be trusted on the streets. "Let me go and I won't steal from you again...I swear I won't..."

"Be quiet," Jack said, in the same even tone. "What is your name, young lady?"

The girl's face, already pale, became almost bloodless as she realised he knew her sex. "Olivia, sir," she said. "I didn't know you were a spark or a toffee; I didn't know..."

Jack smiled, inwardly. Spark was street-slang for magician; toffee was street-slang for upper-class personage, slumming in the poorer areas of the city for pleasures that were denied even to people of their lofty birth. If the girl had identified him as a magician, it suggested some magical talent of her own. It was almost a shame that the Royal Sorcerers

Corps hadn't found her. She would have been brainwashed into serving the order that kept the lower classes in their place, but at least she would have enough to eat.

"I'm looking for Mistress Lucy," Jack said. It was a name from the past, but unless he was very much mistaken she would still be alive and thriving within the underworld. Any woman in a position of power had to be stronger, tougher and more ruthless than any of her male counterparts. The female of the species was far more deadly than the male. "Do you know where she stays?"

He allowed some Charm to slip into his voice. "You will take me to where she stays," he said, as the girl nodded frantically. "Don't try to run away, or I'll turn you into a rat."

The girl's eyes went wide, in surprise and fear, and then she nodded. "Follow me, mister," she said. "I won't lead you wrong."

Jack followed her, shaking his head inwardly at how the locals didn't seem to take any notice of them. But life on the streets was hard; no one would risk their lives to save a street child who would steal from them the moment their backs were turned. Even the handful of preachers who came down into the maze of houses, bridges and slums would turn their backs on a street child. And once she couldn't maintain her manly guise, she'd probably be corralled by a pimp or forced into the brothels. They'd use her up and then throw her out to die. There was no mercy for the poor in London.

The Rookery was more complex than he remembered. It had started life as a set of houses and apartments, but thousands of immigrants from the countryside had taken over and turned it into a mishmash of tiny streets and makeshift houses. The Bow Street Runners wouldn't come into the Rookery without heavy numbers or military support, which meant in practice that the Rookery was controlled by a shifting network of criminal lords. He smiled to himself as he caught sight of a Chinese man striding past, the people moving out of his way to allow him to pass. The Tongs were known for brutally enforcing their will and their smuggling enterprises were legendary. Jack had used the Chinese community the last time he'd been in London, even though he disliked them on general principles. They always seemed to be laughing at him behind their inscrutable eyes.

They are human too, he reminded himself firmly, as the girl stopped outside an unmarked house that seemed to be in remarkably good condition. The sound of laughter and male grunting from inside confirmed that it was a brothel, even before Olivia started to back away, making motions and gestures that seemed to imply that Mistress Lucy was inside. Jack caught her arm before she could start running and pulled her with him as he opened the door. Inside, a line of lovely young women waited for him, trying to look alluring. Jack wouldn't have been tempted even if he'd had time. He knew just how badly they had been used, even if Mistress Lucy treated them as more than cattle.

"Here," he said. He produced a gold coin from his pouch – not his wallet, which had nothing more than a few metal filings to imitate money – and gave it to the girl. Her eyes went wide; the chances were that it was more money than she'd had in her entire life. Given that he'd charmed her, it was a fair recompense. "Wait for me here. Once I have finished, I may have other tasks for you."

He smiled as one of the young women finally approached. Her face suggested a mixture of English and Negro in her blood, part of the great melting pot of lower-class London. She would have been pretty if her eyes hadn't been so tired, if she hadn't known the truth about her existence before she'd grown old enough to try to make her own way in the world.

"Like what you see, sir?" She asked. Her voice was light and breathy. "We have others, far more exotic, if you are a real connoisseur…"

"I'm here to see Mistress Lucy," Jack said, cutting her up. He allowed a little more Charm to slip into his voice. "I'm an old friend. Take me to her at once."

"Well, well," a new voice said. "Look what the cat dragged in."

Jack looked up and smiled. "Lucy," he said. "It is simply *lovely* to see you again."

"I'll give you lovely," Lucy said. She was older than he remembered. "What are you doing here?"

"I'm here to overthrow the government," Jack said, cheerfully. "Isn't *that* a lovely idea?"

Chapter Five

wen rose to her feet as Cannock stepped into the room. Master Thomas had told her that the next series of magical lessons would be coming from her fellow apprentices, who were more skilled with their individual powers than he was with each of them. It wasn't something that entirely pleased her – and it was clear, looking at him, that Cannock bitterly resented having to teach anyone. He would graduate in June and start serving the British Empire in foreign parts. Teaching a young lady wasn't among his ambitions.

He was a short young man with messy dark hair and darker eyes, barely old enough to go dancing on his own. Gwen guessed, from the way his eyes lingered on her chest for just a second or two longer than necessary, that he'd already discovered the pleasures of drinking and wenching, just like her brother. It was a double standard – men could enjoy themselves with whores, women had to be chaste – but it wasn't one she intended to challenge. The thought of sharing her body with hundreds of men was horrifying. If she ever found a husband, someone she could love, perhaps she would feel differently about it.

"Thank you for coming," Gwen said, as graciously as she could. She had already learned that the Royal College and Royal Sorcerers Corps judged by talent, rather than noble blood, but even they couldn't avoid it entirely. Cannock was the younger son of the Duke of Essex and a bad word to his father could lead to unpleasant repercussions for the Royal College. At least he'd earned his awards through hard work and endless practice. She didn't have to worry that he'd purchased his commission. "I am very pleased to meet you."

Cannock gave her a half-bow, rather than kissing her hand.

Gwen was rather pleased about that, although she knew that he had intended it as a subtle insult. Kissing a woman's hand was a way to show respect; a bow suggested a certain reserve. The way his eyes kept dancing over her worried her, even though part of her mind found it amusing. Men never seemed to change. At least a magician from the Royal College wouldn't find her powers intimidating...or perhaps they would. They had spent years practicing to rise in the ranks and Gwen had succeeded merely through an accident of birth.

"Moving is one of the simplest talents and yet it is the most complex," Cannock said, at once. His voice was flat, almost dead. Someone had twisted his arm quite badly – Gwen hoped that that was metaphorical – to force him to teach Gwen his talent. "It basically consists of using your mind to move objects about without actually touching them physically. The more practiced you become at using the talent, the more you will be able to do with it. An experienced Mover can unpick a lock, or even fly through the air. A *really* capable Mover will be able to manipulate objects without maintaining eye contact."

He shrugged, impatiently. "It obviously takes more energy to move heavier objects," he said. "Movers deplete themselves quite rapidly; if you happen to be flying, get down on the ground the moment you feel yourself tiring. You will run out of energy quicker than you will believe possible and then you will fall. A number of Movers have died through hitting the ground at great speed."

Gwen frowned, but nodded. A moment later, she felt an uncomfortable itching under her buttocks. The feeling spread rapidly until she found herself being picked up by an unseen force and lifted into the air. She could *feel* the magic tingling all around her, but it didn't seem to be part of her. The whole feeling was vaguely uncomfortable, even unpleasant. Cannock didn't seem to notice her distaste, but she knew it could be an act. She resolved not to show any signs of distress.

"A skilled Mover can talk as well as holding something in the air," Cannock said. Gwen felt the magic shifting and she found herself gliding over towards the rear of the room. It struck her suddenly that all he had to do was alter her poise a little and he would be able to see right up her skirt. She blushed furiously and then giggled, despite herself. Cannock gave her a puzzled look and started to lower her to the floor. "The more complex the manipulation, the more concentration it requires to actually carry it out without losing control."

Gwen felt the hard stone floor under her legs. The force holding her upright vanished abruptly and she had to catch hold of one of the tables to prevent her from falling over backwards. She saw a trace of amusement in Cannock's eyes and silently vowed revenge at the earliest possible moment. He'd probably enjoyed watching her float under his control. She walked back to the table she'd been seated at and sat down, daring him to try to pick her up again.

"Movers, once they have mastered basic manipulation, practice in the hall by playing Mover Ball," Cannock continued. He was definitely smirking now. "Mover Ball is not unlike the games played by children on the streets, but the balls are thrown though the air by magic, rather than a person's hands. To be hit by a ball, or to be caught touching it with one's bare hands, is grounds for instant banishment from the game."

Gwen smiled. "And the objective is to be the last person on the field?"

"Quite," Cannock said. "People without the right talent can still play by hurling balls at the talented. They are forced to catch them or deflect them with their magic, or risk losing and being mocked by their peers."

He reached out one hand and held it over the bowl of water. There was a shimmer of magic and a ball of water floated out of the bowl and hovered in the air. "And there is another trick we play all the time," Cannock added. "We throw water at each other."

Before Gwen could react, the ball of water flew right at her face. She held up her hands like lightning and the ball of water seemed to explode, drops of water flying everywhere. Enough touched her face and clothes to convince her that it was freezing cold – and that she would have to get some more practical clothes. Cannock looked surprised that she'd even managed to block it – he'd wanted to drench her, she realised – but recovered quickly. Absently, she wondered how long he'd taken to master his single talent.

"Not too bad," Cannock said. "Do you know what you did?"

Gwen shook her head. "You hit my ball with a blast of

pure motion," he said. "You weren't particularly subtle – later, you will learn to catch the water and throw it back at me – but you prevented me from hitting you with the water. Well done."

"Thank you," Gwen said, tartly. Her mother would not have approved. "And why do we use water?"

Cannock grinned, unpleasantly. "Because when we throw stones or something material, someone gets hurt," he said. "The worst that can happen here is that we both end up drenched. Let's see, shall we?"

He pulled a second ball of water out of the bowl and launched it at Gwen. She tried to block it, but this time the ball resisted her efforts. For a moment, the ball of water seemed to flatten into a sheet of water hanging in the air, and then it flew right towards her and smashed into her face. Gwen gasped in shock as the water slid down her front and soaked her dress. Powered by anger, she reached out towards the bowl herself and *yanked* at the water. An entire stream of water rose out of the bowl and came down on Cannock, who held up his hand to deflect it. It seemed to hang in the air for a long moment, and then Cannock pushed it away. The water shattered into droplets that went everywhere, drenching the walls. He laughed and picked up the bowl. It was empty.

"I think we need to work on control," he said, as he turned one of the taps and refilled the bowl. "You are very blunt with your power, very crude. A more experienced Mover could have drenched me while I was holding off your stream of water."

Gwen flushed, feeling cold water trickling down her bodice. She hadn't felt so cold since she'd taken an unplanned dip in the waters down near their country home. Cannock's eyes seemed to light on her for a second and she flushed as she realised that her dress was clinging to her skin. He'd done that purposefully, or her name wasn't Gwen. She ground her teeth as he placed the bowl back on the table behind him and – without any gestures – pulled three balls of water into the air. Gwen was impressed as they spun around his head, and then flew at her. This time, she was ready; one of the balls shattered, while the other two flew back at Cannock. He caught one and tossed it back at Gwen, but the other smashed into his shirt. Gwen had to smile at his expression, just before the final ball of water drenched her hair. The thought of what her mother would have said, if she'd seen her, made her giggle. Lady Mary would *not* have been amused.

They practiced for nearly an hour, until Gwen felt her head beginning to throb. "Time to stop for the day," Cannock said, seriously. He sounded more concerned about her than she'd expected. But then, if anything went badly wrong, Master Thomas would have thrashed him to within an inch of his life. "You don't want to push your talent too far."

Gwen nodded. She disliked headaches at the best of times. "Thank you," she said. "I'll just get changed and then I'll join you for lunch."

Back in her rooms, she glanced at herself in the mirror and burst out laughing. Her sodden dress was clinging to her skin, her hair was a dreadful mess and her skin was covered in droplets of water. Pulling the dress off and dumping it on the floor was not particularly easy – and when she'd done so, she discovered that her undergarments had been soaked as well. The dress was almost completely ruined, even though it had been designed for rougher use than her ballroom dresses, and she made a mental note to insist on wearing trousers. It might not be acceptable in polite society for women to wear trousers, but the Crichton Family weren't so rich that they could afford to keep buying new dresses. Conspicuous consumption wasn't the kind of reputation a reputable older family wished to develop.

She wiped herself with a towel, donned a light-green dress that would be suitable for an afternoon spent in the library, and headed down the stairs for lunch. The lunches in Cavendish Hall were served at noon precisely, with anyone who was late – according to Master Thomas – forced to dine out, unless they had a very good excuse. At least the food was good, although it was a curious mixture of typically British foods and imported tastes from the Empire. Some of the student magicians would be going to India or Africa or even the Americas when they graduated and they would have to learn to eat native cuisine. The Colonial Service frowned on officers who refused to eat local foods, at least outside the network of government officers. It also frowned on British officers who formed liaisons with the local womenfolk, but Gwen had heard enough whispers from relatives of those who had served in India to know that such regulations were tacitly ignored.

The table wasn't as crowded as she had expected. Master Thomas and several of the senior tutors hadn't come to dine, which *was* surprising. A handful of students – including Cannock – sat at the table, tucking into the soup that formed the first course. Anyone who failed to arrive by the time the maids started removing the soup would have to beg and plead to receive a share of roast lamb or beef. Gwen took a seat, accepted a bowl of soup and bread from one of the maids, and started to sip at it. The cooks had produced a rather surprisingly spicy carrot soup.

She glanced up sharply as she felt the first tingle of magic surrounding her. No one seemed to be looking at her; in fact, the group of students seemed to be looking *away* from Gwen. The magic faded away, and then reappeared, right behind her. Gwen frowned and concentrated, trying to understand what it was. A moment later, she felt a sharp pinch on her rear end. There was no one behind her, which meant that someone was using magic to pinch her from a distance. She felt a hot flash of anger as she glared at Cannock and his friends, all of whom were clearly fighting to control the urge to burst into giggles. They could play their tricks on the maids if they liked – she'd already heard that Cavendish Hall had a higher turnover of servants than her father's house – but they couldn't play them on her. A second pinch made her jump, followed rapidly by a third. It felt as if someone was crawling over her body, pinching away at exposed flesh.

"Stop it," she ordered. The students burst into giggles, followed by another series of pinches. Gwen yelped as she felt her buttocks stinging in pain. "Stop it!"

Magic flared through her and the soup bowls in front of the students seemed to explode, showering them in hot soup. It was their turn to yelp in shock, just as another wave of magic – only partly under Gwen's control – slammed into the tureen and tipped it over onto the table. A flood of hot soup spread across the tablecloth and into their laps. She wanted to giggle herself as they jumped up, the stain spreading over their clean trousers, but she was burning with rage. A hot prickling behind her eyes seemed to be overpowering her. Cannock turned and glared at her, no longer so amused now he was dripping with soup. He used his magic to pick up the bread and throw it at her. Gwen caught it with her own magic and knocked it back at him, only to see it come apart as the other students – two of whom were clearly Movers themselves – caught it and shoved it at her. Tiny pieces of bread slashed into her skin, leaving her feeling bruised and sore. Angrily, she sent her own magic billowing out of control across the table, picking up spilled soup, tableware and even part of the table and hurling it at them. Cannock ducked in alarm as a knife narrowly missed him by inches. Maids and kitchen staff scattered, screaming in panic as the magic duel ran right out of control.

Gwen felt Cannock's magic forming around her and pushed it back, slamming her will directly against his. For a moment, she held her own, but his greater experience and skill told and he broke through her defences. A wave of magic slapped into her and sent her staggering backwards; she hit the floor hard enough to hurt as the table started to disintegrate around her. Magic flared over her fingers, slipping from Moving to Blazing, enough magic to burn right through Cannock. If she was fighting for her life.

"ENOUGH," a voice said. *"STOP FIGHTING, NOW!"*

There was enough Charm in the voice to control an entire crowd of angry magicians. Gwen felt her rage dissipate slowly, the magic she had raised to defend herself fading away. Master Thomas was coming down the long flight of stairs, his face as angry as anyone else Gwen had ever seen. It struck her, suddenly, that she was no longer at home. If he felt that she had grossly overreacted to their provocation, she was likely to be in real trouble. Her father had let her run wild, but Master Thomas believed in discipline. It was the key to effective magic.

"I do not expect to see student magicians fighting one another with the food," he said, sharply. Cannock and his friends looked as if they wished to be somewhere – anywhere – else. Gwen, for once, found herself in agreement with them. Her head was starting to pound again, suggesting that she might have overreached herself. How much Moving could a person do before they risked permanent damage? "I would insist on none of you having any lunch, except you will have exhausted yourself through your silly fighting."

For the first time, Gwen took in the scene before him. The dining hall was wrecked, with soup and bread scattered everywhere. The massive oak table had been smashed, while the soup was soaking into the carpet, paintings had been torn from the walls and a set of cutlery was embedded in the stonework. It would take hours, perhaps days, for the servants to clear up the mess, if they didn't give their notice as a body when they recovered from their hysterics. She felt a flash of shame, despite the wooziness that threatened to send her to her knees. They hadn't meant to tear the room apart during their fight.

"You will all spend the afternoon cleaning up the mess," Master Thomas decreed. His voice was flat, perfectly controlled. It was clear that any argument would only make the punishment worse. "You have disgraced yourselves in front of your tutors."

He stepped forward, the tip of his cane tapping against the stairwell. "Control and discipline are the keys to your magic," he said. "I do not want to see any of you lose control, not again. Losing control could mean that someone – perhaps someone innocent – gets hurt. I will not tolerate that on my watch."

It took nearly four hours to clean up the mess. The table was beyond repair – the intersection of two different magical forces had shattered its structure – and had to be sent to the bonfires. Gwen found herself scrubbing the floor for the first time in her life, along with a handful of students who had probably never done a day's real work in their lives. It was a bitter insight into how the servants had felt during her temper tantrums as a young child, with the added threat of malicious magic for those that worked at Cavendish Hall. Afterwards, she had to change again. The green dress had been totally ruined.

She vowed, in the aftermath, that she wouldn't lose control again. The results, she decided, were too dangerous. Magic was far from safe.

Chapter Six

on't look around too much," Lucy said, as she ushered Jack into her living room. "I haven't decided if I want to keep you here yet."

Jack smiled at her as he took one of the comfortable seats. Lucy had done well for herself over the years, but then owning a brothel was always a licence to print money. Her living room had been decorated to her tastes, with a number of comfortable chairs, a drinks cabinet and a double-sized sofa intended to allow her to share time with a lover – if she had a lover. It was luxury on a scale that made Jack think of the people outside, who would have killed for just one of the chairs in the room, but he refused to allow himself to feel guilt. He would do what he could for them by destroying the system that kept their lives hellish.

"I'm sure you're pleased to see me," he said. Lucy shrugged as she poured them both a drink. Jack sniffed the aroma as she passed him one of the glasses and lifted an eyebrow. A bottle of good brandy cost more than the average inhabitant of the Rookery could hope to make in a year through honest labour. He took a sip and placed the glass aside. "It has been such a long time."

He studied Lucy with frank interest. She had once had long red hair and perfect skin. Now, her hair was still red, but her skin was marked by age and despair. She wore a dark dress that contrasted oddly with her hair colour, tight in all the right places, yet decent enough to pass unnoticed in most parts of London. The Bow Street Runners wouldn't move her along if they saw her, although some of them might solicit her for free sessions in the brothel. It was always nice to know which of the Runners could be corrupted at will.

"Too long," Lucy said, as she sat down opposite him. "I had almost given up hope of seeing you again. The French might have wanted to keep you."

"They knew better than to try," Jack assured her. "Whatever differences we might have with King Louis and his Court, anything that weakens the British Empire would be sure of their support."

"Until they discover that the movement is also targeted on the French monarchy," Lucy pointed out. "Don't they realise that the British are not the only people in bondage?"

"Oh, I'm sure they know," Jack said. He grinned at her, mischievously. "That's what makes the game so exciting."

He took another sip of the brandy. "I spoke to the American – Franklin – while I was at Versailles," he said. "He still has high hopes of a second revolution in the colonies and he may be right, but Arnold is still clamping down hard on any expression of dissent. And the savages didn't make it any easier by rising up against the settlers three years ago. They'll forget what the redcoats did for them in a few more years, but right now all Arnold really has to worry about is Shays. And Shays has only a small band behind him.

"No, the only hope for freedom is here, in Britain," he concluded. "Once I did my duty by the French, I set out to return to the land of my childhood."

"And I'm sure you positively *hated* doing your duty by the French," Lucy said, sweetly. Jack flushed. It had been years since they'd been lovers, back when he'd first become involved in the underground movement, but she still had the power to embarrass him. Lucy had always been so delightfully crude, unsurprisingly. Living on the streets did nothing for one's airs and graces. She was so much more alive than many of the aristocratic ladies he had once known. "Do you really trust them to support us when the crowd starts making threatening noises in Paris?"

Jack shook his head. "I think they'll be sending for the troops again," he said. The period following the aborted American Revolution had been followed by popular unrest in France, Prussia, Austria and even Russia. It had been a heady time, with hope burning brightly in the population, but the established order had been able to clamp down and reassume control. The streets of Paris had run red with blood as troops had fired on the crowds, dismantling the barricades and restoring King Louis to his throne. "But until then, we can count on their support."

The French had fought countless wars with the British over the last two centuries – and they'd lost every one of them. France, with its open borders, simply couldn't concentrate its might upon building a navy to match its island rival, rendering it supreme in Europe, but weak at sea. The British Empire had expanded rapidly under Pitt to the point where it ruled nearly a quarter of the known world. There were British missions in China and even Japan, ones that might lead to conquest and settlement. King George and Lord Liverpool were firm believers in expansion. It kept the masses quiet and provided dumping grounds for criminals who could then be worked to death.

Jack didn't blame the French for feeling more than a little frustrated, even though most of their problems stemmed from their own government as well as geography. The French nobility had rallied behind the King in the years of unrest, but they remained determined to cling to their ancient rights, as did the Church. No King had the power to force them to reform, which meant that nothing would ever be fixed. The French could only draw money from a small segment of its society, the poor and powerless. France would suffer a revolution when they finally realised that they were damned to poverty no matter how hard they worked. The threats of ruthless suppression would no longer seem intimidating.

"Right," Lucy said. She took a sip of her brandy. "Most of our networks got crushed by Liverpool and his Dragoons. There aren't that many of the old guard left."

Jack had expected that, but it was still a shock. There had been heady days in the past, when the movement had been gaining ground and sucking in people who could support the demand for peaceful change. And then all hell had broken loose and he'd had to flee for his life. Magic, as his old master had told him more than once, didn't make a person invincible. It often made a person overconfident instead.

"Priestly was transported to Australia," Lucy said. "His wife and family were transported along with him. Jacob and Rowley died in the riots, either gunned down by the Dragoons or lost in the crush. Old Rupert died – pleasantly, if not peacefully – in someone else's bed. Davy is still alive and active, but he's downhearted."

She smiled. "And old Ebenezer is dead," she added. "He died in a stone-cold bed."

"Old Scrooge himself," Jack said. He shook his head. Ebenezer had been a loan shark, lending out money at ruinous interest rates to the poor and desperate. Anyone who failed to pay back the loan in time was visited by his hired thugs and beaten up, or killed if the first beating failed to produce the money. Jack had never known why Ebenezer had helped to fund the movement, but the old bastard had provided more than anyone would have expected. "Who took over the business?"

"Henry Ebenezer, his son," Lucy said. "He's twice the bastard his father was, I'm afraid. Ebenezer had some limits, even though he was utterly ruthless; Henry has none. Most of the sparkers in this part of London are working for him now, along with the pimps, thugs and gutter-trash. He's the uncrowned King of the Rookery."

Jack nodded, sourly. There had always been a magical underground, composed of magicians who were too poor or too weak to attract the interest of the Royal Sorcerers. He was, technically speaking, a member himself, but the underground had never been very united. Most criminals would know better than to lean on a magician – at least one with useful talents – but Henry sounded as if he'd figured out how to control his pet magic-users. Jack could think of a handful of ways, starting with Charm. Henry had never shown any sign of magic, as far as he knew, but it was hard to judge what someone was actually capable of without seeing them in action.

Or Henry could simply be using carrots and sticks. The old ways had worked perfectly for his father. Why should his son be any different?

"We may have to deal with him," Jack said. "Does he get along with Davy?"

"No," Lucy said. "In fact, I believe that Davy is in debt to Henry."

Jack frowned. "We definitely have to deal with him," he said. "Does he ever come here?"

"He knows better than to interfere with me," Lucy said, bluntly. "I still have my talent."

"That's no surprise," Jack said. "You've always been very talented."

Lucy made a rude gesture with her right hand. "But Henry will definitely pose a problem," she warned. "If he hears that you're back, he'll go running to the Runners. The Rookery can't afford to have them pounding the beat through here. A man won't be able to earn a dishonest living."

"And if he happens to live here, he won't be able to earn an honest living," Jack said. The people of the Rookery survived, somehow. It was a dog-eat-dog world. The strong survived and prospered. The weak perished. It was no way for a human being to live. "I think I'll go and have a few words with young Henry. Perhaps I can bring him over to my way of thinking."

"Watch your back," Lucy said. "Are you going to be staying here?"

"I'll find somewhere to stay," Jack assured her. He trusted Lucy as far as he trusted anyone, but this was the Rookery and trust was in short supply. Who knew who could turn into a betrayer, given the promise of enough money to move into a more upmarket part of London? "And I want you to find young Olivia a position here."

Lucy narrowed her eyes. "You haven't become one of...*them*, have you?"

"No," Jack said. "And I'm sure that you're not servicing *them*, even here."

"No," Lucy said. "And what are you going to do with her?"

"She knows the streets," Jack said. "She may come in handy."

He smiled. "I'll do something to show that we can strike back at the oppressors," he said. "You start spreading the word; I want to talk to Davy and start preparing for the revolution. Our time has finally come."

"Yeah," Lucy said. "I heard that from you before, Mister Spark, and it ended badly for all concerned."

"This time will be different," Jack promised. He tipped his hat to her as he stood up. "And call me Captain Swing."

Outside, he took a moment to introduce Olivia to Lucy and offer the young girl a chance to work at reasonably good wages. The child was nervous, unsurprisingly, but Lucy had a way with children; after all, she acted as mother to over thirty whores. Lucy took care of them, ensured that rough clients were shown the door before they could inflict permanent harm on the young ladies, and paid them reasonably well. It had once troubled Jack's conscience to know that his lover was marketing girls of dubious virtue, but he had long since overcome his doubts. None of the girls were forced into the brothel. They had had the choice between selling themselves or starving to death. Besides, Lucy's brothel was relatively safe. The gang wars that threatened to tear the Rookery apart never touched its walls.

The sun was setting in the sky as he strode through the streets, heading for Ebenezer's house. It was surprisingly well-built for the Rookery, but Ebenezer – although he'd been a miser and a ruthless bastard – had loved his comforts. He'd ensured that his home was always heated against the cold night air of London. A pair of thugs stood on guard outside, holding clubs and thoroughly-illicit pistols, daring anyone to challenge their might. Their master ruled most of the Rookery with an iron hand. Few would dare to see him unless they were desperate or already in his grip.

Smiling, Jack strode up to the lead thug and slapped him with a blast of powerful magic. The thug staggered backwards, blood pouring from his nose and lips, and collapsed to the ground. Jack laughed as the second thug drew his pistol, took aim with a shaky hand and fired. The bullet was caught in the magic and deflected back at the thug, who gasped as it slammed into his chest. Jack had added a little extra speed with his magic. Leaving the two thugs moaning on the ground, Jack headed inside, wincing at the heat. Henry had few scruples about showing off his wealth and power, even in the middle of the Rookery. It was a testament to the fear his father had inspired.

Jack lashed out with his magic and the inner door shattered into dust. He strode onwards and was unsurprised to see Henry running for his life, no doubt convinced that King George IV had sent all the forces of law and order in his Kingdom to deal with him. Jack caught him effortlessly and held him in the air with magic, while pushing the half-naked girl out of the office and slamming the door behind her. She'd probably run and alert someone, but who could she fetch? Henry's tame magicians wouldn't be able to do more than delay him.

"I've been hearing some bad things about you, my boy," Jack said. Upside down, Henry looked as if he was going to be sick. His flabby chest suggested that he ate a lot better than the average inhabitant of the Rookery. "You've been squeezing the last drop of blood from people's lives. You're nothing more than a parasite on society."

Henry gasped for breath. "They...they came to me," he managed to say, finally. "They wanted money from me."

"And you press them into taking ruinous interest rates," Jack said. He was enjoying himself far too much. Some people had no choice, but to turn to crime if they wanted to eat. Henry had had a choice and had chosen to prey on his fellow men. "How many sons have you sold into service with the Crown? How many daughters have you sent to brothels when their parents couldn't pay their debts? How many families are destitute because you forced them to repay the original loan many times over? *How many lives have you ruined?*"

He compressed the magic around Henry's neck, choking him slightly. "There's a new man in town now," he added. "If you want to live, you work for me – understand?"

The door burst open and four men hurled themselves through with guns. Jack lifted one hand and sent a pulse of glowing magic right into the leader's head. The others stumbled, just for a second, and Jack hit them with a wave of magic. They fell over backwards, crying out in shock. None of them had expected to face a real magician, let alone one who possessed all of the talents. But then, few of them knew much about magic. They probably believed that the bracelets sold by wise women possessed actual healing powers.

He made a show of clicking his fingers and the second thug burst into flame. The remaining two turned and fled, leaving Jack behind with his helpless victim. He watched the thug burning for a long second, and then fired a burst of magic directly into his head, putting him out of his misery. When he turned back to Henry, whom he'd left spinning in the air, he discovered that the former ruler of the Rookery had soiled himself. The stench was starkly unpleasant against the vaguely perfumed air.

"You work for me or I will take your organisation anyway," Jack said. As fun as it was to torment Henry, there was too much else to do – and besides, he didn't want to develop a taste for tormenting people. "What do you say?"

Henry was still staring at him, wild-eyed. "I'll do it," he

said, desperately. Jack wasn't too surprised. Criminals were rarely brave when confronted by magic. Hopefully, Henry would never have time to realise that magic didn't make one invincible. "I'll work for you."

Jack dropped him onto the ground, slowing his fall just enough to prevent him from cracking his skull. "You're going to forgive all your loans," Jack said. He ignored the brief sputter of protest. "You're going to start thinking about all your upper-class clients, all the nobly-born who use your services – and you're going to start telling me all about them." He drew a little on his magic, enough to make his eyes glow with fire. "And if you defy me, I'll make sure you burn in fire forever."

Henry stumbled backwards, slipping over his own urine. Jack almost smiled at the expression on his face. "I'll do as you say," Henry protested. He was badly shocked; Jack allowed himself to believe that Henry would be too terrified to act against him, at least at first. And the Rookery would know who to thank. "I will…"

"And when they ask why, tell them that Captain Swing sent you," Jack said. "And trust me on this – you do not want to defy me."

Shaking his head, he strode out of the building, leaving the broken man behind. He'd find lodgings in the Rookery, have a good night's sleep, and then start preparing for his first act of resistance. The oppressors of mankind were about to discover that nowhere was safe from Captain Swing.

And then they would discover the meaning of fear.

Chapter Seven

can't say that I am very impressed."

"No," Gwen said. They were riding together in a carriage, the day following the disastrous food fight. She had been expecting Master Thomas to have a private word with her and hadn't been surprised when it had finally materialised. Cannock and two of his friends had looked uncomfortable during the evening meal and seemed to be having problems sitting down. "I'm sorry about it."

"I'm glad to hear it," Master Thomas said, flatly. "I expected a degree of maturity from you – and from young Cannock. His commission to go to India and serve as a sorcerer with the army may have to be delayed."

Gwen said nothing. A dozen arguments ran through her mind – from the marks she'd seen when she undressed in the evening, to the sheer unfairness of three ganging up on one – and she dismissed them. Master Thomas wouldn't be too impressed if she started acting like someone in need of his protection. It was bad enough when her father thought her a foolish female who needed a strong male hand to guide and protect her throughout her life.

"You are training to be the next Royal Sorcerer," Master Thomas continued. "You will one day be giving orders to Cannock and his fellow Movers. Your multiple talents could have made the outcome of the whole affair far worse…"

"I tried to restrict myself to Moving," Gwen protested. "I didn't Blaze them…"

"You came close to Blazing them out of this world," Master Thomas said. "They should have known better than to provoke you – and you should have known better than to lose control. Had you been born a man, we would have taken you when your powers first manifested and spent the last five years teaching you control. As it is, you will have to learn on the job."

"I didn't rule that women shouldn't learn magic," Gwen protested, hotly. "That rule makes little sense if magic is part of a person's body..."

"I didn't make the rules," Master Thomas said. "There is no formal rule against ladies learning to use the magic they have. They are just rarely considered for employment by the Crown."

"But you needed to employ me," Gwen pointed out. "Do all the rules change when situations require that the rules be broken?"

"Of course," Master Thomas said. "Just ask poor King Charles."

Gwen frowned. Charles I had lost control of his country – and his head – after crossing swords with Parliament. His son, Charles II, had finally restored the monarchy, but Parliament's powers had not been diminished. George II had known and understood the power of Parliament – both to fund wars and fight them – yet George III had thought he could control it by fiat. George IV seemed to prefer to allow Parliament to handle its own affairs, while he enjoyed himself at Windsor Castle.

The carriage lumbered to a stop and Master Thomas peered out of the covered window. He'd been remarkably unforthcoming about where they were going, or even why; he'd even insisted that Gwen refrain from practicing magic in the morning. She'd spent the hour waiting for him reading a tome of eldritch lore that seemed to bear no resemblance to magic as she understood it. The Mad Arab's spells seemed to make no sense at all.

"One thing," Master Thomas said, in a gentler voice. "You are about to see sights that...some would say are not suitable for young ladies. And that is strange, because young ladies are often involved. If you want to stay in the carriage..."

Gwen shook her head, firmly. "I'm coming," she said. "Where are we?"

Master Thomas helped her down to the pavement. They were standing in front of a large brick building, situated on the northern outskirts of London. A high fence, topped with unpleasant-looking spikes, sealed off the building from the rest of the city. She could see a handful of people walking on the grass inside the fence, their faces downcast and sad. It looked more like a prison than a reputable home.

"This place has no name," Master Thomas admitted. He led the way to the gatehouse, where a burly man scrutinised both of them before allowing them entry through the double gates. It was starting to look more and more like a prison. "I think most of the nobility are a little ashamed of it. They wouldn't want anyone to know what happens inside these walls."

Inside, Gwen felt a prickling feeling at the back of her neck. The handful of people on the grass seemed to be paying no attention to the two guests. For a moment, she wondered if they were revenants rather than living beings, but they didn't seem to be dead. Their eyes were strange, almost as if they couldn't focus on anything. She shuddered as she saw spit falling from their mouths. Master Thomas caught her arm and led her away from the strangers, up towards the huge doors. A man wearing a white coat greeted them and invited them inside.

"Ward Four," Master Thomas said, bluntly. "At once, if you please..."

Gwen stared around her. Inside, the hallways appeared to be quite deserted. An unpleasant stench hung in the air, suggesting meat that was on the verge of rotting off the bone. The white-painted corridors were blank, illuminated only by gas lamps hanging from the ceiling. As they walked down the corridors, she glanced into a side room and saw a young lady, naked to the waist, chained to a chair. Her eyes were savage and, as she met Gwen's stare, she yanked at her chains and started forward. Gwen was halfway through preparing a magical defence when she realised that the chains had held. Even so, she didn't want to turn her back on the woman. What, she asked herself, was wrong with her?

"This place is a madhouse," the attendant said, noticing her puzzlement. Master Thomas frowned in a manner that promised trouble for the attendant, if he said much more. "The gentry send their mistakes here to be held away from public view..."

"Every family has someone who isn't right in the head," Master Thomas rumbled, his voice drowning out the attendant's comments. "The ones who are too dangerous or too embarrassing to be let out in public are sent here, where they are treated to the best of our ability."

"But none of them are ever healed," the attendant said. "They live out their lives within these four walls and no one ever sees them again."

Gwen was shocked. She'd heard rumours, allusions she hadn't fully understood – until now. It seemed that every aristocratic family produced at least one person who couldn't wipe their mouth in public, let alone look after themselves, but she'd never realised what happened to them. Everyone involved had to keep it quiet, or there would be an almighty scandal. Hadn't there been rumours about George III during the regency? His son might have had him committed to a madhouse, if he hadn't been the King. Parliament would never have stood for it.

Master Thomas stepped back and caught her hand. "The first time I came here, I had nightmares for weeks," he said. "If you want to back out now…"

"No," Gwen said. "I won't let this beat me."

"Then prepare yourself," Master Thomas said. "Remember who you are."

The attendant threw open the door to Ward Four and ushered them inside. It hit Gwen at once, a deafening babble that seemed to appear inside her head without going through her ears first. She put up her hands to cover them anyway, but it was useless. The babble just grew louder and louder until she thought she would be lost in it. She opened her mouth to scream, but somehow she caught hold of herself. And then she remembered who and what she was.

She opened her eyes without fully realising that she'd closed them. Ahead of her, there were a number of men and women lying on beds, their eyes wide open as they stared at the bare ceiling. She somehow knew that their minds were elsewhere, despite their twitching bodies as they struggled against their restraints. The noise within her head started to billow up again and she recoiled, fighting down an urge to be sick. The sound was overwhelmingly powerful, as if it were trying to jam its way into her mind through every possible orifice. She staggered backwards, struggling against the torrent of diverse thoughts and emotions. There were voices in her mind...

A strong hand caught her. "Focus," Master Thomas

ordered. A stinging pain appeared on her face and she dimly realised that he'd slapped her. It was almost lost against the roaring in her mind. "Concentrate. Imagine building a wall against the barrage of thoughts. Imagine something that will keep them out forever..."

Gwen closed her eyes, squeezing his hand tightly. It gave her something to anchor herself in the real world as she concentrated on building her defences. Little girls weren't supposed to play with building bricks, but she'd played with her brother's building set as a child before he'd become interested in toy soldiers and then grown too old to play with his little sister. Brick by brick, she built a wall in her mind. It grew easier with each brick and she almost sagged in relief as the torrent diminished and finally faded away into the background. She realised that she was clinging desperately to Master Thomas and let go of him hurriedly. How close had she come to losing her mind?

"You did well," Master Thomas reassured her. She could see concern in his eyes, concern that he might have pushed her too far too fast. "There are Talkers and Sensors who can't come anywhere near this building without risking madness."

Gwen focused her mind. Every time she looked at one of the patients, the babble at the back of her mind seemed to grow louder. She wasn't looking into their minds, she realised grimly; they were projecting their maddened thoughts and feelings into the air, creating an atmosphere where madness flowed from mind to mind. Each of the maddened magicians added to the madness of the other magicians, and in turn fell further into darkness as they absorbed madness from others.

Her legs felt weak, but she held herself upright through sheer force of will. "What...what happened to them?"

Master Thomas's face was grim. "They came into their powers too early," he said. "They should have been Talkers and Sensors and Seers, but they developed their magic too early and discovered that they couldn't learn to control their talents. The influx of outside thoughts drove them insane. Some of them could be controlled through drugs, but others...others had to be brought here and left to die."

Gwen stared at him, honestly shocked. "Their families just...*abandoned* them?"

"No one wants to admit that madness runs through their family blood," Master Thomas admitted. He looked down at one of the older patients, a man who appeared to be on the verge of death. "That man is twenty-two years old and he looks fifty. There's nothing we can do for them, except make them as comfortable as possible and prevent them from hurting themselves. Some of them do make it out of the madness..."

"And how many of them die because they cannot separate their own thoughts from those of others?" Gwen demanded. The building was evil. How could anyone leave people here to waste away and die? "Can't we do anything for them?"

"It's been tried," Master Thomas admitted. He nodded towards a middle-aged woman, who was lying on one of the beds, giggling to herself. "She was once a trained Talker, with a particular interest in helping to cure the sick. It was easy for her to peer into a person's mind and discover what they were reluctant to tell her, or understand the true cause of their distress. And then she came here, into the mental storm, and opened her mind."

"And then she just lost herself," Gwen said, bitterly. "Why...why do we even *tolerate* this?"

Master Thomas caught her arm. "There isn't a single aristocratic family in the Kingdom who would permit us to...kill mentally disturbed family members," he said. "None of us enjoy watching them suffer, young lady, but there's nothing we can do, apart from watching them die."

He looked down for a long second. "I'm sorry for bringing you here," he admitted. "I needed you to develop mental shields before your training continued..."

Gwen shook her head. "It's forgiven," she said, shortly. She didn't want to know, but she had to ask. "What else is here?"

The next ward *stank* so badly that Gwen had to push her pocket handkerchief against her nose to remain within the room. It was crammed with small beds, each one holding a young child. Like the older patients, the children were restrained, but they seemed to be inhumanly calm rather than traumatised. Only their eyes, staring at nothing, revealed that their minds were elsewhere. A handful of nurses with nervous eyes moved from child to child, changing the cloths that had been hung around their waists. They didn't make eye contact with either of the visitors.

Gwen forced herself to look at the children, even though every nerve in her body called out for her to run. They seemed to be evenly divided between male and female, ranging from five to nine years old. None of them seemed to be in good shape, despite the nurses; she suspected that the nurses did the bare minimum they needed to do and left the children to fester. The aroma in the room was one of death. How long, she asked herself as she struggled to hold back the urge to vomit, did the children live before they died? And what happened to the bodies.

"When I am Royal Sorcerer," she said, flatly, "I will not suffer this to continue."

Master Thomas nodded, slowly. "I thought the same," he said. "Perhaps you will be the one who finds a solution to these poor wretches. Or perhaps you will realise that everything comes with a price."

The atmosphere in the room changed, sharply. Gwen glanced up, uncertain of just what had disturbed her, and saw one of the children staring directly at her. The other children were scrabbling against their restraints, fighting to sit up and add their gazes to the disturbing stare. Every child in the room was fighting to look right at Gwen. She felt a tingling down the back of her spine as their eyes bored into her. They had magic, she realised, magic tainted by madness. Who knew what they could do? The nurses acted as if they were scared of their charges. Perhaps they had good reason to be scared.

"I have seen you," one of the girls said. Her voice was cracked and broken, an old woman's voice in a young girl's body. The effect was chilling. "You will rise so high and then fall so low."

"I have seen your lover," one of the boys said. "He will burn with passion for his cause, yet you will catch his eye."

"You will feel yourself torn and broken," a different girl said. "You will watch as madness and anarchy consume the land."

"You will see your lover die," the first girl said. Her eyes were bright in her emaciated face. "You will watch as he burns to death, consumed by a fire greater than his passion."

"Your choice will save or damn a world," the oldest boy said. Blood was leaking from his eyes as he struggled against the straps holding him in his cot. "You will choose..."

Gwen stumbled backwards. Master Thomas caught her and held her upright. The nurses were lying on the ground, clutching their heads and screaming for mercy, a mercy that might never come. Gwen tried to raise her mental wall of bricks, but it refused to form...and then the mental pressure faded away. The children lay back in their cots and resumed staring at nothing. Gwen risked a glance at Master Thomas and saw his worried expression staring back at her. But what had it all meant?

***

"I don't normally partake at all," Master Thomas said, as he passed Gwen the glass of brandy. "But I think we could both do with a proper drink now."

Gwen nodded. She had never fainted in her life and had always looked down on women who fainted, viewing it as weakness. And she had never come closer to fainting as she had when the children had made their prophecy. The brandy tasted strong against her throat, stronger than she remembered. It helped her to think.

"Thank you," she said. "What did all that mean?"

"Their...youth unlocks aspects of their talent that are denied to older and more stable magicians," Master Thomas said. "I suggest that you don't take it too seriously. Very few of their prophecies have proven valid. In at least one case we discovered afterwards that the foretelling hadn't been for the subject at all."

Gwen rubbed her forehead. "The nurses aren't taking proper care of them," she said, coldly. "They need to be fed and washed and..."

"We have tried," Master Thomas said. "But they are children, with talents that can be very dangerous. It's difficult to give them as much care as we do, let alone what they actually need. We lose a nurse every month..."

Gwen started. "They die?"

"Some die," Master Thomas admitted. "Some are mentally damaged by being so close to the children. Some are humiliated and forced to...*perform* for their amusement. And some just cannot bear to be so close to such power and so little control.

"But don't take their words too seriously," he added. "They see many possible futures. How many of them can actually come true?"

Somehow, Gwen was not reassured. "I'm going to do something about it," she said. "I don't know what, but I will do it."

"I hope you succeed," Master Thomas said. He shook his head, sadly. "If we can't take care of our own, what good are we?"

Chapter Eight

urley Hall glowed brightly against the dark. Jack perched on a rooftop, wrapped an illusion around himself and studied the building dispassionately. Lord Burley had served the British Empire in India and Cuba during the wars and there was an undeniably Indian flavour to his house. After he'd made his reputation as a skilled soldier and an undoubted loyalist to the Hanoverian dynasty, he'd been appointed commander-in-chief of the forces in Britain, where he'd stamped on all rumours of uprisings and rebellions with enthusiasm. The common people had many scores to settle with him.

Lord Burley was clearly aware that he wasn't popular – and he clearly also lacked the faith in capital punishment that upheld the ruling government. His house was heavily guarded, with at least two-dozen private guards, all armed with the latest in military rifles. At a guess, Jack reminded himself, he would have some magicians on his staff as well. A single Talker, even one with only limited powers, could summon the Bow Street Runners or soldiers from the nearby garrison easily. And the walls of the house were tough enough to hold off shellfire for long enough for the inhabitants of the house to escape. Jack's lips twitched into a smile. Lord Burley's confidence would be his undoing. He had no idea what was coming for him in the darkness.

Jack had spent a day chatting to Lucy and a handful of other contacts in the Rookery and the middle districts of London. It had always astonished and dismayed him how the poor followed the affairs of the wealthy with so much enthusiasm, but maybe it made a certain kind of sense. A man who made it as a successful merchant could hope to join the Quality, if only through the traditional method of bribing the King in exchange for a peerage. His children would be mocked by those born to the aristocracy, but their children would be accepted as part of the lords and ladies of England. There was plenty of speculation over who would marry Lord Burley's son. His wife and children lived apart from him, according to his contacts; Lord Burley was as unpleasant to his family as he was to his servants and soldiers. He'd flogged more men than anyone else, even the Duke of India.

Jumping down off the rooftop, Jack ran through the shadows until he reached Lord Burley's wall. It was almost impossible for anyone to climb, but Jack didn't need to climb to get over the wall. He levitated into the air, lifted himself over the wall, and put himself down gently on the grass. The illusion of darkness surrounding him would make him impossible to see, unless there was a Sensor among the guards. Jack doubted that anyone with Lord Burley's tastes would hire a Sensor, but he kept himself moving quickly anyway. The moment they knew that he was there, all hell would break loose. He kept a sharp eye out for dogs as he crossed the lawn and came up to the building. Human eyes could be deceived, but dogs were far harder to fool. No magic could confuse their noses for long.

Up close, he found himself admiring the patterns that had been carved into the stonework. Lord Burley had spent a small fortune – enough money to feed and clothe most of London for a year – on his house. It was an advertisement for his military skill, culminating in a depiction of one of the most savage battles against the Sikhs in India. The British troops and their Indian allies had crushed the Sikhs, but only after a long and savage conflict. And now the Sikhs were flowing into the British Indian Army and being transformed into the tool that would take the British Empire north into Afghanistan, maybe even up to the Tsar's borders. It hadn't been that long since Alaska had been taken from the Russians. Who knew what else could be taken and added to the British Empire?

Gathering his power, he floated up into the air. He wasn't the most capable Mover he'd ever seen, but it was easy to lift his body up to the roof. There were no guards positioned on top of the building, an odd oversight for a competent general who had good reason to fear for his life. Jack suspected that the full implications of magic – and the airships that were coming into service with the military – had escaped his notice. The French had a plan to invade England using airships. It might just allow them to land an army on British soil without having to fight their way past the Royal Navy. They might even win.

The rooftop was flat, almost barren compared to the outer walls. Jack moved over to the skylight and examined it quickly, noticing that it was locked from the inside. It would have prevented any normal thief from getting inside, at least without smashing the glass and alerting everyone, but Jack was no normal thief. He closed his eyes and sent his Sight into the lock, and then carefully used his magic to unlock it. There was a click, loud enough to make him jump, and the skylight swung open. Jack dropped down into the house and landed softly, without making a sound. He listened, but there was no sign of anyone else. His Lordship was clearly still in bed, sleeping off his marathon session of drinking and wenching. The rumours had made him out to be something of a pig.

Jack's lips twitched as he slipped forward, careful to inch along the walls rather than walk down the centre of the corridor. A single creak from the wooden floorboards might wake someone, or alert them to an intruder in the house. There was nothing more conspicuous, his old master had warned him, than someone trying to be stealthy and overdoing it. The tricks of burglary were more effective than magic, if used at the right time. He froze as he heard the sound of someone breathing, before realising that it was nothing more than Lord Burley, storing inside the master bedroom. Jack slipped up to the half-open door and peered inside. Lord Burley lay on his bed, face down on the blankets, one hand gripping the hand of a young girl. She couldn't be older than sixteen. Jack winced in disgust, even though he'd expected nothing less. Whatever the Church of England had to say about adultery and fornication, powerful men always considered themselves above the law. Lord Burley was far from the worst of his class – and at least he'd contributed to the Empire, which was more than could be said for most of the aristocrats.

He slipped into the room. The girl was still awake. She opened her mouth to scream for help, but Jack was on her before anything could reach her mouth. He felt her struggle helplessly against him and cursed mentally, knowing that he might well have to kill her. But she was an innocent. She didn't deserve to die. Jack picked her up with his magic, keeping one hand clamped over her mouth, and put her down onto the floor. Lord Burley snorted and turned over in his sleep, his walrus moustache twitching as it came into view. Jack found himself smiling as he stared into the girl's eyes and touched his lips. If she stayed quiet, he promised himself, he would let her live.

"Stay quiet and still," he whispered, pushing as much Charm into his voice as he could. The girl started, and then relaxed. Her eyes went wide with fear. Charm was often more effective when used subtly, rather than with force, but Jack had no time to gently push her into submission. "Don't move a muscle."

He stood up and looked down at Lord Burley. A single slash of his throat would leave him bleeding out in his own bed, but that would be far from enough punishment for the oppressor of the masses. Lord Burley's men had whipped rioters whose only crime was not dispersing fast enough when the Riot Act was read, after they'd come to protest the latest rise in taxes that made it almost impossible for the poor to escape their debts. He deserved a far more meaningful punishment than simply having his throat cut. Jack reached out with his magic and lifted Lord Burley into the air. The overweight Lord's eyes shot open in shock. He'd clearly been drinking before retiring for the night with his latest lady friend. Absently, Jack wondered how much he was paying her. He doubted it was enough to compensate for everything that was about to happen.

Lord Burley's mouth fell open, but Jack stuffed a cloth into his teeth before he could say a word or shout for help. The Lord tried to struggle against Jack's grip, uselessly. Jack bound his hands tightly and then secured the gag in place. Once Lord Burley was secured, Jack tied up the shaking girl, just in case. He'd spent long enough in the underworld to know that a girl could be twice as dangerous as a man, if only because her opponents would tend to underestimate her. He paused outside the door long enough to check that none of the guards had come upstairs and then turned his attention back to his target. To give him due credit, Lord Burley was showing no sign of fear. His gaze – if he had had the magic to power it – could have killed.

Jack leaned closer to the Lord's face. "You have been judged by a court of your victims," he lied smoothly, "and condemned as an Oppressor of the People. Do you wish to say anything in your defence?" He smiled as the Lord's face purpled with anger. "No? We can proceed directly to the sentencing then."

It was too much to expect that Lord Burley would have provided a convenient hook for the hangman's noose, but Jack could use magic to ensure that he was strangled to death, even if the rope wasn't taut. The first flickers of fear entered Lord Burley's eyes as he found himself floating up into the air, followed by the rope tightening around his neck. He started to struggle for breath as the noose grew tighter, but it was futile. His face darkened as he choked to death. It was not a pleasant way to die…

…But it was how they killed on Tyburn Hill, Jack knew. He'd seen enough executions to know that the condemned– often men and women who hadn't been able to bribe the judges or rely on the intervention of friends in high places – were slowly suffocated to death. A noose was the mob's method of choice too, when it lynched infrequent victims. The enemies of liberty would know what kind of message Jack was sending them, once they saw the body. And they would know what would happen to them if they fell into his hands.

Lord Burley made a final gasp and expired. Jack checked his pulse carefully – it would have been difficult to fake, but possible – and confirmed that he was dead for himself. The girl, who had been watching in terror, cringed away from him as he produced a knife. Ignoring her, Jack cut into Lord Burley's leg and used the knife to pick up the blood, using it to write two words on the wall. When he was done, the words CAPTAIN SWING could be easily made out. Its intended target would know what he meant, and those who didn't know would soon come to fear it. They would come to fear Captain Swing.

He smiled as he checked that the girl could breathe properly and walked out of the door. It would have been easy to slip back out of the skylight, but he had a reputation to uphold. By the time London awoke, everyone would know about Lord Burley's death – and the name Captain Swing would be on every man's lips. Whistling tunelessly, he strode down the stairs, wondering how long it would take for the guards to notice him. A man as paranoid as Lord Burley would never have forbidden his guards to enter the house. They weren't as well-trained as Jack had expected. He heard two guards running up the hallway towards him long before they came into view. The moment he saw them, he rammed a pulse of magic through the first one's head and picked up the second one, slamming him into the wall. Jack heard the sound of breaking bones and nodded in approval. He stepped over the prone bodies, wrapping himself in illusion. The alarm would definitely be out now. He gathered his magic as a new guard appeared, clad in sorcerer's black. Jack chuckled aloud as the sorcerer lifted one hand in preparation to use his magic. It was nice of Lord Burley to identify his pet magicians for Jack.

The sorcerer launched a bolt of energy at Jack, which lit up the hallway a second before it slammed into Jack's magic. A brilliant haze flared out in front of him and then flickered out of existence. The sorcerer gaped, clearly not expecting to see someone who could use two different talents – even if he'd seen Jack using magic earlier, he wouldn't have expected a Master Magician. Jack didn't give him time to adapt; he launched a pulse of energy himself, right into the sorcerer's throat. The smell of burning flesh filled the corridor as Jack stepped over the dead sorcerer and down towards the doors. Outside, he could hear the sounds of men running towards the house. Lord Burley's guards, better paid than the average soldier and therefore more willing to risk their lives for their master, had definitely realised that something was badly wrong. And if there was a Talker among them, the Bow Street Runners would definitely have been summoned.

Jack sent a wave of magic out ahead of him as he approached the doors and they burst into fragments, slamming out and into the small army running towards the house. A handful reacted in time to cover their eyes or drop to the ground, but most of them were hit by flying splinters. Jack knew that some of them would probably be blinded, yet he found it hard to care. They'd chosen to uphold the established order and betray their roots by taking their master's money. They needed to pay for their crimes.

Another pulse of energy shot at him and he ducked, reaching out with his magic to catch the Blazer and hurling him into the air. Even the most capable Blazer would have difficulty hitting anyone while flying – and would die when he hit the ground. The remaining guards seemed to be nothing more than mundane humans, but Jack was careful not to allow his field of magic to drop. One mistake and a bullet would kill him just as effectively as it would kill an ordinary human without a single hint of magic.

He directed a burst of energy at one of the guards, and then switched to a second target. They had to be good and mad by now, but just to be sure Jack sent a concentrated beam of light at the rosebushes. Lord Burley had been a keen gardener, something Jack found a little hard to reconcile with his bloody-handed reputation for extreme conservatism. Or perhaps he had just liked the thought of growing something exactly as he planned. The bushes caught fire and the flames spread rapidly out of control, threatening to spread to the house and incinerate Lord Burley's body. Just for a second, he considered jumping back into the house and rescuing the girl – she probably hadn't wanted to share Lord Burley's bed, but hadn't been given any choice – before he realised that it would be a risk too far. The Royal Sorcerers Corps would have been alerted by now. Besides, he had every confidence that the guards could put out the blaze before it was too late. He'd gone to too much effort arranging the body to have it wasted through burning down the house.

Grinning like a loon, he grabbed at his body with magic and hurled himself into the air with terrific force. As a student, his old master had had to shame him into throwing himself madly around the city, but now he wondered how anyone could bear to walk when they could fly. Gravity reasserted itself and he started to fall, yet all it took was another burst of magic to send his body spinning over the rooftops and away from the house. The fire behind him started to dim as the guards fought it with more courage than they'd shown fighting him, but then none of them had expected to face a magician. And not a Master Magician at that…Jack wondered, as he came down and landed in a darkened street, if he was still officially dead. The forces of reaction would have preferred to believe that, certainly. But his old tutor would never have taken it for granted. Master

Magicians were very hard to kill.

He wrapped his cloak around him and strode off down the street. By the time the Bow Street Runners set up a cordon – if they did – he would be well on his way back to the Rookery. London never really slept, even in the middle-class areas. There were too many whores and criminals out wandering the streets to keep the city quiet. And nothing the Church had tried had managed to slow the spread of prostitution. There were simply too many young women with no other prospects in London. The only way they could earn money was through lying on their backs with their legs open. It disgusted him. So much potential was being lost on the streets.

Slipping back into the little room he'd hired was easy. Few people asked questions in the Rookery. He stumbled over and collapsed into the hard bed. Using magic so often was very tiring. Jack promised himself a late breakfast in the morning, before he headed to find his next target. There were thousands of aristocrats to kill in London. They would all come to fear his name.

Chapter Nine

harm is one of the strangest magical talents," Doctor Norwell said. The theoretical magician, Gwen had discovered, loved lecturing his audience. And he didn't seem to hold Gwen's sex against her, once he'd gotten over the shock. "It is more effective if worked gently, rather than with force. The most dangerous form of Charm comes from a slow infusion of suggestions into the victim's mind. A strong-willed person can break Charm if they realise what is happening to them, but if the effect is subtle they literally never realise what is happening to them."

Gwen scowled, inwardly. She knew what happened when a Charmer came into his or her powers, because Charm had been the first talent she'd used. The young Gwen hadn't had the slightest idea of what she was or what she could do – and the effects had been staggeringly bad, bad enough to ensure that rumours continued to swirl around her even as a teenager. Master Thomas had used brute force to demonstrate Charm, yet she knew that that was far from the most dangerous form, even without Doctor Norwell's lecture. She'd proved it herself as a child.

She glanced over at Lord Blackburn as he sat on the opposite chair, staring at her. He was unmarried, Gwen knew, but he didn't seem to be sizing her up as a possible bride, not like some of the other students. His gaze made her feel as if she was an insect trapped under a glass, unable to avoid his stare – or to resist him when she was finally pinned down and placed in a box. There was nothing, but coldness in his eyes, a coldness that sent chills down her spine. Lord Blackburn was a very dangerous person, even without a peerage that linked him to the highest families in the land.

"Charm is also the most feared of all the talents," Doctor Norwell continued. "The Houses of Parliament have passed strong laws against its use, with a number of cases being brought to the Old Bailey. However, *proving* the use of Charm – particularly subtle Charm – is extremely difficult. As always, it is hard to prove what a magician is capable of doing without actually witnessing them using magic."

"And that concludes the lecture," Lord Blackburn said. His voice was cold, almost dispassionate. He took an interest in politics, Gwen recalled suddenly. It might be worth writing to her mother and asking for a briefing on his life and prospects. Her mother knew everyone who was anyone, or who thought they were. "We will now proceed to the practical part of the lesson. You may leave us."

Doctor Norwell scowled at him, but accepted his dismissal without comment. "Master Thomas wishes to see you after this part of the lesson," he told Gwen, as he picked up his case of papers and headed to the door. "You will report to him before lunch."

"Yes, sir," Gwen said, automatically. Doctor Norwell wasn't usually so rude. Lord Blackburn had definitely put him out of sorts. The door closed behind him with an audible thump and she turned to look up at Blackburn. His face was expressionless, but there was something in his eye that made her fear being alone with him. She couldn't have put it into words, apart from a desire to run for her life.

"Charm requires dedication and focus on the part of the magician," Lord Blackburn said, flatly. His eyes had never left her face. "To reveal that one is using one's Charm is to lose an advantage. The human mind does not take well to having suggestions pushed into it by a Charmer. Even the weakest of souls will fight Charm if they are aware that it is being used on them. And pushing too hard can break their minds."

His gaze fixed on her eyes. "Why don't you stand up and take off your dress?"

Gwen was on her feet and unbuttoning her dress before her mind caught up with him. He'd used his Charm on her...and done it so subtly that she hadn't even realised what was happening, even though he'd spoken his outrageous orders out loud. Her mind hadn't registered them properly...even though she knew what had happened it was still hard to force her treacherous fingers to stop. She buttoned up her dress, sat down and glared at him. The force of her glare made absolutely no impression on him at all.

"You realised that something was wrong," he said. "Had I suggested something a little less...unpleasant, you would probably not have noticed until it was far too late. A suggestion implanted in a receptive mind becomes impossible to distinguish from a genuine thought, rendering it very difficult to notice, let alone defeat. You must always bear in mind that highly emotional people are easier to Charm. A person who thinks through every step, bit by bit, and seeks logical reasons to justify his actions is far harder to Charm. The intent is always to push them into accepting the Charm without thinking or close examination."

Gwen felt...dirty. She'd known that her brother had had some fun with the serving maids, before he'd become respectable, and she hadn't understood. But then, she'd been protected by her birth and the rumours surrounding her and no one had taken an interest in marrying her. Her mother had even talked about marrying the simple-headed Lord Percy, Heir to the Duchy of Northumberland. No one else would have wanted a magical wife. Blackburn had pushed a thought into her head and she'd obeyed. She knew now how the maids must have felt, when they'd been used for someone else's pleasure.

"Don't do that again," she said, more sharply than she'd intended. The whole prospect terrified her. "I'll...I'll..."

"I'll keep doing it until you learn how to defend yourself against it," Lord Blackburn said, flatly. "And until you learn how to use it for yourself. I understand that apart from an...unfortunate incident, you have never learned to practice Charm. Like all of the talents, it requires constant practice to learn how to use it perfectly. And you will be perfect by the time you graduate from this school. Your blood demands it."

He strode over to the door before Gwen could reply and opened it, beckoning for someone to enter the room. Gwen's eyes went wide as she saw a scullery maid, wearing a simple white dress that was stained with food and drink. It was quite common for youngsters to enter family service and rise up through the ranks, leaving their families behind until they were completely dedicated to their masters. She had been surprised to discover that Cavendish Hall used a similar system, but then far too many of the servants handed in their notice after being the target of a handful of magical jokes.

The maid bowed. "You called me, sir?"

"Yes," Blackburn said. His voice sounded as cold and harsh as always, even when the maid hastily lifted her dress in a curtsey. "Take a seat by the table and wait."

Gwen frowned as the maid did as she was told. The maid's body was trembling and her eyes were wide with fear. Somehow, Gwen knew what was about to happen before Blackburn closed and locked the door. They were going to use the maid as the target for their magic, practicing her Charm. And the maid was going to hate it. Cold logic told Gwen that she needed to learn and to understand; human sympathy told her that she should call a halt right now. The maid, she resolved, would be paid enough never to have to work again.

If Blackburn had any similar thoughts, he kept them to himself. "Your task is simple," he said, looking the maid in the eye. "You will remain seated while Lady Gwen gives you orders. You will do everything you can to remain seated. Do you understand me?"

"Yes, sir," the maid said.

Gwen winced at the frightened expression on her face. "What is your name?"

"Fiona, My Lady," the maid said. Her accent was clearer now. She had to come from Ireland, or perhaps an Irish family who had immigrated to London in search of food, work and lodging. There had been riots a few years ago against Irishmen taking English jobs, if she recalled correctly.

"Very good," Lord Blackburn said. "Gwen…you may issue a few orders."

Gwen hesitated. The last time she'd used Charm had been a disaster.

"Go on," he prodded her. "She's here to serve."

Gwen gathered herself. "Stand up," she ordered.

Fiona didn't move. "You need to really *want* her to move," Blackburn said. There was an odd look of almost predatory excitement in his eyes, one that Gwen couldn't understand. "You have to focus your mind on her motion."

"Right," Gwen said, crossly. But she *didn't* want Fiona to obey. Charm had scarred her mind – and she'd been the Charmer. "Stand up."

This time, Fiona half-rose to her feet before sitting back down. Gwen saw her eyes, wide with fear and terrified anticipation, and shuddered. The Church damned Charmers who used their powers on unwilling subjects, although she'd heard that Charmers were sometimes used for social control. And Blackburn...Blackburn's eyes were still gleaming with a hellish light. What was he *thinking*? Master Thomas had warned her that she would probably never be able to read minds – that required a powerful Talker – but she thought she sensed his feelings. Something was pushing him onwards, something almost...unholy?

"Not too bad, but too mild," Lord Blackburn observed. His voice shifted with a snap. "Stand up – *now!*"

Fiona rose to her feet, still shaking with fear. Gwen looked at Blackburn and saw him lick his lips. She shuddered as Fiona broke free of the compulsion and sat back down, her hands tightly clasped in her lap. How could anyone just sit and endure being Charmed by a pair of sorcerers? But then, the maid had no choice. If she didn't obey, she would be put out on the streets.

"Try again," Lord Blackburn ordered. "Focus your mind on something more subtle."

Gwen scowled at him. "Stand up and touch your forehead," she ordered. This time, she felt the subtle magic weaving its way into her voice. Fiona rose and barely stopped herself before her hand touched her forehead. Blackburn snickered at the look of confusion and horror on her face.

"Don't worry about it," he said, directly to her. "You are here to obey."

"I am here to obey," Fiona repeated. She sounded as if she'd been put into a trance. "I am here to obey. I am here to obey..."

Gwen rounded on Blackburn. "Enough," she said, her voice shaking with anger. "Stop it, now!"

Blackburn smiled, amused. "Make me," he said. She could feel his magic woven into his voice, threatening to influence her thoughts. It was a devilishly subtle power – and all the more dangerous for it. "Use your Charm to command me."

He leered at her. Gwen saw red and slapped him before she quite realised what she was doing. He staggered backwards, a bright mark appearing on his cheek. She watched his hands as they clenched into fists, wondering if he was going to hit her back. No gentleman would ever hit a lady, but she'd known long before Master Thomas had invited her to the Hall that few gentlemen lived up to their high standards. If he took a swing at her, she vowed to herself, she'd use her magic and send him flying right across the room.

Somehow, he kept his own temper under control. "You'll regret that," he snarled, as one hand rubbed his cheek. Gwen hadn't thought that she'd slapped him that hard, but if she'd lost control there might have been magic in the force of the blow. "I'll make you regret that..."

"Get out," Gwen ordered. It was tricky to use magic to move two things at once, even though she'd been practicing – and she'd had the unexpected battle with the other students to hone her skills. She pulled the door open and pushed him towards the exit. He cast one last murderous look at her and stormed out, slamming the door behind him. Gwen rolled her eyes, feeling her temper cooling. If Master Thomas felt that she should be punished, she would accept it. But only if he punished Blackburn for his cruelty to Fiona.

The maid cringed away from her as Gwen tried to help her to her feet. She practically ran for the door, as if she expected a bullet to hit her or a charmed voice calling her back. Gwen watched her go, feeling cold bitterness congealing around her thoughts. She was already isolated from the other students because of her sex and age; now she would be isolated from the staff too. But then, she couldn't have shared herself completely with them. It was funny how she'd felt happier alone at home, but not now that she'd found her niche in life. Would she ever have magical friends?

She pulled herself to her feet before she lost herself in self-pity and walked out the door. Fiona was nowhere in sight, thankfully. Gwen headed down into the library, knowing that Master Thomas would probably be waiting for her there. The library was easily her favourite room in Cavendish Hall. It was big, with thousands of books on magic, books that Master Thomas had admitted were largely nonsense. Other books had been banned by various authorities and had only been stockpiled in the hall because the previous Royal Sorcerer had hated the very concept of destroying books. The librarian glanced up at her as she entered, and then pointed to a corner of the room. Master Thomas was seated at a small oak desk, reading his way through a sheaf of papers. He looked up at her as she took the seat facing him.

"You look unhappy," he observed, as he closed the set of papers before she could start reading them. They looked official, with a seal she half-recognised at the bottom. "I thought you'd still be learning Charm."

"I lost my temper," Gwen admitted. The whole story spilled out, from start to finish. "I...why...why did that happen?"

"Charmers have a tendency to irritate everyone else," Master Thomas remarked. He hesitated for a moment. "And Lord Blackburn, who may be the most capable Charmer in the world, has a habit of irritating people. The two don't go together very well."

He looked up at her. "But in Blackburn's case...I'm afraid that slapping him was not the best way to deal with him," he added. "Luckily, with you being an emotional woman, he will probably overlook it once his temper has cooled down."

Gwen flushed. She'd heard her mother say that women were naturally more emotional and sensitive than men, but she'd seen plenty of evidence that the opposite was true. But then, women were more affected by their lives than men. A man who wenched every night was a hero to his fellows; a woman who took a different lover every year was a whore. It didn't seem fair to her, somehow, but no men had ever shown any interest in her anyway. They didn't want to marry the subject of such disturbing rumours.

"He was mentally *raping* her," Gwen snapped. Her mother would have fainted if she'd known that Gwen had even *heard* that word, still less knew what it meant. Somehow, Gwen found it hard to care what her mother thought. "He was enjoying forcing her to be his slave..."

"Lord Blackburn is a Darwinist," Master Thomas admitted. He didn't seem perturbed by Gwen's use of the word *rape*. "I'm afraid that such people have been growing in power lately. And if you hadn't existed, one of them might have been put into the position of Royal Sorcerer."

Gwen blinked. "I thought that the Royal Sorcerer had to be a Master," she said.

"Yes," Master Thomas agreed, "but what if we had *no*

Master?"

He shook his head. "Charles Darwin is a young man with a magical talent; he's actually a fairly powerful Blazer. Darwin believes in the survival of the fittest – and that the fittest is the one who will survive. Magicians have an advantage over mundane humans – and aristocratic magicians are more powerful than common-born magicians. The Darwinist Creed says that magicians are superior to mundane humans and should be ruling the world."

Gwen snorted. "I doubt the King enjoys hearing such talk," she said. "Why hasn't Blackburn been arrested for treason?"

"The man has a powerful family," Master Thomas said. "He also has considerable support among younger magicians who would not normally inherit any titles from their parents. The King...feels that such people had better be ignored until they cross the line into outright treason. No one wants a repeat of the Jacobite Rebellion – the Pretender had a great many friends in high places back in '45. If they'd risen against the King's grandfather, the results could have been unfortunate."

He shrugged, slowly. "I don't know if the Darwinists will become a major problem on my watch, but they will certainly become one on yours," he added. "I'd suggest learning as much as you can from Lord Blackburn. And don't ever forget that he is a very capable magician. I've seen him do far worse than convince a serving maid to take off her dress for him."

"And you allow him to work here," Gwen said, sharply.

"My dear girl," Master Thomas said. "Whatever made you think I got to choose the magicians I have to work with?"

He stood up and picked up his hat and cane. "But we have other matters to turn our attention to," he said. "I received a note from Inspector Lestrade of Scotland Yard. Someone has murdered Lord Burley – and a magician was definitely involved. And that means that we have to investigate."

Gwen frowned. "And you want me to come with you?"

"You may as well see what happens when a magical crime is committed," Master Thomas said. "You'll be investigating them yourself soon enough."

Chapter Ten

wen could barely remember Lord Burley.

They'd met briefly, if she recalled correctly, during a dinner party held at her home. Lord Burley had nodded gravely to Gwen – who had been barely seven years old at the time – and then proceeded to talk to her parents about boring adult matters. He hadn't brought any children with him, so Gwen had been taken back to her room by her nurse once she'd been presented to the guests. She couldn't remember why her mother had held the dinner party in the first place. Her mother rarely needed an excuse to hold a party.

She frowned as the carriage turned the corner and she saw the policemen outside the building. The death of a noted Lord, no matter how disliked by High Society, would definitely attract attention from the police, who would be put under immense pressure to find someone they could convict of the crime. Master Thomas leaned forward and issued instructions to the coachman, who pulled up alongside the pavement and reined in the horses. Gwen followed Master Thomas out into the cold morning air, silently grateful that she'd brought her thicker dress rather than something decorative. Master Thomas strode off towards the policemen and Gwen had to move swiftly to keep up with him. He didn't seem inclined to wait for her at all.

The servants had been gathered by the police and asked to remain on the lawn, inside the walls. Outside the barriers, the broadsheet writers had already gathered, shouting questions to all and sundry. Gwen's mother had often complained that the broadsheet writers either didn't write what they were told or repeated what had been said with embarrassing accuracy, something that hadn't stopped her reading the society papers thoroughly every morning. Gwen herself had enjoyed reading the serialised stories, until her mother had put a stop to it on the grounds that it was unladylike. Part of her still resented her mother's decision, but it no longer mattered. She could read to her heart's content in the library at Cavendish Hall.

Inspector Lestrade was a short, rat-faced fellow, wearing a heavy overcoat from which dangled a truncheon, a whistle and a small oil lamp. Gwen's mother had often said that policemen – the Bow Street Runners, in popular parlance – were not the social equals of noblemen, but merely hired servants to protect the property of the rich. They didn't have a good reputation, although Master Thomas had assured her that Lestrade was the best of a bad lot. Gwen had to smile at how he took one glance at her, registered her sex, and then fixed his eyes on Master Thomas. Perhaps he had mistaken her for a daughter or even a relative of the deceased. A murder scene was definitely not a place for a young lady.

"Master Thomas," Lestrade said. His voice was clipped and precise, oddly accented in a manner Gwen didn't recognise. Scotland Yard recruited from all over the country. "I'm afraid that Lord Burley is definitely dead."

"So I was given to understand," Master Thomas said, calmly. Too calmly; for whatever reason, Gwen realised, he was more worried than he let on. Something about the murder had drawn his attention and the mere fact that a magician might have been involved couldn't have accounted for it. There were far too many criminally-minded magicians on the streets. "Myself and my apprentice will inspect the scene of the crime. You will keep your men outside until I am satisfied."

"Yes, sir," Lestrade said, promptly. Gwen realised that he was glad of the chance to pass the responsibility to someone else. "Should I hold the relatives when they come for the body?"

Master Thomas nodded. "They can have the body once we have finished our inspection," he said. "Make sure you find out where they were last night and get it corroborated if possible. Who knows who might have benefited from the crime?"

Gwen followed Master Thomas up the driveway and through the big open doors at the front of the house. It was cold inside, suggesting that all the windows had been opened by the staff during the night. The hallway was a wreck, with shattered walls and debris lying everywhere. She caught a whiff of smoke in the air and glanced over at one of the walls. It had been scorched by incredible heat. It reminded her of the scene after they'd had the disastrous food fight, only with more malice and different types of magic. Master Thomas bent to inspect one of the bodies and Gwen followed his gaze. She felt sick the moment she saw the body, breathing in the stench of burned flesh.

"Breathe through your mouth," Master Thomas advised, without looking away from the body. Gwen swallowed hard and looked back. The body's throat was completely burned to blackened ruin, a wound that would certainly have been fatal. She tried to remember what she could of anatomy – not a fitting subject for a young lady, according to her mother – and then realised she didn't need any specialised knowledge to understand what had happened. Only magic – a Blazer – could have inflicted such a wound.

"Certainly," Master Thomas agreed, when she said it out loud. He looked up at her suddenly. "Do you notice anything odd about the second body?"

Gwen walked over and peered down at it. The body looked...crushed, even though it seemed to be intact. She had to fight down another tidal wave of vomit as she realised that most of the body's bones had been broken; something or someone had thrown him into the wall with terrific force. Again, magic – a Mover – had to have been involved. She couldn't imagine anything non-magical that could inflict that kind of damage.

"There was a Mover involved as well," Gwen said, carefully. She looked over at him, suddenly. "How many criminals were involved?"

"Good question," Master Thomas said. "The message from Lestrade said that the staff claimed that only one magician was involved. They might have been wrong."

He stood up and headed over towards the stairs. "Or they might have been lying," he added, absently. "They failed their master – or they might have been bribed into betraying their master. Lord Burley was not popular in town."

Gwen followed him, her mind spinning. She had always been taught that servants were reliable, even the ones who were afraid of her and her powers. Even though servants were trusted family retainers, her mother wouldn't have hesitated to fire a servant who displeased her. There were entire families of servants who had served a particular aristocratic family throughout the years. If Lord Burley had been so unpopular…would his own servants have turned on him? But if they had, why had some of them been killed by magic in the struggle?

"Master," she said, slowly, "was Lord Burley a magician?"

"Not as far as I know," Master Thomas said. "All magicians are supposed to be registered with the Crown, but an aristocrat might keep his powers to himself, just in hopes of using them for unfair advantage. Still" – he shrugged – "Lord Burley's career was that of a very honourable soldier. He would surely have used any powers he had in the service of the Crown."

Gwen stopped dead as they reached the landing. A stuffed tiger was glaring back at her, its face twisted in savage excitement. Lord Burley, she realised, had been a keen hunter, taking advantage of his years in India to bag hundreds of tigers. He'd probably been a terror while fox-hunting or grouse shooting back home in England. She'd known young scions of the aristocracy who spent their entire lives shooting harmless birds and deer. It had never seemed a good pastime for her, but while she had been allowed to ride, she had never been allowed to hunt. Perhaps she would have felt differently if she'd been born a man.

"The fellow was an excellent shot," Master Thomas observed, studying the tiger. There was no sign of where the bullet had entered its body. "I couldn't have done it better with magic."

He led the way into the master bedroom and frowned. Gwen followed him in and saw Lord Burley – an older and fatter man than she remembered – lying on the ground. A length of rope was tied around his neck, clearly having been used to strangle him to death. She glanced up at the wall and blinked in surprise. The words CAPTAIN SWING had been painted on the walls in red paint. No, not paint, she realised in shock. The murderer had signed his crime in his victim's blood. This time, she couldn't swallow fast enough to stop bile rising into her mouth and she retched loudly. A metal bucket floated across the room and hovered just in front of her, ready to catch it if she threw up. Somehow, she managed to keep it down.

"Interesting," Master Thomas observed. "What would you say was the cause of death?"

Gwen stared at him. "He was hanged," she said, flatly. He'd clearly died when the rope had been pulled tight around his neck. "His murderer hung him from the ceiling…"

"Look up," Master Thomas suggested. "There's no hook, no rafters…nothing that could be used to hang a man. And yet he was very definitely hanged. What does that suggest to you?"

Gwen stared down at the body, wincing. "Magic," she said. Once she'd made the connection, it was obvious. "They held his body in the air using magic and then let go, holding onto the rope. A Mover was involved."

"Yes," Master Thomas agreed. He prodded the body thoughtfully, but if he pulled any flashes of insight off the body he kept them to himself. "And a Blazer, who killed one of the guarding magicians – and they said that there was only one magician."

He led Gwen back outside and looked up at the skylight. "He got in through the skylight," he said. Gwen frowned, and then understood. A Mover could have opened the skylight from the outside and then jumped down into the building, relying on his magic to land safely. But if there had been only one magician…?

"Captain Swing," she repeated. "Who is Captain Swing?"

Master Thomas didn't answer. He walked back inside the master bedroom and studied the wall thoughtfully. Gwen didn't understand – and then it all made horrifying sense. One magician had been involved, one magician with multiple powers. And that meant a Master.

"It's a message," Master Thomas said, finally. "A message aimed at one specific person."

Gwen looked over at him. He sounded grim – and worried. "Aimed at whom?"

"Aimed at me," Master Thomas said. He stepped closer, studying the word CAPTAIN. "This wasn't a random murder, young lady. This was an act of war – a *declaration* of war – aimed at me. Lord Burley was a known supporter of the Whigs; he was one of their biggest backers. And he controlled several votes in the House. His murder is going to upset several different political factions."

He turned and marched out of the room, not looking back. "There are only a handful of people in the world who could have slipped into this house and murdered its owner," he said. "And one of them was someone we thought long dead."

Gwen blinked. "Who was it?" She asked. "Shouldn't we be chasing him?"

"Not at the moment," Master Thomas said. "You're going to have to learn faster, I'm afraid. Try not to slap any more tutors. They make a frightful fuss."

His tone was light, but Gwen could sense the worry under it. Master Thomas was the most accomplished magician in the world. He shared all of the powers and knew how to use them in combination, making him far more dangerous than any other magician. And yet, whoever had killed Lord Burley worried him. If there had been only one intruder, he had to have been a Master – a Master who knew how to use his powers in combination.

Master Thomas led the way down the stairs and out into the garden. For the next thirty minutes, he interrogated each of the servants and surviving guards one by one. One of them, a girl shivering under a blanket, was apparently under arrest for loose morals. Master Thomas rebuked the policeman who'd arrested her, arranged for her to be taken to a place where she could live and perhaps find a honest vocation, and then interrogated her carefully. She'd been in the room when the murderer had arrived, but she'd seen almost nothing. The murderer's face had been cloaked in illusion. He would have been almost impossible to see in the dark.

Gwen lost interest rapidly and found herself studying the policemen instead. They were glancing at her when they thought she wasn't looking: glances that suggested that she made them nervous in some way. Scotland Yard didn't employ women in any position; even their servants were all male. Perhaps they were unused to the idea of a woman being in a position of power, not when there hadn't been a female Queen for decades. It had been centuries since Elizabeth had proved herself the equal of any man.

She frowned as she saw a strange man talking to Inspector Lestrade. He was tall and thin, wearing a deerstalker hat and a cloak that seemed to cover most of his body. Beside him, a shorter man with a moustache and a doctor's bag was watching impatiently, clearly looking forward to examining the body. Lestrade's voice grew louder as they argued, but Gwen couldn't make it out clearly. He didn't sound happy.

"None of them saw his face," Master Thomas said, grimly. He nodded to the Inspector's two friends, who nodded back. "I don't think we'll find anything here that can be used to trace him back to his lair. You may as well have the body removed and handed over to the clergy for cremation."

"Of course, sir," Inspector Lestrade said. No one was buried these days, not when a necromancer could give new life to the dead. Bodies were incinerated by law and anyone who failed to notify the authorities would face a stiff fine and six months in jail. "I'll let the relatives know."

"I'm sure they know already," Master Thomas said. "It will be all over London by now."

He said nothing until they were back in the carriage, heading back to Cavendish Hall. "I must speak with Lord Mycroft at once," he said. "His brother is a private agent who sometimes takes on commissions for the government. Perhaps he can be of some service."

Gwen looked up at him. "Master," she said, slowly, "who *is* he?"

"That isn't important at the moment," Master Thomas said. "The Fairweathers are planning to host a ball in a week. I trust that you will be attending?"

Gwen was used to sudden changes in subject, but it still caught her by surprise. Master Thomas had never shown any interest in balls before, or the parties that socialites like her mother hosted on a regular basis. Or maybe she'd just missed the signs. It had only been a week since her life had turned upside down.

"I don't think that anyone will take me," Gwen admitted. The thought hurt more than she was prepared to admit. It wasn't the done thing for a woman to go to a ball without a male companion. Most of the young girls she knew either moved from man to man, or formed a relationship with a single man that would inevitably lead to marriage. By then, the parents would have been consulted, negotiations would have taken place and the happy couple would have discovered that they no longer controlled their own lives. "And I wasn't planning to go."

"They're powerful patrons of Cavendish Hall," Master

Thomas said, dryly. "It would be unwise to offend them. Do you wish anyone to invite you to the ball?"

Gwen flushed. The thought of Master Thomas ordering one of the other students to escort her was embarrassing. And yet...she doubted that any of them would work up the nerve to ask her to accompany them to the ball. They'd be reluctant to risk any shadow over their own reputation, even though they'd probably been visiting brothels or seducing the maids since they'd grown old enough to know that the stork didn't bring babies to their parents at night.

"No, thank you," she said, firmly. She would prefer to go on her own rather than have an unwilling companion. But then, maybe they wouldn't be all that unwilling. The Fairweather family wasn't *just* interested in magic. They were major backers of the East India Company and had interests and investments all over the globe. Their parties were *the* major event of the year. Her mother might not be able to secure an invitation.

"You will be coming," Master Thomas said, firmly. "I suggest that you ask one of your fellow students, or a young man of your acquaintance. There will be a chance to meet many of the most powerful men and women in London at the ball. When you become the Royal Sorcerer, you will need contacts and allies in high places if you are to do your job properly."

Gwen nodded, reluctantly. How did he manage to keep making her feel like a child?

"When we return home, I suggest that you apologise to Lord Blackburn," Master Thomas added. "You cannot afford a political enemy in such a high place. Your position is going to be unstable anyway – you don't need darker problems."

"No," Gwen said, flatly. "You didn't see how he was treating that girl. He deserves far worse than a slap."

"I don't doubt it," Master Thomas said, "but if you don't learn anything else from me, learn this. Those with power have to be humoured or they will work against you. And then, if you're lucky, you won't be able to get anything done."

Chapter Eleven

he Government had banned the Working Men's clubs after the long period of social unrest in Britain that had followed the aborted revolutions in America, France and even Russia. People being people, their decree had done nothing more than drive the clubs underground, where working men of the lower classes could drown their sorrows in drink before staggering home to their wives. Jack knew that it was a more subtle means of social control than using Dragoons to clear the streets. The working men spent their day working and drinking and rarely had time to consider the true nature of their place in society. Besides, when the local temperance legion had managed to ban alcohol, there had been riots in the streets. That law had been hastily rescinded.

He smiled to himself as he slipped through the door and into the club. It was a massive room, lit by dim oil lanterns that shrouded the whole chamber in an atmosphere of gloom. A fire burned brightly in one corner, providing heat and flickering illumination for the crowd of heavy drinkers. It was, by common consent, an English-only club. The Irishmen, Welshmen and Scotsmen had their own clubs, where they drank their sorrows away. And, on weekends, the drinkers would often end up brawling with other drinkers, their hatreds blinding them to the fact that they shared a common cause. Jack slapped a copper crown onto the table, accepted a tankard of beer and tasted it carefully. It was weaker than he remembered, but then there was nothing stopping the barman from watering his booze. No one in their right mind would try any of the bar snacks.

The racket grew louder as more and more men crammed into the club. Jack watched as the barmaid, almost certainly the owner's daughter, moved from table to table, replenishing glasses and taking coins from the bar's patrons. The bartender was one of the few totally honest men – if one didn't count the watered-down beer – in the Rookery. Everyone liked and trusted him, which made his participation in the movement essential. Jack took another swig of his beer, winced at the taste, and then stood up. Night was falling, the serious drinking was just beginning and before too long, the camaraderie at the bar would be replaced by violence and drunken fighting. No one would break it up if two drunkards started fighting each other. They'd be more likely to start betting on the outcome.

Jack scowled inwardly as he pushed his way through the crowd of sweaty men, drinking as quickly as they could. He had no illusions about their nature, not like the upper-class women who formed the temperance legions. The poor were shaped by their environment, lying, cheating and stealing to survive, knowing that their lives might be ended at any moment. Life was cheap in the Rookery. Jack was mildly surprised that the recruiting sergeants didn't have more recruits for the army. But then, the army was used to repress urban rioting. The weak-chinned aristocrats who commanded the army wouldn't want soldiers who refused to charge their fellows.

He opened an unmarked door and slipped into the rear room. A smaller number of men were gathered around a fence, watching with interest as two wild dogs fought each other for their amusement. One of the dogs had lost a leg, but it managed to stay on its feet and savage the other with sharp teeth. The sound of bets being exchanged could be heard over their growls; by the time the night was done, a few people would be richer at the expense of their fellows. The game wasn't precisely rigged, but a smart planner could ensure that the odds were tipped in his favour. A cheer went up when the smaller dog managed to sink its teeth into the larger dog's throat and ripped, hard. Blood went everywhere as the larger dog sank to the ground and died. A number of gamblers were sulking. They'd bet heavily on the loser.

Jack shook his head and walked through the third door. Inside, a man carrying a club inspected him before waving him through. Davy had taken care of security, with trusted men posted at all points. If the Bow Street Runners had a spy inside the movement, they might know about the meeting, but they'd never get to the club before the occupants already been warned. Besides, after the death of Lord Burley, the Runners were more likely to be running around looking for his murderer than watching the underground. But then, Master Thomas would have seen his message. He could hardly have failed to understand what it meant.

Inside the inner room, nine men waited for him. Jack exchanged handshakes with the ones he didn't know, hoping – praying – that Davy was still a good judge of character. The last time he'd been in London, he'd trusted the wrong person and ended up having to run for his life. And if he hadn't had something to bargain with, the French might well have killed him rather than trying to turn him into a tool. Four other men, all from the underground, came in several minutes later. Davy himself, who was a silent partner in the club, brought up the rear.

His gaze passed over Jack in silent consideration. Davy was a short man with a cloth over one eye. Years ago, a werewolf in government service had taken his right eye during a brutal struggle and had almost ended his life. Davy had been bitter and resentful long before losing his eye, but he'd grown darker and more determined to succeed, whatever the cost. Jack knew that Davy didn't trust him, but they didn't have time for a conflict within the movement.

"Well," Davy said, finally. "We're here. Shall we begin?"

Jack stood up and walked to the front of the room. It was easy to use a little magic to illuminate his form, even though he knew better than to try; at least two of the underground's leaders had magic of their own and they wouldn't be impressed by his tricks – as well as sensing it if he tried to Charm them. . It wasn't worth the risk. He studied them, as dispassionately as he could. Two of them were union organisers – unions were banned, by law – and three more were former professors turned revolutionaries. One was an exile from the Tsar's Russia, another was a miner who'd lost his job when the mining company had brought in Irish labour and undercut English wages. Years ago, there had been a proper underground movement, but that underground had been shattered. A repeat of that disaster would prove fatal to the movement.

"You all know why we're here," he said, without preamble.

He spoke quietly, but with passion – and with enough force to make sure they all heard the conviction in his voice. Charm wasn't necessary to convince people. "We have struggled for reform the legal way – and we have gotten nothing for our pains. The toffees like us in the dirt, grubbing around their feet for the scraps they throw to us, uncaring about our suffering. We lose children because we have to live in the slums. We lose money through taxes and the high cost of food. We lose our sons to workhouses and our daughters to brothels. We are hectored by churchmen and bossed around by lords and ladies who think that their birth makes them better than us.

"In this world, one thing counts," he continued. "You must have large amounts of money in the bank. But how many people have enough money to have a vote? How many people own enough property to have a vote? The laws are carefully drawn to disenfranchise the poor, the hopeless...the ones like us. And why should we look to our lords and masters for change? They're happy with things the way they are. Why should they change for us?"

He allowed his gaze to move from face to face. They knew this, of course; they would hardly be underground leaders if they hadn't *felt* the pain of poverty. Some of them had seen children die because they hadn't been able to buy food for their families, or watched helplessly as their womenfolk were ravished by petty officials with a little power. They had all felt the endless oppression that pushed down on them, crushing their souls and turning them into slaves. An Englishman was not free in England. The British Empire ruled a quarter of the world, yet it cared nothing for nine-tenths of its population.

And they were all beaten down by the government. There had been brief periods of violent unrest, but some had ended after feelings cooled and others had been savagely repressed by the government's troops. It had bred helplessness into the poor, a sense that they were doomed no matter what they did – and even a sense that their lords and masters had a *right* to be their lords and masters. Their submission – their inability to break their psychological bonds – was the key to their physical bondage. Jack had set himself the task of giving them the confidence to throw off their chains and break free.

"But why should it be that way?" He demanded. "Why

should we not live in vast palaces? Why should we not be allowed to hunt and fish as we please, or avoid paying taxes, or even claiming some of the *benefits* of those taxes? We are told that we belong to a vast and powerful empire, but what do we see of its greatness? We see nothing, save the lights of rich London and the red-coated soldiers who crush us whenever we raise our heads high. We cannot go on like this!

"Last night, I killed Lord Burley," Jack said. "Three nights ago, I...convinced Henry to forgive his debts. I am here to bring down the government and start a new age, an age where people will rise to the positions they deserve and no one will be ground in the dirt, simply for having been born poor. This time, the government will learn to listen, or we will destroy it. We have the power to bring it down."

He held up a hand. Bright light sparkled over it, illuminating the room with an eerie, flickering light. "None of us have ever achieved anything much on our own," he concluded, "but as a group we would be able to beat the government. We can take the toffees down once and for all, if we rise and claim our birthright – freedom, and the rights of man!"

There was a long pause. "We have heard this before," Davy said, finally. "How can we beat the government? We have no weapons, no money – and no security. And they have magic. They see our every move."

"Hardly," Jack said. Everyone believed that Seers saw everything. Jack knew better – and so did any other trained magician. But he would have to start training the sparkers in the Rookery himself, now that Henry had surrendered them to the movement. Ebenezer's son had always lacked imagination, save when it came to grinding more money out of his victims. "I have magic – and magic does not make you invincible. We can beat their magicians."

One of the others, a former professor, spoke up. "And if you're wrong?"

"Then we die," Jack said, simply. There was no point in lying to them. They all knew the risks. "I ask you this: is it better to fight and die on our feet, or live on our knees as slaves? None of us is any freer than a negro from the south of America, working on one of the cotton plantations. We either force them to grant us rights or we will never be anything more than slaves.

"We have numbers, but we don't have weapons? We can get weapons. I have been working on ways to ship weapons into the country from an outside source. We will be able to arm ourselves and when the time comes, we will take control of the city and seize the government. And they will have to concede to us or risk a long civil war which would cripple the Empire.

"And as for magic...?

"You all know what they do," he added. "They come into the poorhouses and they take children with any trace of magic from their parents. The children are fostered with the right sort of people, paid by the Crown; they rarely learn that they are adopted at all. How many of us have lost children to their raids?"

His eyes narrowed. "And if magic appears among the downtrodden and oppressed, does it not put the lie to their claim to be superior?"

Jack smiled at them. "If we work together, if we plan properly, we can win," he concluded. "Join us now or walk away."

Davy frowned at him. "Where are the weapons coming from?"

"A dealer overseas," Jack said. "And that is all that you need to know."

It was a weak link in the plan, but one he couldn't avoid. There were thousands of smugglers along the coast and in London, smuggling in goods from Europe and America without paying the taxes demanded by the excise men. It would be relatively easy to smuggle in the weapons, but if they were discovered it would be a red flag to the authorities. Firearms were not permitted to the urban poor – and to very few people outside the cities, unless they had the right connections. Losing a weapons shipment could prove disastrous. And it was something he couldn't share with the others, because there were already too many weak links in the chain.

He smiled to himself. Henry was a bastard, all right, but he'd had close links with the smugglers and those links could be used for the underground. As long as he stayed good and terrified of Jack, he'd do as Jack ordered. Jack had taken care to frighten him badly, knowing that someone like Henry might go to the authorities. And if anyone drew a line between Henry and Captain Swing...

The argument raged on long into the night. Jack wasn't too surprised, even though he was impatient to move on to the next stage of his plan. The underground had been burned badly over the last century, even before it had become a coherent force – insofar as it *was* a coherent force. It was a bit much to expect the poor to care about abstract political ideas when the rabble were starving, desperate for food. They would sell their children into slavery – or worse – just to keep them alive.

In the end, there was reluctant agreement. It helped that Davy was aging, with only a few years of life left to him in the Rookery. Jack ran through a handful of possible ideas with them – without committing himself to anything – and then started to issue orders. The underground would have to recruit the first warriors from the ranks of the unemployed and arrange for them to be trained. Lucy knew a few former soldiers who could train others, once they found somewhere where they could train in secret. And once the first bunch had mastered military skills, they could teach the others and their former tutors could be eliminated. Jack wasn't going to risk any leaks.

"You killed Lord Burley," Davy said, afterwards. "Don't you feel that that was...unwise?"

Jack smiled. "I had to do something to prove that I could," he said. Davy didn't know about his shared history with the Royal Sorcerer. No one knew that, apart from himself and Master Thomas – and perhaps Lord Mycroft. The overweight civil-servant-of-all-trades might have known part of the story and deduced the rest. "And besides, with Burley having been murdered, there will be plenty of upset nights for his fellow oppressors. How many of them have as many guards as he had?"

"They'll be hiring more," Davy said, flatly.

"Yes, they will," Jack agreed. "And believe me, it works in our favour."

He stood up and clasped Davy's hand. "We won't lose this final chance," he said. "We will plan it properly and hit them when they're least expecting it. We will terrify them into submission."

Outside, the London night was louder than ever. It had

been payday at the factories and many of the younger men were trying to spend it all in one night. The whores and bartenders would probably manage to separate them from most of it before they even managed to take some of it home to their wives. It hardly mattered, anyway. No wages earned by anyone who lived in the Rookery would drag them out of poverty.

He stopped as he caught sight of a half-drunk man molesting a girl. At first, he thought she was a prostitute, but her desperate struggles to escape convinced him otherwise. Once, he admitted to himself, he would have watched dispassionately as he raped her in the street, but he'd been a different man then. Now he walked forward, caught the man's neck with his hand and picked him up, throwing him into the nearest wall with a push of magic. The body collapsed and fell to the ground. By morning, it would have been stripped of everything and perhaps transported to the crematory. Even the hardened inhabitants of the Rookery blanched at the thought of necromancers using discarded bodies as weapons.

Jack took the trembling girl's hand, kissed it gently, and then vanished into the shadows, pulling an illusion around his body. The girl would have seen him vanish into thin air. It would be yet another rumour about Captain Swing echoing through the underworld until it reached the ears of Master Thomas. He would know that Jack was back.

He smiled as he lifted himself up to the roofs and began to make his way back to Lucy's brothel. The coming confrontation would be savage – one of them wouldn't walk away alive. But Jack had his cause to fight – and die – for, while Master Thomas merely upheld the established order. Jack would die for the poor.

It was the least he could do to make up for his crimes.

Chapter Twelve

wen cleared her throat.

The young man – almost a boy – who was reading a book in the library jumped when he heard her behind him. He looked around, hand raised in a defensive pose, and flushed when he saw her. Bruno Lombardi – a young man barely two years older than Gwen – had been assigned to tutor her in infusing...and he'd forgotten. Gwen doubted that he'd forgotten intentionally, unlike some of her other tutors; he'd simply entered the library, found a book and lost track of time. It had happened to her from time to time as well.

He was a handsome youth, apart from the pair of spectacles that were precariously balanced on the end of his nose. Unlike most of the young men his age, personal grooming wasn't practically an obsession, giving him a kind of dishevelled appearance that Gwen found rather endearing. He blinked owlishly at her and she found herself smiling. It wasn't as if she disliked him, after all. He had never shown any sign of dislike – or resentment – of Gwen's presence in the hall.

"You were meant to be in the workshop with me," Gwen said, dryly. He flushed even brighter; as the third son of a minor aristocratic family, he had to learn to live by his wits alone. There would be little more than a few thousand pounds left for him when his father shuffled off the mortal coil. "I've been waiting for the last twenty minutes."

"Oh, crumbs," Lombardi said. He sounded embarrassed. "I quite forgot."

Gwen cast her eyes over the pile of books on his table. "I can believe it," she said. His face couldn't get any redder, but his hands twitched nervously. "If you want to postpone the lesson…"

"I'm just coming," Lombardi said, quickly. He placed the book he was holding on the table and walked quickly out of the door, leaving the pile for the librarian to sort out and return to the shelves. Gwen took one last look at the pile – a handful of scientific treatises and a couple of speculative fiction works – and followed him down to the workshop. The library would have to be left until later.

The workshop was the largest room in Cavendish Hall, apart from the dining room and the lobby. It was bare, save only for a pair of metal tables and a sheet of metal blocking off half the room, almost like a fence. Gwen had inspected the room several times while she'd waited for Lombardi and hadn't been able to figure out why anyone would want to cordon off part of the room. Or, for that matter, why it was so bare when she had expected tools and raw materials scattered everywhere. The door, she realised as she closed it behind her, looked like it had been armour-plated. Someone, she deduced, didn't want to take any chances.

Lombardi waved her to one of the stools and sat down beside her. He looked nervous to be sitting so close to a girl, even though it was unlikely that their respective parents would sanction a match. His eyes didn't seem to dip to her bodice as often as some of the other young men in the building, something else Gwen found a little endearing. He was shy around her – and presumably every other young girl he met. It was better than the bullish bragging that other men indulged in when they were trying to impress a girl.

"The difference between Infusing and Changing is that Infusers place magic *into* an item while Changers use their magic to *reshape* an item," Bruno said. He sounded more confident while he was lecturing, even though Gwen was right next to him. "A skilled Infuser can create objects that can do almost anything, as long as the magic lasts. The more one wants it to do, the more magic it consumes, leading it to burn out quickly. Once the Infuser has created the item, however, a less-skilled magician can replenish the magical supply and keep the item working."

He looked up at her, flushed, and then looked away. "It takes time and practice to become a skilled Infuser," he added. "The Infusers like me tend to apprentice themselves to older, more skilful Infusers and charge their items in exchange for lessons in magic. You may find it difficult to learn more than the basics; I have a feeling that Master Thomas will not want you to waste your skill in creating objects of power."

Gwen nodded, impatiently. "I understand," she said. "You want me to push magic into an object."

"Correct," Lombardi said. He stood up, walked over to the wall, and opened a cupboard. "For reasons we don't fully understand, different materials store different levels of magic; they can be used for different purposes. As a general rule, the denser an object, the more magic it will store."

He walked back to her, carrying a handful of small objects in his hands. "Look at this," he said, passing her one of them. "What do you make of it?"

Gwen turned the object over and over in her hands. It was a small statue of a man, made from clay and then baked in an oven. For some reason, it gave her the creeps as she touched it, even though she couldn't understand why. There was no sense of magic surrounding the tiny piece of pottery. She passed it back to Lombardi, who smiled, took it in his hands, and closed his eyes. Gwen *sensed*, somehow, a shimmer of magic flickering around the object, just before Lombardi put it down on the table. The tiny manikin stood up and ran towards the edge of the table, almost jumping over the edge before Lombardi caught it. It struggled in his palm until its movements slowed to a stop and it collapsed. Gwen told herself that it wasn't alive and had never truly been alive, but it still shocked her.

Lombardi grinned at her expression. "A fairly basic trick, once you learn what you're doing," he said. "Now" – he put a block of wood in front of her – "try to infuse magic into that wood."

Gwen took the block of wood in her hand – and stopped, unsure of how to proceed. "Close your eyes," Lombardi instructed, "and visualise the wood in your hand. Hold the image in your mind and imagine directing your own power into it. Don't try to think of anything more complex, just imagine your power infusing the wood. Focus…"

There was a long pause. Gwen struggled to infuse magic into the block, but nothing was happening. She knew when she was using her magic – to Blaze or Move or Charm – yet she couldn't feel anything shimmering inside her body. The block of wood was really nothing more than a block of wood, useless and dead. She focused on it as hard as she could, her eyelids screwed up in concentration, but nothing happened. It seemed impossible to do anything to it.

"Concentrate," Lombardi instructed.

"I am concentrating," Gwen snapped back. She kept her eyes closed. "Nothing is happening."

Lombardi hesitated. "I want you to focus on your body," he said, and broke off, embarrassed. Gwen managed to avoid giggling, if only because he would certainly die of embarrassment. "Concentrate on your heartbeat; imagine the sound thrumming through your entire body. And then allow your mind to slide down to your fingertips. Feel them pressing against the wood. Feel the magic shimmering over them..."

Gwen gasped. Her fingers were *alive*! No, not alive; magic was crackling into existence around her. She couldn't hurt herself with her own magic, she reminded herself frantically, even as the air started to sizzle. The block of wood was suddenly very large in her mind, almost as if it were part of her. She directed the magic into the wood and felt it being sucked out of her...

There was a burst of heat and she yelped, dropping the block of wood onto the table as her eyes snapped open. The wood was glowing, almost as if it had been plucked from a fire by her bare hands. Her fingers *hurt*...Lombardi reached forward, quickly, and scooped up the block of wood. Before Gwen could say anything, he hurled it over the sheet of metal blocking half the room and pulled her away from the table. A second later, there was an explosion that shook the room.

Gwen turned and saw smoke rising up from behind the metal wall. It was a shield, she realised numbly, a shield protecting young students from the consequences of their mistakes. A magician with only one talent might be expected to be better at handling it than a magician with multiple talents, yet...she found herself looking up at Lombardi with new respect. He'd mastered an art she suspected she would never fully be able to understand or master.

"That happens to pretty much everyone at first," Lombardi said. He grinned at her, even as he pushed his spectacles back into position. "The magic within the item destabilised and then exploded. Young magicians sometimes play with explosions for fun – or for war. My old tutor used to tell us that we might have to use our talents for fighting the French."

"If they ever came over the water," Gwen agreed. It had been less than a century since the Young Pretender had attempted to invade England – and the French, to give them credit, had been working on invasion plans for centuries. None of them had ever even come close to success, but the new technologies that Britain had introduced to the world might change that and give the French an advantage. Airships didn't have to worry about large bodies of water in the way. "What else can you do?"

Lombardi's smile widened. "You'd be surprised," he said. "You can shape thoughts with your mind and infuse them into objects. You can create locks that can only be opened with one specific key. You can create barriers that are impassable, save only to a magician with the right power and skill. You can even create storages for magic, or lights, or even communications devices. A skilled Infuser will be assured of a job for life. There are never enough of them to meet demand."

He picked up a second block of wood. "Time to try it again," he said. "Don't worry about wasting the raw materials. We go through entire forests in the first few weeks of lessons."

Gwen smiled and picked up the wood. This time, she understood instinctively what she had to do. Using the power once had unlocked a door in her mind; this time, it was easy to see the magic and to direct it into the wood. It grew hot alarmingly quickly and Lombardi tore it from her hand, throwing it over the barrier. Gwen watched as it disintegrated in a flash of bright light and shattered, throwing splinters everywhere. The noise alone was deafening. She could see why young male Infusers would like to show off.

"Impressive," he said, dryly. "But you have to learn to funnel the magic into the block. Each object can only hold a finite amount of power before it starts to grow hot and explode."

Gwen scowled at him. "How does one tell the difference?"

"Practice," Lombardi said. He smiled, thinly. "You need practice, practice and more practice. It's no use learning to run before you can walk."

The next hour passed slowly. Gwen went through five

more blocks of wood before she finally managed to work out how to sense when an object was approaching capacity. Her power tended to funnel back on itself when time was running out, warning her that she was about to lose control. It was hard to fine-tune it to the point that she could fill a block completely – without causing an explosion – but she was learning. Given time, she promised herself, she would learn how to do it perfectly.

She smiled, sourly. Cannock had been right about Mover Ball; it did help young magicians to perfect their skills. It had also given him and his friends the chance to extract a little revenge; Gwen hadn't been able to avoid noticing that they tended to direct the ball at her with astonishing force. Only a combination of luck and good judgement had saved her from worse than aching bones – and she had learned more about her powers than she had thought possible. Flying – levitating, rather – under her own power made up for everything else.

"It may need more practice tomorrow," Lombardi admitted, finally. Gwen, who was sweating and uncomfortably aware that she was exhausted, nodded in agreement. A quick wash and a change of clothes, and then she would go to the library and study all afternoon. It wasn't as if she had anything else to do. "But you're doing better than I did when I was in training."

Gwen looked up, surprised. "I am?"

"You have experience in using your other talents already and I think that helps," Lombardi said. "I had to learn to unlock my powers before I could actually use them – and my old tutor used to despair of me at times. He said I'd be nothing better than a grenadier for the army if I didn't improve."

He seemed more confident now, Gwen noted with amusement, even though his forehead was gleaming with sweat. She hadn't realised that the lesson would be dangerous for the tutor as well as for the pupil, but she'd seen how easy it was to cause an accident. If he hadn't reacted so quickly, one of the blocks would have exploded in her hand. The consequences didn't bear thinking about. And so she made up her mind.

"I'll practice," she said. "What are you doing on Friday night?"

Lombardi blinked. "Nothing," he said. Unlike some of the other young magicians, he didn't go out every night to cause havoc in the city. Master Thomas had had to deal with a handful of magicians who had been picked up by the police and, from his expression, Gwen suspected that they weren't going to be enjoying the next few days. "Study, perhaps."

Gwen smiled. "Why don't you come with me to the Fairweather Ball?"

He stared at her, a conflicting mixture of emotions playing over his face. "You want *me* to come with you?"

"I have to go and I am not going alone," Gwen said. She *had* thought about going on her own, even though society would point and talk about it behind her back. It wasn't *decent* for women to go to balls on their own – and a young lady who wanted to find a husband would still need to convince a brother or cousin to accompany her to her first ball. "And I think you'd be a good escort."

Lombardi hesitated. "I can't dance," he admitted, finally. "I have two left feet."

"I have problems dancing too," Gwen said. She held out a hand and clasped his firmly. "Don't worry about a thing. You'll have a good time, we'll dance the night away and then go back home and wake up late the following morning."

Part of her mind couldn't believe how forward she was being. The old Gwen would never have had the confidence to upend protocol and ask a man to walk out with her, rather than wait to be asked. She wasn't really interested in Lombardi, even though he was a good man, but no one would expect them to announce their engagement the following morning. A young lady Gwen's age would have taken a succession of escorts to balls by the time she finally became engaged and married. A married woman could only go with her husband, never on her own.

"If you will have me," Lombardi said, finally, "I will come with you."

He sounded terrified. Gwen had to hold herself under tight control to prevent breaking down into a fit of giggles. "I'll organise the carriage and everything," she said. Lombardi would simply be too shy to organise anything. "All you have to do is find something nice to wear, I think. This is *the* social event of the season, remember? Wear something very nice."

Lombardi flushed. "I don't know what to wear," he admitted. "I really don't think…"

"Don't," Gwen advised, mischievously. She patted him on the shoulder and smiled at his expression. He couldn't have looked more shocked if Gwen had proposed marriage. "Just relax and it will be over before you know it."

She waved cheerfully to him as she walked out of the workshop and headed up the nearest flight of stairs. The building was nearly empty of trained magicians in the morning, with most of the tutors taking their students out to practice their skills elsewhere. A skilled magician with an Infusing or Changing talent would be welcome almost anywhere, even one with a weak talent or a lack of control. There was even a need for a person who could make objects explode.

In her room, she closed the door and stripped down, looking at herself in the mirror. She'd put on a little weight, she noted, and she looked healthier than she'd ever been. There were whispers that magic did help magicians to heal faster than mundane people, but no one – according to Master Thomas and Doctor Norwell – had ever managed to isolate the talent. It stood to reason, Gwen considered, that if such a talent existed, she had to have it – but she didn't even know where to begin looking for it.

She smiled to herself as she walked into the bathroom and started to run a bath. If nothing else, her mother would be awfully jealous. She couldn't hope to receive an invitation to the Fairweather Ball. It would almost make up for having to go. Balls, in her experience, were never fun.

And she wondered, despite herself, what High Society would make of the new Gwen.

Chapter Thirteen

ow do I look?"

Olivia looked at him and giggled. Jack was wearing a bright green shirt, golden trousers and a purple hat that came down low over his brow, making it almost impossible to make out his face. Just in case, Jack had taken the time to use makeup to subtly alter his features to the point that he would be almost unrecognisable – if anyone bothered to look past the outfit. It was a very distinctive style.

"You look," Olivia said, between giggles, "like a ponca."

Jack shrugged as he studied himself in the mirror. Ponca was street-slang for a man who liked other men, rather than women. It wasn't something Jack had ever considered, but while High Society and the Church despised men who liked men, there were plenty of clubs that catered for homosexuals. London had always been a city of sin, even when it had been ruled by the Romans. Besides, compared to some of the crimes that routinely went unpunished because the culprits were too wealthy or too powerful to be challenged, what was a handful of sodomites? God would punish the guilty.

"They'll be looking at the outfit, not at me," he said, as he picked up the small arsenal he'd amassed over the last couple of days. It took only a few minutes to hide almost everything within the outfit. By now, the Bow Street Runners would know who – and what – they were hunting and a display of magic at the wrong time would mean detection. Jack was confident in his own abilities, but he knew better than to underestimate Master Thomas. "And when I strip, they won't recognise me."

He ruffled Olivia's hair affectionately. The young girl was starting to come out of her cocoon, thanks to some care from

Lucy's girls and a chance to eat and sleep properly without fear of being robbed or molested. And her contacts with the gangs of street children that ran wild throughout the streets were invaluable. It was astonishing how little attention the high and mighty paid to poor children, unless they discovered that their pocket had been picked while they were distracted with something else. Jack had seen one of the street children beaten to death for stealing a wallet, knowing that intervention would only reveal his presence. After the government had fallen, he promised himself, there would be a better life for all, even the street urchins.

"Not that it matters right now," he said. "Have you had the word?"

Olivia looked up, suddenly serious. "I have," she said, slowly. "He's there."

"Good," Jack said. "Let's go, shall we?"

Outside, darkness was falling over London, but the streets were as crowded as ever. Jack felt oddly disconnected from the passing civilians as he walked amongst them, hidden behind his ponca outfit. A handful of masked bravos took one look at him before sniggering to themselves, clearly under the impression that Olivia was his catamite. You could get away with anything in the Rookery, if you had power and wealth. The person Jack was planning to visit had tastes that even his fellow aristocrats would find revolting. That, Jack suspected, was part of the appeal.

He looked at the bravos, one hand falling to the pommel of his sword. They looked back and then drew apart, clearing a path for him through the crowd. Anyone who carried a sword openly, on the streets, had to be very well connected, particularly when the private possession of weapons was forbidden to the poor and downtrodden. A street bravo who attacked an aristocrat would be lucky if he were merely deported. Jack ignored them as they headed off in search of easier prey, leaving Jack and Olivia walking down the streets on their own. They were alone in the midst of thousands of people.

The building, when they reached it, was utterly unmarked. A handful of men stood outside it, on guard. Jack knew that they had orders not to allow anyone to enter unless they were vouched for by one of the patrons. If the Bow Street Runners – or even the general public – found out what was happening inside the building, the perpetrators would be lynched on the streets. Even the most hardened of Londoners would be revolted. The entire city would be aflame.

One of the guards stepped up to him as Jack approached the building. Jack stopped, leaned close to the man and whispered in his ear. There was a brief clink as money changed hands, enough money to allow a man to live for some weeks in the Rookery. It was good coin, Jack knew. He'd stolen it himself; just to prove that he could break in and out of noble houses at random. He sometimes wondered how many of his victims even realised that they'd been robbed.

The guard stepped back. Money talked in the Rookery. There would be no warning as Jack entered the house, nodding for Olivia to wait outside. No one would bother her, not after Jack had established himself as a patron. The establishment was protected by powerful links to the great and the good, with enough material on far too many people to face justice. If some of the information ever got out, it would cause a scandal. And then the entire Establishment would quiver.

Inside, it was warm enough to pass for India. Jack pushed the second door open and walked into a room. He saw a handful of children waiting for him there, kneeling on cushions and wearing outfits that revealed far too much of their bodies. The oldest couldn't have been any more than ten years old. Someone had painted their faces and styled their hair until they looked almost angelically beautiful. It was a beauty intended to attract the worst kind of person. He shuddered as he caught the eyes of a young boy, with long fluttering eyelashes. The boy gave him a smile that almost sent Jack fleeing in horror.

Jack had lived in France. He'd seen things that would shock the more straight-laced British public. And he had spent time and money in brothels, enjoying prostitutes from all over the world. But this was the worst kind of perversion. None of the girls were sexually mature, which meant that they would burn out quickly after they were broken to their task. Their owners would throw them out onto the streets or sell them onwards, knowing that there was no longer any money to be made from their bodies.

A door opened and a middle-aged woman looked out, her face puzzled. She caught sight of Jack and stared at him, unsure of who he was or what he was doing in her building. Jack didn't give her time to react; he lunged forward, picked her up with his bare hands and slammed her against the wall. She let out a yelp that tailed off when he tightened his grip on her throat. If she intended to call for help, he was quite prepared to snap her neck and search the building personally. God alone knew how many famous people had secret ties to the building.

"I'm here for one person," Jack growled, pushing his face right up against his victim's nose. "Where is Lord Fitzroy?"

The woman stared at him. "I can't," she said, finally. Jack winced as the smell assailed his nostrils. She'd lost control of her bowels. The children were giggling, but none of them had moved from their position. They'd been trained to behave, rewarded with sweets and punished with beatings that left their skin unmarked. "He'll kill me…"

Jack thrust his face up against hers, allowing a little magic to illuminate his eyes. "I hate you," he hissed. "I want to break you. I want to show you exactly how these children have suffered. I want to boil your blood inside your body. And if you don't tell me where he is, I promise you that you will die in the most horrific manner I can devise…"

The woman recoiled from his eyes. "I'll show you," she said, desperately. Tears were running down her cheeks. He'd shocked her far worse than he'd dared hope. "He's upstairs…"

Jack followed her up the stairs, magic at the ready. The corridors were cramped, barely large enough for a single man to walk with his head bowed. He watched as the woman led him past a dozen doors until they reached an unmarked hatch, and then stopped. Jack smiled as she told him that Lord Fitzroy was inside, and then slammed a pulse of magic into her head. Her lifeless body hit the ground like a sack of potatoes. He'd wanted to make her suffer, but there had been no time for indulging himself. There would be time for that later.

He opened the door and stepped into a warm room. Lord Fitzroy looked up in alarm from his bath, which he was sharing with three naked girls, all well below marriageable age. Jack fought down the urge to vomit as he closed the door behind him, not taking his eyes off Lord Fitzroy. The Lord was reaching desperately for something hidden in his clothes. Jack smiled, despite the cold hatred spreading through his mind, as he saw the pistol. Lord Fitzroy hadn't entirely trusted the establishment to guarantee his safety, after all.

"I wouldn't bother," he said, as Lord Fitzroy took aim. His hand was shaky, so shaky that Jack wondered if he – the target – wasn't the safest man in the room. "That really isn't going to hurt me."

Lord Fitzroy fired. The children yelped as the bullet came to a halt in front of Jack, caught by his magical field. Jack took a step forward, and then another, ignoring the second and third shots. After that, he yanked the weapon out of the Lord's hand with magic and threw it across the room. A second later, he picked up the girls, more gently, and put them down beside the piles of clothing. They looked…traumatized.

Jack smiled at them. "Do you like this man?"

They shook their heads, almost in unison. "Neither do I," Jack said. He grinned at them, enjoying the feeling of doing something good for once. "Get dressed and then I will take you out of here."

He turned back to Lord Fitzroy and chuckled nastily as the Lord rose to his feet, watery foam washing off his body and revealing his nakedness. The Lord was holding a knife in his hand, although Jack had no idea where he'd stashed it, probably in the pile of clothing that had concealed his pistol. Jack gestured with a hand, pulled the knife out of Lord Fitzroy's hand, and angled it back towards the Lord. Lord Fitzroy had no time to scream as the knife slashed at his genitals and cut them right off. Bright red blood flowed from the wound as he staggered and fell back into the water. Jack stepped forward, almost casually, and removed his sword from his scabbard.

"I wish I had time to make you suffer," he said, as he pulled Lord Fitzroy's body out of the bath. "I'll have to leave that to the many thousand minions of Satan."

He cut Lord Fitzroy's head off with one stroke of the blade. He'd designed the sword himself, using magic to sharpen the finest cutting blade in the world. Swords were useless against magic and few people expected a magician to carry a sword, but Jack had seen advantages in concealing his powers. The headless corpse fell back into the water, blood streaming out into the pool, but Jack ignored it. Instead, he wrapped the head in his cloak and turned back to the children. They were all clad in short shirts designed for adults, shirts that came all the way down to their knees.

"Come on," he said. The children were staring at him, their eyes wide. They were thinner than he had expected, although it shouldn't have surprised him. The owners of the establishment wouldn't want to feed them more than the bare necessities. "It's time to go."

Leaving the body behind, he went from door to door, peeking into the private rooms. A number were empty, but a handful held others who had been invited to the perverted establishment. Jack killed them before they had any chance of escape, adding the abused children to his small following. Before he knew it, he had twenty-two half-naked children, girls and boys, following him, looking up at him worshipfully. The sensation of actually *helping* people, even in a small way, made him feel proud. He'd accomplished something concrete for tiny lives, the lives that really mattered.

He knew why the establishment existed. The children hadn't been kidnapped; there would have been no need to steal them from their families. They would have been sold by their parents, who chose to believe promises that their children would be well cared for – and that they would receive good positions. Maybe they knew the truth – maybe they guessed at the truth – but it wouldn't have been enough to convince them otherwise. The money from the pimps and their masters would make the difference between surviving another winter, or the entire family dying in the cold.

It was far from the only place where children were abused. In the workhouses, children as young as three years old were put to work, fed little more than gruel and flogged savagely if they so much as faltered in their work. There was no shortage of replacements when they died – and many did – and those that rebelled often found themselves broken, or cast out onto the streets to die. Jack had seen it all, back when his eyes had been opened, and he hadn't been able to look away. Perhaps his first plan had failed, perhaps he had been forced to flee to France while Master Thomas and the Dragoons thought him dead, but he hadn't given up. And maybe this time he would genuinely change things for the better.

He herded the children down the stairs and into the lobby. Two guards were standing there, eying the children with half-puzzled, half-disgusted eyes. Jack cut them both down before they could react, cursing them as their dead bodies fell to the ground. They'd known what had been happening here, behind shuttered windows and locked doors, and they'd guarded it, rather than raising the alarm. Maybe they had felt that they had had little choice – the visitors to the building had powerful connections and would never be brought to justice – but Jack didn't care. They were just as guilty as the men who came to the building to force themselves into prepubescent girls or fondle young boys. They disgusted him.

"Get some proper clothes," he ordered the children, as he checked through the final two rooms. Unsurprisingly, there was very little suitable for children, making it harder for them to run away. He was mildly surprised that they hadn't been chained like animals. There were brothels where the girls were tied down with their legs spread, making it utterly impossible to resist their customers. It was an old trick for breaking a girl who showed any sign of resistance. "Pull those cloaks around you – hurry."

He looked outside into the darkened streets, waving to the guards. They came up to him – and he burned them both down, nodding to Olivia as she appeared from an alleyway. The remaining guards would be alerted soon enough; by then, they had to be well away from the building. If Master Thomas was on watch – and if he put two and two together – he might realise what had happened. But then, whatever his other faults, Master Thomas wouldn't have patronised the brothel. He might have been a reactionary, using his powers to impede change, yet he did have his limits.

"Take them back to the house and introduce them to Lucy," Jack ordered. He wanted to escort the children personally, but he had another mission. It might have been better to leave the children to die, yet he couldn't bring himself to do that, not when they were innocents. They hadn't volunteered to serve in the brothel. "I'll be along after I've finished with the head."

He glanced down at his cloak, which still held Lord Fitzroy's head. Waiting until Olivia and her string of followers had vanished into the darkness, he turned back into the building and shaped a thought with his mind. Fire leapt from his fingertips and scorched the side of the building, flaring down the corridors and into the lobby. Expensive carpets, imported from Persia, caught fire rapidly, incinerating the wooden walls and paintings someone had hung above the carpets. The building itself caught fire seconds later, leaving the bodies and the evidence to be consumed by the flames. Jack stepped backwards, knowing that the fire could burn him, and used his magic to lift himself up to the nearest rooftop. The fire was already spreading out of control.

A clanging sound in the distance announced the approach of London's fire brigade. The city was justly proud of its fire-fighting service – it hadn't been *that* long since the Great Fire of London – but they wouldn't be able to save the brothel. They'd be lucky if they managed to prevent the fire from spreading to the buildings next door, even if they did have the world's most modern underground water supply to draw on. They might even have to start dynamiting the nearby buildings, just to prevent the fire from spreading out to consume much of the city. Magic might have started the blaze, but no magic Jack knew would be able to quench it.

Jack took one last look at the roaring flames and then turned and started to make his way along the rooftops. It was a long walk to Fairweather Hall. And then, he promised himself silently, the oppressors of the masses would know the meaning of the word fear.

Chapter Fourteen

airweather Hall was beautifully illuminated against the darkness, glowing with magic lanterns. Gwen watched as the carriage slowly drew closer and closer to the stairs leading into the building. By long custom, the guests would be expected to leave their carriages one by one, entering the building and mingling with the other guests once inside. The host and hostess would be waiting for them, allowing them the chance to greet each of the guests personally before they entered the ballroom.

She smiled, wondering what they would make of her. It had taken her hours to decide what to wear, if only because of her changed status. Finally, she had decided to wear a black dress, even though it might cause offence; young ladies were not supposed to wear black unless there had been a death in the family. But black was the colour worn by the sorcerers and Gwen knew that, one day, she would be the Royal Sorceress. Black was her colour. She'd braided her golden hair – shorter now, because long hair tended to get in the way when she was practicing with magic – and tied it up in a ponytail. Lombardi had stared at her when he'd seen her, suggesting at least one person was impressed. Gwen hoped that Lord and Lady Fairweather would feel the same way.

The carriage reached the steps and Lombardi got out, holding up one hand to help Gwen climb down. He looked terrified, but he was still managing to remember his manners. Gwen rewarded him with a smile as they started to climb up the steps towards the waiting Lord and Lady. There was no sign of Master Thomas or anyone else who might perform introductions and the last time Gwen had seen either of them had been when she'd been a child. They knew Lombardi, though, and appeared to take no notice of Gwen's dress. She was almost disappointed.

Inside, they were greeted by the sound of music and happy laughter. Young couples were already out on the dance floor, waltzing to a tune Gwen vaguely recognised. There would be no formal dances for at least an hour, allowing the newcomers a chance to get used to dancing and overcome their nerves. Gwen looked up at Lombardi, who had fixed a slightly pained expression on his face, and smiled. He looked as if he was on the verge of bolting at any second. She held onto his arm gently and pulled him onto the dance floor. He seemed to know almost nothing about dancing – from where he should put his hands without violating protocol to how to move with the tune – but Gwen was patient. She had never tried to teach anyone how to dance before, but she had had lessons as a child and knew the basic steps. All the dancers really had to do was move with the music and remember not to move too quickly or too slowly.

The ballroom was massive, large enough to impress even Gwen. There seemed to be hundreds of guests, the great and the good of London and the British Empire, gathered in one place. She caught sight of a pair of dark-skinned representatives from India – probably from one of the Princely States – and even a handful of Colonials from America, enjoying the music as much as anyone else. But then, the Colonial Government knew that it had to cleave to the British Crown. No one wanted a second war or even a bloody uprising that would have to be crushed by the Redcoats. She grinned as two other couples linked hands with them as the music changed, pulling them into a circle. Lombardi was grinning as well, his nerves forgotten in the excitement; Gwen watched as they exchanged partners in a waltz that would eventually see them meeting again. Who knew? Perhaps she had created a social animal in a shy and retiring young magician. But she still had to prompt him to pick up a dance card for her.

Soon, the music came to a halt and the dancers headed for the side of the room. A trumpet sounded, calling their attention to the stairs leading up into the mansion. Gwen watched in silence as Lord and Lady Fairweather descended, arm in arm, and came onto the dance floor, announcing the start of the formal dancing. She took Lombardi's arm and pulled him out into the gathering crowd as the band struck up a new tune. The leader called out instructions for the first few steps and then sat back, leaving the dancers to manage on their own. Gwen held Lombardi's hand and took him through the steps. Despite some of the glances cast in her direction, she found that she was enjoying the dancing. It was almost too soon when the tune came to an end and a new one began. This time, she found dozens of partners coming up to write their names in her dance card. She made sure that Lombardi had a partner and then threw herself back into the dancing, resolving not to sit out a single dance.

An hour later, her body aching even as she felt surprisingly good, she left her current partner and headed for the stairs to answer the call of nature. Outside the ballroom, the sound of music was curiously muted, giving the mansion an eerie atmosphere that bothered Gwen more than she wanted to admit. A couple of rooms were occupied with young men and women testing the limits of their chaperon's patience, something that would cause a major scandal if they were caught. Gwen ignored them and headed onwards, searching for the toilets. They were never far away from the ballroom. She stopped outside one unmarked door and was about to push it open when she heard a voice coming through the wood. It was Master Thomas – and he sounded angry. Good girls didn't eavesdrop, Gwen knew, but she couldn't resist. Besides, ever since Lord Burley had been assassinated, Master Thomas been consumed with something that he'd refused to talk to her about, even though she was his designated successor.

"It has to be him," he was saying, flatly. "Who else could it have been?"

"This is a pretty rum show," a second voice – Lord Mycroft, Gwen thought – said. "I was under the impression he was dead."

"We never found the body," Master Thomas snapped. "It is quite possible that he managed to escape in the confusion and made it out of the country. The French or the Spanish would be pleased to hide him in exchange for services rendered."

"So he's become a traitor as well as an anarchist," a third voice said. It was lazy, almost languid. Gwen didn't recognise the speaker's voice at all. "I don't think he had much to offer our friends across the water."

"Of course he had something to offer them," Master Thomas said. He sounded like a teacher explaining something to a particularly dim-witted child. "There is one service he could perform for his paymasters that they couldn't find anywhere else. And he would have paid that price willingly. His cause is all."

"He's a Master," Lord Mycroft said. "I have information that King Louis would gladly part with half of his Kingdom to win the services of a Master. The French have yet to breed one from a French mother."

"The French will never gain the services of a French-born Master," the mystery voice sneered. "Charles Darwin has proven that to my satisfaction."

"Darwin's theories may not hold water," Master Thomas warned. "He could only theorise."

"His theories are beyond question," the mystery voice insisted.

"Of course they are," Lord Mycroft said, dryly. "They support your political position."

"The only other theory we have is Perivale's Sleeping Plague," the mystery voice said. "Do you believe that his theory holds any validity?"

"It is a capital mistake to speculate without facts," Lord Mycroft said. "We have too few facts to speculate. We are also missing the important detail – our old…friend has returned to London and presumably made contact with his old allies."

"We scattered the anarchists five years ago," the mystery voice said. "We taught them a damn good lesson."

"And someone with Master-level powers killed Lord Burley," Master Thomas said. "There have only ever been five Masters – and only one of them remains unaccounted for."

"Five that we know about," another voice said. "How old were you when you discovered your powers? How many Masters have lived and died without ever knowing what they were?"

Master Thomas snorted. "How many unknown Masters would have the inclination and the training to cause havoc in London?"

Gwen felt a shiver running up her spine. Master Thomas

had told her that two of the previous Master Magicians were dead – and the third was missing, presumed dead. But what if he hadn't died after all? And...who *was* he? What had happened five years ago?

"Which leads to another point," Lord Mycroft said. "What about Lady Gwen?"

"She should have been sent to the farms," the mystery voice sneered. Gwen felt another chill at the cold loathing in the voice. "She does not conduct herself in the manner befitting a young lady."

"We are not asking her to conduct herself in the manner of a young lady," Master Thomas said, mildly. "And before you raise the issue of her slapping your nephew, the young fool did attempt to Charm her into undressing herself in front of him."

"But..."

Master Thomas ignored the interruption. "There is also the minor detail that she remains too important to be sent to the farms," he added. "We *need* her, desperately. We cannot afford to waste her on a program of dubious value. She is learning magic quicker than I had believed possible and should soon be ready to start coming out on patrol with me. Any small displays of unladylike behaviour are hardly a problem...unless one of you happens to be hiding a Master up his sleeve?"

There was a pause. "I thought not," he said. "Now, if you don't mind..."

Gwen heard footsteps and stepped away from the door, walking down the corridor as fast as she could without running. The door opened behind her and someone came out, heading down in the other direction, away from her. Gwen kept walking until she found the toilets and finally answered the call of nature, her mind spinning as she tried to digest what she'd heard. Who was the mystery voice? Who was the mystery Master? And what were the farms?

One of the questions, she decided, should be easy to answer. The mystery voice had Lord Blackburn as a nephew. It would be easy to look him up in *Who's Who*. And then...what?

Loud cheers greeted her as she re-entered the ballroom; cheers not for her, but for Admiral Lord Nelson and Lady Emma. Lord Nelson, who had won a glorious victory against the Barbary Pirates and forced the rulers of the Barbary States to refrain from plundering British shipping, was still the toast of the town, even though it had been nearly twenty years since he'd last taken command of a naval fleet and gone out to wage war on Britain's long list of enemies. Lady Emma, if Gwen's mother had been right, was actually his second wife – and he was her second husband. They'd been having a long affair before her husband passed away; they'd even produced a child out of wedlock. Nothing illustrated the hypocrisy at the heart of the British Empire more than Lord Nelson. Few would dare to point a finger at England's greatest admiral, even the chattering wives of London.

She made her way over to Lombardi, who had just finished another dance with a girl Gwen vaguely recognised. The girl gave her a sharp look as she invited Lombardi to dance, a look that suggested that she'd had her eye on him as a possible husband. Gwen wasn't too surprised; Lombardi might be a third son, but he was from a powerful family that had thousands of pounds in the bank. A young lady of noble blood and impoverished family couldn't hope to find a better match. And who knew? Perhaps she would make him happy.

Lord Nelson was being pressed into service to lead the latest dance, a march that reminded her of some of the taller tales of military service whispered by the other magicians at Cavendish Hall. Lady Emma, Gwen noted absently, was enormously fat, so much so that the darker side of her mind wondered how they managed to sleep together. But maybe it was love, or maybe they stuck together because they knew that no one else would have them. Or maybe Nelson had his fun with the maids while his wife looked on helplessly.

Gwen followed the dance steps carefully, holding tightly onto Lombardi as they went through the motions. Partners were exchanged and exchanged again as the band changed the tune, forcing the dancers to react quickly to stay in the dance. A handful of couples even left the dance floor, preferring to take a drink from the tables and exchange catty remarks with the other wallflowers. Gwen knew that most of the real business would be transacted behind closed doors, with powerful family members striking deals with their allies – or even with their enemies. This ball would be particularly significant, if only because much of the London nobility was in attendance. She wouldn't have been too surprised to see the King himself.

She almost flushed as Master Thomas appeared in front of her. Gwen's mother would have demanded to know if it was proper for a master to dance with his apprentice, but Gwen didn't care. Besides, it wasn't as if there were many female apprentices. Master Thomas danced with a dignity that showed his years, reminding Gwen that she didn't even know how old he was, not really. He'd been in service to the Crown at least forty years, assuming that he'd served in the wars with France and Spain that had marked the end of the eighteenth century.

"A splendid ball," he whispered to her, as he pulled her around the dance floor. "I hope you're taking the time to see and be seen – and to listen?"

"Yes, sir," Gwen said. It was hard not to flush – all she'd overheard was his conversation with Lord Mycroft and their mystery guest. She glanced around, but saw no sign of Lord Mycroft. It stood to reason he'd want to stay off the dance floor. Being so massive, he was a danger to shipping. "I think I'm enjoying myself."

"I'm glad to know that you're being a credit to your tutors," Master Thomas agreed. He *sounded* perfectly sincere. "And I trust that you will make time to chat with some of the great and the good. They may be the ones deciding your future."

They swapped partners before Gwen could think of a response. If Lord Blackburn and his Darwinists were right, magicians were superior to everyone else. And that meant that they should be giving orders, not taking them. But magic's gifts were fickle and Gwen's brother had shown no sign of magic, even though he had been tested extensively shortly after Gwen had come into *her* magic. In hindsight, it was clear that Master Thomas and the Royal College had known what Gwen had been long before they'd approached her. They'd almost certainly hoped that her brother shared the same magical talents.

But if Lord Blackburn was wrong, and magicians were just people with different talents, what did that mean? So much in the British Empire was decided by birth, not by merit. It took an exceptional man – a man like Lord Nelson – to rise from humble beginnings to achieve a legacy that would live on long after the man himself was dead. And a woman could rarely hope to be more than a daughter, a wife and a mother. Gwen had known that that was her fate until Master Thomas had offered her a chance to serve the crown. And if Gwen could do it, why couldn't other women have the same chance?

The thoughts haunted her as the dance came to an end. She curtseyed to her partner and headed off towards Lombardi. The girl Gwen had taken him from had reached him again and was dragging him back onto the dance floor. Gwen smiled at his retreating back – they weren't supposed to share any dance, but the first and the last – and changed course, heading towards the tables in the next room. They were groaning under the weight of the food, from whole roast chicken, pigs and cows, to a selection of dishes from all over the British Empire. She smelled a spicy scent from one of the curries and helped herself to a small portion, taking some bread and rice to cool it in her mouth. The normal rules of eating in public didn't apply to balls, thankfully. A formal dinner was far more tedious.

She caught sight of Master Thomas sharing a dance with an elderly woman she didn't recognise. Could she be his *wife*? He'd certainly never said anything about a wife, but then he'd said little about his past to her. As far as she knew, he slept in his own set of rooms at Cavendish Hall. Maybe they'd been sweethearts once, before he'd been called away to serve the Crown. Or perhaps she was wrong and he was dancing with her out of politeness. There was no way to know.

The sense of magic suddenly assailed her and she looked up. Above her head – above the entire ballroom – the chandeliers began to shatter. Glass showered down onto the heads of the dancers, forcing them to duck and cover their heads. Gwen reacted as quickly as she could, pulling her magic around her to shield everyone nearby, but it was far too late. People who had been happily dancing a moment ago were screaming as splinters of glass slashed into their faces and bodies, scattering blood over expensive clothes. Gwen started forward as something the size of a ball crashed down in the midst of the ballroom and bounced on the floor. It was a severed head, a head instantly recognisable to many of the dancers. Lord Fitzroy was clearly beyond recovery. Someone had beheaded him and then tossed his head into the midst of his family and friends…

The room dissolved into pandemonium.

Chapter Fifteen

ack was almost disappointed in how easy it had been to sneak into the mansion.

He'd expected to have to fight his way into the building, even though he'd taken time to disguise himself as one of the servants Lord and Lady Fairweather had hired for the evening. They'd be asking some pretty tough questions of the hiring firm tomorrow, he knew, and some poor unfortunate was going to have to explain what had happened to his uniform. Jack had found him, Charmed him into going for a drink in the nearest pub and left him there, half-naked, with no memory of what had happened since he'd left his home. No one had questioned him when he'd walked in the servants' entrance, probably assuming that someone else had already vetted him. He had half a mind to write a very stiff note to whoever was in charge of security after he'd done his business.

No one had tried to stop him as he slipped away from the lower floors – where the servants were being run ragged trying to keep up with the demands for food and drink – and headed up the stairs to the balcony. In his experience, a man who looked like he fitted in and had legitimate business was unlikely to be stopped – and besides, Jack had the ability to Charm anyone who caught him. Nothing blocked his path as he walked up the stairs and looked out over the crowd below. Picking out Master Thomas was easy. His former tutor was dancing with the Dowager of Tunis, the mother of the Duke of Tunis, the man who had claimed a city for the British Empire.

He hesitated, holding his sack in one hand. It had been a long time since he'd stood in a ballroom, clad in fine clothes and sharing inconsequential patter with aristocrats.

Something about the scene called to him, even though he knew the price – the price paid by London's poor. It was tempting him, in a way, tempting him to walk away from his cause, head down the stairs and blend in with the crowd. But then he remembered the children who had been turned into prostitutes and felt sick. Behind the pretty clothes and bright painted smiles – the insincere smiles – there were rotten hearts that cared nothing for those who were trampled under their feet. And the ones who were too brainless to even realise what they were doing was worse. Some of them were mentally unsound because their families had been inbreeding for generations. Others were just too stupid to even realise that they were ignorant.

For a moment, he thought Master Thomas had caught his eye, but it passed without a shout of recognition. Jack was almost disappointed. He summoned his magic and lashed out, almost casually, at the glittering chandeliers. They started to shatter, falling down on the crowd below. Jack didn't hesitate any longer; he picked up the head of Lord Fitzroy and threw it out into the empty air, giving it a little shove with his magic so it would reach Master Thomas. Magic was already shimmering into existence, more than Jack would have expected even Master Thomas to be able to produce. Maybe there were more aristocratic magicians at the ball than Jack had expected.

His former tutor was rising into the air, his dark eyes already hunting for the person he knew had to be watching the chaos from high above. Jack was struck, suddenly, by how old Master Thomas looked. It had only been five years, but he looked to have aged almost twenty. For someone who was in his eighties, Master Thomas was still going strong. Jack wondered just how long it would be before he passed away. He'd once respected Master Thomas – and he still did. If only the price hadn't been so high...

"Up here," he called. Master Thomas turned to look...and Jack reached out with his magic, seeking to disrupt the magic that was holding the elderly magician in the air. Gasps and screams rang through the hall as Master Thomas fell several feet, before he warded off Jack's attack and threw a bolt of lightning towards his former pupil. Jack deflected it easily and abandoned the attempt to send his former master crashing to the floor. Instead, he called out to Master Thomas, knowing that his mocking words would anger his former teacher. Perhaps they would even anger him enough to make him forget prudence and common sense.

"Be seeing you, old man," he called. A second bolt of lightning proved harder to deflect. Old, Master Thomas might be, but his magic was still running strong. "Long live the Revolution!"

He threw a fireball down towards the dancers and turned, fleeing through the door and down the stairs into the rear quarters. Master Thomas reached out with his magic, trying to grapple with him, but Jack managed to evade it with a small effort. He came out of the stairs, knowing that Master Thomas would be in hot pursuit, and almost flew through the kitchens below. Magic billowed out of him, sending pots, pans and great tureens of soup smashing to the floor. A handful of servants who got in his way were picked up and tossed across the room. Jack didn't intend to harm them any more than necessary, but they were blocking his way. Besides, they had taken up service with the noble family rather than joining the fight to bring the establishment tumbling down.

A thunderous roar and a sensation of magic behind him announced that one of the walls had been shattered. Master Thomas flew through the hole he'd created, fire dancing over the palms of his hands. Jack ducked as a fireball flew over his head and slammed into a bowl of water, sending the water flying upwards as superheated steam. He gathered himself and used magic to hurl small objects at his former tutor, aiming them with his mind's eye. Master Thomas had to drop down to the ground to avoid Jack's spray of makeshift projectiles, before picking up a number of spice pots and hurling them back at Jack. One of them was glowing; Jack barely had time to pull his magic around him as a shield before it exploded. Master Thomas had definitely been practicing ever since their last meeting. Jack grinned, despite the seriousness of the situation. Who said you couldn't teach an old dog new tricks?

Master Thomas cleared the remaining tables in one leap and came right at him. Jack raised his own defences and, for a long moment, their magic collided. Flares of magic shot out in all directions, smashing walls and bringing down the ceiling. Jack jumped back as a lump of stone almost crashed down on his head, silently grateful that he'd spent so much time honing all of his talents. Seeing and Sensing seemed less useful than the others, but in the hands of a Master they made him almost invincible. His lips twitched into a smile as the magic storm blew out of control. They didn't make him invincible when he was facing another Master.

Jack jumped forward, feinted with a bolt of lightning...and then used his magic to hurl himself backwards. The magic storm evaporated as Jack smashed through two walls, including one that had been holding up part of the mansion. He doubted that the structural damage would be easy to fix; if he was lucky, most of Fairweather Mansion would come crashing down. Master Thomas hesitated – torn between giving chase and helping the people who were likely to be crushed if the mansion came tumbling down – and Jack took advantage of the moment. Grabbing at his magic, he threw himself into the air and out of sight. There was a final desperate struggle as Master Thomas tried to knock him out of the air, and then he was clear. Behind him, he saw Fairweather Mansion and the guests streaming out into the grounds. They'd be talking about this ball for *years*.

He was still chuckling as he came down to land on a rooftop. Tired, too shaky to stand, he found himself clutching a chimney for dear life. Once he'd jumped from rooftop to rooftop and waved at chimneysweeps as they'd stared at him. Now...now there was no time for such fun and games. He reached into his pocket and found the sandwiches he'd prepared earlier. They tasted odd, but he didn't care. Without food, he would slip away into darkness on the rooftop. They'd be searching the city for him at first light.

Jack smiled as he pulled himself back to his feet and headed back towards the Rookery. No one – not even the King – would be able to hide what had happened at Fairweather Mansion. The entire city would know that someone had walked into the building, deposited the head of Lord Fitzroy on the ballroom floor, and escaped, despite the presence of the Royal Sorcerer. And then they would no longer feel safe in their own homes.

Grinning, he set off for his own room. He needed sleep, desperately. Tomorrow was going to be a very busy day.

***

Gwen hadn't believed it when Master Thomas had confronted the intruder and been stymied. The brief tussle in the air had almost killed her tutor. She'd pushed people aside as she'd run through the corridors, following the sounds of explosions and objects crashing to the ground. And, despite her speed, she'd found herself watching helplessly as the intruder hurled himself into the air and vanished into the dark night.

Master Thomas was looking a little pale as she ran to him. The entire building was creaking alarmingly. Gwen knew little about building and architecture – it had never been considered very feminine, and besides she'd never been interested – but none of the noises sounded very good. It sounded as if the beams high over her head were breaking up, one by one. The magic had dispersed, but the effects remained. And if she had been able to wreck a dining room during her tussle with Cannock and his friends, what damage might have been wrought by two Masters struggling for supremacy? The entire building might have been damaged beyond repair.

"Get everyone out," Master Thomas grunted. It took all of Gwen's strength to hold him upright. Doctor Norwell had lectured her on emergency treatments for magicians who had pushed themselves too far, but his lectures had been long on theory and short on any actual detail. Sugar was supposed to be good, as was tea, coffee and a handful of other things. "Get everyone out, now!"

Gwen looked up. The Butler was standing at the doorway, looking in with disbelieving eyes. He'd probably never seen such chaos outside a battlefield. Gwen barked orders at him and he nodded, relieved to have clear instructions. He could get everyone out of the building and worry about the rest later. Once he had gone, Gwen put Master Thomas down and skimmed through the kitchen. It was easy enough to locate a pot of tea and pour sugar into it until it would be almost painfully sweet. She carried it back to Master Thomas and pressed it against his lips.

Another rumble shook the building and she glanced up, nervously. She knew how much she could lift with her magic, but she had no idea if she could hold the roof up long enough to escape. The sound of falling masonry echoed in the distance, followed rapidly by shattering glass. She could hear screams as the servants and party guests started to panic, heading for the exits. At least the ballroom was close to the front entrance, well away from the worst of the damage. Maybe they'd have time to get out before the building came down on their heads.

Master Thomas was sipping the tea gratefully. "My thanks, Gwendolyn," he said, through halting lips. It was a chilling reminder of his age. His opponent might have been less skilled – although that was doubtful – but he was almost certainly younger. "You would have made a good nurse."

Gwen's lips twitched, just as the ground shook as something heavy came smashing down, somewhere in the distance. "I have to get you out of here," she said. It took most of her magic to lift him up, even though she'd lifted heavier things with less effort. She was puzzled until she realised that Master Thomas's magic was interfering with her own. He was trying to levitate himself up and out of the building, even though his magic reserves had clearly been drained by the confrontation. "Master..."

He relaxed. Gwen managed to hold him in the air and float him over to the exit the rogue magician had made when he'd departed the building. It was just in time; behind her, the roof started to cave in. Flames flashed up from where the cooking fires had spread out of control, threatening to burn down the entire mansion. Outside, the servants had gathered on the lawn; Gwen was able to convince two footmen to help carry Master Thomas away from the fire. He seemed to have lost all of his strength once the rogue magician had vanished into the darkness.

A hand fell on her shoulder and she looked up, startled. Lombardi was looking down at her, his pale face torn and worried. He might once have been attracted to her – or believed that she was attracted to him – but what he'd seen had destroyed it. Gwen was vastly more powerful – and capable – than he could ever hope to be...and few men would accept such a disparity of power between himself and his wife. She hadn't been attracted to him at all, yet losing the thought that he might have been attracted to her hurt – and she didn't understand why. Perhaps she should have spent more time with her mother, socialising with her gaggle of chattering friends, but it wouldn't have been long before she gave into the temptation to incinerate a few of the particularly mindless ones. Some of her mother's friends didn't have the brains God had given squirrels.

"It's going to be fine," Gwen said. She couldn't collapse, not now, or all the people who had whispered that female magicians couldn't handle the pressure would be proved right. It wasn't easy to pull herself to her feet, but somehow she managed it. "How many people are injured?"

Lombardi hesitated. "At least fifty guests were struck by flying glass," he said, finally. "A few more were hit by falling stones as part of the building collapsed. I don't think that anyone was actually killed, but..."

Gwen nodded, sourly. "Why?" She asked. "Why would anyone do anything like this?"

"To humiliate us," Master Thomas said. He looked stronger now, although he was still lying on the grass looking up into the dark sky. London's ever-present clouds of smog were blocking out the night skies. "To show the great and the good that there is no defence against them. To terrorise them into surrendering and making concessions..."

He shook his head, firmly. "Not on my watch," he added. "We'll hunt them down tomorrow and exterminate them."

"I'm coming with you," Gwen said, firmly. She'd spoken before she'd quite realised what she was about to say. "If that...rogue Master shows up again, you'll need help."

"It's no place for a young woman," Master Thomas said, weakly. He didn't seem to be able to sit upright without help, let alone start hunting down the rogue. "You have a great deal more to learn before..."

"You cannot go on your own," Gwen said, feeling hot anger flaring through her. Once again, someone was treating her as a weak female who needed to be guided and guarded from the big bad world outside by a strong male. She was one of the most powerful magicians in the world – and she wasn't entirely untrained. An emotional argument, however, wouldn't impress Master Thomas. Only cold logic and reason would sway his mind. "You're weak, sir; one brief battle drained you almost completely. What will happen when you find him on his own ground?"

Master Thomas smiled, thinly. "I won't be alone, Lady Gwen," he said. "I'll have others with me; men from Scotland Yard and a handful of sorcerers to back me up..."

"But none of them will be Masters," Gwen pointed out, resolutely. "You need another Master – and the only one you have is me."

There was a long pause. "Very well," Master Thomas said, as he pulled himself to his feet. "You can accompany me tomorrow morning."

The police and fire brigade had arrived and were starting to clear the gardens and put out the fires. It would be months, perhaps years, before the mansion was fit for human occupancy. The great and the good of London had just had their noses rubbed in their own vulnerability. Gwen realised that the reaction was going to be profound, and unpleasant. The people who had been killed, or injured, or even risked in the fighting were actually *important*.

Master Thomas looked over at Lombardi, and then nodded to himself. "Take Lady Gwen back to Cavendish Hall and make sure that she goes to bed," he said, firmly. Gwen opened her mouth to argue and then realised that it would be futile. Master Thomas had made up his mind. "Once you have done that, go to Doctor Norwell and inform him that Captain Swing has definitely returned to London."

"Yes, sir," Lombardi said. He looked as puzzled as Gwen felt, but neither of them dared ask Master Thomas who Captain Swing was – or who he had been. "Come on, Gwen. We have to get you home to bed."

Gwen nodded, without speaking: one thing she *had* learned from her mother was that when one was arguing with a man – and when one had actually won the argument – it was a very good time to shut up. Patiently, she allowed him to escort her to the carriages that were lining up outside the gates and into the one that had brought them to the mansion. She caught sight of a line of injured guests being treated by doctors and shuddered. Doctors knew far less than they claimed to know; most people, quite reasonably, were morbidly afraid of medical treatment.

Master Thomas had been right, she realised. The aim had been to terrorise...

...And there was no doubt that it had worked perfectly.

Chapter Sixteen

 want you to take this," Master Thomas said, the following morning. "If you feel that your life is in danger, use it without hesitation."

He passed her a small pistol, perfectly designed to fit her hand. Gwen studied it with some surprise. She had taken part in shoots at her family's country estates, but she'd never actually fired a pistol. Women weren't actually expected to fire the guns. Besides, she had her magic. What did she need with a pistol?

"You may find yourself running low on magic," Master Thomas explained. He looked down at her, sternly. "I'm taking you with me against my better judgement, so listen carefully. Do exactly as I tell you to do, without hesitation. If I tell you to head back to the Hall, do so at once, whatever the situation. Do you understand me?"

Gwen nodded, without speaking. She'd been woken early in the morning, allowing her to eat some bread and jam for breakfast before dressing in her new outfit. Master Thomas had had it made for her, clearly anticipating the moment when Gwen would start taking over his official duties. It was a pair of loose-fitting trousers and a shirt, both black as the night. Gwen's mother would be horrified – respectable women didn't wear trousers, it just wasn't done – but Gwen found it hard to care. If she was going onto the streets to serve the Crown, she was going to look the part. And trousers meant that she didn't have to worry about someone looking up her skirt while she was levitating through the air.

"Good," Master Thomas said. "If you'll follow me...?"

A gust of cold wind struck her in the face as they walked outside, carrying with it the scent of smoke and fire. In the distance, she could see smoke rising from the direction of last night's fire. The fire brigade would have done their best, but the fire had been started by magic and would be fiendishly difficult to quench without draining half the Thames. Master Thomas would probably have detailed a handful of sorcerers to assist the fire brigade in putting out the blaze, or at least in confining it to the mansion. All of London would know what had happened by now. The rogue magician had humiliated them and the great and the good intended to make him pay for his crimes.

Outside, she saw three carriages, drawn up in front of the gates. The first one carried five men wearing sorcerer's black, looking grim as they checked the weapons they carried on their belts. Their badges proclaimed them to be a mixture of Blazers and Movers. A man standing beside their carriage was clearly a Charmer. Behind them, the other two carriages carried men wearing dark blue coats and grim expressions. They carried firearms and truncheons. She was startled to realise that she recognised one of the shorter men – and he recognised her. Inspector Lestrade tipped his hat to Master Thomas as they came up to greet him. Gwen felt a flicker of tension as Master Thomas exchanged a few brief words with the policeman. This was serious. They were going out to wage war on a rogue sorcerer.

"Into the carriage," Master Thomas ordered, shortly. Gwen obeyed, climbing up without assistance from any of the sorcerers who were already in the carriage. It was important not to pose as a helpless female, not in front of men she might find herself commanding one day. Their expressionless faces betrayed no surprise at seeing her, although tension hung thickly in the air. Gwen realised that they were nervous and trying not to show it. A Master Magician was a formidable opponent – and one who was clearly half-insane would be even worse. They might be going to their deaths.

Her stomach churned as Master Thomas climbed into the carriage behind her, nodding briefly to his subordinates. He was holding his cane in one hand, as if it were a sword, as he leaned forward to shout to the driver. The horseman cracked his whip and the horses snorted as they started forward, heading away from the hall. There was already plenty of traffic on London's streets, even though it was alarmingly early in the morning, but they cleared a path for the carriages. It took Gwen several moments to realise that the onlookers were scared, unwilling to be noticed by Scotland Yard – or the formidable men in black. The common folk, Doctor Norwell had told her time and time again, believed all kinds of nonsense about magic. They believed that magicians could turn a person into a frog with a snap of their fingers. A Changer *could* turn a person into a frog, or so Gwen had been told, but it would be incredibly difficult and a waste of magic. It would be far easier to kill the victim outright.

The carriage picked up speed as it headed into the poorer areas of town. Gwen was struck by the sudden change in the citizens of London. They moved from wearing rich clothing to clothes that looked as if they had been repaired, several times, or passed down from elder siblings to younger siblings. She caught sight of a girl so thin that Gwen could see her bones through her clothing and shivered. There, but for the grace of God, went Gwen. The dirty and smelly inhabitants of the poorer parts of the city were fundamentally little different from herself. Lord Blackburn, she knew, wouldn't agree with her. *He* believed that magicians were inherently superior to everyone else.

She wrinkled her nostrils as the wind changed, blowing the stench into the carriage. It smelt of horses and unwashed human bodies and something she preferred not to speculate about, at least not in front of anyone else. How could humans live in such filth? She saw a group of elderly women following a small pack of dogs through the street, scooping up their wastes into bags they carried over their shoulders. The dogs themselves looked thin and mangy, very unlike the dogs her father owned and kept at his country estate. *They'd* been well fed and trained to assist the fox-hunting local squires. Gwen felt pity, even as she looked away from the elderly women. It struck her suddenly that the women weren't that old. They'd merely lived in conditions that aged them quickly.

The carriage turned the corner, passing a group of street children who made rude signs at the rear of the vehicle. Gwen sensed anger among her fellow magicians, even though none of the rude signs were dangerous. The carriage drew to a stop outside a surprisingly clean building; Master Thomas led the magicians out onto the streets, cane raised as if he expected to be greeted by a blast of magic at any moment. Gwen followed them, bringing up the rear, just before there was a set of growls from the direction of the police carriages. A trio of oversized wolves were jumping out of the carriages and landing neatly on the pavement. Gwen shrank back, despite herself. The wolves were the size of lions, far larger than any dog she'd ever seen. Their handlers didn't seem to have them under very good control. One of the wolves eyed her with disturbingly human eyes and licked its teeth. Gwen gathered her magic, only to dispel it a moment later. There was no real threat.

She turned and looked up at the building as Master Thomas issued orders to his men. It was a small business, she decided finally, a small business right on the edge of the poorer part of town. Her brother had often bored her into a mindless stupor by talking about how location was important for businesses; the owners of *this* business would be able to combine lower rents with an address that wasn't too downmarket for the customers. Or so she thought. The smell hadn't gone away, not really; she'd just grown used to its presence. She made a mental note to have more outfits made up by the seamstresses; the one she was wearing would probably have to be washed several times before the stench was finally removed for good.

"Follow me," Master Thomas said. He lifted his hand and fired a bolt of magic at the door. "Stay behind me."

The door smashed open, allowing the lead policemen to charge into the building, followed by two of the wolves. "Police," the leader shouted. "Put your hands in the air, now!"

Gwen followed Master Thomas into the building. The door opened right into a warehouse, with piles of newspapers stacked up against the wall. A handful of shocked-looking men were ruthlessly grabbed by the policemen before they could react. They were pushed to the floor, their hands firmly cuffed behind their backs, and then left there to wait for the policemen to return. Gwen followed the policemen through the second door and saw a large printing press, one of the machines that had revolutionised the world. In the past, producing manuscripts had been the work of years, but now anyone could produce a book. Gwen, like so many others, had learned to read using books that had been mass-produced for young children. The policemen didn't show any signs of caring about the machine as they stormed forwards, using their clubs to knock down any sign of resistance. Once they'd rounded up the staff, they marched them back out to the first room.

A door slammed open and a red-cheeked man looked out. "This is an outrage," he thundered, his voice loud enough to be heard over the crashing as the policemen searched the building for more staff or visitors. "Do you have a warrant for this raid?"

"I have my warrant," Master Thomas informed him, grimly. "You have been printing seditious materials, in defiance of the Dangerous Publications Act, and advocating armed rebellion, in defiance of the..."

"And what do you call your act here, today?" The man – Gwen guessed he was the editor and perhaps the owner – showed no sign of fear. She was impressed. "Why, one might as well be in Russia, facing the might of the Tsar's secret police..."

Master Thomas did not look impressed. "We are taking you and your staff into custody," he informed him. "I have only one question. Where is Captain Swing?"

Gwen looked up, sharply. The editor's eyes rested on her for a long moment and then turned back to Master Thomas. "I have no idea where he has chosen to make his habitations," he said, in a mocking upper-class voice. "But he sure embarrassed you yesterday, didn't he?"

Master Thomas motioned to two of the policemen. They took the editor by the arms and dragged him out. The editor didn't struggle, but as he passed Gwen he hissed, loudly enough for the entire room to hear, three simple words. "Wilkes and Liberty!"

Gwen looked over at Master Thomas, who was contemplating the printing press. There was a sudden sense of magic and then the entire press seemed to come apart. Gwen barely saw what had happened before it collapsed into a pile of junk. Master Thomas had far better control over his powers than she had of hers, even though he'd forced her to practice every day. It made her determined that she would always continue to practice. One day, she would have to take his place.

The sound of growling from outside convinced Master Thomas to head back out of the building, with Gwen following in his path. Outside, the wolves were growling at the prisoners, who were sitting on the pavement watching helplessly as a small army of policemen swarmed into the building. Beyond them, a crowd was starting to gather, watching silently as the Master Thomas moved from prisoner to prisoner, checking their faces against his memory. Gwen doubted that the rogue Master would be caught so easily, but perhaps he felt differently. Or maybe he was just trying to intimidate them. Perhaps they believed that Master Thomas could read their minds.

Gwen looked up sharply as she heard a feminine scream. A moment later, two of the policemen dragged out a young woman, wearing nothing more than a tattered dressing gown. Behind her, two young children – a boy and a girl – followed, held firmly by two additional policemen. The editor started to call out to the woman, only to be silenced by a blow from one of the police officers. He flinched back as one of the wolves advanced, growling nastily.

The woman hit the ground, hard, as one of the policemen shoved her to her knees. Gwen was moving forward before she'd even realised what she was about to do. It only took a little magic to hurl both of the policemen away from their victim, sending them crashing back into the brick wall. Master Thomas said nothing as Gwen checked the helpless woman. Blood was streaming down her cheek from a cut where she'd been backhanded by one of the policemen.

"That is *enough*," Gwen said. A little Charm slid into her voice, even though she knew it would be useless. Policemen were trained to resist Charm – and Master Thomas's men would be immune to it, unless it was far subtler than Gwen could manage. "Let the children go."

The policemen looked up at Master Thomas, who shrugged and nodded. As soon as they were released, the children ran to the editor – their father. Gwen helped their mother to her feet and escorted her over to her husband, looking around for something to shield her from the crowd's stares. Eventually, she pulled her cape off her back and passed it to the young woman. She was ready to lash out at anyone who dared comment, but no one said anything.

"Search the building and remove all of the paperwork," Master Thomas said. Gwen had expected an angry lecture on how to behave in front of the police, or the public, but he hadn't even scowled at her. She couldn't decide if he approved of what she'd done or planned to yell at her later, once they were back at Cavendish Hall. "I want it all presented in front of the judges this afternoon."

"You'll see what the judges say," the editor said. With his wife and children clinging onto him, he seemed more confident in himself. "You're trampling on the rights of Englishmen…"

"Your rights came to an end when you printed your seditious drivel," Master Thomas informed him, flatly. The wolves came closer, their sharp teeth glinting nastily in their dark mouths. Gwen had to force herself not to shudder. They really did have disturbingly human eyes, eyes that eyed her knowingly. "The judges will take a full account of your printing when they decide your case. I have no doubt that you will find yourself heading to a far less hospitable country. You may not even be able to take your wife and children with you."

Gwen winced inwardly, feeling an odd spark of sympathy, as the editor crumbled. What would happen to his family if he were transported to Australia or South Africa? They'd become nothing better than beggars, particularly if the editor's funds were confiscated by the state. What would happen to them? She looked down at the woman's pleading eyes and shivered. There were many things that could happen to poor people in London, few of them good. But her husband had encouraged plots against the peace of England. He'd printed broadsheets that had attacked the King and his Government.

A fourth carriage arrived and the policemen herded the prisoners up into its confining bars. It was a mobile jail, Gwen realised, one capable of holding all of the prisoners in some discomfort. The woman and her children were pushed in at the end, sharing what little time they had left with their husband and father. Gwen wondered what would happen to them, again. Perhaps Master Thomas would know…but his forbidding look forced her to hold her tongue. She didn't want to be sent back to Cavendish Hall.

She glanced over at one of the wolves and almost jumped out of her skin. The wolf was standing up on its hind legs, almost like a human would stand. Slowly, the fur faded away and the pale flesh below was revealed. The doggy face receded and became human, a naked human male. Gwen saw his manhood, flushed brightly and looked away. When she glanced back, the werewolf was donning a coat thrown to him by one of his fellow officers. His hands, Gwen couldn't help noticing, were incredibly hairy. It was one of the overt signs of his magic.

"I couldn't pick up his scent, Master," the werewolf said. His voice was disturbingly deep, almost as if he was struggling to remember how to talk. In his human form, his eyes looked remarkably wolfish. Gwen found herself wondering how he controlled his animal form. Far too many werewolves – and other hybrids – found it difficult to control their animal's emotions. "If he was here, he was not here within the last few days. The scent they used for the printing was too strong."

"They masked it," Master Thomas said. He sounded thoughtful, rather than angry. "It doesn't really matter. There are other places to look."

The werewolf dropped to his arms and legs in front of him. A moment later, his spine arched and twisted, black fur sprouting out of his back as the coat was pulled away from his body. Gwen felt sick, even though she knew it was safe – but then, werewolves were never really safe. A few seconds of raw animal rage or fear, and blood would be scattered all over the vicinity. And then the Royal Sorcerers Corps would have to hunt down the werewolf before he killed and killed again. A werewolf without control combined human intelligence with wolfish desires. It was a lethal combination.

"Come on," Master Thomas said. He noticed her expression and smiled. "I won't be asking you to do that, I'm afraid. We should have that power, but only one Master was able to develop it properly. And that one is quite definitely dead."

Chapter Seventeen

ow who is that, I wonder?"

Jack watched from a rooftop as Master Thomas led the raid on the printer's shop. In truth, Jack was mildly surprised that it had taken that long for the police to begin their raids, even though only a few hours had passed since he'd fled the burning mansion and vanished into the darkness. It suggested that someone with forethought and patience was directing the forces of reaction and repression – someone rather like Master Thomas. He would know better than to allow his enemy to push him into a mistake.

Most of the horde of policemen and sorcerers were mundane, he saw. He knew a couple of the older sorcerers from when he'd been studying under Master Thomas, but the other three were new. Jack wondered absently how capable they were with their powers, before dismissing the thought. Master Thomas wouldn't have brought along untrained sorcerers if he believed that there was a chance of facing Jack or magicians from the underground. The sorcerers would be trained to the highest possible standard and experienced in working as a team. They would only have one of the talents, but by combining their skills they could be almost as deadly as a Master.

But one of them was clearly not a typical magician. Jack leaned forward, half-convinced that he was seeing things, as if he'd been spending time in Chinatown's opium dens. The magician was female, wearing sorcerer's black; her short blonde hair, cut in a very unladylike fashion, shining against the sun. Jack frowned, remembering why so many Movers liked to shave their heads; long hair provided something for an enemy Mover to grab and pull hard with their magic. But the magician was definitely female, even if long hair was the fashion. He found his gaze following the curve of her body and the shape of her breasts, before looking away sharply. The female magician shouldn't be there at all. Logically, Master Thomas would never have brought a female magician into Cavendish Hall. The only female magicians used by the Royal Collage were Seers and Sensors and neither talent was noted for being reliable.

He frowned, studying the girl as the policemen hauled out the editor's family. It was a shame to know that they would probably be pushed in front of a judge, and then shipped down to Southampton or Liverpool to board a transport ship heading away from the green hills of England. They'd be lucky if they survived the trip, let alone hard years of backbreaking labour paying off the debts they would incur by being transported away from their homeland. Jack wanted to run down and free the prisoners, confronting Master Thomas for the second time – but it would be the final time. The only reason that Master Thomas had showed himself so clearly was obvious. He wanted to lure Jack into a second encounter – an encounter where he would be backed up by five, possibly six, trained sorcerers. There could only ever be one outcome of such a mismatched fight.

Gritting his teeth, he was just about to head away from the scene when he saw the girl confronting the policemen who were pushing the editor's wife around. Jack couldn't hear what she said, or even if she said anything, but Master Thomas didn't seem inclined to object. It was a rare gesture of mercy from someone who rarely showed mercy to his enemies – and that meant that the girl's opinion was important to him. Jack stroked his chin, puzzled. Who the hell was she? And what was she doing in the midst of a group of policemen and sorcerers?

She has magic, Jack thought. But that wasn't uncommon. There were plenty of women with magical talents – and not all of them were scooped up by the Royal College before they hit puberty. Lucy's own talent had remained undiscovered until she'd stumbled across it herself, and Jack was certain that Master Thomas knew nothing about her. If he'd known, he would have spared no effort to capture her, if only because Doctor Norwell would have pushed him into hunting Lucy down. The old researcher had been a dedicated student of magic since before Jack had been born and old age wouldn't have mellowed him.

It struck him almost like a physical blow. The girl didn't just have one talent – she had *all* of them. There had only ever been four Masters when Jack had been studying under Master Thomas – and two of them were dead. And Master Thomas was hardly a young man. He would be slowing down now as old age took its toll on him. If he hadn't been able to find a male Master to take his place, he wouldn't have any choice, but to forget any concerns he might have had about pushing a girl forward and into Cavendish Hall. It made perfect sense – and it would be easy to check. One of the things that he'd been careful to keep from Master Thomas the last time they'd skirmished was the extent of the underground's spying network.

Down on the ground, the werewolves had returned to their human forms and were making their reports to Master Thomas. Jack smiled to himself, knowing that the reports would be negative. There was nothing particularly ingenious about using a powerful scent to drown out a more subtle human scent – and besides, he'd used his magic to fly away from the building once he'd left. The werewolves would be the most disciplined and focused in England – Scotland Yard wouldn't trust them unless they displayed formidable discipline – but they wouldn't be able to track a flying man. Or, for that matter, one who took a swim in the River Thames to break his trail.

As Jack watched, the policemen returned to their carriages and headed off back towards the richer areas of London. They'd be shadowed, at a distance, by a bunch of street children Olivia had rounded up and promised good food and better pay. Jack smiled at the thought of ensuring that some of the children received better food than they'd ever been able to dream of eating, even though he was using them for his cause. The chances were good that some of them wouldn't live to see the next year, not if they were caught by the Bow Street Runners. They'd probably be transported without the bother of a trial.

The crowd was slowly dispersing, muttering angrily. Jack nodded, without surprise. It had only been five years since the Unrest, when the Dragoons had put an end to a series of uprisings that had threatened to burn London down to ashes.

Jack had escaped by the skin of his teeth, but many others hadn't been so lucky. And if he hadn't been able to escape to France, perhaps he would have joined so many others dangling from nooses at Tyburn.

Jack turned and started to run along the rooftops. Once, as a young man, he had been amazed by the hidden walkways that allowed an entire society composed of younger children and even some adults to thrive here, above the streets. Now, as a man with a cause, they served him as a way of getting around London without attracting attention. There was no need to fly in broad daylight, not when someone would see him and perhaps report it to the authorities. Besides, the childish part of his mind revelled in running along the rooftops. He wasn't ashamed to admit that it was exciting.

He smiled as one of the watchers stepped out of the shadows, gun in hand. "It's me," Jack said, before the man could say a word. "I'm back."

"Good to see you," the man grunted. Like seven others, he was watching for any sign of a move towards Lucy's brothel. The underground's nerve centre was protected by the positions in Society of some of its customers, but Jack knew better than to rely on that. If Master Thomas had any vices at all, besides tobacco, Jack's spies had never picked up on them. He would have no compunction about raiding the place. "The young lads have returned to report to you."

Jack opened a hatch a few yards from the guard and slipped down into the darkness. He closed it behind him and generated a small light, filling the room with an eerie, glimmering illumination. The door yawned open at his approach, revealing another guard holding a crossbow. It would actually be more accurate than some of the firearms the underground had obtained over the years – and there was no law against commoners possessing bows and arrows. The legacy of Agincourt had yet to fade from Britain's collective mind.

"Welcome back," Lucy said, flatly. She didn't sound happy. "You'll be pleased to know that they raided five of Davy's hideouts. Seventy people have been taken to the dungeons. Nineteen more have been taken to the graveyard."

"And forty have been taken prisoner from the printer's shop," Jack said. It was a blow – but he'd expected as much. No one, not even Master Thomas, could shut down all of the printing shops in the city. The underground's broadsheets would still go out to upset the great and the good. It was a pity that more of their intended readership couldn't read, but the authorities tended to frown upon efforts to combat illiteracy. An illiterate working class was one that couldn't understand just how badly the game was rigged against them. "Did we lose anyone important?"

Lucy glared at him. It did interesting things to her chest, reminding him of times when they'd shared pleasure while plotting the downfall of the British Government and the creation of a new world for the poor and downtrodden. But Master Thomas had won that round and the dreams had been crushed by the Duke of India and his Dragoons. It was a shame that Jack couldn't assassinate the Duke, but he was well guarded. There were thirty sorcerers assigned to protect him from underground assassins.

"No one who knows everything, if that is what you mean," she said, shortly. "We did lose a couple of recruiters. They didn't know anything beyond the meeting points, but..."

"We'll have to switch warehouses," Jack said. He hung up his coat and passed Lucy, heading into her sitting room. Davy was seated in one of the chairs, drinking what looked like a cup of tea with added alcohol. Jack picked up one of the bottles of wine and poured himself a large measure. A sorcerer should know better than to get drunk, Master Thomas had said, but one drink wouldn't kill him. "I trust that you have burned all of our bridges?"

Davy nodded, wearily. "I sent one of your boys to order the warehouses evacuated," he said. "Luckily, the *Aurora* and her master were already up at their harbour. One of the horsemen will reach them before they return to London."

"Good," Jack said. Captain Mordecai Smith – and his first mate Tonga, a former cannibal from the Andaman Islands – were only slightly involved with the underground, but they knew too much to risk them falling into enemy hands. Someone with imagination might be able to take the handful they did know and deduce Jack's grand design. And then the Dragoons would be on the streets and the entire plan would become impossible. "I'll head up that way tomorrow and meet with Ruddy. He can brief me on progress at the estate."

"We'll have to cut back on recruiting," Davy said, sourly. The recruitment plans had been proceeding faster than Jack had dared hope – but then, the relentless press of modern technology had turned hundreds of thousands of young men off the lands and out of work. They had started to gravitate to London and the other cities, only to discover that there was no work for them there either. Jack and his recruiters had found it easy to meet their quotas; so, unfortunately, had the Army. The government's final weapon against the urban poor had enough manpower to pose a quite serious problem for the rebel underground.

"Or move to Manchester or even Colchester," Jack said. There were thousands of urban poor in every city. Spreading out the recruiting would ensure that they weren't dependent on a single city, even if it did run the risk of exposure. "I'll leave you to handle that."

"You'll have to be careful when leaving the city," Lucy warned, from her corner. She still looked grim. "The Dragoons have watchers on all of the city gates. You won't get through without a great deal of luck."

Jack grinned. "I was thinking of taking Olivia," he said. His lockup, with his store of clothing and makeup, hadn't been touched by Master Thomas and his servants. Jack would find it easy to pose as a nobleman. It hadn't been difficult in the past. "The lass has never seen the countryside – and besides, she would be mistaken for my ward."

Lucy nodded, slowly. "Don't get yourself killed," she said. "The toffees are terrified of you right now. If they find your body..."

"They won't," Jack promised her. "Speaking of which, there is a new player in the game."

He described the girl he'd seen with Master Thomas briefly, unwilling to admit to Lucy or Davy that he'd felt a flicker of attraction when he'd realised that the girl had to be a Master. There had never been anyone else, apart from Master Thomas, who knew what it was like to hold and use all of the talents – and it had been years since he'd been able to share a drink and a relaxed chat with the Royal Sorcerer. The girl might be someone well worth getting to know – particularly since he'd seen her defend the editor's wife. Master Thomas would do whatever it took to uphold the government, no matter how personally repulsive he found it; the newcomer might have more doubts and scruples. She might be just like Jack himself...

The thought was banished quickly as a pair of messenger boys ran in from outside, carrying a warning that Dragoons had been seen searching a set of brothels only a few blocks away and rousting out all the customers. Jack smiled as he donned his hat and headed up to the hatch that led out onto the rooftops; some of the Bow Street Runners might find themselves in a nasty situation if they happened to encounter someone of noble blood. There was no shortage of aristocrats with a taste for slumming – and not all of them were as perverted as Lord Fitzroy.

His smile grew wider as he considered how Lord Fitzroy's family would take his death. Some of them had probably hated him; he hadn't been the kind of man to make friends easily. And the others might try to conceal where he'd been when he died, knowing that Master Thomas or one of his subordinates would be following up on that, trying to discover where Jack had killed his prey. The brothel had been burned to the ground – Olivia had reported that the firemen hadn't been able to quench the blaze – and they would find no leads there, but there would be a great deal of embarrassment for Lord Fitzroy's family. There were some perversions that would never be accepted, even by High Society.

He waited, patiently. Patience had been one of the first lessons Master Thomas had caught him, back when the world had been a simpler place. An hour passed slowly, finally broken by another messenger boy informing him that the Bow Street Runners had gone to raid another building on the other side of the Rookery. Jack was mildly surprised that they were showing so much energy. No Runner would want to be in the Rookery after dark. They'd never be seen again.

"I know who she is," Lucy said, once they were back in her room. Davy had gone off to roust out a handful of stevedores to help move boxes once darkness had fallen. The underground would have to scatter its supplies, just in case the Bow Street Runners had a stroke of luck. Or, for that matter, just in case a Seer managed to locate the rebel hideout. "She's Master Thomas's new apprentice."

Jack nodded, without surprise. He had already deduced that the girl had to be a Master. Nothing else, after all, would have qualified her for her position. Master Thomas was showing a remarkable degree of flexibility in one so old, but then he'd witnessed more change in a long lifetime than had Jack – or his new pupil.

"Rumour has it that she's a witch, with powers over common folk," Lucy continued, dryly. Jack snorted. There were all manner of rumours about magic and magicians; indeed, everyone he asked came up with a new – unfounded – rumour. "She was kept in near-seclusion until Master Thomas visited her father and convinced him to allow her to study with him at Cavendish Hall. I don't know what they said to each other..."

"Probably Master Thomas crossed his palm with silver," Jack said. The thought made him scowl. "Anything interesting in her family tree?"

"Nothing too much; minor quality," Lucy said. "The father works for the government – he may be getting a promotion in the next few months, if my source tells me true. It might have been the father's requirement for giving his daughter to the Royal College. The mother is a party creature, just like most of the rest of High Society. And her brother seems to be a staid and respectable businessman. There may have been some...questionable deals in the past – her father used to be in business before going to join the government – but nothing my sources could dig up."

"Bribes – or something else," Jack mused. He shook his head. "Anything else?"

"Her brother is celebrating a birthday in a fortnight," Lucy said. She caught sight of Jack's expression. "Let me guess; you're going to send him a birthday present?"

"I thought I would go pay my regards," Jack agreed. "I should be back from the country by then."

Chapter Eighteen

eady?"

Gwen braced herself. She was standing in the centre of the garden, a heavy blindfold covering her eyes. Darkness had enfolded her, to the point where she wasn't even sure where she was in the garden. Master Thomas had spun her around after he had blindfolded her and she was unpleasantly aware that she probably looked like an idiot. Cannock, thankfully, had the wit not to laugh at her. He'd been much more respectful after their brief and violent confrontation two weeks ago.

"Ready," she said, and tried to open her mind. Master Thomas had said that combat sense – using Sensing, one of the least understood and least reliable talents – was something that came with practice. Right now, Gwen had little confidence in her own abilities. "Go."

There was a pause and then something smacked against her arm. Cannock, Lombardi – who still blushed every time he saw her – and Master Thomas were hurling small beanbags at her, pushing her to develop her own abilities so that she could dodge them or use her powers to deflect them from her body. They wouldn't inflict permanent harm, she'd been assured, but there *would* be bruises. Master Thomas was a great believer in the school of education through hard knocks; besides, as he'd admitted after he'd explained the rules; the only real way to learn was through practice, practice and endless practice. Gwen was a quick study, but Sensing continued to defeat her. Even the Sensitive admitted that they didn't really understand or control their abilities.

Gwen grunted in pain, determined not to scream like a foolish female as the second beanbag impacted against her leg. A third smacked to the ground near her, followed rapidly by a fourth; someone – she suspected Lombardi – was deliberately aiming to miss. She overhead Master Thomas handing out a lecture in a sharp whisper and smiled inwardly. The next beanbag passed so close to her head that she felt it the force of its passage through her hair.

"Concentrate harder," Master Thomas said. He hadn't been able to put the skill into words, nor had any of the magicians whose sole talent was Sensing. They'd just explained to her that understanding would come, if she concentrated hard enough on her practice. Gwen was starting to suspect that they didn't realise that Masters tended to focus on the easy powers and therefore found it harder to develop the more complex and less understood talents. Or maybe they were just trying to reassure her that success wouldn't come easily. "Focus on the beanbags with your inner eye."

Another beanbag smacked against her buttocks. Gwen felt a hot flash of anger, remembering the time that Cannock had used his abilities to pinch her bottom, and closed her eyes. Somehow, it became easier with her eyes closed, despite the blindfold. The air around her seemed to be shimmering with potential. She was suddenly very aware of the garden around her, of the life buzzing from plants and trees that ran through the air. The sensation was so overpowering that she felt weak at the knees. She gasped as something intruded on her senses, followed rapidly by a jolt of pain against her chest. It took her a moment to realise what she'd done; she'd sensed the passage of the beanbag before it struck her body. And as soon as she'd realised what she'd done, her abilities seemed to slide into place.

She looked up as she felt another beanbag passing through the air, and then stepped forward sharply. It missed her and thumped down somewhere in the grass. Gwen lifted a hand as she felt a third beanbag, but failed to catch it before it hit her. The more she used the ability, the harder it was to comprehend the sensations – and then she realised that comprehension simply took too long. By the time she'd worked out what was happening it was already too late to avoid being hit. She had to allow her mind to wander freely and guide her body by instinct. It sounded easy, when she shaped the thought in her mind, but trying to put it into practice was difficult. She'd spent a lifetime learning to control herself – without the benefit of a tutor – and how could she surrender control to her instincts?

Her lips twitched, remembering one of the few lectures her mother had given her that had turned out to be actually useful. "Listen to your intuition," her mother had told her, firmly. Gwen hadn't taken much notice at the time, something that – in hindsight – she realised had probably worried Lady Mary. "You won't often know *what* is wrong, but you will know that *something* is wrong. And don't then fail to act on it."

Gwen scowled as more beanbags came hurtling out of the darkness. She just couldn't react in time. By the time she sensed them, it was almost too late to do anything. A hail of beanbags – thrown by Cannock, the Mover – slammed into her back and she found herself falling forward onto the grass. The impact stunned her for a long moment, not so much because of the pain as the sudden sensation of being so close to the natural world. Her enhanced senses were overwhelmed by the life surrounding her.

"Enough," Master Thomas said. "Gwen – can you get up without taking off the blindfold?"

Gwen scowled, but obeyed. She could still feel her body – and she could feel where she was in relation to the garden. It was almost as if she was watching herself from a far distance, even though she had never been able to develop Sight, one of the most fickle of the talents. Once she was standing upright, she reached for the blindfold and pulled it off. The sunlight streaming down on her forced her to use one hand to cover her eyes before she became accustomed to the light.

"You were getting somewhere," Master Thomas said. He didn't sound as if he was angry or disappointed. "And you have the benefit of a teacher. I had to discern most of the rules on my own."

Gwen nodded, wiping sweat off her brow. In truth, she was starting to suspect that having a tutor for this particular talent was not really helpful. Master Thomas had learned through doing – and had formed his own way of using the talent. Gwen found herself crippled by inadequate explanations. The Royal College would have to come up with a whole new set of words merely to explain the talent to prospective students. Very few of them came to Cavendish Hall before they had acquired at least some control over their talents.

"Thank you," she said, finally. It was a talent she needed

to develop, quickly. She'd seen Master Thomas pick a bullet out of the air, but Gwen couldn't even catch a beanbag. A bullet would kill her just as surely as it would kill a mundane from the streets. "I think we should do more work on this later today."

"Perhaps," Master Thomas said. She'd barely seen him for the last two days, ever since the raid on the printer's shop. They'd found nothing, or at least nothing that pointed the way towards finding the rogue Master. They *had* found enough evidence to have the printer and his staff transported to Australia as convict labour. At least their families would be going with them. Gwen had insisted and, somewhat to her surprise, Master Thomas had agreed. It seemed that he had far more authority than Gwen had ever realised. "Or perhaps you need a rest and a hot bath. You can study your books after lunch, if young Lombardi is unavailable to assist you with developing your other talents."

Lombardi blushed. Cannock snickered, unpleasantly. Gwen glared at him, trying to convey a threat with her eyes. Cannock looked at her, sneered, and then looked away, quickly. Gwen had to bite down the urge to lash out at him, even though she felt magic boiling through her blood, demanding that it be used. The bully wasn't worth the effort involved in squashing him, or so she told herself. She didn't want to admit that she didn't want to start a fight in front of Master Thomas.

"I'm sure that my studies will prove fruitful," Gwen said. If Master Thomas recognised the underlying sarcasm, he said nothing. "Will I be seeing you this afternoon?"

"Perhaps," Master Thomas said. He'd been busy for most of the afternoons, assisting Scotland Yard with its raids on suspect locations within the poorer parts of town. The aristocracy had had a nasty shock when Lord Fitzroy's severed head dropped in their midst – to say nothing of the hail of broken glass – and they were demanding action. Master Thomas had been forced to assign some of his reserve sorcerers to various mansions and houses, just to serve as guards. The King had apparently decamped to Windsor Castle, which was much easier to guard. "The Prime Minister and Lord Mycroft will require my presence to discuss security matters. I will probably be back later."

Some of the aristocrats Gwen had known would have

boasted of their relationship with two of the most powerful men in Britain – and hence the world. Master Thomas sounded almost as if he regarded it as a nuisance, an obligation that he would sooner avoid. Cannock, who sensed the same thing, seemed surprised, almost horrified. *He* would have died to have the ear of men who could bind and loose at will. Even the King, Gwen had heard, didn't have the same level of power and influence as Lord Mycroft. He was truly the indispensable man – but then, so was Master Thomas. Gwen doubted that she could ever live up to his example.

Lombardi blushed as Gwen motioned for him to follow her. He'd been dreadfully embarrassed for the first day after the ball; in her eyes, he'd been the perfect gentleman, but spending more time with other woman than one's escort was not regarded as polite by High Society. Gwen didn't really blame him, not when she had no intention of allowing their friendship to bloom into romance. Besides, as a third son there was no need to choose his wife so carefully; his prospects weren't too bad at all. There was no shortage of aristocratic women who would be happy to marry him. Marrying for love was rare; marrying for position or status was much more common.

"Don't worry," she said, as soon as they were alone. "I don't mind at all."

"You read my mind," Lombardi accused. He sounded shocked; there *were* Talkers who could read minds, but Masters rarely developed that talent to such a level. "You…how did you know?"

Gwen smiled, concealing her confusion. What did Lombardi think that she was talking about? "Female intuition," she said. Understanding clicked in her mind. He'd found someone he liked enough to court, someone who would be a good and supportive wife, without a flicker of magic. "What's her name?"

Lombardi's blush deepened. "Kate," he admitted. It was probably a diminutive of Katherine, part of Gwen's mind noted. "We were dancing at the ball – and then she invited me to the next ball, three days from now."

Gwen smiled again. "Have fun," she said. She didn't want to go herself, even though she'd enjoyed the dancing more than she wanted to admit. "And don't worry about it. Just concentrate on having a good time."

She walked up the stairs to the private rooms before he could think of a response. Away from him, she couldn't help feeling bitter, a feeling that made little sense to her. She hadn't wanted him as a husband, or a lover; she'd only asked him to the ball because she needed a partner. A young woman couldn't go on her own, even though God knew she'd broken enough conventions in the last few weeks. There was no reason for her to be upset, let alone jealous. And yet she felt...unhappy, rejected, even abandoned. Why did she feel that way?

Her new senses seemed to expand as she let her mind wander. Outside, she'd been aware of the garden, and of the life surrounding her. Inside, she could feel the stolid wooden walls – and stone, masked under the wood – that had been used to build Cavendish Hall. Magic infused into the stone, making the building stronger than any other in England, was easy to sense. In some ways, she was sure that she could tap it for power if necessary. Lombardi had warned her that that was incredibly difficult – and dangerous, if you hadn't been the magician who had infused the power into the stone in the first place – but Gwen could see how to do it, safely. She was halfway towards touching the wall when she caught herself. Master Thomas would not be pleased if she drained the stone. Besides, for all she knew, it was what held the building upright. She made a mental note to study buildings and builders when she had the time – if she ever had the time – and walked into her room, closing the door behind her. No one apart from the maids had entered her room, even Master Thomas, but Gwen knew to be careful. Cannock and his friends wouldn't hesitate to do something nasty if they thought they could get away with it.

She stopped as she saw the envelope lying on the ground, where it had been left after someone had pushed it under the door. It had surprised her to discover that mail was taken in by the staff and then distributed privately, but she guessed that it allowed Master Thomas a chance to check the letters before they were given to their intended recipients. Gwen simply hadn't had many letters since she'd arrived, leading her to wonder if her parents had chosen to forget that they had a daughter. Lady Mary probably found having a magical daughter deeply embarrassing in Polite Society.

The envelope was stiff and formal. Gwen opened it –

noting the cost of the paper – and frowned as she unfolded the letter. It was very simple; David Crichton, son of Lord and Lady Crichton, requested the pleasure of Gwen's company at his birthday dinner. Gwen hesitated, and then smiled to herself. Her brother David might have been a stuffy pain in the posterior most of the time, but he'd never picked on her. And he'd even stood up to their mother several times for Gwen's sake. Gwen disliked parties – a treacherous part of her mind reminded her that she'd enjoyed the dancing at the ball, before the rogue Master had appeared to cause havoc – yet she would go to her brother's dinner. As his sister, she could go alone.

Putting the letter on her dressing table, Gwen headed for the bathroom. The maids, at least, knew better than to meddle with her small collection of expensive bathing supplies. Pouring a hot bath, Gwen undressed and examined herself critically in the mirror. There were bruises on her arms and legs where beanbags had struck her body. A dark mark on her abdomen, just above her groin, showed where one had struck with savage force. She was lucky that it wasn't worse, she told herself, as she gritted her teeth against the pain. Her determination to succeed – to excel – had only grown stronger. It was the only way she could prove herself worthy of the trust that had been invested in her.

Climbing into the bath, she closed her eyes as the steaming hot water enveloped her body and slowly started to soak away the aches and pains. She was tired, even though it was barely noon; she found it hard not to relax into slumber. Only the thought of accidentally slipping below the water and drowning kept her half-awake. No magic could save her from drowning, at least as far as she knew. There were no recorded humans who could shift to a marine animal form. They might not have survived their first transformation. God knew there were enough weird tales out there that might – stripped of the lies and exaggerations – have represented a failed transformation.

Her mind started to wander, slowly. It drifted out of the bath and floated into the bedroom. Gwen was only partly aware of what was happening, which made it easier. Her awareness shimmered towards the door and passed through its wooden frame, unbothered by the magic running through the barrier. One of the maids was just moving up the stairs, carrying a basket of washing, unaware of Gwen's ghostly presence. She walked right through Gwen and, for a second, Gwen found herself looking into the maid's brain. No wonder, part of her mind realised, that researchers had discovered so much about the human body. Seers could look right *into* a body and, with the proper medical training, perhaps know what was wrong. And if they could *look* into a body, could a Changer not *heal* a body?

She found herself choking as she snapped back to her body. Gwen thrashed about in the tub, almost panicking before she hauled her head out of the bath. She'd slipped down while her mind had been wandering elsewhere, almost drowning, just as she'd feared. What had happened to her? Understanding came slowly, but surely. Her mind hadn't wandered; she'd learned how to use her Sight. No wonder Seers were so useful to the Crown. A trained Seer could spy on anyone, and only another sorcerer could even sense that it was happening.

Slowly, she leaned back in the bath and closed her eyes. This time, she imagined her awareness detaching from her body and floating up into the air. The ceiling provided no barrier as she kept heading upwards, into the uppermost levels. She spun, imagining that she had a ghostly body, and found herself looking at Master Thomas. He was standing at a table, reading a letter. It looked official, even though it carried no golden seal.

He turned and looked at her. Gwen was invisible – she wasn't really there at all – but he could still see her. "You're a very naughty girl," he said, with a sudden smile. Gwen wasn't sure how she could even hear him. The words echoed oddly in her translucent ears. She flushed horribly as it dawned on her that she was effectively naked. "It's very bad manners to spy on your master."

Gwen panicked, her awareness sharpening up...and she fell back into her body. As she climbed out of the bath, she found herself reflecting on her new ability. Used properly, it could help her – and perhaps she had found the key to unlocking a new ability as well. She was still smiling to herself when she went down for lunch. Who knew what the future would bring?

Chapter Nineteen

t's green!"

Jack smiled at Olivia's surprise. The young girl – wearing male clothing, as always – had been born in London, abandoned in London and forced to learn to live on her own in London. She had never seen Hyde Park or any of the great gardens patronised by the rich and powerful; she had certainly never left the city. The green farmlands that surrounded London, supplying the city with food and drink, were completely new to her. Jack, who had seen them before, found himself reflecting, instead, on their other aspects. If something were to happen to the farms, London would starve.

Their little steamboat was heading up the Thames, away from London. Jack had been worried about navigating the endless series of locks and canals, but Mordecai Smith – the Master of the *Aurora* – had assured him that it was perfectly safe. Besides, there were thousands of vessels plying their trade on the river every day. Who was going to look at a single boat?

"It's what the land ought to be everywhere," he assured her, with a smile. "But the factories have been taking their lands and people for generations."

The thought was a chilling one. In the five years since the Unrest, the rich had been consolidating their hold on the poor. There were thousands of farmers and farmhands leaving their lands now, even though some of them had been offered the chance to stay on and work for their new masters. The rebellion might have failed, but America still offered the poor a chance at a better life – if they managed to make it across the Atlantic and into the sprawling untamed wilderness of the New World. Jack knew that much of America was still inhabited by redskins, but no one in London or New York would care if the savages exterminated the colonists. It would remind them not to be too independent of the British Army.

He pursed his lips as he remembered meetings in Paris, just after the Unrest. Franklin – a descendent of the legendary Benjamin Franklin, one of the few rebels to escape the noose after the destruction of the rebel army – had told him that French officers suspected that the British had been quietly encouraging the savages to raid American settlements. It sounded absurd, until one considered that the Viceroy would be quite happy to see the settlers reminded of how much they needed military protection – and if a few thousand redskins were killed into the bargain, so much the better. The last time the American settlers had thought they no longer needed the British Army, there had been a rebellion. No one wanted to repeat that disastrous episode.

Olivia sensed his mood and looked away, studying the green fields as the boat headed upstream, towards the west. A large mansion was coming into view, near a jetty already waiting for the puffing steamboat. Jack allowed himself a brief smile as Smith brought the boat in to the jetty, and his black servant – who had been brought to England as a curiosity and then abandoned in London – jumped ashore and secured the boat to the stone harbour. Olivia hadn't been able to avoid staring at Tonga; she'd never seen a black man in her life. it had only been a few years since the Cotton Gin had made slavery profitable in the American South; Blacks were commonly regarded as savages, fit only for slavery. Jack knew better than to believe such lies. The rebellious blacks on Haiti had soundly thrashed two French armies before the third had finally achieved an uneasy peace. They bled red too, just like white men.

"Thank you," Jack said, as he scrambled ashore. "Stay with the boat; I'll have food and drink sent out to you."

Smith nodded. He was a sour-faced man with very little to say, not least because his eldest son had been caught up in a riot and killed by the Dragoons. His wife disapproved of him assisting the underground, but she had done nothing to stop him or his younger son. The younger son had even enlisted in the rebel army. Jack helped Olivia up onto the jetty and strode up towards the manor. Kelmscot Manor, a house built by minor gentry back in the 16th Century, had fallen on hard times. The current owner was a drunk, who had no idea that his estate was serving as a recruiting and training base for the underground. His butler, a common-born man who had climbed through the ranks by dint of hard work, had been Jack's ally for years. Jack trusted the resentment he felt at knowing that higher positions would be barred to him because of humble birth. An intelligent and capable man, trapped by circumstances beyond his control, tended to develop resentment. It was a dangerous combination for his lords and masters.

The air smelt fresh and clean as they passed through the garden and up to the gates. A man was waiting for them there, wearing the pristine clothes and faintly disapproving expression of a Butler. Butlers, in Jack's experience, often turned out to be bigger snobs than their masters, offsetting their low birth with an attitude that would have done Lord Fitzroy credit. This one, at least, didn't take himself too seriously. Jack respected him for his willingness to get his hands dirty, even though his master simply couldn't afford to hire additional staff. The owner of Kelmscot might have been spendthrift and a drunk, but at least he wasn't checking the grounds and wondering why some of his fields had been turned into parade grounds.

"Welcome back to the house," the Butler said. His voice, at least, was perfect; richly upper-class, with just a hint of disdain when he saw Olivia. Jack was wearing an outfit that suggested he was minor gentry himself – and Olivia was his son – but a snob would probably have been able to see through the disguise. "The General is waiting for you in the lobby."

Jack frowned. "Chancy," he said. "Is your master not awake?"

"He won't be up until afternoon," the Butler assured him, as he led Jack through corridors that had once held fine paintings and expensive artworks. They'd all been sold, one after the other, to keep the house's current master on his steady course towards drinking himself to death. "The sleeping draught I put in his drink will see to that."

"Good thinking," Jack said. It was lucky that such a man wasn't on the other side – but then, if the government had allowed competent and capable men to rise, there would be no need for the underground. Or Jack himself, for that matter. What would he do, Lucy had asked him once, when they won? Jack hadn't been able to find an answer. "Let's see the General, shall we?"

The Butler led him into the lobby, standing aside so Jack could see the man he'd made a General. Ruddy – his real name had been forgotten, not least by him – had once served as a recruiting sergeant in Colchester, a position that would have made him a target for Jack and the underground if he'd remained in the army. But he'd watched in horror as the Dragoons charged a mob of unarmed women and deserted later than evening. Jack had taken the opportunity to Charm him into total loyalty, just in case the former soldier thought better of working with the underground.

He was a tall man, only slightly shorter than Jack; his unshaven face darkened by exercise and hard living. They clasped hands for a long moment, reminding Jack that Ruddy was stronger than him, at least physically. The former sergeant had lost none of his strength, or the skills that had allowed him to start turning the scum of the earth – as the Duke of India had affectionately called his men – into proper soldiers. Jack disliked knowing that anyone was indispensable to the underground, even him, but there was no one else like Ruddy, with the skills they needed. The former sergeant knew that he was needed. Jack only hoped that he didn't know how much.

"Good to see you again," Ruddy grunted. He looked down at Olivia. "And this is…?"

"My assistant," Jack said, firmly. Ruddy would have been able to see through her disguise, if anyone could. He had had plenty of years of experience dealing with recruits who tried to lie about their pasts or exaggerate their skills. "How is the army?"

Ruddy shrugged. "We've put five thousand men through the training course," he said. "We won't know how good they will be until we actually have to fight, of course. I had to put a couple in irons for drinking while in training and a couple more needed to be knocked about before they learned some discipline, but the rest are coming along nicely. You selected good men."

Jack nodded, although it had largely been Davy and his recruiters who had selected the prospective soldiers.

Smuggling them out of London hadn't been easy, all the more so because they needed to conceal their destination. Some would be captured – or desert – and the less they knew, the less they could reveal. The real challenge was in finding a place to hide them in London, a place where they could pass unnoticed until the time came to start the uprising. And then the Establishment would know just how well they'd prepared the groundwork for revolution.

"They've fired off enough rounds to learn their trade," Ruddy added, after a second. "Once they get their weapons, they'll be ready to move."

"Excellent," Jack said. The first shipment of smuggled weapons was already in London, concealed in a warehouse near the Thames. It wasn't unknown for ships to bring in cargos and leave them in London until they were needed, but the longer they remained unused, the greater the chances of discovery. "Are there any major problems?"

"We need more space to train," Ruddy admitted. "There just isn't enough room for real training – and none in a city."

Jack nodded, slowly. He'd watched the skirmishes between France and Prussia from a safe distance two years ago and had been shaken at the bitter fighting that had raged through a medium-sized town. The advantages of the French Army had been offset by the Prussian willingness to fight from cover and force the French to destroy the town section by section. In the end, the struggle had been settled by a treaty and both sides had retreated to lick their wounds and learn their lessons. Jack, who had found it hard to choose a favourite between the Prussians and the French, had drawn his own conclusions. Half-trained troops could hold off an army if they were fighting in a city.

The Unrest had failed to cause the ruling class to make concessions for three separate reasons. It had largely taken place in the countryside. There had been no coordination between the different groups. And the government had not been weakened; despite the chaos, it had never lost its grip on events. In a way, they'd had a fourth advantage; they'd had magic, the Royal Sorcerers Corps. Jack scowled, remembering the bloody skirmishes and how they'd ended. This time, he promised those who had fallen when London's cobblestones had run red with blood, it would be different.

"We may have to improvise," he admitted. Finding one

estate to use as a training ground had been a stroke of luck. Finding a second would require a miracle. "Can we start moving the combat units into London soon?"

Ruddy frowned. "You intend to move soon?"

"Sooner rather than later," Jack said. Upsetting Master Thomas and scaring the aristocracy had been fun – with the added bonus that Jack now knew about Master Thomas's new apprentice – but it had also put them on alert. There would be more guards in London for the next few months, rendering similar raids far harder. "Time isn't on our side."

"We can start moving the first few companies within the week, if you have a place to hide them," Ruddy said. "But you will have to ensure that they're fed and watered, or they will be useless."

Jack nodded. There were a few more points, but the important one – preparing for the uprising – had been settled. He didn't have a firm date yet – plans never survived contact with reality, let alone the enemy – yet he knew that he could start thinking about a date. If they weren't betrayed…if they weren't exposed…if they weren't discovered. Jack had worked with Master Thomas and the Royal Sorcerers Corps for years; he knew their strengths and weaknesses. One leak would be all it took to destroy his entire plan.

And then the walls of aristocracy would never come tumbling down.

He allowed Ruddy to lead them outside, heading down towards the fields on the other side of the estate. Guns were rare in the countryside – at least for the commoners – but the nobility were allowed as many guns as they liked. No one would take any notice of gunshots from the estate, even if it *did* sound like a small army of men drilling for combat. Up close, it would be a different story. It was lucky that Lord Wooster had plenty of acres of fields and forest to conceal Jack's men.

The underground had used Ruddy and a handful of others to train a cadre of soldiers. Those men had, in turn, trained others, who now marched about in the field as if they were real soldiers. Certainly, no regiment of the British Army could have marched with more pride. Guns in their hands and a chance to actually fight back against their oppressors had done wonders. Jack would have bet on them against a regiment commanded by chinless wonders whose sole qualification for command was aristocratic birth, some of whom would have served their country better by charging the enemy and getting themselves killed at the earliest opportunity.

"Soldiers!" Ruddy barked, in his parade ground voice. Beside him, Jack was aware of Olivia flinching. She would know to be wary of soldiers wandering away from their barracks, looking for beer, whores and gambling. They tended to start fights and rough up anyone who got in their way. "Present...arms!"

The soldiers snapped to attention. Jack had watched French soldiers on parade and hadn't been too impressed, but his men looked more determined – and tougher – than the Frenchmen he'd seen. Perhaps it was the rough uniform, barely more than a green overall and metal hats. British officers wore red so that the blood wouldn't show and upset their men, a theory that had suited the Duke of India just fine in the endless series of wars that had won the subcontinent, but Jack preferred something that didn't make an easy target for enemy snipers. Some of the Frenchmen he'd seen with rifles had been deadly, swift to slaughter unprepared enemy commanders. The green tunics made his men harder to see, especially against the grass, but they'd have to find something else for the coming uprising in London.

Jack inspected them one by one, checking weapons and supplies. Ruddy, at least, had a good grasp of logistics; the men would have their weapons cleaned and ready for use at all times, on pain of heavy punishment. Jack disapproved of flogging men and it was true that the more successful British commanders boasted about how rarely they had to flog their men, but a soldier who didn't take care of his rifle was more of a danger to his fellows than the enemy. And Jack knew that when the time came to strike, the vast might of the British Empire would be brought to bear on his rebel army. A single lost battle would mean destruction.

A handful of the men had done particularly well and Jack – prompted by Ruddy – singled them out for special attention. Their fellows would see and emulate them, he hoped. The small number of miscreants looked downcast as Jack glanced at them and purposely looked away, fighting to hide his smile. At least they hadn't had any deserters, but then they'd chosen their men carefully. The more they brought in, the greater the chance of one of them becoming dissatisfied and trying to slip away into the night. And one deserter could betray them all.

"Excellent," he said, finally. The soldiers in earshot straightened up noticeably at his words. "I would bet on them against anyone."

"So I would hope, Governor," Ruddy said. The old sergeant's gaze met Jack's. "They're ready for action. Boredom is our greatest enemy now."

Jack nodded, shortly. "We will act as soon as we can," he promised. Taking some of the men back to London would help ease the pressure, but young men who had been taught to fight would tend to grow restless. And London offered so many temptations for a would-be deserter. It didn't take any imagination at all to know how badly things could go wrong. "Did you have a chance to think about Aldershot?"

"Yes, Governor," Ruddy said, as they walked away from the troops. The other sergeants – men Ruddy had trained – could handle the next few hours of training and exercising. "It's not going to be easy, even with surprise. The Duke of India is there half the time and he's a right hard-ass about preparation."

"True," Jack agreed. Oddly, given the size of the British Empire, the British Army was relatively small. There were garrisons scattered through North America, India and a handful of other places, but most of the Empire was upheld by native troops. The reserves in Britain itself were all that could be deployed to a trouble spot, something he suspected worried Lord Liverpool – and the Duke of India. Those men were the only reserve the Empire could deploy quickly. The militia – and the Trained Bands of London – weren't worth their uniforms. "We may need to find another way to pin down the garrison."

"And then there are the smaller barracks," Ruddy added. "You do know just how many there are, don't you?"

Jack smiled. "Don't worry," he said, affecting a confidence he didn't feel. "I will deal with them all in due course."

Chapter Twenty

y name is John Wellington Wells," the man said. He held out one hand for Gwen to shake. "I'm a dealer in magic and spells."

Gwen frowned, studying the man closely. He *looked* the part, she had to admit. Dressed in a black evening suit, with a top hat, and carrying a silver-topped cane, he reminded her of Master Thomas when he was wearing his formal clothes. He was handsome, with dark hair and a strong chin: almost *too* handsome. There wasn't a blemish anywhere on his face. His handshake was strong and firm. He looked too good to be true.

"He's a fake," Master Thomas said. It had been his idea to visit the store, promising to teach Gwen something new about magic – or magicians. Gwen wasn't sure what she was intended to learn, other than the fact that people in magician's clothes weren't always magicians. There had been a tendency for black to go out of fashion for a few years – at least according to the maids – because magicians and sorcerers wore black. The tendency hadn't lasted long, Gwen knew, if only because black was required at funerals.

"I resent that," Wells said, letting go of Gwen's hand and pulling himself up to his full height. "I am a dealer in magic from many a source." He reached forward to Gwen's ear. When he pulled his hand back, there was a golden coin held in his palm. "Magic is my stock in trade."

"Slight-of-hand," Master Thomas informed Gwen. "Only the credulous would believe in him, I'm afraid. And that goes for all of his stock."

He waved an elegant gloved hand towards the shop's merchandise. Gwen studied it, unsure if she should laugh or cry. A hundred bottles of coloured liquid, marked as everything from love potions to healing potions, dominated one shelf. Beneath them, glittering crystals that promised to help a person concentrate, or learn quicker than they might expect. There were silver talismans that promised to ward away evil and dusty parchments that offered to teach someone how to curse their enemies. On the other side of the shop, there were relics from religious organisations, each one claimed to have magical power. Gwen picked up a splinter of the True Cross and looked at it doubtfully. Whatever accommodation had been reached between the Church and the Royal College, she doubted that it extended to obvious fakes.

"If you put all the pieces of the True Cross together," Master Thomas observed, archly, "you would have enough wood to build a brand new ark."

"It's belief that is important," Wells protested. He no longer sounded impressive, at least to Gwen's ears. "People believe – and that brings the magic."

"Really?" Master Thomas enquired. He picked up a box. "The skull of John the Baptist," he said. He put it down and picked up another one. "The skull of John the Baptist – as a young man. Do you really believe that anyone would be fooled?"

"You might be surprised," Wells said. "People *want* to believe."

He picked up one of the coloured bottles and held it out to Gwen. "This is a love potion," he said. "In one sense, it's just coloured water; in another, it gives a young man the courage to make the first move. Perhaps the girl would be interested in him if he actually asked her for her hand – and the potion encourages him, gives him confidence."

Gwen shuddered. The thought of a potion that would make her – or anyone else – fall in love with someone against her will was chilling. A Charmer could presumably make someone fall in love with him, but that could be resisted. The idea of a love potion...she shook her head in disgust. Looking around the store, she realised that almost everything was fake. There was no magic in the room at all, except what they'd brought in with them. Wells made a living by fooling his customers into believing that he could work magic.

A small pile of books caught her eye and she glanced down at them, curious. They promised to teach her all kinds of magic, along with Latin and Arabic words that could be used to focus and harness the power of the natural world – or summon demons from the pits of Hell. One of them, written by a character known only as the Mad Arab, promised to put its owner in contact with beings from another space and time, beings so powerful that they could destroy the human world in the blink of an eye. The illustration – a giant mutated octopus – didn't give her any confidence in the book's value. Besides, if the book was genuinely that powerful, why wasn't Wells already ruling the world?

"Hope springs eternal," Master Thomas said, when Gwen asked. "Particularly in the minds of the deluded."

He chuckled and picked up one of the parchments. "This allows you to curse your enemies," he said. "You'd be better off spending the money on drink, getting them drunk, and then cutting their throats while they are unable to resist. The murderer would still face the gallows, but at least he wouldn't run afoul of the Demonic Powers Act."

"I provide a valuable service," Wells protested.

"You take money from the gullible and convince them that they can do magic," Master Thomas said. He seemed more amused than annoyed. "You have them paying through the nose for worthless parchments and tin talismans you claim are silver."

Wells picked up a silver dagger and held it out to Master Thomas. "Designed to stop a werewolf," he said. "It's pure silver."

"It's shiny tin," Master Thomas countered. "You wouldn't leave a silver dagger out here, would you?"

He stamped towards the door and headed out into the street. Gwen followed him, realising that they weren't entirely alone. A small crowd of curious onlookers had gathered on the other side of the street, watching with awe as the Royal Sorcerer departed the magical shop. They'd believe in Wells, she realised sourly, now that they'd seen the Royal Sorcerer himself visiting his store. Whatever irritation Wells had felt over their visit, it would be more than amply compensated for by the new custom – and the money it brought to his coffers.

"A fake," Master Thomas said, as the carriage rumbled to life and headed down towards Cavendish Hall. "Still, he serves a useful purpose. It just isn't the purpose he thinks he serves."

He eyed Gwen, expectantly. She frowned, considering. Master Thomas hadn't said anything about *why* they were visiting a fake magic store, let alone why they were not shutting it down for practicing illicit magic. But then, Wells *hadn't* been practicing illicit magic; he'd been nothing more than a fake. That might not impress a jury; God alone knew how many people had been conned out of their hard-earned money by Wells and other frauds like him.

"He convinces people that magic isn't what it is," she said, finally. It was the only answer that made sense. Before Master Thomas had recruited her, she hadn't known much about real magic – and a great deal of nonsense. Anyone trying to learn without the Royal College's assistance would be at a severe disadvantage. "It cuts down on the number of underground magicians."

"Quite," Master Thomas agreed. "And he helps to confuse people about what magic can actually do. It keeps them respectful."

His lips twitched. "Would you care to guess how many people among our lords and masters patronise his store?"

Gwen looked up, surprised. They weren't exactly in the Rookery or one of the other poor – and therefore criminal – parts of town, but Wells had his store on the edge of respectable London. Gwen had heard of it long before becoming Master Thomas's apprentice; the younger gentry often dropped hints of roguish dealings on the edge of respectable London, apparently under the impression that it gave them an air of mystery that women would find irresistible. The ones who did patronise the area were always careful to be out of it before night fell. There were limits, even for men born and bred to consider themselves the lords and masters of the world.

"Hundreds," Gwen said, finally. Master Thomas nodded. "But why?"

"As I said," Master Thomas said, "hope springs eternal in the minds of the deluded."

He settled back into his seat as the carriage rattled across one of London's bridges. Gwen caught sight of a ship waiting for the bridge to rise so it could carry on down towards the sea. It was surrounded by a flight of seagulls looking for scraps they could scoop up from the river and eat while flying through the sky. Once, she'd envied the birds their freedom. Now, she understood how they had to feel. They were dependent upon humans feeding them to survive.

"I have a question," Gwen said, finally. She hadn't dared ask before, but Master Thomas seemed to be in a good mood. "Who trained the rogue Master?"

Master Thomas stared at her, just long enough to make Gwen uncomfortable. "You'll know all that when you are ready to hear it," he said. "You're not ready to hear it now."

Gwen stared back at him, refusing to be intimidated or browbeaten into silence. "He's loose in London and he may know about me," Gwen said. She had no doubt of that. Master Thomas's apprentice would have kept the aristocracy gossiping for months even if she'd been a male; a female apprentice was unheard of. "I need to know now."

There was a long, chilling pause. Gwen was just starting to wonder if she'd gone too far when Master Thomas nodded, finally. "We'll talk about it in my rooms," he said, firmly. The carriage rattled as it passed through the gates and up the lane towards Cavendish Hall. "And you're right. You do have a need to know."

Gwen was still puzzling over that as he led her through the doors, up the sinister staircase and into his rooms. Had he been waiting for her to ask, to see if she had the confidence to proceed against his silence, or had he merely changed his mind when she pressed for information? She pushed the thought aside as she entered his rooms, glancing around to see what luxuries were afforded to the Royal Sorcerer. Gwen had never been in his rooms – at least not physically – and she was almost disappointed. There were a small set of bookshelves, a rug that had come from India and a pair of paintings covering one wall. The remainder of the rooms were almost barren, as if Master Thomas had no time for luxuries. It was an attitude her mother would have found incomprehensible.

A maid – an elderly woman, wearing the black and white formal dress beloved of London's society – appeared out of a side room. Master Thomas ordered tea as he motioned for Gwen to sit in one of the comfortable armchairs. Spartan the rooms might appear to be, but Master Thomas enjoyed his comforts. It struck Gwen, again, that Master Thomas was *old*. He'd been a young man at the dawn of magic, perhaps the oldest surviving magician from the days when magic had saved the British Empire from the American rebels. How much history had he seen, Gwen asked herself, and how much did he know that had been kept from the British public?

The maid served a small pot of tea and handed Gwen a china cup. She sipped it slowly, waiting for Master Thomas to drink his own tea before speaking. He seemed to be lost in his thoughts, so she looked away towards the paintings. They showed three young men, wearing sorcerer's black; they seemed young, confident...looking towards the future and daring it to do its worst. One of them, Gwen was shocked to realise, was Master Thomas. His chin was unmistakable. The other two were strangers.

"There were three of us in those days," Master Thomas said. "Myself, Master Saul and Master Luke. We designed the Royal College in the days when High Society and the establishment weren't quite sure what to make of us. We planned to change the world."

His eyes closed, as if he was looking into the past. "We succeeded," he added. "We got what we wanted. It didn't make us happy."

He opened his eyes and looked at Gwen. "Masters are rare – but then, you already know that," he said. Gwen nodded. If there had been a male Master of her age, Gwen herself would never have had the chance to learn magic properly. "I saw my friends die; one died in an accident, when we didn't fully understand our powers; the other died in combat against the French, back during the wars at the turn of the century. I wondered if I was the only Master left alive – and if there would ever be a fourth. It delighted me when I discovered Master Jackson. He was much younger than me and I allowed myself to be convinced that he would be able to take over the position of Royal Sorcerer when I retired."

Master Thomas shook his head, slowly. "But there was too much I didn't know about him," he added. "I didn't know that at the time, but afterwards...he was a perfect pupil in many ways. He learned quickly and well, faster than anyone else – I expected no less from a Master. He even taught me more about how the powers worked together than I expected."

He stared down at his hands for a long moment. "But there was too much I didn't know about him," he repeated. "I didn't see the signs of trouble for years – and then I

convinced myself that I was mistaken. He had sworn an oath
to the Prince Regent to serve and uphold the establishment,
but in the waves of unrest sweeping the country he chose to
forget his oath and join the rebels. I tried to stop him five
years ago." He hesitated. "I believed that he was dead."

Gwen leaned forward. "But if he escaped," she asked,
"where did he go?"

"He was – is – a Master," Master Thomas reminded her.
"If he'd gone to the French or the Russians, they'd have been
delighted to have him. God knows their magical programs
have always been behind ours. And then there's the wretched
Corsican who made himself the Sultan of the Ottoman
Empire. He would sell his entire harem for the services of a
Master Magician. Or he might have gone underground in
Britain itself. I thought he was dead and that the matter was
at an end."

He shook his head, very slowly. "Master Jackson hates the
establishment," he said. "I don't know why – something
happened, something that he never chose to tell me. But he
turned against the government when the unrest started
sweeping through the cities, forcing the government to crack
down harder and harder. Magic had to be used against
Englishmen. There are a great many people out there who
hate us for that, even if they understand why we did it..."

"And people like Lord Blackburn, who think it was our
birthright," Gwen said. Master Thomas nodded, sourly.
"Was Master Jackson ever a Darwinist?"

"The Darwinists were barely a concept during the unrest,"
Master Thomas said. "Charles Darwin's work helped to
justify everything we did retroactively. I sometimes wonder
if some people accepted his words out of guilt; it's a great
deal easier to crack down on people if you regard them as
subhuman, unworthy to be considered one's equals."

He shook his head. "I swore an oath," he said, firmly.
"England is still the finest country in the world; it has the
finest ships, the finest trade, the finest magicians...even the
finest government. There is more freedom in England than
anywhere else on the globe. Even Cromwell was unable to
alter that truth."

Gwen frowned, inwardly. The official story about Oliver
Cromwell was that he had been a regicide, who had murdered
King Charles I with his own hands. She'd read enough to

doubt that the official version of history was actually true, but asking the wrong questions would draw unwelcome attention – even for a prospective Royal Sorceress. After meeting the King – and realising how power was finely balanced between the Monarch, the aristocracy and Parliament – she thought she understood how he had felt. The wrong people in power could do untold damage to the country.

"Master Jackson was always headstrong," Master Thomas added, slowly. "What he did – confronting me directly – was a declaration of war. By harming so many rich and powerful people, he has made it impossible for any compromise to he formed – exactly what he wanted to happen. His ultimate goal is to tear down the establishment and replace it with a democracy, to hand the country over to the poor. Men and women who are not bred or trained to rule can only drive the country to ruin."

His lips twitched. "Indeed, had the American rebels concentrated on uniting their forces, rather than squabbling, George Washington might have become their first King, rather than hanging from a gallows in Philadelphia," he said. "I watched him die. He died bravely, unlike some of his fellows. And that opportunist Arnold managed to change sides quickly enough to avoid joining him on the scaffold."

He glanced over towards the paintings. "You may encounter Master Jackson again," he said. "When you do, remember one thing; he isn't entirely sane. He had no sense of the long-term view when I knew him and I don't think he has changed at all. You cannot trust him to think of anything, but his cause and his goal. Don't turn your back on him."

"I see," Gwen said. She trusted Master Thomas – and yet it was obvious that he wasn't telling her everything. "Do you think that we will ever find him?"

"He's probably plotting his next move," Master Thomas said. "Someone like him will not be able to remain underground forever."

Chapter Twenty-One

arkness fell over London like an enveloping shroud.

Jack perched on a manor's rooftop, cloaked by the shadows, watching Cavendish Hall. It was strange, staring at his old home – the first place in the world where he had truly felt happy. But the happiness had been a lie, the result of his own arrogance and ignorance, the ignorance when he hadn't known the truth about his origins. And when he found out, he'd known that he could no longer stay at Cavendish Hall.

He moved his gaze from window to window, wondering which room held Master Thomas's apprentice. Where had she come from, he asked himself, and what did she make of it all? Master Thomas wouldn't repeat the same mistakes he'd made with Jack, yet he had had no choice but to take on an unconventional apprentice. A girl would discover some unsavoury truths about magicians on her own, but would she break free of her mental shackles? Or perhaps Master Thomas would have Charmed her into obedience. Charm was deadly, even though it wasn't anything like as spectacular as Moving or Blazing. A person who had been charmed carefully enough would never realise what had happened to them. Their thoughts would simply flow into the channels created by the Charmer.

A movement caught his eye and he smiled as a dark-clad figure exited the side of the building. He didn't go down to the main gate, but walked through the gardens to the fence and scrambled over the top, showing remarkable skill. Jack turned and slipped from chimney to chimney, shadowing the dark figure as he headed away from Cavendish Hall. Few people, in his experience, bothered to look up, even when they were trying to remain unseen and avoid hidden watchers. This man was no different. He moved with the precision of an expert, but without the habits that a reconnaissance patrol would have learned in the field. The Duke of India would have been upset if any of his men had shown so little tradecraft.

Jack caught sight of his face, briefly, and his smile deepened. Lord Blackburn himself, heir to one of the most powerful families in Britain – and a Charmer, perhaps the most powerful Charmer in the world. There were whispered stories about Lord Blackburn, stories that suggested that all of his friends were under his spell and all of his servants had had their minds twisted until they could do naught but obey. Jack knew that such stories were, if anything, understatements. Lord Blackburn had been a manipulative little shit even before he'd developed his Charm. The Darwinists had projected themselves onto the universe and had come to believe that they had a right to rule. It said more about their insecurities than it did about God's grand design.

Lord Blackburn moved with easy confidence through the darkened streets. There was little need to fear footpads, robbers and drunkards in the richer parts of town. The Bow Street Runners patrolled heavily, just to ensure that their lords and masters remained undisturbed in their beds. In other times, Jack would have taken the opportunity to rid the world of a few collaborators – men who helped their oppressors control the poor – but he had other business right now. Unless he missed his guess, Lord Blackburn was heading to the farm. And Jack, whatever else he'd been able to pull from the rumours that surrounded Cavendish Hall, had not been able to locate the farm. There were times when he suspected that aristocratic embarrassment, far more than anything else, helped conceal some of the nation's darker secrets. The truths were buried under a mountain of nonsense.

He nearly lost Lord Blackburn twice before his quarry finally reached an old house on the edge of the Thames. It was closer to one of Jack's warehouses than he cared to think about, but it hardly mattered – at least as long as the Royal College didn't draw attention to the area by mounting patrols around their building. The handful of night watchmen on duty looked properly slovenly; only their posture, and the weapons ill-concealed around their persons, suggested that they were anything more than urban poor working for pennies. Few people trusted night watchmen in London. The guilds controlled the manpower and most of them were corrupt. Jack knew that warehouses and stores had often been burgled by their own guards.

Lord Blackburn stopped outside the doors and spoke briefly to one of the watchmen. Jack wished he had time to concentrate and use his Sight to spy on them, but it was alarmingly possible that Lord Blackburn would sense his intrusion. Charm shouldn't allow it, yet it had happened. Master Thomas had speculated that all powerful magicians were sensitive to magic, even if they lacked all of the talents. It was as good a theory as any other. He would have to rely on his own senses.

Jack drifted through the air and came to rest on top of the suspicious building. Lord Blackburn had vanished inside, leaving Jack searching the building for a way to enter without being seen. It quickly proved to be impossible. The one hatchway leading down into the building was guarded; he could hear muffled voices from below, suggesting that at least two guards were on duty. He could have broken through and killed them before they had a chance to raise the alarm, but it would not have passed unnoticed. Master Thomas would have known that someone had broken into the building – and it wouldn't be hard to guess who.

Instead, he took a gamble and floated silently down to one of the windows. It had been painted black, preventing anyone from peering inside, but Jack had very sharp ears. The sound of male grunting could be heard, faintly, accompanied by feminine gasps. Jack smiled, sourly, as he floated back up to the rooftop. He'd located the farm, or at least one of them. All he had to do was decide what to do with the information. Breaking in and wrecking the place, as tempting as it seemed, would be hazardous. There were too many magicians in the building.

Shaking his head, he drifted off into the air and headed down the Thames. There were still boats on the river, including a handful that were clearly smuggling while the excise men were tucked up in bed. London had thousands of docks, jetties and warehouses on both sides of the Thames. It wouldn't be difficult for smugglers to smuggle in anything they wanted – and once they'd converted their goods to money, no one would be able to prove what had happened. London's importance didn't just come from its position. The bank vaults in London were regarded as the safest in the entire world. Even New York didn't come close. Jack made a mental note to plan a bank robbery and drifted down to one of the smaller barges. The crew didn't notice him as he touched down on the deck, not until he allowed his cloak to rustle through the air. They looked up in alarm, and then relaxed. Jack had promised them he'd visit, after all.

The barge was larger than he'd expected, but the crew managed to muscle it into the dockyard without problems. London's docks never slept; bright lights, powered by magic, illuminated the entire scene. It would have seemed impossible to a man living in the era that had birthed Professor Cavendish and Master Thomas, but it was real. Jack shrugged off his cloak, revealing the tunic of a stevedore underneath, and started to help the crew to unload the boxes mounted on the barge. The paperwork said that they were carrying foodstuffs from France; the aristocracy, no matter how much they might dislike the French, had a yearning for French food. If someone happened to examine the barge, there would be considerable embarrassment – and alarm. The boxes held something a great deal more harmful than French pastries and cheeses.

He carried one of the boxes into the warehouse and placed it down on the stone floor. A handful of his men gathered around the box, opening it up with giant crowbars, revealing the weapons hidden within. The French had done them proud; whatever else could be said about the French, their gunsmiths were the best in Europe. There were hundreds of rifles and pistols, a smaller number of machine guns – invented by the French and used on the Prussians, where they had changed the face of warfare – and a handful of cannons in the barge. They'd be scattered throughout London over the night, hidden away from watchful eyes. Even if one cache happened to be discovered, the remainder would be safe.

A smaller box was opened with care. It contained explosives, enough to blow up several large buildings. Jack knew that this one would have to be moved quickly, if only to ensure that no one realised what it contained. Rifles and pistols were one thing, but people tended to get nervous around explosives. It hadn't been *that* long since Guy Fawkes had tried to blow up the Houses of Parliament. Master Thomas and the Dragoons wouldn't have to get warrants to search the city if they suspected that the underground was concealing explosives somewhere within London. There would be absolute panic among the high and mighty.

Two hours passed slowly as the barge was unloaded and the various crates earmarked for different destinations. The business was legitimate; anyone who happened to cast an eye over its paperwork would see a receiving firm selling its services to a handful of smaller importing business that didn't want to purchase their own warehouses in the docklands. Jack changed his clothes, posing as a security guard, and mounted one of the wagons as the horses were urged out onto the streets. That too wasn't unusual in the docklands; indeed, many preferred to move their goods at night in hopes of avoiding the crowds. It was a fool's hope outside the richer parts of town.

Jack watched dispassionately as the driver cracked his whip, moving the horses onwards. He'd never liked horses, even when he'd thought that the world made sense. They were nasty brutes; he'd never met one that hadn't been skittish whenever he'd tried to climb into the saddle. Some dogs sensed magic on magicians – no one knew how – and some magicians had wondered if horses had their own version of the same sense. But Master Thomas had never had difficulty riding a horse. Absently, he wondered if Lady Gwen loved horses. It would fit in with what little he knew of her upbringing.

A group of footpads strolled out onto the streets, took a look at Jack and the other guards, and thought better of trying to hijack the wagon. Jack was almost disappointed. He preferred fighting with his fists – and clubs – to using magic, even though a skirmish on the streets risked attracting attention from the Bow Street Runners. The police might just think to enquire about what was in the wagon and then Jack would have to kill them, or risk losing his supply of weapons. And killing Runners would definitely attract attention.

He was still scowling as the wagon pulled up outside a furniture store. London still produced a fair number of skilled craftsmen, who produced handmade furniture for the nobility. It wouldn't be long before technology drove them out of work, Jack was sure, just as it had done for many other once-traditional trades. They knew it, too. The craftsmen hated their masters with a passion unmatched by many others who *had* lost their jobs. Fear was a remarkable stimulant. The small crowd of apprentices appeared from the darkened building and started to unload the boxes. They'd keep what they saw to themselves. Their masters would see to that.

Jack nodded to the guards and slipped away, into the darkness. There was another small warehouse not too far away, officially owned by a Newcastle-based shipping company. It was guarded too, but the guards allowed Jack to enter the building once they recognised him. Inside, it was a small military base; the rebel soldiers had spread out their blankets on the stone floor, spending their days sleeping, eating and exercising. Boredom would be driving them out of their minds, but they'd be in London when the time came to strike. And, as far as they knew, they were the only group in the city. Jack knew that there were ten other buildings being prepared as advance bases for the rebellion.

He inspected the troops quickly and efficiently, before consulting briefly with their commander and slipping out of the rear entrance. The plan had worked well so far – almost perfectly – but the chances of exposure grew higher as he brought more and more of his people to London. A single mistake could alert the government and Lord Mycroft, at least, would understand the seriousness of the situation. Jack had thought about trying to assassinate him, but he was well protected and his brother would stop at nothing to hunt down his murderer. The last thing the rebels needed was London's most famous consulting detective on their trail.

Outside, a wavering band of light was beginning to appear in the distance. Dawn was rising over the city. Jack pulled his cloak around him and levitated up to the rooftops, starting the long walk back to the Rookery. Parts of the rooftops had been altered since the days when he used to sneak out of Cavendish Hall, he noted, almost regretfully. But he'd been a young man then, unaware of the price he would pay for his powers – and unaware of the price that others would pay. He almost missed a step and narrowly avoided plunging down off the roof with a touch of magic. Jack was in good shape, but he knew that he was no longer a young man. Life on the run had hardened him, yet it had exacted a toll.

He dropped down to the streets as he reached the edge of the more prosperous part of London. It was a short walk to the Rookery, one he had already determined would be walked on the ground. There might just be a chance for some excitement. He was almost disappointed until he walked past an alleyway and a hulking bravo stepped out, intent on causing trouble. Jack promptly beat the hell out of him with such vicious thoroughness that the bravo's friends, hardly unused to violence, backed off and headed off at speed. The man Jack had beaten to within an inch of his life lay groaning in the gutter. Jack fought back the temptation to urinate on his body – though it would have reminded the bravo of his defeat – and headed onwards. No one else tried to block his path.

The memory made him smile as he walked into the Rookery. He felt little sympathy for the footpad. Instead of helping his fellow man, he had robbed them, taking money from those who had little and offering nothing in return, not even security. The beating would hopefully convince the bastard that there were changes coming, changes Jack intended would completely reshape the city. Or maybe the coward would just go to a brothel and take his temper out on a whore. The thought disgusted Jack. How could a man call himself a man when he beat a helpless and defenceless woman?

He entered Lucy's brothel through the back window and walked into the lounge. Lucy was waiting for him – she never slept, as far as he could tell – a grim look in her eyes. Jack braced himself for the lecture he knew was coming. She never hesitated to tell him when she thought that he was being a fool.

"You were out there doing something stupid," she said. She'd exploded in rage when she'd heard what Jack had done at Fairweather Hall. It would only provoke the high and mighty, she'd objected. That had been the point, Jack knew, but he'd kept that thought to himself. Lucy in a rage was more fearsome than much else. Any woman who could make her own way in a man's world was formidable. "How many did you kill this time?"

"None," Jack assured her. The bravo might not have survived his beating – particularly if one of his other victims took the opportunity to slit his throat – but he decided not to mention him. Lucy would not have seen the funny side. Starting a vendetta with the street gangs would only render their position insecure. "I watched Cavendish Hall and I located the farm."

"Nicola will be glad to hear that," Lucy said, coldly. She knew that he was hiding something, all right. "And do you think you can take the place?"

"Not at once," Jack said. He finished removing his cloak and hung it neatly on a stand. Lucy would have told him off for leaving it anywhere else. "There are too many magicians on guard, even though they think that no one knows where it is."

He remembered Lord Fitzroy and smiled, darkly. High Society would have crucified him – perhaps literally – if they'd discovered the true nature of his crimes. What would they do, he wondered, if they learned the truth behind the farm? All the little uncertainties and fears surrounding magic would explode at once. And then...who knew? It would present all manner of opportunities for the underground.

"They'll be suspicious," Lucy reminded him. "Master Thomas knows that you know, doesn't he?"

Jack nodded, without speaking. That was not a memory he wanted to recall.

"Get some sleep," Lucy ordered, standing up. "You're going to need to be rested when you crash the party."

"That's two days away," Jack said, but he obeyed. Lucy was right about the need for rest, even if he hadn't fought his way through a group of sorcerers. If Master Thomas attended the birthday dinner, he'd have sorcerers backing him up. The handful of magicians with reliable precognition – insofar as precognition could be considered reliable – might have warned him about Jack's plans. "You get some sleep too. I'll see you in the evening."

Chapter Twenty-Two

wen," a voice called. "How lovely to see you again."

Gwen smiled as she clambered out of the carriage and up to the speaker. Laura Crichton was a short, rather plump girl with extensive family connections. Gwen's father had arranged the match, but rather to everyone's surprise it had worked out remarkably well. David – a rather stuffy person at the best of times – occasionally needed someone to prick his pomposity and Laura never took anything too seriously. Gwen rather liked her, even though they hadn't had much time together since she'd married Gwen's brother.

"And you," Gwen said. Laura had been the closest thing she had to a real friend. They exchanged hugs as the carriage rattled away, to the back of the house where the coachmen would wait until they were summoned. "I trust that you have been taking care of my brother?"

Laura winked at her as she led Gwen into the gardens. "I've been doing more than that," she said. She rubbed her abdomen meaningfully. "I think you may expect a newcomer to the family in the next five months."

Gwen stared at her. "You're pregnant?"

"Of course," Laura agreed. She winked, again. "Your brother is quite enthusiastic between the sheets."

Gwen blushed, bright red. She wasn't ignorant, but she didn't know everything about sex; it wasn't a proper subject for young ladies. The textbooks she'd read over the years concealed and obfuscated rather than revealed, something that puzzled her. There were nurses and midwives working for a living; how were they meant to learn when their textbooks were actively misleading? And some of the misinformation had been easy to disprove. She'd only had to take a look in the mirror.

"Believe me, he is," Laura said. Gwen's blush deepened. Her mind refused to imagine her brother copulating, let alone her parents. There were some things that just couldn't be thought about, at least not by her. Gwen's parents had had their children, no doubt, by some neat method that didn't involve bodily contact. "And he was looking forward to seeing you."

Gwen shrugged. David had always been good to her, even if he had been dreadfully stuffy and reserved. He meant well, she knew, but she'd always found his lectures rather trying. Laura kept hold of her hand as they rounded the house and entered the gardens. A dozen tables had been placed on the grass. A number of people moving between them chatting to their fellow guests – and the birthday boy. Gwen's smile deepened at the thought of David being called a boy. He was in his early thirties, old enough to have a household and career of his own. His path, she'd been led to understand, had already been mapped out for him. David would probably never rise to become Prime Minister, but it was quite possible that when he left the business world, he would find a seat in Parliament or even on the Cabinet.

She found herself attracting more than a few looks from the guests. In deference to her brother, she hadn't worn the black dress that Master Thomas had had produced for her. Instead, she wore a simple green dress that had been cunningly tailored to allow her legs to move without constraint – and, if necessary, to allow her to rip the skirt free and move in her underclothes. It would cause comment – even if her underclothes would have served as perfectly decent clothing for someone from the lower orders – but at least she would be able to fight. No one had seen anything of the rogue Master since the attack on Fairweather Hall, yet everyone knew that he was still out there. God alone knew what he was thinking, or planning.

David Crichton, in Gwen's sisterly perception, had been born old. She couldn't remember a time when he had played in the mud with her, or chased her around the gardens when they'd both been younger – although, to be fair, there was fourteen years between them. He was as tall as Gwen, with short blonde hair and a plain but not unhandsome face. Gwen noted, as he gave her a restrained hug, that he looked older than she remembered. It was all she could do not to check his head for signs of grey hair. But then, like their father, he would probably age well.

"Gwen," he said, quietly enough so that the other guests couldn't hear. "Thank you for coming."

Gwen smiled, feeling oddly relieved. High Society wouldn't have known what to make of a female magician – even though common sense told her that there would be a great many women with magician talents. And a woman who would find herself holding the most important magical position in the land...? They'd be torn between trying to ingratiate themselves with her and expressing their disapproval by shunning her. David wouldn't let them get away with that at his own birthday party, at least. She *was* his sister, even though convention insisted that she should be married off by now and producing children. Girls always married sooner than boys.

"I couldn't stay away," she whispered, herself. "I heard about you and Laura..."

David seemed to stiffen, just slightly. He was still the same stuffy prude that Gwen remembered, even if he was a decent man under his demeanour. "We're going to announce it today," he said. "Laura just didn't want you and mother to be surprised."

"Gwen," a new voice said. Gwen didn't need to turn to recognise it as Lady Mary, their mother. Her mother's voice had been ingrained in her ever since she was born, since not an hour would go by without Lady Mary trying to turn her into a proper young lady. "I'm so glad you came."

Gwen exchanged a last look with David and allowed her mother to haul her through the crowd and up towards the house. David had bought a mansion on the southern side of London for his wife, although Gwen had heard that he also had a flat in Pall Mall to conduct his business affairs while in London proper. Even for an aristocrat, London tended to be difficult to navigate early in the morning. It was a fine house, even though Gwen had heard that it had a bad reputation. The previous owner had lost most of his fortune in a disastrous investment in the South Seas and had had to sell it to recoup most of his losses, before winding up in debtor's prison. It was a chilling reminder that failure could come to anyone, even an English aristocrat.

Lady Mary was wearing a frilly pink dress that made her – in Gwen's private thoughts – look rather upsetting. As the mother of the birthday boy, she was second only to Laura, but she'd dressed to attract attention. Gwen had never had any time for the social circle that her mother effortlessly dominated, regarding it as rather silly, the worst display of foolish females in the country. It had often struck her that women would get more respect – and opportunities – from the men if so many women didn't waste their lives on the social whirl. Lady Mary had a fine mind, when she chose to use it, but she preferred to use her position and knowledge as a weapon. Gwen had no intention of ever becoming like her.

"Gwen," she said, as soon as they were inside. "I trust that you have managed to find yourself a husband?"

Gwen gaped at her, openly surprised. Her mother had to know that she hadn't found anyone – and wasn't even looking. Sure, she'd taken Bruno Lombardi to the ball, but that didn't signify that they were going to get married. Besides, Lombardi had been lucky enough to meet a girl who might even make him happy. Gwen was hardly going to stand in his way, not when they hadn't had anything, but friendship – insofar as a boy and girl could be friends.

"You're alone in a house of male magicians," Lady Mary said. "Do you not see your opportunity?"

For a moment, Gwen couldn't understand a word that she'd said. Alone in a house of male magicians...what in the world did she mean? And then it struck her. Master Thomas, as far as Gwen knew, was unmarried – and probably the most eligible man in the city. Did her mother expect her to try to seduce a man old enough to be her grandfather? Or, perhaps, what about the younger magicians? Lord Blackburn wasn't married. The nasty part of Gwen's mind had wondered if anyone would want to put up with him, if they knew what he was like. Her mother couldn't expect her to marry one of them, could she?

"Mother –"

"Gwen," Lady Mary interrupted, talking over her daughter, "I have agreed to allow you to study and learn magic. I have even agreed to allow you to live at Cavendish Hall."

Gwen scowled at her. It had been her father who had agreed to allow her to study magic – and he'd been under immense pressure from some of the most powerful men in the realm. The decision hadn't been taken by Lady Mary – and, as a wife and mother, she would have had little say in it anyway, at least officially. A wise husband would learn to listen to his wife, if only to ensure peace and harmony at home. And her mother, whatever her faults, was very strong-willed. If only she had spent her time storming the bastions of male supremacy rather than carving out an empire of foolish females for herself.

"I have agreed to that against my better judgement, for society *judges*," Lady Mary continued. "It is not *decent* for a young woman to live on her own among men. It is not *right*."

"Mother," Gwen said, as patiently as she could, "there are plenty of young girls my age who go to finishing schools in Switzerland where their brains are turned to mush. How exactly am I any different?"

She knew what her mother would say before she opened her mouth. "Those girls are chaperoned by their teachers – and they are not alone. You are alone in a household of men."

"Men who know better than to try to lure me into their rooms," Gwen snapped. Her mother always brought out the worst in her. "And there are female maids and servants and – "

Lady Mary snorted. "Servants cannot be relied upon to guard a young girl's reputation," she said, sharply. "You need to start looking for a husband. I have a list of suitable young men –"

Gwen felt her temper flare. "I am not interested in marrying anyone," she said. Anger burned through her voice, threatening her stability. She felt magic flickering into life behind her eyes. It wanted out; it wanted to be discharged. Somehow, Gwen kept it under control. The last thing she wanted to do was lash out at her own mother.

"There is no one who would be interested in me –"

"You are a magician and of good birth," Lady Mary said. *That* was absurd. Being a magician, even an untrained one, had ruined her prospects long before Master Thomas had invited her to train under him. "I have no doubt that you would find a partner..."

There was a cough from behind her. Lady Mary spun around to see a young girl, wearing a maid's uniform. The maid, looking embarrassed to have stumbled into an argument between two of the guests, curtseyed. "Begging your pardon, madam, but the dinner is about to commence," she said. "The master would be pleased to see you in the garden."

"Thank you," Gwen said, before her mother could launch into a furious tirade at the poor maid. She'd never beaten Gwen – or David, as far as Gwen knew, even though the rules for bringing up young men were different from those for young women – but Gwen knew that she had beaten a number of maids over the years. It was the same casual unconcern for the lower orders that Lord Blackburn and his fellow Darwinists shared. "We'll be out in a moment."

The maid bowed and vanished. "Come on, mother," Gwen said. "The master of the house has called us to dine."

Lady Mary scowled at her and then smoothed out her face as they walked back out into the garden. It was just past noon, with the sun hanging high overhead; Gwen could have almost convinced herself that they were in the midst of the country, rather than on the edge of London. Bees and birds flew through the air, searching for pollen and prey; in the distance, she could see the smog that hung over London. She didn't care what the factory owners claimed. Something that smelled so bad couldn't be harmless to the poor humans trapped underneath.

David – or, more likely, Laura – had laid out the tables carefully. Gwen, as David's sister, had been allocated a seat on the high table, where she could see the other guests as they received their bowls of soup from the servants. David wouldn't have experimented with exotic dishes from India or the Americas, somewhat to Gwen's regret. The soup was a conventional chicken and vegetable: tasty enough, but not particularly exciting. Gwen supped it gratefully, her mind turning her mother's words over and over again. Lady Mary had to be joking, surely. She couldn't seriously expect Gwen to marry Master Thomas?

But then, Lady Mary hadn't had much choice in her own martial arrangements. Her parents had pushed her into marrying Gwen's father; Gwen's father hadn't been offered much choice either. It made perfect sense to have parents choose their children's partners, if only because parents were more given to cold calculation than youngsters in the hot flush of youth. But Master Thomas...how could anyone expect Gwen to marry him? Gwen liked him and respected him, but he was *old*! And Lord Blackburn was a monster in human form.

The thoughts kept dancing through her head as the servants removed the bowls of soup and set out the next course. As Gwen had expected, it was ruthlessly conventional; roast beef, potatoes, boiled vegetables and gravy. A set of Yorkshire puddings – the sole gesture of unconventionality – was placed below her, inviting anyone to take one if they so wished. The servants carved the meat themselves, setting out dainty portions for each guest. As a child, Gwen had thought it hideously unfair that the servants didn't get to share the meal; as she'd grown older, she'd realised that the servants probably ate up the scraps as well as having a little of the meal reserved for them in the kitchens. It was just never officially acknowledged.

David had gone to a boarding school, Gwen knew, and it had shaped his tastes. Laura would probably have wanted to experiment more, but not at a dinner party. Gwen smiled at her sister-in-law, realising just how happy she looked. Oddly, she felt a dull ache within her heart. She had known that she wouldn't find such happiness even before Master Thomas had convinced her father to allow her to study magic. Was it a bad thing to wonder if Laura didn't have the intelligence to be unhappy, or should Gwen regret having the intelligence to realise that there was more to life than parties and children? Gwen's horizons had been wider long before she'd ever met Laura.

She chewed her meat slowly, noting which of the guests risked a glance at her before returning to their food. Some of the younger men – all unmarried, or their wives would have come with them – might well have been invited by Lady Mary, rather than David. Laura would have known better than to arrange casual encounters between Gwen and any young man, particularly without telling her in advance. Her mind kept returning to her mother's words, desperately trying to parse out the meaning behind them. Had someone asked for her hand in marriage? And if so, who? Or had someone rejected her firmly enough to sting her mother? *That* would make a great deal more sense.

The meal was finally cleared away and small bowls of ice

cream placed in front of each of the guests. Ice cream was expensive, Gwen recalled; her father had sternly limited the amount they could eat as children. David was making a statement to his guests, confirming that his business interests were as strong – and profitable – as ever. Gwen smiled in memory, nodding towards her elder brother. David had pleased her parents; maybe they could be convinced to let her chart her own path in life. She remembered her mother's face and shook her head. Lady Mary wouldn't be happy until both of her children were married off to good matches. And then she'd probably start matchmaking for her unborn grandchildren.

David tapped his knife against his glass and quiet fell over the garden. "I would like to thank you all for coming," he said. His voice seemed to echo oddly in the silence. His expensive school had taught public speaking, training the children to mimic the words and styles of a Greek or Roman orator. Cicero's speeches were still studied in public skills, as were the writings of Caesar and Pompey. "My wife and I are very pleased to see you all."

There was a long pause. "It is my pleasure to announce that we had good news yesterday evening," he said, after a moment. "My wife and I are expecting our first child."

Gwen smiled as cheers rang through the air from the younger – and less well-behaved – men. The older people smiled and nodded. Beside Laura, Lady Mary was beaming. A grandchild was someone she could spoil – and perhaps use as a pawn in her endless games. Gwen made a resolution to spend time with her coming niece or nephew. She wasn't going to allow her mother to mould the newborn child in her own image.

She glanced up, sharply, as she sensed magic. It was shimmering above her...no, it was coming down! Tables shattered under the impact; guests screamed and scattered as broken glass and splinters of wood fell everywhere. Gwen jumped back, using a little magic to direct her flight, and glanced upwards.

The rogue Master was standing on the roof, staring down at the chaos.

Chapter Twenty-Three

hat are you...?"

David's voice broke off as he saw the intruder. Master Jackson was standing on the roof, wearing a black cape and a top hat that mimicked the one worn by Master Thomas. Gwen knew, without a doubt, that there were no other magicians at the party. The servants and guards that David had hired wouldn't be able to stop the rogue. He'd go through them like a knife through butter.

The guests were panicking, running in all directions. Gwen saw one young man, one of the ones who had been casting glances at her, fleeing towards the bushes at the end of the garden. Others were fleeing into the mansion, although Gwen knew that that wouldn't provide any real safety. The rogue had wrecked a far stronger mansion in the centre of London. If he was to be stopped before he slaughtered the guests, Gwen was the only person who could do it.

"Call help," David said, quickly. "Call Master Thomas."

He was holding Laura, something that touched Gwen's heart even as she returned her gaze to the rogue. Master Jackson was posturing, mocking her by standing on the roof, daring her to do something about him.

Gwen said nothing. She hadn't learned to use mental communication yet. A Talker could have summoned help instantly, but Talkers tended to go insane unless they were trained very carefully. Gwen had been reluctant to risk learning to use that talent and Master Thomas hadn't pressed. In hindsight, that had been a mistake. And she would bet half of her legacy that the rogue Master knew that she couldn't call for help.

She gathered her magic and threw a fireball up towards the

rogue. He leapt into the air, right over her head, and came down amidst the wreckage of the tables. The fireball missed completely. He lifted one hand and fired a burst of red-gold light towards David. Gwen raised her magic and deflected it barely in time. Cold anger – and fear – ran through her mind. She hadn't faced anyone who shared her powers before – and she'd barely been trained to fight. Dodging or catching beanbags was no substitute for actual experience, and she had none.

"Get Laura inside and head out the other side of the building," she said. David had to understand that he couldn't help her. A man wasn't supposed to desert a woman who needed help, but there was nothing David could do, apart from dying bravely. "Now!"

The rogue Master smiled and nodded, his mocking gaze never leaving Gwen's face. It struck her that David and his guests weren't the real target; Gwen herself was the target. If he killed her, Master Thomas would have to start looking for another Master. He'd never be able to retire. The rogue's smile grew darker, as if he were reading her thoughts. Gwen had no experience in shielding her mind, but she pulled her magic around her anyway, hoping that it would provide a barrier.

There was a moment's warning – and another blast of energy came blazing towards her. It was strong, strong enough to knock Gwen backwards even though it impacted on her defences rather than directly on her body. A wave of heat struck her as the magic dissipated harmlessly. It seemed hot enough to burn her skin. The rogue was far more experienced than her, yet he seemed almost to be pulling his punches. He was mocking her! Rage flashed through her and she lifted her hand, throwing a burst of magic back at him. It broke up just before it could touch him and started a number of small fires amidst the wreckage. The rogue Master danced back, his smile daring her to follow him. David, Gwen noted with relief, had made himself scarce. The other guests had scattered.

Master Jackson launched himself into the air. Gwen remembered what Master Thomas had taught her and reached out with her magic, seeking to disrupt the power that held her enemy aloft. It seemed to work, just for a moment, before the magic recoiled on her. He'd disrupted her grip while flying!

Gwen launched herself into the air after him, throwing a series of fireballs towards his position. He ducked and dodged, hopefully too busy guarding himself to try to knock Gwen out of the sky. She sensed a brief flicker of magic and dropped, just before something tried to shimmer into existence around her. It closed harmlessly above her head as her feet touched the ground. Despite herself, she felt excited. She could win this!

She looked up and around, but there was no sign of Jackson. He'd vanished. Gwen wondered if he'd found her a harder target than he'd expected, but he'd duelled with Master Thomas – and Gwen knew that she wasn't anything like as capable as her tutor. Master Jackson would never have a better chance to remove her from the field and he had to know it. Closing her eyes, she tried to sense...and ducked, just before a blow slashed through the air. It would have decapitated her if she'd allowed it to hit. Now she knew roughly where he was, she could see the glimmer of magic that was concealing his position. It wasn't perfect invisibility, but it would have made him impossible to see at night. Even in bright daylight it was still hard to see him.

There was a wavering shimmer in the air and he materialised, only three yards from her. Gwen had expected him to be carrying a cane, just like Master Thomas, but his hands were empty. He was taller than she had expected, with dark hair and a rough, handsome face – and very bright eyes. Despite herself, she felt a flush of attraction – and damned herself for it a moment later. Master Jackson had turned on his tutor and killed hundreds, perhaps thousands, of people. He was a traitor to his country and to his family.

He nodded to her, a gesture of respect that oddly warmed her heart. They stared at each other for a long moment, and then he hurled himself back into the air. The next mansion, a smaller building clad in pink stone and surrounded by statues of weeping angels, was easily within reach for a Master. He landed on the roof and gazed at her, daring her to follow him. Gwen reached down and tore her skirt free, before jumping into the air herself. It had never occurred to her to try jumping from rooftop to rooftop, but perhaps a practiced magician would have other ideas. She landed neatly on the roof, her eyes searching out and finding Master Jackson. He lifted a hand and a blow struck her in the stomach. She found herself tottering backwards, on the verge of stumbling over the edge and falling down to the stone below. Desperately, she caught at the air around her and threw herself upwards. Master Jackson jumped back as she formed fireballs and threw them at him, hoping to distract him while she came down and reached out with her magic. She pulled a chimney away from the roof and launched it at his back. He evaded it barely in time.

Gwen cursed her own mistake as she prowled forward. He'd developed his own combat senses, just like her...and he was far more practiced. There was no need for him to look to know what was behind him. He could probably read her mind and know what she was planning ahead of time. Maybe he intended to Charm her into submission, or...there were simply too many possibilities for someone who controlled all of the talents. She kept inching forward and sensed the trap, a moment too late.

The roof exploded around her and she found herself thrown into the air. She'd acted without quite realising what she was doing, or why. Master Jackson hadn't just been evading her; he'd been infusing his magic into the roof, daring her to step on the charged slates. It was clever, all the more so as she'd never anticipated it even though Lombardi had taught her how to make grenades. She gritted her teeth as she fell back to the rooftop, uneasily aware that her clothing was torn and ripped. She'd have to make something more durable if she was to make a habit of fighting on rooftops, part of her mind insisted. And what would her mother say if she came back in rags, covered in soot?

She smiled as the thought led to a second thought. Catching hold of the debris with her magic, she threw it right at him – and followed up with a set of fireballs. She'd practiced enough with her own senses to know that they could be overwhelmed, or given too many problems to react to them all in time. One of the fireballs struck his magic and sent him flying backwards in a blaze of light; Gwen knew a moment's exultation before she realised that he'd used her magic to aid his escape. The debris crashed down onto the ground far before, leaving her unable to see her foe. She looked, but there was no tell-tale shimmer...

...And yet she was sure that he hadn't abandoned the fight. She stepped forward, bit-by-bit, watching carefully and trying to sense his presence. He had to be somewhere...she stopped, just before she reached the edge of the roof. She couldn't sense him, but she knew where he was hiding. He was waiting for her to come close and then hit her before she could react. Grinning to herself, she directed her magic down into the rooftop, shattering it and sending the levitating Master down towards the ground. The building seemed to be coming apart around her, so she jumped up into the air, floating over the garden. Her enemy had caught himself just before he slammed into the ground. She saw an elderly gardener shaking his fist at her just before her enemy started to run. He was in the air, propelled by his own motion, seconds later. Gwen watched him fly almost naturally, and then gave chase. The next rooftop was only yards away. They landed on the building and stared at each other.

"Master Thomas chose well," Master Jackson said. His voice was calm, yet intensely focused. He sounded, Gwen realised, like Master Thomas. There was none of the assumed superiority of Lord Blackburn, or the earnest shyness of Lombardi. "You're not too bad at this."

Gwen flushed. Praise always disarmed her, if only because she'd had so little in her life. "Thank you," she said, seriously. "Please would you come with me...?"

"I'm afraid not," Master Jackson said. His smile grew wider. Gwen wondered, just for a moment, if he was sane. Some magicians went mad, like the children Master Thomas had shown her. And Master Thomas had certainly implied that his former pupil was insane... "Things to see, people to do – you know how it is."

He leapt into the air, over to the next mansion. Gwen followed him a second later, watching as he landed neatly on the roof, before leaping to the building after that. Scowling, Gwen leapt after him. He turned and half-bowed to her, before tossing a blast of magic that she had to duck. It would have burned through her magic if it had hit her. He hadn't even used his hand to shape the magic, she realised, numbly. Even Master Thomas had to use his hands...unless he'd kept a few secrets to himself. Gwen knew that she was far from practiced enough to take his place. Master Jackson leapt to the next building, and then the next, daring her to follow him. Gwen could no more have stopped than she could have accepted her mother's choice of husband; if she arrested the rogue Master herself, or killed him, no one would question her right to become the Royal Sorcerer. Or Royal Sorceress, in her case.

The city grew darker as they moved further and further into London. Gwen realised that the smog had stained the buildings, despite the best efforts of their inhabitants. A small bunch of children hiding on the roof – no, she realised; *living* on the roof – scattered as the two magicians passed through their territory. The next rooftop held a finely dressed woman carrying an umbrella and chatting to a chimney sweep. She nodded to Gwen and raised her hat to Master Jackson. Gwen had hardly any time to notice her before leaping onwards to the next building. Master Jackson was moving with terrifying speed.

He settled on a rooftop and dived into a hatch leading down into the building. Gwen followed him through the hatch, pausing long enough to generate and throw down a grenade ahead of her. The explosion illuminated a dark interior, a building that had been consumed by fire and abandoned by its inhabitants. Master Jackson, half-hidden in the shadows, threw a burst of magic at the roof. Gwen raised her magic to cover her head as the roof came tumbling in, giving Master Jackson just enough time to catch himself and fly out of the building, heading up into the cloud of smog. Muttering a word her mother would have been appalled to think Gwen knew, Gwen followed him. By the time she pulled herself into the open, he was several buildings away and heading towards the Thames.

Heedless of the dangers, Gwen followed him, drawing on her magic to the limit. She flew through the air, giving chase and hoping that he wouldn't sense her presence until it was too late. It was a vain hope; he turned, pointed his finger at her – and, a second later, she felt him attempting to disrupt her magic. She fell towards the ground and only caught herself moments before she would have crashed into hard stone and died. Master Jackson hovered in the air above her, his bright eyes mocking. Gwen reached up with her own magic and tried to pull him down to the ground, but nothing happened. His control was far finer than hers. But then, he'd had years to study under Master Thomas and more years just to practice. Gwen had had barely two months. It wasn't anything like enough time.

A hand caught onto her dress and yanked her backwards. She gasped in shock as she saw a ruffian wearing rags pulling her backwards, one hand grasping towards her breast. Pure rage ran through her and she shoved with her magic, sending the street thug flying into the nearest building. Gwen heard the sound of bones breaking and saw blood splashing out where he'd hit the building, feeling sick as she saw her would-be rapist fall to the ground. Dear God in Heaven – had she *killed* him? She had never even seen a dead body in her entire life. The thought of killing someone, no matter how unpleasant...she found herself being violently sick, throwing up everything she'd eaten at David's dinner party. How could she have killed a man? She'd killed a man...

She looked up sharply as Master Jackson landed near her. "It gets easier," he said, seriously. Gwen stared at him, wondering why he hadn't taken advantage of her weakness to end her life. "You'll find that there are those who deserve death – and so you give it to them. I assure you that that man would not have been merciful to you, had you been helpless and powerless. He would have forced himself into you and spent his lusts on your body. You would have been lucky if he left you alive afterwards."

He sounded...regretful. Gwen gritted her teeth, spitting out the remains of the vomit from her mouth. It tasted awful, mingled with the bitter awareness that she'd killed a man. Surely, there had been a better way to handle him...but her body felt dirty where his hands had touched her and part of her knew that it would have been far worse. There were whispered rumours shared among young girls, rumours that Gwen had heard despite being a social pariah. Rumours about what happened to girls who fell into the wrong hands.

"Damn you," Gwen growled, although in truth she wasn't sure who she was damning. Master Jackson...or herself. "Why?"

Master Jackson shrugged. He didn't sound concerned. "Why not?"

Gwen felt hot rage billowing through her and she launched herself at him. For a moment, their magic collided on a dozen different levels, and then he jumped backwards and up into the air. Gwen followed him, too angry to care about the dangers any longer. She'd killed a man...what would become of her now? Master Jackson jumped to the next rooftop, then casually ripped it apart and threw the debris at her. Gwen ducked and dodged desperately, feeling the blows as several pieces of debris struck her body. Her arm hurt where one of them had caught her a glancing blow, but she was still able to hurl a fireball at his position. He dodged it, almost effortlessly, only to run into the second. His form flashed with light as he fell off the roof and down towards the ground. Gwen, who remembered what had happened last time, dropped to the ground and ran around the house, only to see him lying on the ground, a broken man. She ran towards him, wondering if she'd killed a second man, only to realise her mistake an instant too late. He'd been pretending to be dead, merely to lure her into a trap.

Magic flared around her, as if she'd run right into a wall. Pain slammed into her a moment later; just for a second, she was completely – and helplessly – aware of her body. Her bones were breaking apart inside her flesh, shattering to dust. She had a moment to think of Master Thomas – and how she had failed him – before darkness fell over her mind. And she knew, with absolute certainty, that she was dead.

Chapter Twenty-Four

he felt...odd. Her head was swimming, as if it was a dream, yet she couldn't wake up. Thoughts seemed to flicker across her mind, only to vanish before she could quite grasp their importance. Something bad had happened, she knew, and yet...what? And who was she?

A voice echoed through her mind. *You've been badly hurt*, it said. She couldn't tell whose voice it was, or where it was coming from. It might have been an angel's voice, an angel carrying her to Heaven. Or maybe it was a delusion brought on by her injuries. *Relax and let me take care of you. You're going to be fine.*

Gwen's mind swam again and she plunged back down into darkness.

***

Lucy removed her hands from Gwen's temples and looked up at Jack. "She's going to be fine," she said, briskly. She hadn't appreciated the call to leave her brothel and come to a building Jack had hired for his plans, but she'd come. If she hadn't...well, Jack knew that magicians were often tougher than mundane people, yet Gwen had been badly injured. She might not have survived the night. "You do realise that you're taking one hell of a risk?"

Jack nodded, shortly. Lucy's talent was rare; indeed, she was the only Healer Jack knew to exist. The Royal College had heard rumours of her abilities, enough to make them suspect that the talent existed, but they had never come close to finding Lucy or another Healer. Jack had heard a story that a French girl in Southern France had developed the talent, yet she'd been burned to death by a mob of priests, after being formally accused of witchcraft. No wonder most magicians in France kept their talents to themselves. And Jack, who should have shared the talent, had never been able to master it for himself. Healing was rather more tricky than Changing or Infusing.

"It's a worthwhile risk," he said. He hadn't expected Master Thomas's apprentice to give chase so enthusiastically and he'd had to hold back, just to avoid harming her before she fell into his trap. He'd also expected bodyguards and it had taken nearly an hour before he'd concluded that no one had been sent to escort her. Master Thomas was slipping – or, perhaps, he hadn't realised that Gwen would need a bodyguard; he would certainly have been profoundly insulted at the suggestion that he might need such protection himself. "She might come over to our side."

Lucy quirked an eyebrow. She was no Talker, able to read minds, but she was expert at reading people. Whores learned quickly on the streets, or they died when one of their clients turned out to have nasty tastes and no respect for limits. And Lucy had known Jack for over a decade. They'd never been lovers, but they had been close friends and allies. She knew that there was more involved than his cause. Gwen *was* attractive and she was clearly more skilled than anyone, even Master Thomas, had realised. Masters tended to develop instinctive understandings of their powers, something that rarely happened to magicians with only one talent. Or so the Royal College believed.

"I still think it's too big a risk," Lucy said, flatly. She looked down at Gwen as the girl's breathing grew stronger. "You should have left her to die."

"We would never have a better opportunity," Jack said, calmly. "Can you wake her up?"

"Yes," Lucy said, after a moment. "If *you* are sure you want her awake, I can wake her. Or we could leave her here and she'd recover on her own."

Jack shook his head. "Wake her," he ordered. Lucy touched her fingers to Gwen's forehead and there was a brief sparkle of magic. Healing was a very complex talent, but Lucy was skilled; after all, she'd had lots of practice. Few people in the Rookery could afford a doctor; Lucy was all they had, which was why they kept her talent to themselves. "And then leave her to me."

Lucy gave him a sharp look, and then withdraw her hand. "She's awakening," she said, coldly. "Good luck."

***

Gwen was suddenly very aware of her own body. It ached, reminding her of the last moments before she'd blacked out. Her memories were hazy, but she remembered feeling her bones breaking – and knowing that she was dead. And yet...she hurt too much to be dead, surely. She had never taken religion too seriously, but surely that wasn't enough to condemn her to Hell. Her eyes, she realised, suddenly, were closed, so she opened them. Bright yellow light flared down and she gasped in pain, squeezing her eyes shut until she felt that she could take the light. When she opened her eyes for the second time, the light had faded slightly. She found herself lying on a bed, her tattered clothes around her.

Two people were standing next to the bed, looking down at her. One was a proud confident woman, wearing a simple dress that drew attention towards her heart-shaped face and long red hair. The other...Gwen started as she recognised the rogue Master. She'd been captured by the enemy! She was astonished to discover that she wasn't tied down, but the moment she reached for her powers her head started to hurt badly. Gwen groaned aloud and saw them both looking down at her, concerned. The woman picked up a glass of water and pressed it to Gwen's lips. She drank gratefully, realising a moment too late that she hadn't asked if it had been boiled. Only a fool in London drank water without knowing if it had been boiled first.

"Don't worry," the woman said, softly. "I purified it myself."

Gwen coughed as the glass was removed from her lips. The woman had known what she was thinking, which meant that she might be a capable Talker. Gwen didn't recognise her, but there were hundreds of magicians she'd never encountered – and quite a few unregistered magicians in the underground. Or she might have simply made a lucky guess. Few in London would not share the same thought, ever since Doctor John Watson had proved the existence of bacteria and viruses in water. Boiling water before it was drunk, she'd learned, had saved thousands of lives. London no longer had to fear the outbreaks of Cholera that had once terrorised the city.

"You're not in any danger," Master Jackson said. "We *will* return you to Cavendish Hall, if that is what you want. However, we must ask for your word of honour that you won't fight us now."

His voice was smooth and reasonable; too reasonable. Gwen's head still hurt every time she thought about using her powers, but she was sure that there was some Charm within his words. Without her own powers, she was almost defenceless – but Charm wasn't all-powerful, or Lord Blackburn and his friends would be ruling the world. The thought crossed her mind that she might have lost her own powers completely – some magicians had lost their talents after taking blows to the head – but she pushed it away before it could linger. She didn't even want to *think* about the possibility.

"I..." She said. Her voice felt rusty from disuse. How long had she been unconscious? Was Master Thomas searching for her? What had happened to her brother's guests? "I...won't fight you for now, as long as you don't try to harm me."

The woman chuckled. "She knows you, Jack," she said, not unkindly. "He won't threaten your body, my dear. He might just threaten your mind."

Master Jackson scowled at his companion. "We won't try to harm you," he promised. He held out a hand and Gwen took it gingerly. It felt warm, almost too warm. Her hand, when she pulled it back, was mottled with oddly coloured skin. It felt almost as if she had been burned. "We mean you no harm."

Gwen flushed, remembering the chase across London's rooftops. She'd made a dreadful mistake. She should have held back and waited for Master Thomas, or a squad of trained combat magicians, rather than giving chase herself. And now she was a prisoner of the underground. God alone knew what they had in mind for her, but she was sure that it wouldn't be pleasant, no matter what they said. She looked down at her arm and saw that the reddish skin was fading away. What had they done to her?

"I'm going to turn my back," Master Jackson – Jack – informed her. "Lucy will help you to get out of those rags and into something more comfortable. Please don't try anything stupid – take it from me, you're in no condition for a fight."

Oddly, he sounded as if he genuinely cared about her. Gwen reminded herself that he was probably using Charm and watched him carefully as he turned his back. Lucy helped her out of bed and held her upright as her head started to spin, almost as if she was recovering from a cold or the flu. She'd been ill as a child, Gwen remembered, and had been bedridden for nearly a week. The doctors had promised that she would recover, but Lady Mary hadn't believed them. She genuinely did love Gwen, in her way. The thought made tears prickle at the corner of Gwen's eyes. Would she ever see her mother again?

The dress she'd worn to her brother's dinner party had cost nearly two hundred pounds. It was lucky that Master Thomas had given her a clothing budget, or else she would have been dependent upon her mother's tastes in clothing. The dress was now a wreck, with much of the fancy embroidery ripped apart and great slits reaching up her legs. She flushed as she realised that she must have shown parts of London her underclothes, even her bare skin. No wonder the man she'd killed – and she shuddered at the thought – had taken her for a whore.

Her bare skin looked strange. The mottled pattern she had seen on her hands was all over her body, slowly blurring into the original skin. She'd felt bones breaking, yet she now felt intact and well, apart from the dizziness. Holding up her hands in front of her face, she studied them, puzzled. They'd broken when she'd hit the ground, and yet...she was alive and well. It made absolutely no sense at all. She caught Lucy's eye and silently asked a question. The older woman merely winked at her.

Gwen's mother would have thrown a fit if anyone had expected her to wear the dress the underground had provided for her daughter. It was dark brown and looked dirty, even though a quick examination revealed that it was surprisingly clean. Gwen felt like a shapeless lump as soon as she donned the dress, glancing down to realise that it concealed almost all of her body. It would have been decent almost anywhere –

and made her almost unrecognisable.

"You can turn around," she said, as strongly as she could. Her mother would have exploded even more violently if she'd heard that Gwen had changed in the same room as a man. "I'm ready for you now."

Jack turned and smiled at her. He really was handsome, part of Gwen's mind noted. Too handsome, really. She disliked anyone who touched her heart in such a way. He'd changed his own clothes sometime between their rooftop chase and now, wearing a simple factory worker's outfit. There was nothing to mark him out as a magician, not even one of the silver-topped canes affected by Master Thomas and some of the other magicians. He wasn't even wearing sorcerer's black. Gwen realised, grimly, that he could walk right past the policemen searching for the underground and they'd never even realise that their target was right next to them.

"I'm sorry about the way we brought you here," he admitted. "We would have sent an invitation, but it would have gone astray somewhere along the line. Master Thomas has been reading your mail, I'm afraid."

He grinned at her, as if he was expecting her to share the joke. Gwen was outraged. How *dare* Master Thomas read her mail? Her face flushed, before she remembered that she was technically his apprentice and he had every right to read her mail, if he felt that someone unsuitable would be writing to her. The life of an apprentice was not very easy at the best of times.

But then, who would be writing to her?

"I wish I could tell you I was glad to be here," she rasped, finally. "What did you do to me?"

Jack and Lucy shared a glance. "That's our secret, I'm afraid," Jack said, finally. "Suffice it to say that we saved your life. You came very close to death, I'm afraid. The Grim Reaper will have to wait for your soul, thanks to us."

Gwen didn't doubt him. The memory of her bones breaking was crystal clear. And yet...if her bones had broken, why wasn't she dead or crippled? Had she imagined everything, or...no, that couldn't be possible. There had always been rumours of a Healing talent, but Doctor Norwell had always insisted that they were just rumours. And yet she knew that she'd come very close to death...

"Doctor Norwell insists that there are only rumours of a Healing talent," she said, finally. Lucy seemed oddly concerned; Jack only smiled. "Did you...did you master the talent?"

"Ah, Doctor Norwell," Jack said. His grin widened. "Is he still a long-winded bore?"

Gwen ignored the sally. Doctor Norwell could be long-winded, but he'd been the first tutor who had actually tried to teach her something useful. She would have forgiven almost anything from a teacher who wanted her to learn. Her other tutors had acted as if they were humouring her, or, more accurately, humouring Lady Mary.

She looked up at Lucy, suddenly convinced of it. "You're the Healer," she said. "You Healed me."

"I did," Lucy said. Her head tilted, oddly. "And if you would like to thank me, please keep that to yourself."

Gwen hesitated, caught between duty and gratitude. It was her duty, as Master Thomas's apprentice, to report the existence of a Healing talent – and a living Healer. As a Master, she should logically possess the talent herself. But gratitude – Lucy had saved her life – told her otherwise. If Lucy wanted to keep her talent to herself, who was Gwen to say otherwise? And besides, she owed Lucy her life. Another Healer would appear soon enough, surely.

"I will," she said, finally. "How do you do it?"

Lucy hesitated, just long enough for Gwen to realise that she was having difficulty putting it into words. She'd seen similar pauses on the part of Changers and Infusers, magicians whose talents were at least partly intuitive. They couldn't explain what they did, or how they did it, either.

"The body wants to heal," Lucy said, finally. "I push myself into the body and allow it to guide me in healing itself. The magic within you helped, which is why you healed so quickly..."

She broke off. "They're going to know, aren't they?"

"Depends," Jack said. "We have much to show our guest before she returns to Cavendish Hall."

He looked up at Gwen, smiling. "I have to show you a few things," he said. "After that, you may not want to return to Master Thomas."

Gwen scowled at him. "How long was I out of it?"

Jack pretended to be surprised by the question. "It's early

evening," he said. "All over London, the little ones are being tucked up in bed, while the big bad folk are going out into the street, to drink and carouse and burn away their pay before going home to their miserable wives and even more miserable children. Drunkards, robbers and thugs are wandering the streets, looking for targets..."

Lucy coughed. "But if you're feeling better," Jack said, "we can go out and join them. You have a great deal to see and very little time before you have to return to Cavendish Hall – if you still want to return, that is."

"They'll be looking for me," Gwen said. "All of the Seers will be hunting for me..."

"Of course," Jack agreed. He grinned, again. "The trouble with Seers is that they're not always very reliable. A tiny amount of magic infused into stone will prevent them from seeing you" – he nodded upwards towards the ceiling – "or us, for that matter. Poor Master Thomas will be worried sick about you. He's in his eighties, you know. He really should have retired long ago."

Gwen stood upright. The pain in her head had faded, although she still felt rather faint, as if she hadn't eaten for a long time. Lucy silently produced a set of cheese rolls and handed them around. Gwen's mother would have turned up her nose at such simple fare, but to Gwen it tasted rather like manna from heaven. The cheese was surprisingly tasty and the bread a perfect complement to it. She finished one roll and took a second.

"Just because we're in the underground," Jack said, "it doesn't mean that we can't eat well."

He grinned, before changing the subject. "Did you ever hear of Perivale's Sleeping Plague?"

Gwen started to shake her head, and then stopped. She *had* heard of the Sleeping Plague, but where? A moment's thought reminded her that Lord Blackburn's uncle had mentioned it at the Fairweather Ball, back before they'd known that Jack was still alive and intent on causing trouble. It had passed out of her mind, forgotten about in the press of events that had followed the ball.

"Look it up," Jack said, flatly. "You'll find a copy of his book in Cavendish Hall's library."

He stood up and grinned at her. "Come on," he said. "I'm

going to take you on the streets of London. And I will show you something to make you change your mind."

Chapter Twenty-Five

ear this," Jack said. He passed her a gold-painted crucifix. "You'll need it."

Gwen took it, puzzled. It was wooden, without any real value at all. She turned it over and over in her hand, looking for some sign or reason behind his choice, but she couldn't think of anything. The young boy with short blonde hair who'd met them downstairs was scowling at her, almost as if he was jealous. But of what?

"The Little Sisters of Christ are the only people who actually give a damn about the people on the streets," Jack said. There was an undertone of cold anger in his voice, but it wasn't directed at her. "They're also the only untouchable people, the only ones that everyone will rise to defend. No one will touch you while you're wearing that cross."

He opened the door as Gwen put the cross around her neck. "Come on," he said. "It won't get any easier the longer we delay."

Outside, night had fallen over London. Gwen had never been on the streets so late and she was astonished by how many people were still wandering around, looking for drink or whores. A group of sailors were staggering along one side of the street, singing a bawdy song that made Gwen blush the moment she realised what the words meant, while a handful of women were eyeing them reluctantly. They would be sailors home from the seas, Gwen guessed, looking to spend their pay before returning to the water. The women – the whores – would try to seduce them into spending their pay.

Jack led her through the twisting alleyways and streets without showing any sign of fear. He glared at a group of thuggish men who saw the look in his eye and decided to seek easier targets elsewhere, stepping over a dead or dying body with magnificent unconcern. Gwen almost felt sick, again. The body turned over and groaned, revealing that someone had stabbed a knife in its back before making off with its wallet. It took Gwen several moments before she could determine that it had been a male victim. The clothing could have belonged to either sex in the poorer areas of London.

A group of street urchins ran past her, their hands snatching out at her dress as they passed. Gwen ignored them as best as she could, even though it was clear that they had wanted to rob her – and would have robbed her, if she'd had anything worth stealing. The crucifix wasn't real gold, she reminded herself – and besides, even street urchins would have hesitated to steal something like it. It was certainly worthless to them. They turned a corner and stepped into a pub, where hundreds of men were drinking beer as if it were going to be prohibited tomorrow. A handful of drunkards had been tossed out and left to sleep it off on the pavement. She paused as she felt one of the drunkards clutching at her dress, before falling back into a stupor. God alone knew what had been going through his mind.

Jack caught her arm as they passed out of earshot of the pub. "The men here have nothing in their lives," he said, flatly. "They have no hope of ever earning more from the factory owners – and when they get injured, they get put out on the streets and left to die. So they come here every evening and drink themselves into a state where, just for a while, they can forget their lot. They rarely care about their wives and children."

He shook his head. "Would you like to guess how many wives end up dead on the streets?"

Gwen shook her head. "The men come home, drunk, and their wives yell at them for spending all their pay," he said. "And they turn on their wives and beat them – and their children too, for all that it's worth. They often beat their wives to death and no one gives a damn. Life on the streets is nasty, brutish and short."

His scowl deepened. "And do you know what? Even if they didn't drink, even if they saved all of their money, they'd never get out of the trap. What's the point in struggling if you can't hope to win? They keep fighting to stay alive, but that's all they can do. There's nothing to live for, not in London. It's a strange world where the best thing that could happen to them is that they get transported to America or Australia."

They passed through another couple of streets until they reached a lighted building. There were a handful of women outside, some younger than Gwen; others older, looking as if they were on the verge of dropping dead on the spot. One of them called out a suggestion to Jack that made Gwen blush furiously, which Jack ignored. Instead, he nodded down an alleyway, barely illuminated by an overhead light. Gwen saw a woman on her knees in front of a man, her lips wrapped around his penis...she looked away, frantically. She'd never even dreamed that a woman could do that to a man. Certainly, it had never been mentioned in any of the biological textbooks...

"There are countless young women with no prospects," Jack said. "Often, they have children and families to feed, and the only things they have to sell are their own bodies. So they go out on the streets, find men coming home from work and offer them sex in exchange for money. And if the man just happens to beat them to death afterwards instead of paying...well, there's never any shortage of whores."

He nodded towards a grim-faced man smoking in the darkness. "One of the pimps," he said, flatly. "The women who don't have pimps soon find that one will take them into his service, or cripple them if they refuse. He will keep most of their earnings and give them a pittance, if anything at all. And if a stronger pimp comes along, the women will pass to his service while the old pimp is turned into a beggar – or killed. What does it say about a world where a woman in a whorehouse is safer than one on the streets?"

Gwen caught a flicker of magic and barely had time to react before Jack smashed the pimp against the nearest wall. The pimp's head was crushed, leaving his body to collapse to the ground. Gwen felt sick, yet...surely, the pimp had deserved his fate. He'd sent women out onto the streets to work for him, without caring what happened to them after they died...

"There will be a new one soon enough," Jack said, darkly. "No judge has ever judged a pimp too harshly, not when half of them use pimps themselves. But the women...they're convicted of prostitution and sent to jail, or transported overseas. And yet it isn't really their fault if there's no other way to make a living. How can anyone judge them too harshly?"

He shook his head, bitterly. "What would have happened to you, I wonder, if you'd grown up on these streets?"

Gwen said nothing. It had honestly never crossed her mind that the poor lived so badly. The servants who had worked for her mother, or worked at Cavendish Hall, had had good clothes and good food; Gwen had never wondered if they might want anything better. She cursed her own oversight even as her eyes stung with tears. How could anyone live like this?

"A few years ago, the Church sent a party of Ministers into the streets to try to put an end to prostitution," Jack said, as they passed an old church. "They had the idea that the women could work at spinning or weaving instead. But they forgot that machines had replaced women and that they only paid women a few shillings for their work. Even the pimps paid better! And so they went back to their churches and loudly declared that the women were whores who deserved no better than they got. I wonder if they remembered that Jesus spent more time with the poor than with the wealthy?"

Gwen didn't answer the question. "But surely...someone could do something..."

"Of course they could," Jack said. "All they would have to do is care. But they don't care – and why should they? People like your friend Lord Blackburn think that the poor are poor because they deserve to be poor – because they were born poor. The Indians have a caste system, one that confines their lives by patterns of birth. I wonder how long it will be before the poor here discover that they're trapped in a caste system every bit as brutal."

He grinned at her, savagely. "I never knew either," he said. "I was twelve when they discovered my magic; I was twelve when I was taken away and apprenticed to Master Thomas. I never knew about the poor, or what had happened to them. I never knew that the machines we'd invented had pushed so many people off the land and into the cities. I never knew...

"I committed terrible crimes," he admitted. He looked down at the cobblestones for a long chilling moment. "And if they catch me, they will hang me – but they won't hang me for any of my crimes. They'll hang me for wanting to make a difference."

There was a long moment where he seemed to be lost in his memories. "Come on," he said. "There's something you have to see before you decide where you want to go."

Gwen followed him through the streets, inwardly recoiling at the poverty and squalor all around her. Windows opened and buckets of human waste were tossed out onto the streets, with blithe disregard for anyone underneath when the waste was thrown away. Rats, cats and dogs ran feral, hunting each other and weaker humans; the rats, in particular, carried diseases through the streets. There were a handful of dead bodies lying on the ground, their clothes long since removed by the street gangs along with anything valuable they might have had with them. A small girl, wearing a pretty dress that looked oddly out of place, was selling flowers, offering them to the hardy sailors and workers who were trying to drink themselves to death.

"The girl's parents will send her out to sell her wares," Jack explained, as he gave the girl a coin and collected a bunch of flowers, which he made vanish inside his clothes. "The men here are tough bastards, but they often have a soft spot for young children. But there are also men on the streets who want to use children for their sexual games – and if the child dies, no one will care. There are plenty more where she came from."

He paused, and then looked at her. "Do you know where I found Lord Fitzroy?"

Gwen shook her head. No one had mentioned that at all, which – in hindsight – struck her as odd. But the Fitzroy family was well connected and if they'd wanted to bury something, it could have been buried without the rest of High Society ever guessing at the truth. It would hardly be the first time a nobleman had died under mysterious circumstances.

"I found him in a brothel," Jack said. Gwen looked up, sharply. She knew that many male noblemen were given to visiting brothels, though she wasn't supposed to know about them, or even what a brothel *was*. "But this was no ordinary brothel. This one catered for a very select clientele." He leaned forward. "The people who visited this brothel wanted to have sex with children, girls and boys so young that they hadn't even begun to mature."

Gwen stared at him, unable to believe her ears. "They forced their way into the children," Jack said, sharply. "They were often injured – and the injured were thrown out onto the streets to die. Lord Fitzroy was one of the brothel's most powerful patrons."

Abruptly, he turned and headed down the street. Gwen followed him, her mind spinning. If Lord Fitzroy had been having sex with children...she felt revolted, disgusted. She'd been introduced to him, socially, and he'd kissed her hand. It was irrational, but she wanted to scrub her hand thoroughly, scrape off the skin and remove all traces of his lips...Jack was moving faster now and Gwen almost had to run to keep up with him. How could *anyone* do that to a child? How could anyone...?

She looked around her and, for the first time, understood what Jack was trying to tell her. The urban poor had literally nothing to lose, but their chains. Savage repression and ignorance – and magic – was all that kept them from rising up against their masters. And Gwen, if she became the Royal Sorceress, would be a part of that repression. And...what had they done to deserve such suffering? Gwen prided herself on being intellectually honest – and the only thing they'd done wrong was being born to the wrong parents. What was the difference between Gwen and the girl who had been selling flowers, but an accident of birth?

Jack stopped outside a building on the edge of the wealthier part of town. "I'm going to show you something that many people would say wasn't fit for female eyes," he said. "Which is very strange, because the things in this building are happening to females."

He leapt into the air and rose up to the rooftop. Gwen followed him, her mind still spinning, and watched as he opened a hatch and reached down into the darkness. He motioned for her to wait while he dealt with the sentries, and then called for her to come down into the building. The air seemed thicker somehow, glowing with the scent of magic. Gwen watched as Jack created a light with his magic and illuminated the hallway. A handful of doors lay ahead of her, each one with a tiny glimmer of light coming from just above the carpet. Jack slipped forward, listened at one of the doors, and then opened it a crack. Gwen followed and looked inside.

It took her a moment to understand what she was seeing. A pair of naked buttocks – male buttocks – were heaving up and down on the bed. She flushed, almost looking away despite a kind of queasy fascination, and then realised that there were two pairs of feet. There was a woman under the man, gasping as he thrust deeper and deeper into her...Gwen skittered away, flushing bright red. She had never seen a man and a woman having sex before, not ever. It seemed louder than she had expected...

Jack smiled as he opened a second door. This time, the girl was bent over the bed, the man standing behind her and thrusting into her. It looked painful; Gwen was sure that the woman wasn't enjoying herself at all. Magic rose inside her, only to be dampened by Jack's presence. He pulled her back to the hatch and they floated up and out, leaving Gwen stunned as one thought kept spinning through her mind. She'd *recognised* the second man. Lord Blackburn was unmistakable.

"The women here aren't here of their own free will," Jack said, twenty minutes later. They sat together on the rooftops, looking over in the direction of Buckingham Palace. "Every poor child who shows signs of magical ability is taken by the Royal College. The street gangs get paid for each child they deliver to Master Thomas and his subordinates – very few magical children escape the net. Each of the boys is adopted by a wealthy family, one who can meet his every need. He is encouraged to forget his real parents. The girls are taken to one of the farms, like this building here. They are raised carefully, and then...bred with male magicians, each one eventually becoming pregnant. A pregnant woman is well cared for, but her children are taken from her at birth. The males, again, to be raised by good families and eventually become magicians; the females to be raised in...other establishments before being sent to the farms."

Gwen found it hard, almost impossible, to comprehend. "But why...?" She managed, finally. "Why all...this madness?"

"It isn't madness," Jack said, seriously. "The great advantage Britain has over the rest of the world is an organised magical system. It won't last and Master Thomas knows it. Here, in places like this, they're breeding the next generations of magicians. They hope that by...cross-breeding the talents, they will breed more magicians with multiple talents. The results weren't too successful when I was still working for Master Thomas, but they've had plenty of time to experiment since then."

He looked up at her. "I came out of one of those programs," he said, softly. "I never knew my real mother or father. I was raised by a wealthy family until Master Thomas came for me. He may even have been my father, Gwen; every male magician in the Royal College is expected to do his bit for the program. Lord Blackburn is far from the only one to come here and attempt to impregnate the girls. None of the poor women have any choice about what happens to them...

"When I found out, I knew that I could no longer stay with Master Thomas," he admitted. "If you had been born to a poor family, you would have wound up here – or dead."

He shrugged. "But it's time for you to head back to Cavendish Hall," he said. "If you still want to go back, that is..."

Gwen hesitated. "I don't know," she admitted. She felt terrible, and confused. "I just don't know."

"I understand," Jack said. He pointed towards Big Ben. "You can find your own way home from here?" Gwen nodded. "We'll see each other again, sooner or later. And I hope you make the right choice."

Gwen stared at him. "But what is the right choice?"

Jack chuckled. "The right choice is the one that allows you to sleep soundly at night," he said. "I wonder just how well Master Thomas sleeps these days."

Chapter Twenty-Six

here the hell have you been?"

Gwen ignored Cannock as the guard showed her into Cavendish Hall. It had been a difficult walk back to the Hall, if only because her mind was spinning. She'd seen Lord Blackburn forcing himself on a woman – and how many others, she asked herself, had done the same over the years? Cannock was a powerful Mover, even though he was a complete pain in her posterior. Had he been ordered to impregnate any number of unwilling women?

"You're lucky Master Thomas isn't here," Cannock said, getting in front of her. Gwen had started to walk towards the stairs, ignoring him. "He's out on a raid for the police – but he was worried about you. We've had all kinds of reports."

He placed a hand on her shoulder. "Where the hell have you been? And what the hell are you wearing?"

Gwen fixed him with a look that would have done her mother proud. "Take your hand off me, now," she said, icily. Cannock let go of her and stumbled backwards, either shocked by his breech of etiquette or suddenly reminded that Gwen had far more talents than he possessed. "I am going upstairs to my rooms. You will inform Master Thomas, when he returns, that I am catching up on my sleep. He will doubtless wish to talk to me himself."

She walked up the stairs, silently daring Cannock to follow her. He shouldn't have been in charge at Cavendish Hall, but she could see him assuming control if all the senior magicians were out of the building, looking for her. Or perhaps Master Thomas was somewhere other than on a raid. He had made little fuss about her attending David's birthday dinner...perhaps he was at one of the other farms, impregnating other women. The thought chilled her to the bone as she stumbled into her rooms. She locked the door behind her, even though she knew that any magician with a hint of magic would be able to break through the locks and force his way in. How many women had been sacrificed on the altar of necessity?

Despite herself, she yawned. It had been a long day, even though she'd been unconscious for part of it. She pulled at her outfit, suddenly aware that she must look a sight, and undressed rapidly. The mottled pattern of new skin that she remembered from when she'd been with the underground was rapidly fading. By morning, she suspected, it would be gone completely. The aches and pains still haunting her body were all that remained of injuries that should have killed her outright. Lucy's talent was a miracle, a miracle that Master Thomas and his men would have done anything to acquire. Absently, Gwen wondered if Lucy had any children – and, if so, if they shared the healing talent. How many other talents were known to the underground, but not to the establishment?

She crawled into bed without bothering to don her nightwear and closed her eyes. The next thing she knew was that she was being shaken, firmly. She opened her eyes and saw one of the maids, staring down at her anxiously. Her long curly hair was falling down to tickle Gwen's face.

"You have to wake up," the maid whispered, urgently. Gwen, still half-asleep, couldn't even remember her name. How long had she slept? Bright sunlight was pouring in through the windows, suggesting that it was early morning. "Master Thomas wants to speak with you."

Gwen allowed herself an inner sigh of relief. At least Master Thomas hadn't come charging into her room demanding answers, although it would have been a gross breech of etiquette. A master had ultimate power over his apprentice, but Gwen could count on the fingers of one hand the number of women who had been apprenticed in male professions. Master Thomas wouldn't have violated her privacy so blatantly. On the other hand, he was certainly going to demand answers the moment Gwen showed her face.

"You have to come," the maid insisted. She sounded worried. Master Thomas had clearly put the fear of...well, himself into her. "Please..."

Gwen pulled herself upright, ignoring the maid's blush as

Gwen's bare breasts were revealed. "Please inform Master Thomas," Gwen said, in a tone her mother would have recognised at once, "that I will attend upon him as soon as I have finished my toilet. And then inform the kitchen that I would like a late breakfast."

The maid fled, leaving Gwen to pull herself out of bed and splash water on her face. Gwen had never taken long to dress – her mother took hours before going out to a ball or even a simple meal with a few friends – but she paced herself as she pulled on her apprentice's uniform. It gave her time to clear her head and decide what she could – and would – tell Master Thomas. She wasn't going to tell him the truth, at least until she'd sorted out her own thoughts and feelings. The memory of Lord Blackburn flashed in front of her eyes and she shuddered. Master Thomas was the most powerful magician in Britain, at least as far as anyone knew. He would have been called upon to father hundreds of children.

"It is vitally important that no one questions the paternity of your children," her mother had said, once. The young Gwen had realised that David had been allowed far more freedom than she, and had demanded answers from her mother. In hindsight, she cringed at the memory and wondered why her mother hadn't slapped her face once or twice. "You must remain like Caesar's wife, above suspicion. What contact you have with *men*" – her tone had suggested that Gwen would want little contact with men – "must be carefully chaperoned to ensure that your name is not brought into disrepute."

Gwen scowled at the memory as she checked herself in the mirror. The King was known for having bastards, at least three according to her mother's gossip. Queen Caroline might have been favoured by the British public, but she had never been allowed such liberty. Gwen could see how the scheme had worked for so long. No one would question the origins of a child, provided that they were adopted as very young children. Indeed, no one would have to know that the child had been adopted at all. The child himself might never know that the people who had brought him up weren't his real parents.

She stopped dead as a thought crossed her mind. How did she know that Lady Mary was her real mother? How did she know that her father was really her father? The thought of

Lady Mary adopting a young girl...but no, Gwen hated to admit it, but she did have her mother's face. Lady Mary had the same blonde hair and face as Gwen; only Gwen's eyes had come from her father. And she could see her father objecting to allowing someone else to father a child on his wife. It would have been more understandable if Lady Mary had had children from her first husband, if she'd had one. No one in High Society would have asked questions about that; indeed, the second husband would be expected to adopt the children formally.

The thought tormented her as she gathered herself and walked downstairs. She'd delayed as long as she dared, even though her thoughts weren't complete. If she lied to Master Thomas and he caught her at it, he would never trust her again. But if she told the truth, she would put Jack and Lucy in terrible danger. And yet they were rebels, rebelling against the establishment. And they had a very good cause.

Master Thomas looked tired as she entered his study. He had a small office on the ground floor which he used for official business. Gwen had seen it once or twice before, but hadn't spent any real time in it. He was seated behind a massive desk, reading a file of papers and checking off names against a list on the table. Gwen stopped in front of the desk and waited, uncomfortably aware that it was far too similar to facing her father after a childish prank. Master Thomas had every right to discipline her as he saw fit.

He looked up and fixed her with an unblinking stare. "What happened to you last night?"

Gwen swallowed, hard. There would have been plenty of evidence of the desperate chase and fight across the rooftops of London. They might even have found the dead body, the body of the man she'd slain. It would have been obvious that he had been killed by magic – and Master Thomas might deduce that Gwen, rather than Jack, had killed him. If he saw through her lie, she knew that he wouldn't be merciful. Jack had betrayed him too badly for him to trust another apprentice completely.

"The rogue attacked my brother's dinner," Gwen said, finally. It dawned on her that she truly was as selfish as her mother had called her, long ago. She hadn't even thought to ask after David and his guests. The guilt gnawed at her mind as she faced Master Thomas. "I gave chase across the rooftops and…"

She broke off. "He did something to me," she admitted. "I blacked out and collapsed. When I recovered, it was midnight and I was lost somewhere in London. I made my way back to Cavendish Hall and went to bed."

"He just left you there," Master Thomas said. Gwen flushed. She knew how weak it sounded. Jack would have wanted to kill her if she hadn't listened to him, if only to deprive Master Thomas of a powerful ally. "Where did you get the street clothing?"

Gwen hoped that he'd believe that her flush was embarrassment, rather than shame. "My clothes were rags," she said. "I gave them to a street beggar in exchange for something I could wear back to Cavendish Hall."

She had always hated it when men thought of her as a foolish female, a phobia she'd had ever since she'd become aware of the difference between men and women. It was ironic, she admitted in the privacy of her own mind, that that very phobia drove her to commit foolish acts. Chasing Jack across the rooftops had been foolish; not taking a bodyguard to her brother's dinner party had been foolish…and then giving away her clothes would have been foolish. As explanations went, it wasn't one that could be easily disproved. Her ruined clothes would still be worth far more than a labouring woman's outfit.

"You should have known better than to give chase to him," Master Thomas said, flatly. He sounded as if he was angry, but not at Gwen. Gwen wondered, absently, what else had happened since she'd been knocked out. Jack might have shown himself to her as a diversion, to distract attention from something else. "You risked your own life."

"Yes, sir," Gwen said, tightly.

"You're strong and adaptable and you have much less to unlearn than your fellow students, but you're not ready to fight another Master," Master Thomas said, sharply. "You didn't just put yourself at risk, Lady Gwen; you put the future of the Royal Sorcerers Corps at risk. Who could have replaced you if you'd died on the streets?"

His eyes met hers, boring into her very soul. "You will not risk your life again," he said. "Do you understand me?"

"Yes, sir," Gwen said. She felt…uncertain. Master Thomas had always been good to her, yet the memory of the farm mocked her – and him. How many women had he slept with in the hopes of producing talented children? And how willing had those women actually been? "I understand."

"A male student would be feeling the sting of my displeasure," Master Thomas said. "As it is, you can go to the library and study for the next few hours. An urgent matter has come up and I must attend to it. You can return to your practice tomorrow morning."

Gwen nodded and left the study, not trusting herself to speak. Most of her fellow students would have regarded being banished to the library as a punishment, but Gwen rather enjoyed the chance to study the collection of books – and pick out the numerous misconceptions about magic put forward by various authors. Lombardi loved the library too, yet when Gwen entered there was no sign of him. There was no sign of any other students either. The library was as dark and silent as the grave.

She glanced around to be sure that she was alone and then started to hunt for a particular book. Jack had told her the name of the author, but she had no idea where it would have been shelved – or even if it had been left on the shelves. There was a section of restricted books that could only be read with permission from Master Thomas and Gwen knew, without needing to ask, that permission would not be forthcoming. She was on the verge of abandoning her search when she spotted the book she was looking for, hidden away amid a set of mathematical treatises. It was a small pamphlet, dated 1801. The author, she realised, might well have known Professor Cavendish personally. They might even have been friends, although Professor Cavendish, according to his official biographer, had been a very shy and retiring man. It was a minor miracle that he'd even been able to convince the establishment that magic existed.

The book's title confused her at once. It read *The Sleeping Plague and the Origin of Magic*. Below, written in red ink, was a note that read *BANNED BY ORDER OF THE CROWN*, suggesting that there were only a handful of copies in existence. The Church and the Government, if Gwen recalled correctly, had considerable powers to ban publications they didn't like, something that had often led to embarrassment. Even Gwen had heard of the shady circumstances behind the death of John Wilkes. Concealing the book in a larger tome, she found a private seat and opened the volume. It launched straight into text at once.

The origin of magic has confused numerous scholars since Professor Cavendish outlined the principles of magic thirty years ago. In theory, magic should have existed throughout the ages, but historical accounts of magic simply do not match the discoveries of Cavendish and his fellow researchers. The power to turn men into frogs, to kill someone at a distance through symbolic magic and powerful curses simply does not exist. Merlin's legendary magic remains unmatched by modern-day sorcerers. And no attempt to summon the devil from his fiery realm has succeeded.

Gwen frowned, puzzled. She had heard about the misconceptions surrounding magic; John Wellington Wells and his friends had made a fortune exploiting the ignorance of common people, but she was surprised to see that they'd existed for so long. But maybe that wasn't surprising. People had believed in magicians long before real magicians had come into existence. She skimmed through a section relating to Darwinists – or what had probably become the Darwinists, once Charles Darwin had outlined Darwinism – before coming to the meat of the matter. It took her several moments to understand what it said.

The general belief that magic is limited to the upper classes is demonstrably incorrect, as is the belief that magic is somehow limited to Britain. Indeed, there are very definite signs that there are French, Russian and even Turkish magicians. This leads us to consider that the origins of magic are nowhere near as clear-cut as suggested by Professor Cavendish. We must therefore ask ourselves the obvious question. What do all magic-users have in common?

On the face of it, the only thing that they appear to

share is that they are all human. There have been no reported cases of magical animals or even humans who can shift into animal forms. What else do they have? There are both male and female magicians; there are magicians from all civilised countries; there are old magicians and young magicians...what do they have in common? Careful research suggests that there is one factor linking all magicians together.

During the Seven Years War, doctors in Britain became aware of something that became known as the Sleeping Plague. The victims would act as if they had been mesmerized, muttering to themselves or sleepwalking through life. Some of the victims, the ones with wealth and servants, were put in bed and left to recover on their own. Others, without money or property, died while they were affected with the plague. They were unable to take care of themselves. The plague seemed to fade as quickly as it had arrived, leaving a mystery that baffled doctors.

But one thing is clear. Every known magician was either affected by the Sleeping Plague, or is descended from someone who was affected with the Sleeping Plague. It has proved hard to gather information from the poorer sections of society, but I believe that the evidence connecting the two factors is impossible to refute. The Sleeping Plague created the first magicians – and the reason there were more upper class magicians than lower class is that upper class people were cared for while they were affected by the Plague.

Gwen stopped reading in shock. The writer hadn't known about werewolves – they'd been isolated around 1810, if she recalled correctly – but his words made sense. Charles Darwin hadn't written for at least two decades after Perivale had studied the Sleeping Plague, yet he'd never even considered the possibility that there might be a connection. Darwin had believed in the survival of the fittest, with magicians on top of a triangle that led down to the lower orders. He had provided the justification Lord Blackburn and his fellows used to keep themselves on top of the pile.

And that meant…what?

She pulled herself to her feet, carefully returned the book to the shelves, and settled down to more mundane studies. Inside, her mind was spinning. She needed advice, but whom could she trust? Master Thomas wouldn't listen to her…

Gwen called for a servant and asked him to deliver a message. She needed to see David anyway, if only to check up on him and Laura. And there was no one else she trusted who could give her advice. In all of her life, isolated from her peers, she had never felt so alone.

Chapter Twenty-Seven

ack watched Gwen floating off into the darkness and shook his head, sadly. She'd need time to process what she'd learned, time she might not have. Jack had no illusions about Master Thomas's capabilities; the old magician might have had his own reasons for leaving his apprentice on her own. God alone knew what he might have in mind, but Jack doubted he'd approve of it when he finally found out. Standing up, he smiled as he saw Lord Blackburn – his task completed – heading out of the farm and back towards Cavendish Hall.

He must have finished quickly, Jack thought, as he walked back to the hatch. Gwen would not have approved of what he had in mind, but there was no other choice. He'd returned to the farm once since discovering its current location and he was pleased to discover that the supplies he'd hidden on the rooftop were still there. It was disappointing – if he'd known that there was a rogue magician on the loose, he would have ensured that there were guards on the rooftops – but perhaps it was understandable. High Society – at least the part of it that had no magic – would have disapproved strongly of the farm. The whole idea was repulsive.

Jack scowled as he unpacked the gunpowder and reopened the hatch. It hadn't taken long for him to realise that High Society was composed of hypocrites, even before he'd discovered the truth of his own origins. Men were allowed to go out drinking and whoring as much as they liked, while raising hell if an unmarried woman happened to be seen alone with an unmarried man. And when there were little accidents – illegitimate children – very few noblemen had the decency to arrange for their upbringing. King George might be a fat and thoroughly useless roly-poly of a man – with an inability to keep his sausage in his pantaloons – but at least he did take care of his bastards. It was a pity that the same couldn't be said of most of his more ardent supporters. There were quite a few children of middle-class men who had been born on the wrong side of the blanket.

The interior of the farm was as dark as ever. Jack checked the sentries and was relieved to discover that they were both still sleeping it off. He hadn't killed them in front of Gwen, if only because he didn't know how she would have reacted to outright murder. Lord Blackburn had clearly missed their slumbering forms, something that wouldn't please Master Thomas when he discovered the truth. Jack made a mental note to ensure that Master Thomas found out, in the hopes that Lord Blackburn would find himself in hot water. The Charmer deserved to feel lonely and afraid at least once in his life. His crimes were far worse than anyone else Jack knew – and, unlike Master Thomas, he didn't even have the excuse of upholding the established order.

Jack placed the gunpowder, lit the fuse and floated up and out of the farm. The first glimmer of dawn could be seen along the horizon as he rose in the air, heading back towards the Rookery. London slumbered below him, the streets as empty as they ever were, with only a handful of drunks sleeping off their night's boozing in the gutters. It wouldn't be long before the Bow Street Runners started feeling their collars. The workhouses were always short of men for manual labour and convicts were cheaper to feed than free men. Jack had learned to hate the system a long time before he'd finally deserted Master Thomas and the Royal College. It did him no honour to recall that he'd once had a great deal in common with Lord Blackburn.

There was a thunderous roar as the gunpowder exploded below him. Jack smiled as the shockwave caught him and pushed his body through the air, a fireball rising up to challenge the dawn. Below, he caught sight of men staring at the flaming remains of a once-proud building. The fire brigade would probably be called off before they could find any evidence of what had actually occurred inside the building, although Jack hoped that a few pointed questions would be asked. Lord Blackburn and his fellow Darwinists might find themselves having to answer questions from those they considered their inferiors.

The thought of Lord Blackburn spurred him on through the air. Down below, the Charmer had turned to stare at the fire, almost certainly aware that he'd escaped death by seconds. If he'd lingered with the girls – Jack was sure that some of the magicians cared about the women, even if they didn't think of them as anything like a wife – he would have died in the explosion. Jack dropped down towards him and landed behind the Charmer, allowing the sound of his landing to echo through the air. Lord Blackburn spun around, one hand on his cane, and saw him. He didn't seem to recognise Jack. But then, it had been years since they'd seen one another and he might not have realised that Jack had been flying. Footpads loved to hide until they could surprise their targets.

Jack grinned, nastily. "Well," he remarked, "here's a well set up follow indeed. Sir; your money or your life."

Lord Blackburn's eyes narrowed. "I have a better idea," he said. Charm flowed into his voice, dark and powerful. It would have hit a mundane person like a hammer, leaving them aware of the Charm, but unable to fight it. "You can go and drown yourself in the river."

Jack had to exert himself to stand his ground, but he had the pleasure of seeing Lord Blackburn's eyes widening before he stepped forward. "I took the precaution of blocking my ears," he lied, smoothly. "Your magic is powerless if I don't hear you, isn't it?"

Lord Blackburn lifted his cane, almost as if it were a sword. It clicked ominously, the wood falling away to reveal a blade. Jack was almost impressed, even as he caught hold of the sword-stick with his magic and snatched it out of Lord Blackburn's hands. The Darwinist's eyes opened wide as he realised who he was facing, and then he turned to run. Jack's magic caught him before he managed to travel more than a yard, yanking him up into the air and turning him upside down. He would have expected the Charmer to try his Charm – after all, he had nothing to lose – but Lord Blackburn merely stared at him. Jack made a show of stroking his chin in contemplation, keeping one ear open for the Bow Street Runners. He was mildly surprised that they hadn't shown up already. The people who lived in this part of London were actually *important*.

"You know," Jack remarked, almost conversationally,

"your logic says that magicians are superior to mundane people, and more powerful magicians are superior to less powerful magicians. By that logic, you should be genuflecting at my feet by now."

Lord Blackburn glared at him. "You think I'll ever kiss your feet?"

"I'd be worried about you if you wanted to," Jack mocked. "My feet do get pretty smelly after a week of actually working for a living – but then, you wouldn't know much about that, would you? What use is Charm to the Army?"

"If you think you can intimidate me," Lord Blackburn began, "you are wrong..."

"I'm sure that I am not wrong," Jack countered. "Your entire philosophy speaks of a deep-seated insecurity. And yet you have the power to twist men's minds around and turn them into your slaves. Do you still have the harem of women you turned into your devoted servants?"

"I'm not going to tell you anything," Lord Blackburn said. "You might as well kill me now and save yourself some trouble."

Jack shrugged. "And why would I want to kill you?" He asked. "You're worthless to me. You're beneath my notice, just like the men and women you trample on every day – the men and women you twist with your Charm. I don't care about you, My Lord; I merely want you to pass on a message to Master Thomas. You can do that for me, can't you?"

Lord Blackburn gasped in pain as Jack let go of him and he came down face-first in a puddle. Jack hadn't cushioned the blow at all. The Charmer staggered to his feet, blood pouring from his nose, and came forward. Jack held up a hand and stopped him in his tracks. Charm was very useful in the hands of a skilled Charmer, but it was useless against someone with the strength of will to resist it. And it didn't really add to a Charmer's ability to fight. No wonder Lord Blackburn, unlike most of the Sorcerers Corps, had never served a term with the Army. Charmers were of very little use on campaign.

"In fact, you can be the message," Jack said. He lifted one arm and Lord Blackburn was hurled backwards into a hedge. "I'm coming for him."

He threw himself up into the air, leaving Lord Blackburn behind. The Charmer would have to explain himself to

Master Thomas, even though – for once – it hadn't been his fault. A man like Lord Blackburn would be offended that his enemy hadn't thought him worth the effort of killing. Jack was curious to know what manner of lie Lord Blackburn would invent to explain it to himself, but there was no way to know for sure. Lord Blackburn's Charm was powerful enough to prevent him from being Charmed in turn.

The sun was rising into the sky and so Jack headed back to the Rookery. He'd established a handful of small apartments scattered on the edges – no one asked questions in the Rookery, as long as one paid in cold hard cash – and one of them was nearby. Out of habit, he hadn't told many people about them, let alone their locations. If someone was arrested – and recognised – the Bow Street Runners would do whatever it took to get information from them, so the less they knew the better. Jack dropped down to the ground in an alleyway, adjusted his coat, nodded to a handful of drunken men who would hopefully decide that he was a figment of their imagination, and strode out onto the streets. The Rookery seemed quieter than usual, he noted, absently. Alert for trouble, he walked up to the tenement and headed inside. There were no night watchmen in the Rookery. The very idea was absurd, if only because the people living in the building were too poor to have anything worth stealing. Jack wrinkled his nose as he made his way up a creaky staircase, wondering if it would collapse under his weight. The Rookery wasn't big on public safety either.

He pressed his hand against the lock and it clicked open. There had only ever been one key – at least officially – and he'd given it to Olivia. The young girl had needed somewhere to bed down away from Lucy's brothel – some of Lucy's customers might have thought that she was a whore – and Jack had given her permission to use the apartment. She'd been grateful, although Jack had been amused to note that she'd searched the room the moment he'd left her alone in it. Old habits learned on the streets, living from hand to mouth, were the hardest to overcome.

"You're back," Olivia said. She looked as if she hadn't been sleeping well, much to Jack's surprise. The young girl knew enough to catch sleep whenever she could. "I thought you'd be busy with *her* until later."

Jack frowned, opening one of the bags he'd left in the

room. It was a shame that magic couldn't supply extra energy, but no one had ever discovered a talent that offered anything of the sort. Infusers had tried to infuse energy into water, yet the first time someone had drunk the potion the results had been lethal, putting a stop to that. And the potions supplied by street magicians were little more than coloured water.

"She had to go home and think about it," he said, briefly. He'd half-hoped Gwen would join him at once, but it hadn't been too likely. After all, he *had* attacked her brother's dinner party and forced her to show off her powers in front of his guests. A noblewoman with magical talents tended to keep them to herself; Gwen had been forced to display them all, shattering whatever claim to normality she had had in the battle. "I don't know which way she'll jump."

"I didn't like her," Olivia said. The child's voice was dismissive, but firm. "She looked at me as if I wasn't there."

"I thought that was what you wanted," Jack reminded her. "You know that attracting attention could be dangerous."

He studied the young girl for a long moment. Lucy had been treating her almost like a daughter – Lucy had never had any children, even before she'd discovered her talent – and Olivia was putting on weight. A few more years and she would be unable to pass for a boy any longer, and then the trouble would start. Most women on the streets had to find a male protector – a pimp – or they'd rapidly find themselves being victimised by other men. If Olivia ever developed her talent, perhaps she would be able to carve out a niche for herself, but that carried its own risks. Master Thomas's men might come for her and take her away to the farms. The building he'd destroyed wouldn't have been the only farm in London.

"I just didn't like her," Olivia repeated. "What does she want with us?"

"Truth, perhaps," Jack said, after a moment. He pulled on a different overcoat and checked his appearance by glancing up and down at himself. There was no point in installing a mirror, if only because it wouldn't be there when he came back to the apartment. Jack knew of people who had had to watch helplessly as hawkers sold off their property, stolen from them by thieves and placed on sale. The Rookery had one law, the law of the strong. Lord Blackburn would have approved. "But she will have to make her own mind up. We can't force her into a decision."

Olivia stood up and picked up her coat. "I think that she will betray us," she said, firmly. "You shouldn't trust her so much."

"I showed her nothing, apart from one talent," Jack said. Olivia sounded almost as if she was jealous. But that was absurd. "There have always been rumours of Healers. Lady Gwen won't be able to lead the Runners to our lair, for the very simple reason she never saw it. She cannot really hurt us."

He smiled as he opened the door. "Coming for some breakfast?"

Olivia followed him down the stairs and out into the streets. They were filling up rapidly as the Rookery came to life. A handful of street-sellers were selling meat and bread, although Jack knew better than to ask what was in the stew or sausages. There were people in the Rookery who made a living by catching rats – or cats – and selling them to the cooks, who turned them into stew. No one in the Rookery objected; very few of them would ever have tasted beef, or lamb, or pork. There were chicken coops on some of the roofs, but chicken was pricy. Only the criminals could hope to eat it on a regular basis.

The first time Jack had eaten something cooked in the Rookery, he recalled, he had spent the rest of the afternoon with a very upset stomach. He was a little stronger now, but it still shocked him to see Olivia eat with apparent relish. She wouldn't have had anything regularly before she'd joined up with the underground, yet...Jack shook his head, remembering – once again – why he was trying to overthrow the government. No one should have to live in such conditions. A pack of wild dogs ran through the streets, hunting rats; they too sometimes ended up in the stew pot. Sentiment wasn't worth much in the Rookery. Jack had sometimes wondered if some of its denizens were actually cannibals. It wasn't as if life was worth much in the Rookery either.

He waited for Olivia to finish, sipping a bottle of beer he was fairly sure was safe to drink, and then led her through the maze of streets towards Lucy's brothel. As soon as they turned the corner, he knew that something was badly wrong.

The Bow Street Runners rarely came into the Rookery, but when they did they came in force. There were hundreds of policemen on the streets, surrounding Lucy's building. The men and women inside were being marched out in cuffs. Jack saw a handful of steady customers, a couple of underground messengers...and Lucy herself. He felt magic building up within his body, only to clamp down on it as hard as he could. The policemen were escorted by an entire team of Combat Magicians. Somehow – and Jack had no idea how – they'd tracked the underground down to Lucy's brothel.

"I told you," Olivia insisted. "That snooty bitch sold us out!"

"She couldn't have known," Jack said, flatly. He could think of several ways the Bow Street Runners – or the sparkers – could have tracked them down. A lucky break, a police informer in the right place – or even magic, a more than normally reliable Seer. "Damnation."

He thought, rapidly. If there hadn't been any Combat Magicians, he could have jumped in and scattered the police, giving the underground members a chance to run and hide. But they were there – and Master Thomas might be there too, not too far away. It might even be a trap for him.

"Come on," he said, catching Olivia's hand. They would need to find somewhere to hide, at least until he thought of a plan. Lucy didn't know everything, but she did know enough to expose his overall plan. And then they'd bring in the Dragoons and the plan would fall apart before it had even begun. "We need to get out of here."

Olivia looked up at him. "But what are we going to do?"

Jack had no answer for her. Not yet.

Chapter Twenty-Eight

'm afraid that Master Thomas is in a meeting," Doctor Norwell said. The theoretical magician seemed to have assumed control, somewhat to Gwen's surprise. "Do you wish me to take a message for him?"

It was on the tip of Gwen's tongue to ask about the Sleeping Plague, but she had the feeling that that would be a very bad idea. "I intend to visit my brother," she said, as grandly as she could. Her mother had taught her that arrogance and a total refusal to listen to reason could go a long way. "I would appreciate it if you informed him that I will probably be back late at night."

Doctor Norwell blinked, owlishly. "I think I had better check with him first," he said, slowly. "London is not safe for young magicians at the moment."

Gwen rolled her eyes as he knocked on Master Thomas's door and pushed it open. Gwen glanced through and saw Master Thomas, Lord Mycroft, Lord Blackburn and a man she didn't recognise. Lord Blackburn's face was marred, as if he had come off worst in a fight while making his way home. Gwen flushed and looked away, remembering what she'd seen at the farm. Lord Blackburn couldn't know that she'd seen him. He'd been very busy at the time.

"Lady Gwen would like to visit her brother," Doctor Norwell said. He sounded rather perplexed, as if he couldn't imagine why anyone would want to visit their family. Gwen wondered, rather spitefully, if he *had* any family. He was certainly old enough to have outlived his parents, perhaps even any siblings. "Do you feel that that would be appropriate?"

"Certainly not," Lord Blackburn said. He sounded angry,

although Gwen suspected that the anger wasn't directed at her. "We have far more important matters to worry about right now."

Master Thomas gave him a look that quelled a second protest before it could emerge from his mouth. "One moment," he said, and stood up. He walked out the door, pulling it closed behind him, before he faced Gwen. "You must know that London isn't safe right now."

Gwen nodded, thinking hard. Was he genuinely concerned about her, or was he worried about what she might discover on the outside? She wasn't supposed to know about the farm – and she suspected that she would never be supposed to know about the program, even when Master Thomas finally retired. But she had to talk to someone and David was the only person who would give her a fair hearing.

"Yes," she said, "but I'll be fine."

"We captured some...underground rebels this morning," Master Thomas said. He looked down at her and she was surprised to see real concern in his eyes. "They may want to strike at us again – and you are their most likely target."

"I can take care of myself," Gwen insisted. "I should have gone to see my brother earlier..."

"And you can go with an escort," Master Thomas said. He cocked his head to one side and Gwen felt an odd pressure in her temples. She realised, in surprise, that he was in mental communication with another magician. She'd never seen it demonstrated before. "I'll have a combat team assigned to escort you."

He held up a hand before Gwen could say a word. "Either take the escort or stay here, where it's safe," he said, firmly. "There are plenty of books that you need to read while I'm busy."

Gwen nodded, reluctantly. "Very well," she said. "I'll go under escort."

Master Thomas smiled. "Doctor Norwell will escort you to the carriage," he said. "And I trust I'll see you tonight for dinner."

Outside, the sun was shining down, trying to drive away the London smog. A carriage was waiting for Gwen, painted in the black colour used by the Royal Sorcerers. She saw two young men, both dressed in sorcerer's black, seated up by the horse, waving to her. They carried silver-topped canes and wore evening suits, although Gwen could tell that they had been tailored by the same person who'd designed her garb. The suits allowed their wearers to move freely and could probably come off in a jiffy, should it be required. Both of the men – and the two others inside the carriage – looked reassuringly competent. Their insignias marked them as a mixture of Blazers and Movers. There was no Talker, which struck her as odd, but then few would dare to rob a coach protected by magicians.

But Jack would, she thought, as she allowed one of the magicians to help her into the carriage. Inside, it was surprisingly roomy – and filled with the shimmering presence of magic. She touched one of the seats and sensed that someone had carefully infused it with magic, magic intended to protect the people inside the vehicle. The King himself couldn't be protected any better. And the King, she suspected, was safely inside Windsor Castle, under constant guard by the Royal Sorcerers. Jack wouldn't have a chance to go after him.

The carriage lurched to life as one of the magicians up front cracked the whip. Gwen watched as the horse pulled the carriage out of the drive and onto the streets. London seemed as crowded as ever, although the traffic seemed to clear a path for the sorcerers. London's cabbies were an imprudent lot, given to risking their livelihoods just to get their passengers from place to place as quickly as possible, but even they wouldn't risk the anger of a group of magicians. The pedestrians on the pavement turned to stare, some looking surprised, others fearful. Gwen winced inwardly as she saw the fear in their eyes. Magic was terrifying – and daunting – to those who not only had none of their own, but knew nothing of its limits.

She sat back in her seat and studied her two companions. They both looked handsome, if a little hard-worn. One of them looked old enough to have seen military service against the French; the other might have served in the wars against the Red Indians in America, or the Sikhs in India. Gwen had never truly considered the cost of empire before, but then – why should she? No one had ever expected her to be anything more than a daughter, a wife and a mother. Her magic might have opened new vistas for her, yet it had also closed others. She would never know domestic bliss.

But then, had her mother ever known it? Lady Mary's insistence on proper behaviour might have masked something else, a fear that she wasn't in a secure position at all. Few were, in High Society; only the Queen and the King's legitimate children could hope to be considered secure. Lady Mary's fortunes weren't even under her own control. She wouldn't be the first woman to discover that High Society would turn its back on her if her husband lost the family inheritance by gambling, or unwise investments. Equally, Society would not tolerate someone unable to prevent a daughter from flaunting her magic at every opportunity.

The thought bothered her as the carriage rattled over London Bridge, past the Houses of Parliament and down towards her brother's apartment in Pall Mall. Gwen hadn't bothered to give an address to the driver, which suggested that he'd already known where to go. Master Thomas could have told him, but how had he known where David would be? Or perhaps it had been obvious. David's fancy mansion had been badly damaged in Jack's attack and Laura would want to go somewhere safer. There were few places safer than Pall Mall.

She glanced out as the carriage came to a stop beside the pavement. One of the magicians held up a hand to keep her in her seat and jumped out, glancing around with instincts that had to have been honed while on campaign. There was no sign of trouble, apart from a handful of people who were clearly part of High Society, taking the air and chattering to one another as they walked down the street. Gwen clambered out of the carriage, shot the women a cheerful glance, and then headed towards the apartment door. The flats in Pall Mall were hugely expensive, even though they were fairly small. Gwen could have bought a house on the edge of London for the rent that David paid every month. But location was everything, as David had once told her, and Pall Mall had the best location in the world. The Houses of Parliament and most of the important clubs were only walking distance away.

"Wait here," she said, firmly. The combat magicians didn't look happy, but they nodded in agreement. Gwen rapped on the door, identified herself to a burly footman wearing a fancy uniform, and was waved in through the door. David rented a five-room apartment on the second floor. Gwen remembered that she'd once called him an idiot for spending so much money on it. Now, it seemed the wisest thing he'd ever done.

The door opened when she tapped on it, revealing David. Her brother looked surprised to see her, but he opened his arms and enfolded her in a bear hug. Gwen couldn't help herself; she studied his face, looking for traces of their mother and father. David had very definitely inherited his father's nose and his mother's eyes. He might not have been particularly handsome, but he had a solidly reassuring appearance. Inside, Gwen saw no one. Laura had clearly decided to stay elsewhere.

"She went to stay with her parents for a few days," David explained, when Gwen asked. He walked over to a small drinks cabinet and produced a couple of glasses. "Can I get you anything?"

Gwen shook her head. One of the few lessons about proper behaviour that her mother had drilled into her head was that young ladies should not get drunk. Gwen had known of women who did drink to excess, but she had no intention of joining their number. Besides, the Scotch that David – and their father – bought from Scotland was hideously expensive and unpleasant, at least to her palate. She suspected that most people drank it to show off their wealth, rather than out of enjoyment.

"I need to talk to you," she said, once David had poured himself a drink. "Can I ask you to keep it to yourself?"

David paused, as if in contemplation. Gwen took the opportunity to glance around the apartment. It was clean, too clean. David's bedroom at home was messy, with papers and books scattered everywhere, but here...the apartment was meant for business, rather than pleasure. The bookshelves looked dauntingly packed, yet Gwen suspected that he had never read a single volume. And the seats were formidably uncomfortable. It wasn't her idea of a place to live.

Her lips twitched. If David had kept better care of his books, she would never have been able to borrow them and read them without her mother remarking on how poor her choice was for a growing young lady. She sometimes suspected that David knew all about her 'borrowing' of his books, without bothering to ask permission first. He'd certainly never made a fuss over missing a volume or two.

"I'll keep it a secret," David promised. He leaned forward. "So…do you want me to speak to the parents of some lucky fellow?"

Gwen flushed. "It isn't that kind of secret," she said, shaking her head. Young ladies sometimes asked their brothers to speak to the parents of a boy they found interesting, although society tended to frown on it. Youngsters found it dreadfully romantic, in line with running off to Gretna Green and marrying there, without their parents' permission. "It's…political."

David's eyes narrowed. "You must know that political issues could…impact on the family," he said. "Father's position in the government isn't secure…"

"I need to talk to someone," Gwen said. "Please…"

"I won't breathe a word of it," David promised. "But I expect you to listen to my advice in return."

Gwen nodded. Whatever else could be said about her brother, he was a man of his word. A reputation for not keeping his word would have destroyed his business career – and his chances of entering government once he'd passed the business on to his children. High Society admired a man who kept his word, if only because he could be relied upon to keep secrets. Besides, David was her brother. And he had always looked out for her.

"It started after I chased the…rogue magician away from your house," she said. The whole tale came pouring out, save only Lucy and her Healing talent. That was something Gwen intended to keep to herself, if only until she had managed to figure out how to use the talent herself. Logically, it should be part of her abilities. David listened in silence as Gwen told the story, ending with a brief description of the Sleeping Plague. "I don't know what to do."

David frowned, thoughtfully. "Master Thomas will not be happy when he finds out that you didn't tell him about this," he said, slowly. "Withholding evidence is a criminal offence."

"I know," Gwen said, miserably. "I don't know what to do."

"The anarchists struck last night, according to the newspapers," David said. "They blew up a building in the middle of London, just to irritate the government. Apparently, it was a very important building, even though no one seems to know why. Maybe one of those places where they hold secret talks with the French or the Russians…"

Gwen frowned. She'd seen a certain building in the middle of London last night…and Lord Blackburn had been injured. What if…?

"This building," she said, carefully. "Did they say where it was?"

"I dare say they did," David said. He stood up and rooted through a mass of papers on an otherwise clean table until he found a copy of *The Times*. "There wasn't much point in keeping the details to themselves. An explosion in the heart of London wouldn't be easy to miss."

Gwen looked down at the paper…and muttered a very unladylike word under her breath. Unless she was much mistaken, the farm – the building where female magicians were impregnated by male magicians – had been destroyed. The newspaper story didn't say how many people had been killed, or why, but Gwen suspected that there had been at least ten women kept there. And Jack – she had no doubt that it was his work – had killed them all, almost killing Lord Blackburn in the process.

"David," she confessed, "I don't know what to do. I don't even know which side I'm on."

David put a hand on her shoulder. "What do you mean?"

"I saw…I saw the way people live," Gwen said. The memories would stay with her for the rest of her life. "I saw men driven to drink because they could do nothing else with their lives. I saw women selling their bodies because it was the only way to make ends meet. I saw children wandering the streets, becoming pickpockets or worse, learning to survive in a harsh and utterly unforgiving environment. And I saw magicians taking women who had magical talents and breeding them…"

She broke off. "No wonder they call it the farm," she said, bitterly. "They farm women and children."

David considered it for a long moment. "But without magic," he said, "what would have happened to the Empire?"

Gwen stared down at her hands. "I understood him," she confessed, miserably. "I understood the rogue, despite what he did to you. He fights people who can't fight for themselves…he was once Master Thomas's apprentice, just like me."

"If what he told you is true," David pointed out, "he might be Master Thomas's son."

Gwen flinched. Jack had made the same observation. "David...did you ever get taken to the farm?"

Her brother flushed, answering her question without speaking a word. Gwen could understand the logic behind the farm; David's sister had powerful magic, therefore David might just be able to sire a magical child. And unlike any child he had with Laura, no one would know about one he'd sired on one of the captive magicians. The establishment could do what they liked with such a child. But they couldn't be doing something right, or they would have more Masters and Master Thomas wouldn't have needed Gwen.

"I thought...I was wrong," David said, finally. "I..."

"I know," Gwen said. She'd known that her brother had used whores, but she'd never imagined the farm. "I'm sorry."

"I could have a child out there," David said, distraught. "I could have a dozen children I don't even know I have."

"True," Gwen agreed. She fought for control, fought to keep her mind steady against the helplessness threatening to drive her into depression. What could she do? What *should* she do? "I don't know what to do..."

"I was in France a few years ago," David said. Gwen nodded, remembering how she'd begged and pleaded with her mother to be allowed to travel with her brother. David hadn't yet married Laura when he'd gone. "I met one of the men who'd organised the crushing of the Paris Commune, back in the 1790s."

He shook his head, slowly. "The French rebels wanted revenge on the aristocracy," he added. "So they killed the police and they took the city and they killed every aristocrat they could catch, burning their homes to the ground. And then they killed the merchants, the Jews, the money-lenders...and everyone else they didn't like. And then..."

David looked up at her, grimly. "They ate themselves alive," he said. "The rebels tore Paris apart long before the army arrived to restore order. Can you imagine what would have happened if they'd had a chance to take the entire country? They would have spread a bloody red terror over France, slaughtering everyone who knew how to make the country work...

"And now France is a despotic state, with fat King Louis on

the Throne, mandatory Church services and no representation from the people at all," he concluded. "And if your friend Jack happens to win, that's what will happen to London."

Gwen closed her eyes, wishing – for the first time – that she'd never been born with magic.

"So," she said, finally. David was right. She knew that he was right. "What do we do about it?"

"I don't know," David admitted. "I just don't know."

Chapter Twenty-Nine

o one had ever escaped from the Tower of London.

Or at least that was the official story. Historically, the Tower of London had served first as a Royal Residence, and then as an arsenal, a garrison and a prison for certain select prisoners. Elizabeth the Great, in the years before she'd succeeded Bloody Mary as Queen, had spent many days in the Tower, as had Sir Walter Raleigh and John Wilkes. Jack wasn't surprised to discover that Lucy and the other prisoners had been sent to the Tower. It had always held political prisoners. Besides, unlike any of the other prisons in London, it was effectively impregnable. Maybe a few had escaped, over the years, but the Tower's reputation remained intact.

Disguised as a beggar, Jack slowly made his way around the outer wall. The Tower of London had been renovated in 1801 after the first wave of unrest had begun lapping at the foundations of British society. It was now the main garrison for British troops in the City of London, with enough supplies and men to hold against anything up to a full-scale assault. Jack could see ways in which airships could be used to outflank the tower's defences, but capturing an airship would be difficult.

There were enough troops manning the defences to deter any offensive from the civilian population. Jack had gone up against worse odds in the past, but the presence of at least a dozen combat magicians gave him pause. The Tower of London was also the only prison in Britain to hold magicians, the result of years of careful construction work by the Royal College. There was enough magic infused into its structure to hold any magician, even a Master. Jack knew that most rogue magicians were simply executed after capture, but some were kept alive for years. And if they knew what they had, the establishment would be sure to keep Lucy alive. Healing was a very useful talent, but it wouldn't help her to escape captivity. They could cross-breed her with their magicians and see if her children were Healers.

He scowled as a pair of Bow Street Runners passed him, threatening to kick him into the Thames if he didn't go beg somewhere else. Mimicking the stoop of a wounded war veteran from North Africa or India, he hobbled along back around the tower and out onto the streets. Beggars were not welcome in London, but the establishment generally tolerated their presence. There were even a handful of charities set up to try to help the poor and destitute. They would be more popular if they weren't run by people more interested in preaching to the helpless than helping them learn a trade or recover from their injuries. The thought ground at him as he caught sight of Traitor's Gate, the Tower's private dock. Its prisoners were brought up the river and into the tower without ever having a chance to escape. Only a madman – or someone desperate to escape – would risk swimming in the Thames after the factories established upstream had started to flood the river with their wastes.

Cursing under his breath, Jack kept inching away from the tower, stopping every passer-by to beg for alms. A handful of people gave him coins, but most of them shuffled away as soon as they saw him. Jack rolled his eyes inwardly as he made his way down the street and away from the Tower of London. Behind him, he knew, Lucy and a handful of his friends were rotting in captivity. The Tower was famous for its array of torture equipment – and everyone broke, eventually. And if they made Lucy talk...the consequences could be disastrous.

It took him nearly an hour to make his way out of the richer part of the city and into a cramped alleyway. A passing policeman took a few moments to harass him, clearly intent on shaking him down for whatever money the helpless beggar had collected. Jack wanted to kill him – it would have been so easy – but he had to settle for using Charm to convince the policeman that he had nothing worth taking. He promised himself that he would remember the policeman's face. There would be a reckoning some day in the future.

A loud roar announced the presence of a bear, chained to the wall. Jack blinked in surprise, and then remembered that London had recently developed a passion for bear-baiting. The bear would be poked and prodded until it was enraged, whereupon it would amuse the crowd as it tried to get at them with its teeth and claws. Jack remembered, bitterly, the days he'd spent fox-hunting, back before he'd learned the truth about his birth. It shamed him to remember that he'd once enjoyed tormenting a helpless creature. Where the poor had lost limbs for daring to poach in the vast estates owned by aristocrats, the noblemen had thought nothing of cutting vast swathes through the animal population. Jack had even heard rumours that they'd hunted men – convicts – through their hands, although he'd never participated. It was astonishing how much evil a person could inflict on another if they thought of that person as less than human.

Five minutes later, he had changed his clothes and looked more like a poor manual labourer. The bear roared again and Jack had an idea. Pushing the beast back with his magic, he pressed his hand against the chain and Changed its composition, carefully weakening it. When the bear started to pull against its chain, it would break, giving its tormentors a nasty surprise. He was still grinning when he walked out of the alleyway, abandoning the beggar's stoop, and headed down towards the docks. Davy and his subordinates should be waiting for him there.

And one of them was a traitor, he thought, bitterly. The stench of the docks – the mixture of raw fish, labourers and exotic goods from all over the empire – reached him and made him cough, even as he mulled the problem over and over in his mind. One of them had betrayed the cause – or had he? Magic could have made someone talk, or perhaps one of the Seers had picked up a hint of the coming struggle. And yet...the information hadn't been very precise, or they would have known about Lucy's talent. Maybe Master Thomas and the reactionaries had simply gotten lucky.

He checked around the warehouse first, watching for unpleasant surprises. There was a pair of urchins stationed around the building, standing guard where they would alert the inhabitants if the police or the army arrived in force. Jack was privately very pleased with that part of his plan – no one would think anything of seeing a few dozen street urchins scattered around the docks, where thousands of them tried to scavenge a living – and it was almost a relief when he saw that two of them were paying close attention to him. He looked just like a police spy to them.

The warehouse door opened when he tapped on it, revealing two burly men carrying staffs and pikes. No one would be surprised to see manual weapons, while firearms would draw immediate attention. Jack pulled off his cap, revealing his face, and smiled as they waved him through into the office. The business was real, thankfully; no one would see anything suspicious as long as they didn't go into the warehouse itself. And even the Bow Street Runners would hesitate before forcing their way into the building. A successful businessman could make real trouble for them.

"Jack," Davy said. The underground's nominal leader scowled at him. "I heard they got Lucy."

"They did," Jack confirmed. "They have her and the others in the Tower."

Davy nodded, reaching for a bottle of wine and pouring two glasses. Jack was of the opinion that the wine would be better off poured back into the horse, but he took a glass anyway. The underground fighters would respect a hard-drinking man.

"Someone talked," Davy said. "Who talked?"

"I don't know," Jack admitted. He'd turned the thought over and over in his mind. If any of the inner circle had turned – or broken under torture – they would have betrayed far more than just Lucy's brothel. And yet...who had known about the brothel, but not about anything else? It didn't make sense. "Someone talked to someone; maybe they didn't pick up a complete picture."

"Perhaps," Davy agreed. "This ruins our plans. If they make Lucy talk..."

"They will want her to do a great deal more for them than talk," Jack said, flatly. If they knew what they had...a thought struck him and he shivered. Perhaps Lucy and the handful of others were nothing more than bait in a trap. And *he* was the only logical target for a trap. "We have to get her out of there."

Davy stared at him. "It's the time for pulling in our horns," he said, sharply. "We have to evacuate, now!"

"No," Jack said, equally sharply. "We have got to push

ahead, before the whole plan comes undone."

"You're mad," Davy said. "You *do* know how heavily defended the Tower of London happens to be?" Jack nodded, but Davy went on regardless. "They have at least six hundred Dragoons in the barracks, twenty Sparkers and probably others held nearby, in reserve. And you want to knock it over as if it were a coach on an isolated highway?"

"I have been a highwayman," Jack said, truthfully. He *had* raided coaches on his way out of England, back when his life had disintegrated around him. "It wasn't that hard, as long as you watched your back. Plenty of highwaymen felt it was safer to rob other highwaymen than gentry on the roads."

"You're mad," Davy repeated. He leaned forward. "I pulled the underground back together after we had our butts soundly thrashed five years ago. I managed to build up a new force, one that would push for reform and force the high and mighty toffees to change. I built up..."

"You did nothing," Jack said. He'd known that Davy resented him. Indeed, the only thing that kept him from suspecting Davy was the simple fact that Davy could have unravelled the whole plan with a few words in the right ear. "You kept your head to the ground and avoided attracting attention."

"And you fled to France," Davy thundered. "You lived in luxury while we had to cower underneath the whip! Where were you when the widows and children had to sell themselves into indenture merely to eat? Where were you when Francine Macomb was raped by the Dragoons because her husband had been caught on the barricades? Where were you when they transported thousands of people to some godforsaken island hellhole in the middle of the ocean, just for daring to aspire to something better than..."

"Shut up," Jack said, controlling himself with an effort. Magic boiled behind his eyes, a mocking reminder of the day he'd come into his powers. "In all the years you were in sole control of the movement, what did you achieve? Nothing of any consequence at all. The best you did was arrange for teachers to enter the slums in the hopes that learning to read would help to mobilise the masses. They didn't crack down on you because they didn't *need* to crack down on you. You were nothing to them!"

"And you have gone and gotten Lucy arrested," Davy

snapped. "I heard you'd had something for her, back in the day. Where were you when she was taken away to the Tower?"

Jack swallowed, hard. "I was busy," he said. "I was needed elsewhere."

Davy glared at him. "Where?"

"That's something I have to keep to myself," Jack said. Davy was right; he *should* have been with Lucy. But there had been combat magicians – and perhaps Master Thomas himself – in the force that had arrested her and they would have overpowered him. Jack knew that he wouldn't have died easily, but he would have died. "In the years since I left the country, has anything gotten better for the poor?"

Davy started to speak, but Jack spoke over him. "Nothing," he said. "Back then, there were a number of liberal MPs in Parliament. We could hope for change, but they broke the movement when we merely asked for a say in how the country was governed. Now...there are few liberal MPs and Lord Liverpool can crack down on us however the hell he likes. And he feels that he can do it without needing to fear our response."

"You didn't grow up in a slum," Davy snapped. "You never had to struggle for food. You never had to listen to your children crying because they couldn't find anything to eat. You never had to explain to them that they couldn't have fine clothes because you couldn't earn enough to pay for them..."

"I know," Jack said, as evenly as he could. "Davy...I know that we were never close, but you know as well as I do that we have to get Lucy out. The alternative is to abandon the plan and hide, leaving behind all the supplies we amassed for the uprising. And if they work out what we had in mind, it will be much harder to overthrow them in the next few decades. Perhaps there will be another revolution in America, or another rebellion in India, but I don't think that we can count on it. The time is now."

Davy sighed, all the fight slowly seeming to seep out of him. "But they're in the Tower of London," he said. "I have a few contacts with the Warders, but they won't help us get them out..."

Jack nodded. "I have a plan," he said. An idea was slowly forming inside his mind. "How many men could you get to the Tower without being noticed?"

Davy snorted. "I think the government would notice an army marching through London," he said, dryly. "It is the kind of thing that tends to draw attention."

"Maybe they'd be too shocked to react," Jack commented. The last time London had been seriously threatened by an army had been during the Civil War. And that affair was very embarrassing, as no one was quite sure who had won. "But I have a better idea."

"They're going to keep them under guard," Davy said. "You know how many men they'll have watching the prisoners..."

"Just find out where they're being kept," Jack said. "And then I want ten men who are willing to risk their lives on a thoroughly crazy plan."

Davy snorted. "I'm going to hate it, aren't I?"

"Don't worry," Jack said. "You don't have to come along. You'd better stay here and stay in contact with our army. We don't want someone starting the uprising before we're ready for it."

***

Night was falling over London by the time Davy returned to the warehouse. Jack had spent the time sitting on the roof, turning the concept into a workable plan. If nothing else, he told himself firmly, it would have the benefit of being unthinkable. No one in their right mind would expect Jack to stake everything on one throw of the dice. But Master Thomas knew him...the Royal Sorcerer would have to be diverted, somehow. And only one person could do that...

He'd thought of contacting Gwen, but she wouldn't have made up her mind which way to jump. Besides, if – when – she worked out that he'd blown up the farm with the girls inside, she wouldn't be happy. Jack knew that there had been no way to get the girls out, even if they'd wanted to come, but Gwen wouldn't see it that way.

Instead, he'd studied a copy of the latest Bradshaw railway and airship timetable, considering each step bit by bit. Breaking down a concept into multiple sections was something he'd learned from Master Thomas. Somehow, he doubted that his former tutor would approve of what he did with the lesson.

"They're being held inside the Tower's upper levels," Davy reported. "The Warders are in a right royal sulk over the presence of so many combat magicians – and the Dragoons are irritating the hell out of them. It seems that some of the soldiers have been flirting with their wives and daughters..."

"If you can call it flirting," Jack agreed. The soldiers of the British Empire were not known for delicate manners. They'd won an empire, defeating uppity local rulers and crushing rebels, but their behaviour off campaign left a great deal to be desired. It was one of the reasons why the government tried to keep the regiments overseas. They tended to cause colossal local resentment whenever they were billeted on any part of the country.

"...And some of them feel that the Prime Minister has overreached himself," Davy continued. "But they probably wouldn't agree to help us openly."

"No," Jack said. "We don't need them anyway."

He stood up. "We have to move as quickly as possible," he said. "We'll have everything in place within the next two days. And then we will rescue them..."

"Or die in the attempt," Davy pointed out. "Are you sure that this is going to work?"

"Probably," Jack said. "I want you to gather all of the magicians in the underground at...Clark's Pub. They're going to be needed for the diversion. And then I want one of the Welsh mining experts..."

Davy held up a hand. "You're going to dig a tunnel into the Tower of London?"

Jack grinned at him. "Of course not," he said. The Tower of London would have magical protections against someone trying to dig an escape route out of the castle. A number of very prominent people had been imprisoned there over the years and most of them had had allies on the outside. "My plan is far crazier than that. No one will see it coming."

"I really hope you're right," Davy said. "And what happens if you should happen to die in the attempt?"

Jack allowed his smile to widen. "That really won't be my problem, will it?"

Chapter Thirty

y name is Irene Adler," the woman said. "Perhaps you have heard of me?"

Gwen frowned. Irene was tall, with a face that seemed too elegant to be beautiful. Long dark hair framed her pale face, falling down her back to her rear. She wore a simple dark dress, topped by a bonnet that called attention to her face. Lady Mary would have envied her poise, Gwen suspected, but there seemed to be something about Irene that didn't quite make sense. And Master Thomas had introduced Gwen to her and then left the room.

Something clicked in Gwen's mind. "You're a magician, a woman magician," she said. "I thought I was the only one."

"The only openly practicing one," Irene corrected. Her voice was soft, almost musical. "Can you identify my talent?"

Gwen, who disliked being tested, scowled. "You're not a Master – unless you've been hiding your light under a bushel," she said, tartly. "You have to have something special, or…"

She felt an odd tickling at the back of her mind and looked up, sharply. "You're a Talker," she said. "And you're trying to read my mind."

"Very little to read," Irene said, but she was smiling as she said it. "I am one of the most powerful and capable Talkers in the world. I spent several years in Europe, moving from Austria to Prussia to France, reading minds and gathering intelligence for my superiors. If I hadn't run afoul of a nobleman in Bohemia, I'd be in France still. No one suspects a girl whose only known talent is to sing like an angel and push her chest out at the right moments."

Gwen had to smile. "And so you read their minds," she said. "What have you found out?"

"That men lose the ability to think clearly when they're trying to keep their eyes off your breasts," Irene said, and winked. Gwen flushed. "Am I too crude for you? I've never regretted being what I am, not when Lord Mycroft pays me through the nose to gather intelligence for him. Would you like to know what the Crown Prince of France has in mind for his reign when his father finally shuffles off the mortal coil?"

"Not particularly," Gwen said. The tickling at the back of her mind was still there. "Why are you reading my mind?"

"Force of habit," Irene said. Her smile widened. "That...and Master Thomas has asked me to help you develop mental shields. You're going to need them when you become the Royal Sorcerer."

She waved Gwen to a seat – as grandly as any queen – and took the seat facing her. "One thing about acting is true of mental powers as well," she said. "It isn't enough to say something; you have to deliver the lines with conviction – you actually have to *become* the person you're playing. Have you ever seen a play?"

Gwen shook her head. Going to the theatre – even the renowned Globe Theatre in London – was not ladylike behaviour. And besides, she'd never been particularly interested in acting, or even dressing up, as a child. Lady Mary had been quite concerned about that, although the older Gwen suspected that her mother's performance at balls and parties was at least partly an act. Few people were that confident naturally.

"You should go see a few," Irene said. "Would people admire a Romeo who declared his love for Juliet in flat, unconvincing tones? You have to put yourself in the character's shoes and play the role to perfection – and if you can't, you're in the wrong career."

"Women rarely take to the stage," Gwen pointed out. Even she knew that, although she also knew that at least one of the bawdy actresses had become one of the King's mistresses. "And I don't know how to act."

"Wear one dress; become a noblewoman," Irene said. "Wear rags; become a sewing woman sitting in a room, weaving dresses for pennies. It's all about presentation, really."

Her eyes narrowed suddenly. "And what were you doing last night, young lady?" She demanded, in stern tones. "Were you properly escorted when William walked you home?"

Gwen had to laugh. Irene had changed, becoming the very picture of a stern mother of aristocratic linage. The Talker laughed and relaxed back into her confident poise, although Gwen had to remind herself that that might just be another act. Just who was the real Irene?

"It hardly matters," Irene said. Gwen flushed, feeling…violated. Irene could invade her thoughts. "You don't have to worry about that, I'm afraid. All you have to do is worry about keeping nosy parkers like myself out of your mind."

She reached out and took Gwen's hand in hers. "Talking requires discipline, right from the start," she said. "Those who cannot build mental shields in their minds often go mad, unable to separate their thoughts from the thoughts of everyone else within range. Even when you do learn to control the ability, it can be hard to lower your shields and listen to another person's thoughts. A person with very strong thoughts might overwhelm you and you might find yourself lost in their mind."

Gwen frowned. "Like a Charmer can slip a thought into your mind," she said, slowly. "You wouldn't be able to tell the difference between one of your thoughts and one of theirs."

"Basically," Irene agreed. "Most Talkers can only really link their minds to other Talkers. The ones who can actually read mundane minds…well, they're rare. I don't think that you will ever develop that ability for yourself, but you will be able to send messages around the world. I believe that that would come in handy, wouldn't it?"

She winked. "I heard about your rooftop chase," she added. "Wouldn't it be useful to be able to send a message to someone when you're attacked by rebels?"

"Yes," Gwen said. Irene's words reminded her of things she had to keep secret – and why Parliament was so concerned about Talkers. "Can you teach me to do that?"

"Of course," Irene said. She sat upright and winked at Gwen. "I want you to close your eyes and slowly relax every part of your body."

Gwen frowned, puzzled. "Why…?"

"Because the body is the house of the mind and must be relaxed so that the mind can follow likewise," Irene said. "Now…please close your eyes and relax."

Gwen did so, as best as she could. Thoughts kept surfacing in her mind, reminding her of things she had to keep secret – either because they were dangerous, or embarrassing. The day she'd started her womanly cycles had been one of surprise and horror, when she'd believed that something was dreadfully wrong with her. Her mother hadn't told her anything about being female and the textbooks she'd read had only mentioned monthly cycles in the most elusive language. And then there was her brief meeting with Jack…everything she wanted to keep to herself bubbled up into her mind, there for Irene to read. Cold determination flowed through her as she concentrated on her breathing. She *would* learn to master this talent, if only for her own safety.

"Breathe in…and out," Irene said, gently. "Breathe in…and out. Let your body relax, bit by bit. Relax into the chair; let all the tension fade away from your muscles. Breathe in…and out; breathe in…and out. Breathe in…"

Gwen was suddenly very aware of the pounding of her heart. Slowly, it started to fade, dropping down to a slow, but steady beat. In the darkness, she could almost feel sleep prowling at the corner of her mind. Irene's voice – urging her to breathe in and out – seemed to be coming from very far away. It would be so easy to fall into sleep.

"I want you to visualise your own body," Irene said. Gwen concentrated, recalling what she'd seen in the mirror after dressing herself. "I want you to think of yourself floating in the midst of a vast ocean, all alone in the night. Focus on the image; concentrate until you can almost feel your presence. Allow your mind to drift, but hold the image in front of your mind's eye. Breathe in…and out. Breathe in…and out."

Gwen felt as if she were drifting, her mind slowly sinking into a vast ocean of thought. Now that she had grasped it, she was suddenly aware of whispers at the back of her mind. Automatically, she reached out towards them, only to find her mental tendrils falling apart in her mind. She heard what she was sure was a giggle, although she couldn't place its origin. It didn't feel like part of her mind. A second nexus of thought was right in front of her, glimmering in the darkness of her mind's eye...

...And then there was contact.

Hello, Gwen, Irene thought. *Can you hear me?*

Gwen started...and the contact broke. It left her feeling unsettled, as if something vitally important had been lost. Her eyes snapped open and she saw Irene looking back at her, a sparkle in her devilishly green eyes. The spy grinned at her as Gwen started to close her eyelids, reaching down inside her for the quiet place she'd found. Instead, she could sense tendrils of thought reaching out from Irene towards her. They were probing into her mind.

You can stop me, Irene said. Her mental voice sounded vastly amused. *All you have to do is keep me out.*

But how do I do that? Gwen thought. Her thoughts seemed to dance in the air between them; Irene was a presence within her mind. It was confusing, as if Irene was all around her and within her...almost a part of Gwen's mind. *What do I do?*

She remembered, suddenly, visiting the madhouse with Master Thomas. He'd taught her how to build a barrier within her mind. Slowly, recalling the image of herself floating in a vast ocean, she built a mental barrier around her. The thoughts kept fragmenting, as if the barrier was built out of eggshells, but she learned rapidly. If the barrier's strength depended upon what she chose to use to construct it – what mental representation she used within her mind – she would build it out of the strongest possible materials. Great bricks of cold iron materialised within her mind and started to form into a wall. Irene's mind seemed to hop back, and then she was within Gwen again. And the wall was still in place.

This isn't real, Irene thought. She was definitely laughing now, Gwen realised. Cold anger flared through her mind. *This is the realm of the mind. Your wall may shield one angle of attack, but there are so many of them...*

As if Irene's thought had showed it to her, Gwen realised that she was right. The wall she'd built might block anyone walking down a path, but Irene could climb over the wall or dig under it. Thinking rude thoughts, Gwen rebuilt the wall all around her mind, a solid sphere with no way in – or out. Irene – and the whispering at the back of her mind – snapped out of existence. Gwen blinked in astonishment and then realised that she'd been picking up on outside thoughts without being fully aware of what she was doing. If she'd been nothing but a Talker, she might well have gone mad before anyone realised what was wrong.

She opened her eyes and saw Irene smiling at her. "Not too shabby," Irene said. "And now...let's see if you can keep the wall in place."

Gwen had no time to react before Irene's power slammed into her mind. It was a metaphorical battle, fought – or thought – with concepts rather than real weaponry, but none the less real for all that. Her mental barrier – a solid sphere of iron – melted as Irene created a blazing stream of fire and started to burn her way through the wall. Gwen couldn't believe it, and then realised that because she'd created her barrier out of iron, it could be melted. She hastily imagined the barrier as composed of water instead, and then switched back to Iron.

The battle seemed to spin out of control. Irene would lunge forward, threatening to crack the barrier, and then alter the angle of her attack, forcing Gwen to think rapidly to keep up with her. Maintaining the barrier in the face of a determined onslaught was mortifyingly difficult, even when she realised that there was nothing stopping her from deeming the barrier unbreakable. But then she had to hold it firmly in place, or her confidence would weaken and the barrier would be destroyed. She quite lost track of time and was surprised when Irene called a halt. They'd been skirmishing for over two hours, and yet it had felt like nothing.

"You have the home ground in your mind," Irene said, as one of the maids brought them tea and cakes. Irene poured Gwen a cup and she sipped gratefully. "You determine the mental terrain, something that gives you a powerful advantage. But it only works if you train yourself to recognise when someone is trying to peek into your thoughts – they have to enter your mind – and to keep a barrier in place at all times."

Her smile widened. "But you also have to avoid concentrating too hard on the barrier," she added. "Can you guess why?"

Gwen hesitated, unsure. She'd had to hold the barrier firmly in her mind when Irene had been reaching into her, or it would have shattered. If she'd had to keep the barrier in place while chasing Jack across the rooftops...she realised what Irene meant and swore aloud. No one, not even Master Thomas, would be able to maintain a formidable barrier in the heat of a battle. Her thoughts could be raided while she fought her opponents in the physical world.

"Not too far wrong," Irene said, once Gwen had finally put it into words. "But there's another point."

She reached forward and tapped Gwen lightly on the forehead. "You were concentrating on stopping my mental assault so hard that you couldn't have stopped me if I'd punched you in the throat," she said. Gwen flushed with embarrassment. Irene was right. "Something I've noticed about magicians is that they tend to become dependent upon their magic to protect them, thinking that it makes them invincible. But a bullet will kill a Blazer as surely as a burst of magic; a Mover cannot concentrate on more than a few items at once...and a Charmer's powers are useless, if his opponent happens to be deaf."

Irene smiled. "If you happen to want to kill a Charmer, block up your ears," she added. "And a Talker can be distracted by too many people surrounding him..."

Gwen nodded, impatiently.

"I think you need to learn to fight hand-to-hand," Irene said. "I'll speak to Master Thomas about finding you a trainer. It isn't particularly lady-like, but being able to fight with your bare hands may save your life one day."

"I know how to fire a pistol," Gwen said, flatly. Master Thomas had insisted that she learn, pointing out that pistols could be reloaded, while using magic could lead to exhaustion. "And I know how to use a dagger."

"And you'll know how to use everything else once we get you a proper trainer," Irene said, remorselessly. "Now...it's time to start focusing on sending a mental message."

She looked directly at Gwen. *Hello Gwen,* she thought. *You can hear me.*

Gwen nodded, not trusting herself to speak.

"I pushed my own thought at you," Irene said. "It's the basic Talker talent; only a handful of Talkers can do any more than send messages to other Talkers. When I was trying to read your mind, I opened a link between us; if you can't open that link for yourself, you won't be able to read minds."

"I see," Gwen said. "Can Master Thomas read minds?"

"If he can, he's kept it to himself," Irene said. "You'd be surprised to know that a number of aristocrats have empathic talents. They keep them to themselves, using them for their own advantage. I...never really wanted a life of fancy gowns and vapid chattering about the weather. My parents disowned me ten years ago."

Gwen had to smile, sensing that she'd found a kindred soul. She'd never really had a proper friend, not when she'd been kept at home ever since her magic had flared into life. Who among High Society could have understood her?

"I used to sing in the opera before going to Austria," Irene added. "My parents never got over the shock.

"But enough of such thoughts," she concluded. "Try to send a message to me."

Gwen concentrated. *Irene*, she thought. *Can you hear me*?

"You muttered the message aloud," Irene said. "That's a very bad habit, so try to lose it at once. This time...think the message aloud, without speaking."

Irene, Gwen thought. It was harder than it seemed, but she felt part of her mind unlocking as soon as she shaped the thought. She had to speak without speaking...it took a moment to work out how to do it. *Can you hear me*?

Yes, Irene sent back. *Can you hear me?*

Gwen nodded. "I want you to listen to the next thought," Irene said, "and tell me what you make of it."

Gwen, Irene thought. *You have dark hair.*

Gwen recoiled. The thought was...unclean. No, it was a lie; her blonde hair wasn't dark. And that meant...?

"It's very hard to deliberately lie mind-to-mind," Irene explained. "The sender knows that he is telling a lie and something of that will leak through to the receiver. But..."

"If the sender doesn't know he's lying, it won't feel like a lie," Gwen said. Irene nodded in agreement. "It will feel like the unvarnished truth."

"It's something to watch," Irene said. "When things have gone wrong, it normally happens because the sender genuinely thought he was telling the truth."

She clapped her hands together and settled back into her chair. "And now...it's time to see if you can reach someone else," she added. "Why not give Master Thomas a call?"

Gwen looked at her. "If I sent a mental message to someone," she said, "could someone else intercept it?"

"Only if your mind leaked," Irene said. "We'll cover that in a later session. Now...give Master Thomas a call. He's been waiting to hear from you."

Chapter Thirty-One

mpressive, isn't she?"

"That she is," Jack agreed, gravely. The airfield boy was keen, determined to impress his charges with the sheer majesty of the *Britannia Clipper*. Jack remembered being just as fascinated when the first airships had been launched into the air, great ugly bags of hydrogen gas that promised a global revolution. "I have never seen a more exciting airship."

Despite himself, he *was* impressed. Two hundred and fifty yards long, the airship was a giant among a flock of minnows. She'd been built to make the long journey over France, across the Mediterranean, through Egypt and finally to India, a record-breaking journey that linked the different sections of the British Empire together into a seamless whole. A second airship of her class was reputed to be intended to go from London to New York, but so far she hadn't entered service. The passengers tended to balk at the idea of spending so long above the ocean.

She was a massive cigar, painted with the colours of the British Empire and a hugely idealised set of images of its subjects. George, the King-Emperor, was followed by a Red Indian, a Sikh and a yellow-skinned Chinaman, all looking up worshipfully towards the British lion. Jack happened to know that all three of the followers had not only been beaten, but crushed by British military force. Given time, China would no doubt follow India into the British Empire. The airship wasn't just a flying monument to British aeronautical engineering, but a triumphant acclamation of the deeds that had built the empire. It was nothing more than a distraction, Jack suspected, to keep the poor from realising that the British Empire served no one, but its aristocratic masters.

He smiled as the long line of passengers slowly advanced into the airship. The tickets were enormously expensive even for the aristocracy and the *Britannia Clipper* was always undersubscribed. It had been easy to purchase ten seats on the airship, even without papers that proclaimed Jack and his men to be aristocrats. Besides, successful businessmen could hope to be ennobled and conscripted into the ruling class. The airship staff wouldn't show them any disrespect, at least not in public. A businessman would have the money and the contacts to make their lives very unpleasant.

Darkness fell over him as he walked into the airship's massive shadow and up the steps into the gondola. The sound of its engines warming up slowly made him smile, even as he glanced up at the mighty blades thrashing through the air. The *Britannia Clipper* was supposed to be able to make the trip from London to Cairo without refuelling, although the flight plan stated that there would be a brief delay in France to allow the richer customers a chance to visit Paris. Jack and his men were the only ones who knew that the *Britannia Clipper* would never leave England. In the end, as they filed on board the airship, Jack was almost disappointed by how easy it had been to get into the ship. No one had even insisted on checking their papers.

Inside, the entire aircraft was luxurious. Wood panelling covered the bulkheads, while comfortable seats were strategically positioned next to portholes. The richer passengers could, for a small gratuity, even walk out onto the balcony and feel the wind blowing against their faces. Jack had a feeling that any aristocrat who couldn't use magic to save himself would probably refrain from going outside. The wind might blow them off the airship and down towards the ground far below.

The cabin crew bustled from seat to seat, offering drinks to the passengers and answering their questions. One middle-aged woman was almost a nervous wreck, to the disgust of the woman next to her and her two small boys. The grandma finally snapped at her daughter to shut up and keep her brats under control. Jack smiled to himself as he buckled himself in, even though there was supposed to be no need to do so on an airship. Safety came first, or so the pamphlets advertising the flights claimed, even though they were disingenuous. A single spark in the wrong place and the hydrogen would go up like a bomb. No one would escape an explosion in mid-air.

A dull thrumming ran through the airship as it slowly started to rise into the sky. Jack allowed himself a tight smile as he beckoned to one of the hostesses, a young woman wearing a skirt that would have outraged the Church if she'd worn it in London. Londoners could be surprisingly puritanical at times, but as always laws that applied to the poor didn't apply to the rich. Besides, the airship was well away from London's streets. It was almost a different world.

"I'd like to see a list of passengers," he said, allowing Charm to slip into his voice. The hostess nodded in agreement. Airships had often served as quiet meeting places for people who would never have been seen together on the surface. She slipped away and returned two minutes later with a long list of names. Jack's smile deepened as he scanned the list. There were over thirty rich and powerful citizens on the ship, each one a hostage to his plan. No one would take risks with so many important lives at stake.

He nodded to his men and stood up, making the walk towards the bridge. A cabin boy stood there on guard, but Jack gave him a silver crown and he stood aside, convinced that Jack and his party were merely men who wanted to watch as the airship rose over London. The hatch opened, revealing a complex system of controls linked to the steam engines that powered the fans driving the airship through the air. He'd once read a paper talking about the possibilities of heavier-than-air flight, but that would be some years in the future. Airships were here and now.

The airship's captain looked up in surprise. He was older than Jack had expected, wearing a uniform grand enough to satisfy an Admiral. Jack had expected as much. Passenger liners at sea always ensured that their men had fancy uniforms – even the engineering crew who normally remained below decks – and the airship lines had copied their fashion. It was just another way to convey the feeling that one was travelling on a luxury flight. One day, Jack promised himself, the entire population would be able to afford airship flights.

"Gentlemen," the Captain said. "I'm afraid that we have to ask you to leave..."

Jack chuckled and produced his pistol from his belt. The

Captain's eyes went very wide. No one had ever dared to hijack an airship before, even though they often carried very rich passengers. Airships were simply too difficult to rob while they were in the air, leaving the criminals nowhere to run. It wasn't enough to deter a magician who could effectively fly, but Jack wanted to keep his magic to himself as long as possible. It would serve as an ace in the hole.

"Good morning, Captain," he said. Below them, London was illuminated by the rising sun. They were high enough to see no traces of the squalor that most citizens were forced to endure. It almost seemed a magical city from above. "I'm afraid that we're taking you and your airship hostage. If you cooperate, none of you will be harmed."

The Captain scowled at him, angrily. "You won't get away with this, you scoundrel," he growled. Jack was almost impressed by his pluck. The anarchists – he wouldn't take them for anything else – would probably want a victim to show that they were serious. "You'll be caught and damn well hung."

"Perhaps," Jack agreed. He looked up at the three officers manning the controls. "I want you to cooperate with us. If you do as you're told, you will be released unharmed."

He laced Charm into his voice, enough to keep them biddable. Charm wasn't entirely reliable in such circumstances, but it would have to suffice. Besides, they had to know that Jack couldn't escape. There was literally nowhere to go, as long as one was bound by conventional thinking. Jack smiled as the Captain and two of his officers were tied up and positioned against one of the bulkheads, out of the way. The third officer, the steering master, had to be kept in position. Jack had no idea how to fly an airship and he didn't have time to learn.

"Take us over London," he ordered. The orders would be reassuring to his captives, he knew. They weren't scheduled for a flight to Cardiff or Southampton and the people on the ground would know that something was wrong. Wherever they flew, the Bow Street Runners would follow. And that would make them complacent. "Take us right up the Thames."

He left two of his men guarding the bridge and walked through the airship. The passengers had only started to realise that something was wrong, far too late for any action that would allow them to retake the ship. Jack and the rest of his men herded them into lockable compartments – it was odd that the airship's interior had almost been designed as a prison – and sealed them in. A pair of hostesses and several of the female passengers were having hysterics. Jack ignored them once they were all secured, ensuring that they wouldn't be able to interfere. They'd be safe enough once the crisis was over. Only God – and whoever was in command at the Tower of London – would determine if they survived the day.

The airship creaked as it turned and headed up the Thames. Jack recalled reading that some airship flight paths were determined by rivers, rather than dry land. It made a certain kind of sense – a crashing airship would devastate the surrounding territory – but very few airships ever flew up the Thames. Jack smiled and forced his heart to slow down, breathing deeply until he was calm. It wouldn't do to lose control too early, not when the plan had only just begun. Besides, win or lose, they were about to shock the hell out of the established order. Nothing would ever be the same again.

Norton met him near the great cargo hatches that were supposed to allow cargo to be disembarked from the airship. "I've gathered everything I can," he said. Jack had given him very specific orders, orders that only Norton and Jack himself could follow. "It seems a shame to waste it."

"We'd never be able to spend it all anyway," Jack reminded him. The underground had occasionally hijacked trains, but the pickings had been slim and often lost to criminal organisations. "We need to keep the bastards guessing as soon as we reveal ourselves."

He strode back through the airship, checked the locked doors out of habit, and then returned to the bridge. The Captain was still outraged, threatening the hijackers with everything from keelhauling to slow torture and death. Jack eventually silenced him by stuffing a filthy cloth into his mouth before turning to his men. The Tower of London was slowly coming into view in the distance. Below them, the shipping on the river was already picking up. There would be hundreds of ships on the river by the time they launched their attack.

"I want you to hover over the Tower," he ordered. There was no time for risks, so he pushed as much Charm as he could into his voice. The pilot would eventually break free, but by then it would be a moot point anyway. "Take us low, so low that they cannot shoot at us without risking a crash."

He closed his eyes and expanded his mind. Below him, the garrison would be reacting slowly to the airship's presence, assuming that they realised that something was badly wrong. He had to assume the worst, but the garrison wouldn't be able to simply open fire on the ship. Quite apart from the danger of the airship crashing on top of their position, they would be sentencing a number of very rich, powerful and well-connected individuals to death. Any of the garrison who survived the crash would find themselves being called to account by relatives of the victims.

The combat magicians would pose another problem, he reminded himself. There was so much magic infused into the Tower of London that he literally couldn't send his astral presence through its walls. The magicians would include Movers who would be able to fly up to the airship and board it, or Blazers who might try to bring it down. And if they worked out what was going on, they might even be able to kill the prisoners before Jack and his team could rescue them. He was counting on them being too surprised to react effectively. Now, with the airship slowly lowering itself onto the Tower of London, he felt almost nervous. He'd been in worse situations, he told himself, but it didn't work. No one had ever tried using an airship to mount an aerial assault in the past, even when they'd first been invented. And no one had used one of the flying craft to bombard a garrison from well out of reach of the defenders' weapons.

"Keep us here," he ordered, and headed back to the cargo bays. Norton had already opened them, revealing the Tower of London below the airship. The pilot had been reluctant to go lower, pointing out that they might come down on top of the tower and die in the explosion. "Norton, are you ready?"

"Yes," Norton said. He nodded to the first batch of items. "They're ready for you."

Jack grinned. Norton was an Infuser, an Infuser who had developed tastes that only the underworld could supply. He'd paid for his habit by creating magical artefacts for a series of crime lords, until Jack had finally recruited him into the underground. His drug habit was expensive and Jack had offered a massive payment for the raid on the Tower of London, but the Infuser looked nervous. The whole enterprise was insanely risky and capture would mean certain death.

"Good," he said. Magic rose to his fingertips as he contemplated the small pile of items, each one glowing with magical power. "Let's go."

He picked up the first item with his magic and hurled it down towards the barracks below. Soldiers and combat magicians were scurrying around like ants, staring up at the immense airship. They had no time to run as the first item hit the ground and exploded. There was no particular skill in creating magical grenades, after all; Jack could have done it for himself if he'd had the time. The Royal Airship Corps had devised plans to drop bombs on enemy targets from the sky. Jack had taken their concept and improved upon it. Bomb after bomb struck the ground and exploded, scattering the defences. The handful of soldiers positioned on the roof of Traitor's Tower – as it had been renamed after the years of unrest – were unable to even shoot back. Jack chuckled as they scattered, even reaching out with his magic to pick a couple up and throw them into the open air. The guards would be running around like headless chickens, while he and his men got on with the next part of the plan.

"Keep shooting at any combat magicians who show their face," Jack ordered. The commanders of the soldiers below had either scattered or been killed in the bombardment. Some of them – the smart ones – would be trying to remove their uniforms. They might have looked splendid on parade, but they were nothing more than targeting marks for the enemy in combat. "Don't let them recover while we're up here."

He picked up another grenade and hurled it down towards the ground. It exploded with a deafening sound, scattering chunks of stone everywhere. Jack laughed at the chaos and nodded to Leo, passing command of the airship detachment to him. His second would keep up the pressure, while Jack himself moved on with stage three of the plan. Gathering his magic around him, he leapt into the air and flew down towards the roof of Traitor's Tower. Someone on the ground was watching him – a combat magician attempted to disrupt his magic and send him hurtling to the ground – but it was far too late to kill him. Besides, they had to keep their heads down to avoid Jack's snipers. They wouldn't dare show themselves, even though a Mover could shield himself against bullets. Jack suspected that they would hold back and wait for Master Thomas. Or Gwen, he reminded himself. He still had no idea which way Master Thomas's apprentice would jump, when the crunch finally came.

A shot snapped out behind him, almost taking his head off. Jack spun around, magic shimmering into existence around him, to see a guard holding a pistol. Magic flared from Jack's hands and picked the guard up, tossing him over the edge and down towards the ground, far below. There was no one else on the roof, apart from Jack himself. A handful of dead bodies were testament to the sheer surprise and power of the assault. No one had expected an assault from the skies.

Grinning, Jack walked over to the door and pressed his hands against it. It was locked, and infused with enough magic to make unlocking it difficult. Jack nodded in appreciation of the skill of the unknown Infuser, before Changing the structure of the lock. It crumbled to dust and Jack kicked the door open, staring down into the Tower of London. An explosion shook the building as Jack walked through the door and down into the Tower. A pair of guards tried to stop him, only to be blasted down with tiny bursts of magic. Neither of them posed a real threat to a magician.

The suborned Warder had kindly provided a map of where the prisoners were being held. Jack took out the locks of their cells with bursts of magic and threw them open. Lucy stared up at him in disbelief. They had all been told that no one had ever escaped from the Tower of London. The authorities rested a great deal of faith in the impregnability of the Tower – and, under normal circumstances, their faith would be entirely justified. But they'd never prepared for a rogue Master.

"Come on," he said, grinning. They were all staring at him, unable to believe their eyes. "It's time to get out of here."

Chapter Thirty-Two

ow...?"

"I told you I was a genius," Jack said, cheerfully. Lucy hugged him tightly and he was suddenly very aware of her breasts pushing against his chest. "And they never saw me coming."

The entire building shook, again. He could hear men shouting below, working up the nerve to come running up the stairs and confront the rebels. It wouldn't be long before someone in authority realised that the rebels could hardly bring the Tower down without killing themselves in the process. He let go of Lucy – reluctantly – and motioned for the others to come out of their cells. They didn't look as if they'd been tortured, which argued that the authorities had never known who they'd held. If they'd known about Lucy's talent, they would never have shut her up in the Tower of London. They would have taken her away to the farms.

"They're coming up the stairs," Owen reported. The burly Welshman had been one of Lucy's hired toughs long before he'd joined the underground. "I think they're only two floors below us."

"Head up to the roof," Jack said. "Once you get up there, climb up the ladders to safety."

He reached out with his mind and sensed two presences making their way up the stairs. The Tower of London had been designed as a fortress, the stairs carefully designed to prevent attackers from using their sword arms or advancing up in numbers. Jack took up position at the top of the stairs and readied his magic. The moment he saw an advancing skullcap, he threw a bolt of magic down towards the oncoming soldier. It dissipated in a bright shimmer of light and he swore aloud. A moment later, a twisting beam of magic missed him by seconds. Two combat magicians then, he told himself; one Blazer to attack and one Mover to cover him. It wasn't a bad tactic at all. He infused some magic into a stone, kicked it down the stairs and ran for cover. The explosion might not harm the combat magicians – the Mover was clearly covering the Blazer – but it would force them to keep their heads down. There should be just enough time for him to get himself and the captives back to the airship.

He paused, long enough to infuse more magic into stones and even parts of the floor, and then ran for the stairs. Behind him, he was grimly aware of the oncoming magicians. He'd forced them to be cautious, but they'd have to know that time was running out. He picked up one of the bodies with his magic and hurled it backwards, throwing it down the stairs. It should give the magicians something else to worry about, hopefully winning Jack a few more seconds. He felt the pressure in his mind that indicated the presence of a Talker, probably screaming to Cavendish Hall for help. Master Thomas should still be hours away, assuming that part of the plan had worked, but he did have an apprentice. He hoped – prayed – that Gwen wouldn't become involved. Jack didn't want to have to fight her before she decided which side she was on.

Lucy stopped as she reached the roof, catching sight of the airship for the first time. The Tower of London was surrounded by fires blazing upwards from where Jack's magic-infused bombs had struck the ground. Down below, the guards still looked confused and helpless, even though someone had clearly taken command. Luckily, they still appeared to be reluctant to fire on the airship. A single shot in the right place – or a burst of magic – would bring the entire plan crashing down in flames.

"My God," Lucy said. "What have you done...?"

"Stolen an airship," Jack said, casually. His team on the massive ship were already lowering rope ladders. They'd been intended for emergency evacuations, just in case the airship threatened to fall out of the sky, but Jack and his men intended to put them to much better use. "Get up the ladders, quickly. I'll cover you."

An explosion from below announced the detonation of one of his booby-traps. There was a scream, hastily cut off, suggesting that one of the magicians had been injured. Jack allowed himself a tight smile as Lucy staggered up the rope ladder, her body swaying as the wind blew across the roof. The others followed her, scrambling up into the airship's belly. None of them would ever have ridden on an airship before and Jack hoped that the prospect wouldn't terrify them into immobility. He'd once read that every airship flight had at least one person who became overwhelmed with terror when they realised that they were going up into the sky, high above the ground. It would be precisely the wrong timing if one of the rebels became frozen on the airship.

He fired a burst of magic at a magician who had appeared in the sky, flying towards the airship. The magician ducked down as the blast flashed over his head, firing back towards Jack with the pistols clutched in his hands. Jack knew that the latest pistols were renowned for being inaccurate except at close range, but he had to admire the tactic. The bastard forced him to shield himself when he had to get into the air. Behind him, the combat magicians were making their way up the stairs. They would soon be on the rooftop – and then Jack would have to fight them or lose everything.

"Get up there," he yelled, as the sound of the airship's engines grew louder. The wind was threatening to push it away from the Tower and over the Thames. "Move it!"

He didn't wait for the others to finish scrambling into the airship before he levitated himself up into the air and floated up to the hatch. A magician on the ground tried to disrupt his magic, but failed. Jack silently counted his blessings as he reached the hatch and swung himself into the airship. The remaining prisoners were helped on board the craft as the noise of the engines grew even louder. They couldn't remain hovering much longer. Norton had continued to create grenades and hurl them down towards the roof, one exploding with shocking force and seriously damaging the castle's battlements. The entire city would be able to see evidence of the raid whenever they looked at the Tower of London. There was no way that the authorities would be able to prevent word of his deeds from spreading across the world, giving new hope to those who laboured in bondage.

Lucy was staring down through the hatch as bullets started cracking through the air, alarmingly close to the gasbags. "What happens if they see us landing?" She called. It was hard to hear her over the engines. "Won't they see where we land?"

"Of course," Jack yelled back. "I'm counting on it."

He motioned for the former prisoners to leave the hatches open and hang on to the railings as he made his way back through the airship. The hostages were clearly panicking even though they didn't have any way to know what was going on outside; he could hear them screaming and banging at the sealed doors, demanding to be freed. Jack ignored them. They'd be safe enough unless someone on the ground decided to order the airship shot down and to hell with the lives of the important hostages on the craft. Instead, he reached the bridge, waved cheerfully at the fuming Captain, and spoke to the pilot. The terrified man obeyed without question.

"Take us up the Thames, as low as you can without hitting any of the bridges," Jack ordered. He'd seriously considered crashing the airship into the ground – or perhaps one of the bridges – before dismissing the thought. There was too much chance of bringing it down in one of the poorer parts of London, scoring an own goal. Besides, the authorities wouldn't hesitate to brand him and his followers as anarchists and nihilists, men and women whose only goal was chaos. "Don't worry about the magicians trying to follow us; just keep us in the air and on course."

Down below, he saw the docks as the airship slowly staggered up the Thames. The wind was growing stronger, so much so that Jack wondered absently if Master Thomas or the Royal College had discovered a weather-control talent. Or perhaps it was plain bad luck; the winds often did blow down the Thames and send a chill over London. It hardly mattered, anyway. In a few minutes it would be time to abandon ship.

Returning to the hold, he looked down at the churning water far below. He could hear horns as boats reacted to the airship's presence, only a few yards above their heads. A large ferry bringing in workers from upriver hooted as the airship continued to slip lower, its passengers cheering and waving at the ship. They had no idea what was going on, but they loved staring at the airships. Jack had seen hundreds of small boys watching airships and recording their numbers in tiny notebooks, a craze he might have shared if his life had been different.

"Grab the lifejackets," he ordered. The airship carried a number of cork jackets intended to help people remain afloat if the airship had to come down in the ocean. Jack suspected that they were there more for peace of mind than any actual benefit to the passengers, but they'd come in handy now. "We're going to slide down the ropes and jump into the water."

Lucy and the others stared at him. Only a madman would *want* to swim in the Thames, but Jack hadn't been able to think of any other way to get out without making their landing point far too obvious. He could sense unseen eyes watching them, hostile magicians following their progress and no doubt reporting to their superiors. Coming down in the water, where a boat was waiting to pick them up and deposit them on the shore was the only way of escaping their invisible scrutiny. Once they were in the docklands, with their endless warrens of warehouses and alleyways, they would be able to slip away before the Bow Street Runners took up position on the ground. There was no other way to escape.

"Hurry," he snapped. The airship's labouring was growing even louder. Jack had the feeling that soon they would be blown back down the river and out over the ocean. "Get the lifejackets on and get down there."

Lucy tore at her clothes, revealing her legs as she pulled her skirt off, and then grabbed at one of the rope ladders. She barely managed to scramble down a yard before she lost her grip and fell down towards the water below, hitting the surface with an almighty splash. It honestly hadn't occurred to Jack to ask if all of the former captives could swim, but it was far too late to worry about that now. The other captives followed suit, two jumping off the hatch rather than trying to scramble down the rope; the remainder trying to get down as far as possible before they fell and landed in the drink. Jack nodded to his team to follow and then returned to the bridge. One of his men, who had remained on guard with a pistol pointed at the pilot's head, was dismissed and ordered to jump himself. Jack said goodbye to the pilot, wished him luck in saving the ship, and ran back to the hatch. Tired through he was, he didn't bother with a lifejacket. He merely threw himself over the side and used his magic to slow his fall. The Thames came up and hit him, drenching him as he fell under the surface and found himself choking on foul-tasting water. He reached the surface a moment later, swimming towards the nearest boat. A magician, hovering overhead, was an easy target. Jack disrupted his magic and sent him falling towards the water, directing his fall so that he came down on top of a barge. The resulting crash would almost certainly have killed his victim.

He turned and saw the bridge looming in front of the *Britannia Clipper*. The pilot was desperately fighting to control his ship, but it couldn't rise fast enough to avoid the bridge, even though the wind was trying to push it downstream. Jack found himself praying for the first time in years – he hadn't actually *wanted* to kill his hostages, let alone the airship's crew – but God wasn't listening to him. The underside of the airship scraped against one of the bridge's spires, the cloth ripping under the impact. It might just survive...

...A spark ignited the gas and the airship blossomed into fire. Jack ducked under the water as the fireball billowed out in all directions, sending the bridge tumbling into the water far below. A towering inferno rapidly consumed the remains of the airship, forcing him to remain underwater as he swam towards the shore. Debris was striking the water with terrific force, sending deadly shockwaves racing towards him. He lifted his magic to shield himself as the fireball started to contract, even as fires started to spread out of control on both sides of the river. No one, he knew, would have survived on the *Britannia Clipper*. The entire airship, a symbol of British power and industrial sophistication – and of how magic could aid the development of science – had been destroyed.

He pulled himself ashore on the docks, spitting out water as he slapped at his clothes. A crowd was already gathering to stare, even though the fire posed a danger to the entire city. The fire brigades, at least, would have no problem using the Thames as a source of water. If they were lucky, they might even manage to quell the blaze before it consumed half of the city. London had nearly burned to the ground once before and no one would want to repeat the experience.

A group of magicians flew overhead, right towards the blaze. Some of them held their comrades in the air; others used their magic to pick up great waves of water and drive them right into the fire. It was a crude, but effective trick,

Jack noted; the flames were already being driven back and quelled by the water. The magicians moved closer, some of them pulling entire streams of water out of the Thames and directing it towards the strongest parts of the fire. Parts of riverside London would be drenched by the time they were finished, but it would be enough to save the remainder of the city. Jack caught sight, briefly, of the airship's tail before it vanished below the waves. There was little left of the once-proud craft.

It was a shame, but his plan had worked. Grinning to himself, he started to walk back towards the den. Somewhere along the way, he knew, he would have to get a change of clothes. The Bow Street Runners would be looking for people who looked like drowned rats and Jack, now that he was calming down from the excitement, knew that he was exhausted. He might not be able to use his magic to defend himself if they caught up with him.

He took one final look at the plumes of smoke rising up from the fire and then kept walking. As he had hoped, a street thug stepped out of a doorway and demanded a toll before allowing Jack to pass. It was a typical protection racket, the sort of operation that thrived where there was no effective law and order. Jack reached into his reserves and used his magic, striking directly at the thug's brain. His victim screamed aloud and collapsed to the ground, hands clutching at his head. Jack had heard of a number of men in Europe who had died without any trace of illness or violence. A Mover with only a small talent, barely enough to lift a matchbox, could still tear a person's mind apart, assassinating their victim without any obvious signs of what had happened. Master Thomas wouldn't have hesitated to allow his subordinates to work as assassins. After everything else he'd done, merely to maintain the status quo, assassination wouldn't even cause him to hesitate for a moment.

Jack stripped the groaning thug, tore off his own clothes and pulled on the thug's overall and cap. They stank – his would-be mugger clearly didn't know how to bathe – but they were dry, enough to allow him to avoid notice. He kept a sharp eye out for Bow Street Runners as he headed down the street, watching as a handful of broadsheet sellers started shouting the news. It would be hours before the new editions were printed and on the streets, but that had never stopped them from advertising before and it wouldn't stop them now.

"Hear all about it," one was yelling. "Airship crashes in the Thames!"

"Daring robbery of the Tower of London," another was selling. "Crown jewels under threat!"

Jack laughed to himself. By now, the rumours would be all over London. The Tower of London was used to house the Crown Jewels and anyone robbing the building would be assumed to have designs on stealing the nation's treasures. It wouldn't be long before they realised that someone had attacked the Tower and liberated a number of captives. There was no way that it could be covered up – and no one, not even Lord North, had been able to silence rumourmongers. The entire city would be certain that the Tower of London had been smashed by the end of the day. They'd probably be talking about fire-breathing dragons or foreign armies outside London.

Shaking his head, he kept walking. No one tried to bar his passage. He hadn't intended to destroy the airship, but it had served as a suitable distraction. The city's authorities would have far more to worry about than a handful of rebels. And that was the way he wanted it.

It was so much easier to win if you took your opponent by surprise.

Chapter Thirty-Three

e saved the entire city!"

Gwen listened as Cannock and his friends boasted of their great success. Every Mover in Cavendish Hall had been ordered up the Thames to assist in fighting the fire; Gwen had volunteered to go, only to be told by Doctor Norwell to return to her studies. Instead, she'd climbed up to the roof and watched the flames rising up over London before they were finally quenched. Cannock was known for being boastful, even if he had stopped trying to harass Gwen, but it seemed that for once he was right. The fire had come alarmingly close to spreading out of control and becoming a second Great Fire of London.

"The flames were so hot that my clothes were scorched," he continued, bragging to the other magicians. Even Gwen was listening closely. "I picked up the entire Thames and turned it on the flames like a powerful hose, driving the flames back until they were finally quelled. The remains of the bridge were cooling down once we covered them with water; we had to…"

"That's quite enough bragging," Master Thomas said. Cannock jumped and then tried to pretend that he hadn't. His ultimate superior had come up behind him so quietly that he hadn't heard his passage. "You did well. Go upstairs and get some sleep."

"Yes, sir," Cannock said, quickly. He always deferred to Master Thomas, even if he refused to defer to anyone else. Gwen had seen such behaviour before in social climbers; they were fulsomely flattering to anyone superior to them, while cruel and unpleasant to anyone below their level. Lady Mary often acted in such a manner herself. "We *will* catch the anarchists, won't we?"

"I'm sure that we will," Master Thomas assured him, gravely. His gaze swept the room. "Classes are cancelled for today. Movers are to go upstairs and sleep it off; everyone else is to study unless I call for them personally. Gwen, you're with me."

Gwen nodded, not trusting herself to speak. She had been isolated in the crowd of magicians, both by being a Master and by being a woman. They might have forgiven her being born a Master, but they would never forget that she was a woman. She would never know true companionship from the other magicians, or even from mundane humans. There was no one else quite like her.

The crowd dispersed rapidly. Gwen had been at Cavendish Hall long enough to learn that Master Thomas was often impatient when his orders weren't carried out at once. Apart from Gwen herself – and Jack, when he had been a loyal servant of the Crown – the younger magicians were replaceable. Master Thomas could fill all of the billets at Cavendish Hall merely through using his name. Gwen had been looking at some of the registers, trying to deduce how many magicians had been born in the farms, and ended up concluding that thousands of magicians were known to exist. The Darwinists, who claimed that magicians were born to rule over mundane humans, were almost certainly the driving force behind the farms. If farmers could breed stronger horses, or larger sheep, why couldn't they breed stronger magicians?

But magic didn't seem to obey understandable rules. Logically, a magician born of two other magicians – a Mover and a Blazer, perhaps – should share both talents. And yet it didn't work that way. A magician either had one talent or he had them all; cross-breeding magicians only seemed to produce weaker magicians with a single talent. It made no sense to Gwen, but Doctor Norwell – clearly unaware that Gwen knew about the farms – had once commented that magic clearly obeyed its own laws, even if the magicians didn't understand them. One day, he'd told her, everything would be discovered. Knowing *why* something happened was often more important than knowing *how* something happened. It was the difference between original science and merely using someone else's work.

Gwen had her own theory on the differences between rich and poor magicians. The rich ate regularly and well; the poor often had to scrape for their daily bread. It made sense, to her at least, that the ones who ate well would have more energy for use in their magic, giving them an advantage over the others. The Darwinists wouldn't thank her for such a theory, she knew. They believed that birth alone made them superior.

Master Thomas's office was surprisingly crowded when he led her into the room. Lord Mycroft was seated on the sofa, his oversized chest heaving alarmingly. Lord Blackburn was seated on an armchair, scowling at everyone – even Master Thomas. A number of men she didn't recognise were either sitting in their own chairs or standing in front of the fire. Gwen was the only woman in the room. Even Irene, who might have been able to contribute all kinds of ideas to the meeting, had been excluded. She had a nasty feeling that that didn't bode well.

"The fire at the bridge has finally been quenched," Lord Mycroft said. Gwen, who had heard that Lord Mycroft hated to alter his daily routine, could hear the irritation in his voice. "I am afraid that our former prisoners escaped without loss."

There was a long pause. Gwen had only heard that an airship had crashed into one of the many bridges crossing the Thames. Prisoners? No one had told her anything about prisoners.

"They managed to break their fellows out of the Tower of London," one of the men she didn't recognise said. He looked older than Master Thomas, with a long white beard that reminded her of her grandfather, before he had passed away. "No matter how we look at it, it was a total disaster. Losing so many well-connected people in the explosion..."

"To say nothing of morale at the Tower garrison," a younger man said. He wore no uniform, but he had a military bearing. Gwen saw him as he glanced towards her and realised that he reassembled the Duke of India. The great conqueror's son? "They could have taken the airship down in seconds, if they hadn't had to worry about the human shields."

"The Prime Minister is due to address Parliament this evening," Lord Mycroft said, shortly. "We need to have something to advise him by then. The last thing we need is another rebellion on the backbenches."

Gwen smiled, inwardly. She knew more about politics than the average noble-born girl, if only because her father had been given to discoursing at length on the subject to anyone who would listen. Lord Liverpool was aging; a successful challenge from one of the younger MPs might bring his government down, forcing a series of elections that would put a new government in power. And until the new Prime Minister was settled in office, Britain would be effectively leaderless. The ship of state would drift out of control while attention was focused elsewhere.

"This was intended as a challenge to our authority," Lord Blackburn said, flatly. There was no Charm in his voice, Gwen realised. Master Thomas would have detected it instantly and attempting to Charm some of the most powerful men in the land would be considered Treason. Lord Blackburn would meet his end on Tower Hill, where all of the traitors were executed, before his body was cremated and the ashes dumped into the Thames. "It demands a harsh response."

Master Thomas snorted. "Against who?" He asked. "We raided the known centres of underground activity after the...unfortunate incident at the Fairweather Ball. The underground is careful to keep its cells separated from each other, making it harder to penetrate and break them. They learned a great many lessons since they last mounted a challenge to our authority."

He paused, just long enough to draw attention. "This was a carefully-laid plan, conceived by a madman," he added. "They used underground magicians to distract me and keep me out of London while they raided the Tower. I fear that we must face the fact that one of our worst fears has come true. The magical underground has found a charismatic leader who has united it against us."

"And has allied it with the other underground movements," Lord Mycroft said. "We must assume the worst; that we're facing a more dangerous challenge to our authority since King Charles and the Long Parliament had their deadly falling out. Parliament and the King could talk and try to find a compromise. We cannot compromise with anarchists."

"You should be able to find your former student," one of the other men said. He was younger than David, but older than Gwen – and trying to appear older than he was. "I thought that you magicians could sense one another's presence."

"If Master Jackson was using his powers constantly, we might be able to use Sensors to track him down," Master Thomas said. Gwen realised, suddenly, that it wasn't just the government's power that was being challenged. Her tutor's position as the foremost magician in England was being threatened. They couldn't replace him...or could they? There was another Master in Cavendish Hall now; Gwen herself. But she didn't have his years of experience yet. She couldn't hope to fit into his shoes. "But he is careful and very capable. He won't allow us to track him down so easily."

"And in any case he has the assistance of other magicians," Lord Blackburn added. "The underground has something else that they didn't have five years ago – they have someone who can teach them how to master their powers. We knew that it was getting harder to track down unlicensed magicians even before Master Jackson returned from the dead."

"Begging your pardon," one of the older men said, "but I don't like joking upon such matters."

"It is hardly a joke," Lord Blackburn said, tightly. His face flushed alarmingly. "We believed that Master Jackson was dead. If we'd taken precautions..."

"We did what seemed best in the circumstances," Lord Mycroft said. He sounded tired, almost on the verge of sleep. "There is no point in arguing over decisions that were made years ago. We have to deal with the world as it is, not as we would like it to be."

He tapped his cane against the wooden floor. "We have to track the underground down, rapidly," he said. "If Parliament feels that we cannot beat the underground, they may feel inclined to offer concessions to the lower classes rather than keeping them firmly in their place. I submit to you that allowing such concessions to be made would spell the end of the British Empire. The Americans, the Australians, the South Africans...they would all demand equal rights on the border of empire. We would see the end of the greatest force for civilisation and advancement in our lifetimes; the empire destroyed."

"Not the South Africans," Lord Blackburn pointed out. "They require our support for facing the savages. Even with the Ferguson rifles that broke the tribes, they're still fighting more often than not. We blood the new regiments in Africa before deploying them elsewhere."

"And rounding up more slaves for the plantations in Dixie," Master Thomas said, flatly. "I have never seen the honour in slave-trading."

Gwen couldn't disagree, even though she knew that her father and brother had made fortunes by selling black slaves to the American South. There had been hundreds of antislavery campaigns in and out of Parliament, but slavery was simply too important to the British Empire's economy to be abolished. A handful of colonies in West Africa had been founded by ex-slaves who had had their freedom purchased by religious and moral pressure groups, yet none of them were particularly successful. The Darwinists pointed to those failures as evidence that the black man was not civilised and could never be turned into a rational man. Slavery was for their own good. Privately, Gwen wondered how anyone could believe such a claim when it was clear that the ex-slave colonies had been set up to fail, but it wasn't something she could say publicly. There had to be a caste at the bottom to help keep the empire stable.

There were other reasons, she'd come to realise after she'd moved to Cavendish Hall. Slave rebellions were common in the American South, where frustrated and hopeless young bucks had turned on their masters. The British Army's garrisons were often called upon to put such rebellions down, demonstrating to the Americans just how much they needed the presence of the British military. It was convincing to the aristocratic plantation farmers – and the opinions of anyone else simply didn't matter.

"That debate is one that can be saved for another time," Lord Mycroft said. "What do we advise the Prime Minister?"

"That we can keep the situation under control," Lord Blackburn said. "We do have forces we can call upon in England. It's time to show the vermin the uncovered fist."

He stood up and paced around the room, stopping in front of a table on which was spread a giant map of London. "We know who we are looking for," he said. "We move in the troops and seal off the entire poorer area of London. Once in control, we crack down hard, bringing pressure to bear on the...less savoury residents of the area to expose underground hide-outs to us. Everyone we catch goes under the gaze of the Talkers; we use the intelligence they develop to go after other hide-outs, building up a picture of the underground. We push factory owners to bring pressure on their workers; those who tell us useful information about the underground will be rewarded, those found to be concealing information will be sacked and thrown out onto the streets to die."

Lord Blackburn's dark eyes narrowed. "We *can* win this by a simple and effective response; brute force on a scale they could not hope to match. And if they bring themselves into the open, we could smash them like foxes caught by the hounds."

There was a long pause. "It seems to me that such repression will only alienate the working class further," Lord Mycroft said. "Our system worked for so long because it offered the chance for a working class person to rise to the middle class, to own and operate his own business – or even emigrate to a settlement in America or South Africa. If we come down too hard..."

"They hit the *Tower of London*," Lord Blackburn thundered. "They are not scared of us, not even slightly! We cannot let them get away with this or we will lose control of the country by the end of the year."

Gwen spoke up before she thought better of it. "Tell me something," she said, her feminine voice drawing their attention like nothing else. "How many of the working class have risen to the middle class in the last five years?"

Lord Blackburn glared at her, not bothering to conceal his dislike. If they had been alone, she was sure that he would have told her to run back to the kitchen and mind her own business, leaving politics to the men. But they weren't alone and while some of the men might have shared his opinion, it would have been utterly impolite to say so out loud.

"Those who have earned the rise have done so," he said, finally.

"You don't know," Gwen said, tartly. If she was to have the disadvantages of being a female in male company, she might as well claim the advantages too. "Let me guess; only a handful of men have managed to rise out of poverty?"

"That is of no concern," Lord Blackburn blustered. "I think..."

"I think that it is of very great concern," Gwen said, cutting him off ruthlessly. "As far as I can tell, the poor will always be poor, with no chance to better themselves. Is that not correct?"

"Those who have ambition and capability are often offered the chance to strike out overseas," Lord Mycroft rumbled. "The remainder have no fire in them..."

"They have nothing to lose, but their chains," Gwen said. Jack would have said the same thing, she realised. And who knew what Master Thomas was thinking behind his impassive face? "If they have no hope of lifting themselves up, should they not try to force their way up? What exactly do they have to lose?"

"Their lives," Lord Blackburn said, sharply. "We are the rulers of Great Britain and her Empire. We cannot be seen to bow to anarchist threats. It's time to show those scum who's in charge."

***

"Opposing Lord Blackburn like that was not wise."

Gwen didn't turn. She stood on the roof, staring out over London. The streetlights were coming on, illuminating the richer parts of the city. They stood in odd contrast to the poorer regions, which were barely lit. It was easy to see why Jack had found so many converts. If she'd lived in such conditions, forced to sell herself to survive, she would have wanted to change places too.

"He has far too many friends at court," Master Thomas said. He stood just behind her, his presence easy to detect. Gwen could feel his mind pulsing as he stared past her and out into the night. "You will need to watch yourself."

"You told me that before," Gwen said, tartly. She was sorry almost at once. Master Thomas didn't deserve her scorn. "I thought we were supposed to defend the British Empire, not..."

She shook her head. "I don't understand," she admitted. It wasn't entirely true. She understood Jack better than she wanted to admit. "Why does no one care?"

"They care about their interests," Master Thomas said. "It was far simpler when I was young, when Pitt led us to war against the French. Magic was nothing more than superstition back then..."

He shook his head. "Our goal is to protect the Empire," he reminded her. "Whatever else you decide, remember that. We exist to protect the Empire."

Gwen turned and looked up at him. Master Thomas looked old, as if something had gone out of him. "And what is the Empire," she asked quietly, "without its people?"

Master Thomas said nothing. But then, there was nothing to say.

Chapter Thirty-Four

are," a man was shouting. "The Dragoons are coming!"

Jack stumbled awake and pulled himself out of bed. He'd slept in after they'd made their escape, trusting that the Seers and more conventional enemy agents wouldn't be able to locate their hide. Lucy had joined him – her brothel would have been closed down – and somehow they'd found themselves in bed together. He glanced back at her as he staggered over to the windows, feeling pain trickling through his head. His body always extracted a price for pushing his powers too far.

People were scattering on the streets below, looking for cover or running into buildings. A line of troops came into view, decked out in the bright red uniform worn by British soldiers. Their commanders rode in front of the men, riding horses and daring anyone to try to take a shot at them. The red uniforms – red as blood – glimmered menacingly in the sunlight. There was no doubt that they intended to occupy the Rookery and dare the underground to challenge them directly. Jack wasn't particularly surprised. The authorities would have to find some way of hitting back after the raid on the Tower of London and without any clear targets, pushing troops into the poorer parts of London was probably their best option. It was amazing how many people thought better of revolution after coming face to face with the government's mailed fist.

"Cossacks," he muttered, as he splashed water on his face. Hunger was growling inside his chest, but he ignored it. He would have to eat after he'd checked out the soldiers. "The bastards will pressure the civilians into betraying us."

Lucy rolled over and looked up at him. "What's

happening?"

"They've put dragoons on the streets," Jack said. The cold water was clearing his head. He ran one hand along his chin to check the stubble, before shaking his head in private amusement. There was no time to shave, even if he'd had the tools. "I think they're going to start looking for us."

The thought made him smile. London was the largest city in England; Manchester, Newcastle and even Liverpool didn't come close to the sprawling immensity of London. Searching the entire city was going to take weeks, particularly when the searchers didn't know precisely who or what they were looking for. It would give the underground time to think and plan, but the chances were good that the searchers would stumble over one of the caches of arms. And then the chaos would really begin. Weapons were forbidden to the lower classes, if only to prevent them objecting forcefully to the way they were treated by their lords and masters. An arms dump would reveal the plans for violent revolution.

There was a knock at the door. Jack braced himself, reaching for his magic despite the throbbing pain at the back of his head, before he opened the door. Olivia stood there, carrying a basket under one arm. Jack motioned for her to come in, silently praying that the soldiers on the streets below never saw through her disguise. She'd find herself raped and worse; the army was notoriously prone to savage repression and utterly intolerant of any attempt to rein them in and treat civilians decently. The Duke of India and a handful of other commanders had kept their men under control, but others hadn't even bothered to try.

"I brought food," Olivia said. "Davy sent you a note too."

Jack took it and read it quickly. Davy's network of spies – mainly street urchins, who could go anywhere in the Rookery without inciting comment – had reported that soldiers were taking up strategic positions throughout the city. There had already been some incidents of violence when soldiers had clashed with factory workers, intimidating them as they made their way to the factories in the morning, where they were told that the harassment would continue until the underground was rooted out and destroyed. Worse, their wages had been docked for lateness, even though it hadn't been their fault. Jack scowled as he crumpled up the message in his hands. Someone on the other side was thinking two or three steps ahead; knowing that the factory workers needed their wages, they had used them to pressure the helpless men into betraying what they knew of the underground. The handful of leaders who had tried to create unions would already have been rounded up.

Lucy took the basket and opened it, revealing a hunk of bread and cheese. Jack ate his share absently, thinking hard. The soldiers had to be driven out of the poorer parts of the city before they gained complete control, or the underground would have to scatter and hope that the soldiers eventually left. Jack's network of underground leaders would be broken up even if no one important was arrested by the authorities, for whatever trust had linked them together would be gone. An idea crossed his mind and he smiled, even as he took another sip of cold water. They would have to provoke a far more serious incident between the soldiers and the civilians before it was too late. And he knew just who to ask.

Pulling on his coat and picking up a set of stolen papers that claimed that he worked in a nearby factory, Jack nodded to Lucy and strode out of the door. The plan was already unfolding in his mind as he reached the street and walked down the middle of the road. It felt odd, almost deserted. The hawkers and traders, the drunkards and the whores, they all seemed to have slipped into the shadows, intimidated by the presence of the soldiers. He crossed an intersection and glanced down the side street, shivering as he saw the mounted horsemen patrolling the district. The intimidation would be enough to keep most of the underground in their place, unless rage broke through and destroyed the fear. And if it failed...

Jack had no illusions about the high cost of freedom. He'd been willing to pay it ever since he'd discovered the truth behind his origins. And yet...so many others had never been consulted. They had never made the choice to risk their lives for freedom. Jack hesitated, on the verge of turning around and slipping out of the city, and then his resolve firmed up. It was war, a war that had been waged since time out of mind. Freedom was worth any price.

***

Her name was Flora McDonald, a legacy from her Scottish

father who had made his way to London to find work. He hadn't found anything better than manual labour and had drunk himself to death before Flora had reached her tenth birthday. Despite being young and pretty – with fiery red hair and a seductive smile – Flora had been one of the luckier women in the poorer parts of London. She had never been forced to sell her body just to remain alive; indeed, her husband, one of the handful of teachers and labour organisers in the city, treated her surprisingly well. Flora had come to share his passion for his cause and hadn't hesitated when she'd been asked to help the underground. The soldiers, mercifully, were less interested in harassing the women near the factories. There were simply too many other problems to tackle.

The factory was a massive black building, stained with soot and a hundred by-products of British ingenuity. Flora had been inside several factories – always without the permission or knowledge of the management – and she'd found them hellish, places where men worked to produce Britain's vast catalogue of mechanical goods for small wages. A man who was injured on the job would find himself out on the streets. The factory owners didn't care about the constant stream of cripples from among their employees. There were always more where they came from. Flora had helped tend men who had lost arms or legs to industrial accidents and it had torn at her soul to see how helpless they'd become. None of them had ever found other employment.

She braced herself as she walked up to the soldiers outside the gate. It was lunchtime at the factory, which meant that about half of the workers would be off-shift, waiting for their wives or daughters to bring them their lunch. None of the factories fed their workers; it was yet another expense that helped keep men in the gutter. Flora had had no difficulty in joining the stream of women making their way towards the factory, holding a basket in one hand. None of the women would recognise her, but they'd say nothing; new employees often arrived without notice, their wives unknown to the rest.

Most of the women were looking away from the soldiers, unwilling to make eye contact with the leering men at the gate. Flora braced herself and smiled at the soldiers, trying to make herself seem as inviting as possible. Far too many wives would sell themselves while their husbands were at work, trying to earn extra money to feed their children. The soldiers responded to her smile, grinning at her as the line slowed to a crawl. Flora knew that it was now too late to run. If something went wrong...

She reached the end of the line and paused, licking her lips as the soldiers smiled at her. They'd been asking the wives the names of their husbands, a question that would have made them feel harassed even though it was easy to answer; instead, the leader stepped forward and leered at Flora. Instead of checking her basket, he put his lips close to her ears and whispered a rude suggestion to her. Flora, pretending to be shocked, slapped him and ran for the gate, screaming for help. Confused, the soldiers gave chase.

Inside the factory gates, hundreds of men were milling around. They'd been bullied by the soldiers before they were allowed to enter the factory and then informed that their wages would be docked by the management. Mutiny and violence were in the air, even before the men saw one of their wives being chased by soldiers. One of the factory workers yelled aloud and charged at the soldiers. The others followed his lead. They were hardly weaklings – factory work was physically demanding – and the soldiers had no time to react before the workers were upon them, beating them to death. The soldiers at the gate lifted their weapons, only to find themselves swarmed by a mass of angry women. There was no longer any fear. It had been driven away by anger and resentment.

The soldiers were rapidly killed, but the riot was spreading. As Flora watched, the workers swarmed back into the factory, smashing their way through the building. The manager came out of his office and tried to speak to the crowd, but it was already too late. None of them had liked him even before he'd docked their wages, making his contempt for them all too clear. They ripped him and the clerks apart in seconds, setting fire to the paperwork that chained them as surely as cold iron. And then they headed out onto the streets, racing towards the soldiers and the other factories. The chaos spread faster than any warning.

***

Jack watched from his rooftop vantage point as the riot

spread further. The handful of agents he'd inserted into the crowd were doing their job well, directing the factory workers towards the soldiers and their checkpoints. They could have been broken by quick and decisive action on the part of the soldiers, but they'd been caught by surprise and hadn't been able to react in time. Each riot would spark off other riots as long-held resentments erupted to the surface, challenging the soldiers directly. The government would find itself faced, not with a limited series of riots, but with a serious uprising. They'd be forced to send extra troops into the poorer parts of the city, stripping their defences bare.

He smiled as he leapt from one rooftop to the next. An officer was trying to take command of a small detachment of soldiers, showing remarkable presence of mind in the face of an oncoming storm of rioters. The crowd was too angry to be deterred by anything other than force, yet the soldiers were clearly nervous. They hadn't signed up to crush urban insurrection in London itself. Their officer might have been able to get them into position, given time, but Jack had no intention of allowing someone to take control. He reached out with his magic, despite the pain in his head, and picked the officer off his horse. The redshirt struggled against his invisible tormenter as he rose several yards into the air, before Jack finally lost his grip on him. He plummeted to the ground and shattered both of his legs. His men, realising that they were facing magic as well as an uprising, started to retreat. But there was nowhere to go. The smart ones scattered into side streets and tried to lose their uniforms before they were caught. The others died before they could escape.

Years of pent-up hatreds were exploding. The troops found themselves bombarded by slops and stones from the windows, forcing them to take cover even as they tried to retreat. Thousands of unemployed men – and even a few women – were coming onto the streets, baying for blood. Jack's inciters were doing a wonderful job; the soldiers, despite their weapons, couldn't hold the line against the crowds. Barricades were already being thrown up in the streets, each one cutting off the soldiers and breaking them up into small isolated detachments. They'd be screaming for help from the government, Jack knew; there would be a handful of Talkers assigned to the force. And there was only one place where the reinforcements could come from; the Tower of London's garrison.

***

Major Thomas Keighley was no coward. Indeed, he had won several medals for bravery during campaigns in India against the Sikhs. As the second son of middle-ranking aristocracy, he'd been sent into the army after an undistinguished educational career and, rather to his surprise, discovered that he enjoyed the army life. He prided himself that he understood his men – like Mark Antony and many others from the classical period, he had shared their hardships rather than insisting on special treatment – and that they knew that he would never ask them to do anything that he wouldn't do for himself. Besides, what sort of officer issued orders from the safety of the rear?

He'd seen war...but this was different. The streets seemed to have come alive with angry civilians, each one intent on dragging down one of his men and tearing them apart. His men had killed a handful of rioters, but it hadn't quelled the riot – somehow, it had only made it worse. One of his officers had been brought down by a woman wielding a meat clever who had cut down his horse and then killed the man himself before anyone could react. Keighley himself had had to abandon his horse after a thrown knife had injured the poor beast, a horse that had served bravely in India. The entire world seemed to have gone crazy.

Another hail of stones crashed down among them from the rooftops. A gang of street children were pulling slates from the houses and throwing them down at his men. Keighley prided himself on never having killed a child in his life, but this was too much. His men fired back at the children, knocking several of them off the roof. But the others kept throwing stones and his men were running out of ammunition. What would they do once they ran out? The only thing keeping the crowds from swarming them was their weapons – once they were gone, the crowd would overrun them and they'd all die.

He led his men around a corner and froze. A street barricade had been erected in front of them, blocking their escape. Hundreds of men were swarming over it, some carrying weapons that had clearly been taken from other – less fortunate – detachments of soldiers. Keighley had been in the midst of the sack of Lahore, but this was something different. He could almost sense the morale of his soldiers dropping as they saw the barricade. If they could have surrendered...but blood was in the air. They couldn't surrender to the rioters. The bastards were so enflamed that his men would be cut down before their enemies even realised that they were trying to surrender.

Bracing himself, he did the only thing he could think of – and charged. He led the charge in person, running towards the barricade with sword in one hand and a pistol in the other. His men followed him, firing on the rioters with brisk efficiency. For a moment, he thought that they could drive the enemy off the barricade and make it out of the affected part of London, before enemy reinforcements streamed out of the nearby house. He saw a woman die, her head smashed open by a bullet at close range, before he found himself and his men surrounded by the enemy. His sword was torn from his hand, seconds before he was knocked to the ground and trampled under the feet of the advancing rioters. There was a brief moment of pain and fire, and then nothing.

***

"We've got most of the bastards," Davy exulted. Between the rioters and the rebel soldiers, the dragoons had been largely wiped out. Their weapons were already being distributed to rebels, who were pushing the barricades out throughout the city. "We're winning!"

"We haven't won yet," Jack said. "Send a runner to the outer detachments. It's time to move."

He scrambled up to the rooftop and stared out at London. Flames were rising up from all over the city, great pillars of smoke reaching up into the sky. The rioters wouldn't stay in the poorer parts of London for long, he knew; they were committed now. If the government won, they would be shown no mercy.

Jack smiled and leapt into the air. Whatever happened, he told himself, the world would never forget the day that it had turned upside down.

Chapter Thirty-Five

avendish Hall shook, violently.

Gwen, who had been reading in her room, stumbled to her feet as a second explosion shook the building. She could sense minds flaring with alarm as she stumbled over to the window and peered outside. Flames and smoke were rising up from the outskirts of London, while there was a small plume of smoke rising up from the gardens. She turned, unsure of what was going on, just before the window smashed inwards, scattering glass everywhere. Gwen shielded herself automatically, throwing herself down to the floor. Now the window was gone, she could hear the sound of gunshots; seconds later, there was a third explosion. The building was under attack!

Abandoning her book, she crawled towards the door and used her magic to pull it open. Outside, one of the maids was having hysterics, even though she appeared to be in no immediate danger. Gwen slapped her hard and she stared up at her, her eyes wide with fear. Who would dare attack Cavendish Hall? Gwen suspected she knew the answer. A man's face danced in her mind, a reminder of the man who had shown her the farms and exposed the true cost of Britain's Sorcerers Corps. Jack would dare, of course. He'd attacked the Tower of London – and Cavendish Hall's defences were flimsy in comparison. But there were hundreds of magicians in the building...

"Go down to the basement," she ordered the maid. Gwen helped her to her feet, pointed her in the direction of the rear staircase, and then headed towards Master Thomas's rooms. A quick tap on the door produced nothing, so she twisted the knob and tried to open the door. It refused to open for her, even when she tried using magic to Change the lock. Master Thomas protected his privacy very well. She tried to concentrate, to send her mind out of her body and into his room, but she was too nervous to focus. Instead, Gwen headed for the stairs herself and walked down towards the lower levels. The sound of shooting was growing louder; a loud thump had her drawing magic up to shield herself before realising that it was only a door slamming. Below her, an elderly magician walked out of a side door and headed down the stairs. Gwen followed him, bracing herself for the worst.

Master Thomas was on the ground floor, speaking to one of the guards. The big stained-glass windows that had once depicted the first magicians – the ones who had served with General Howe in the Battle of New York – had been shattered. A cold wind was blowing into the building, bringing with it the stench of smoke and fire. Outside, she could see a handful of bodies lying on the lawn where they'd fallen, twisted and broken. Her gorge rose and she had to swallow hard to prevent herself from being sick. Master Thomas finished talking to the guard and turned to look at her. He looked older and grimmer than she'd ever seen him.

"There won't be any help from the garrison," he said, tightly. "There's a war going on all over London."

Gwen looked up at him, sharply. Jack was powerful – and not a little insane – but how could he have sparked off a civil war in the heart of London? Master Thomas seemed to be listening to a voice in his head, perhaps one or more of the Talkers serving with the army. His face grew longer and longer as the seconds ticked by. Gwen realised that the situation was far worse than anything he'd seen in his long career. It struck her, suddenly, that her parents – and her brother and his wife – might be in danger. The depravation suffered by England's poor and unhappy citizens wouldn't leave them filled with friendship for those who had grown rich at their expense.

"The streets are on fire," Master Thomas said. "I'm not hearing from several of the Talkers. They must have been killed..."

Cavendish Hall shook again. This time, Gwen heard the sound of falling rubble. Whatever was being used to attack the Hall, it was clearly powerful enough to upset the magically strengthened stone that had been used to build the building. The shockwaves alone would do a hell of a lot of damage. She remembered the books in the library and blanched. What would happen if they caught fire? Some of them were unique, never published openly or withdrawn from publication after the Church or the Government objected. Jack wouldn't want to destroy them, not when he could use them to complete his education, but his allies might not have the same attitude.

Master Thomas shook his head. "The reports I'm getting are confused and contradictory," he said. "Windsor Castle and Buckingham Palace are apparently under attack. The Tower of London is being shelled. Entire armies are advancing through the streets...the French have apparently bombarded the coast...we don't know what's actually going on."

Gwen narrowed her eyes. "This building is under attack," she snapped. Another explosion underlined her words. "We have to get the staff out of here."

"I'll deal with the gunners," Master Thomas said. "You start people moving down towards the jetty. We'll have to take a boat downstream and get out of the line of fire."

Other magicians were starting to come down the stairs. Gwen couldn't tell if they'd only just realised that the building was under attack, or if they'd spent several minutes running around like headless chickens before recovering control of themselves. She had certainly never anticipated an attack on Cavendish Hall.

She pushed the thought out of her mind and raised her voice, thinking hard. "I want Movers and Blazers up front," she bellowed. They might hesitate to accept orders from a woman, in which case she intended to use her powers to enforce obedience. "Movers are to shield everyone from attack; Blazers are to fire on the enemy. Move down to the rear doors and prepare to depart from there!"

No one argued, not even Cannock. Gwen would have laughed if she'd had the time; the attack had stunned them so badly that they weren't even bothering to care about who was issuing orders. Besides, some of them had heard Master Thomas putting her in charge. They would know better than to argue in the midst of a gun battle. Gwen hurried them down to the rear doors, sending several of the magicians to the servant's quarters, looking for others to evacuate down to the ship. There were over four hundred servants in Cavendish Hall, but only ninety could be found. Gwen cursed under her breath as they assembled near the rear doors. The others would have to be left behind if they hadn't been located by the time they left.

Another explosion shook the building, followed rapidly by the sound of falling masonry. Cavendish Hall was on the verge of collapse. Gwen barked orders and reached out with her magic, blasting the rear doors open and revealing the path leading down to the jetty. Like most buildings on the riverside, Cavendish Hall had its own place for boats to dock, allowing magicians to land in London without having to make their way overland. It had always struck Gwen as the ultimate in lazy thinking, but it would save their lives now. The boat, a medium-sized yacht, was waiting just ahead of them. Gwen thought, for a moment, that they would be safe, just before the sound of shooting rang out and bullets started to crash into the magical field covering the escaping magicians. The Blazers turned and fired bolts of magic back towards the attackers, trying to keep them back. A fireball rose up from the gardens, followed by a sound like thunder. Someone was firing heavy artillery at the hall.

"Get everyone into the boat," Gwen ordered Cannock. "Once everyone is on board, cast off without waiting for me. Do you understand?"

Cannock stared at her, and then nodded. Gwen took the opportunity to leap into the air and float high above Cavendish Hall, searching for the enemy gunners. They had taken up position in several nearby buildings and were pouring fire down onto the hall and anyone who showed their faces around it. One of the buildings was already on fire; the others were still firing, ignoring the flames that Master Thomas was directing in their direction. Gwen saw a flash of light out of the corner of her eye, just before another shell crashed into Cavendish Hall. The magical protection failed and part of the hall caved in, starting a collapse that sent the south wing crashing down in rubble. Gwen felt a flash of bitter grief – Cavendish Hall had been home to her, far more than the mansion her father had purchased in London – and then anger overrode her sense. She swooped down on the gun team and scattered them with her magic, careful to destroy the gun and its shells. The explosion sent a massive plume of smoke into the air, deafening her.

Something reached out and disrupted her magic. Gwen found herself falling towards the ground, barely catching herself before she hit the ground head first. There was an enemy Mover out there, she realised, perhaps more than one. If he'd been well fed and well trained, he would certainly be more powerful than her. Instead of taking to the air again, she wrapped her magic around her as a shield and inched forward, looking for the enemy magician. There were several enemies gathered near one of the other houses, but none of them seemed to be magicians. It took her a moment to realise her mistake – and it almost killed her. Two of them were Blazers and they almost burned through her shield before she jumped back.

Gwen kept moving backwards, cursing her own stupidity. There was no law that stated that magicians had to wear Sorcerers Black – and the rebel magicians would have defied it anyway. Their magicians would be almost impossible to separate out from the common herd, at least as long as they kept their magic to themselves. A Mover would be impossible to detect; even a Blazer would be tricky, provided that they were careful. Her blunder had almost managed to get her killed. She was still moving backwards when someone dropped to the ground behind her; Gwen spun around, expecting to see Jack. Instead, Master Thomas scowled at her. He didn't look happy.

"I thought I told you to get out of here," he said, sharply. The sound of nearby gunfire was getting louder. Gwen realised, in a flash of horror, that one of the plumes of smoke was coming from near the Tower of London. Jack was clearly attacking it again, daring the warders to stop him. "There are too many rebel magicians here for us to defeat without help."

Gwen stared at him. He sounded...defeated. There was no reason to give up, surely? Cavendish Hall might have been partly wrecked, but most of the magicians had escaped with their lives and they were far from the only magicians in Britain. Jack was dangerous – and his questionable sanity gave him an unfair advantage – but he wasn't unstoppable.

"But..."

"No buts," Master Thomas said. "We need to get back to the river."

They made their way slowly back towards Cavendish Hall. Gwen took one glance at the building as it came into view and wished that she hadn't. Flame was spreading through the upper levels of Cavendish Hall, consuming the books, artefacts and even Gwen's clothes. She had never been obsessed with clothes, nothing like her mother, but seeing the dresses she'd had designed especially for her work burning left her feeling bitter, almost as if she was losing a part of herself. Cavendish Hall could be rebuilt, she told herself, but the Royal Sorcerers Corps might never recover from the blow to its prestige.

On impulse, she hurled herself into the air, spinning around to take in London. The city was burning; she could see fires everywhere, with gunfire echoing out in the distance. An airship was heading away from the city slowly, struggling through the air as the wind changed rapidly. Gwen wondered if it would come down amidst the city before it finally managed to stagger off into the distance. A group of magicians were flying through the air towards the Tower of London. She couldn't tell if they were friendly or hostile. Jack's rebels wore no uniform.

Her eyes narrowed as she saw something else, something she should have noticed from the start. There were dead bodies lying everywhere. Ever since necromancy had been demonstrated and undead monsters had become a deadly threat, all bodies had to be cremated. Doctor Norwell had even said it was the one law that had widespread public approval. There was something utterly wrong about seeing so many dead bodies on the street. No one was even gathering them up for incineration. When she'd been younger, she'd read a horror story about the outbreak of undead on Haiti, years ago. Was London staring at a similar possibility?

She felt a gentle pressure in her mind and dropped back down to Master Thomas. He looked more worried than angry, thankfully, and she took the opportunity to outline what she'd seen for him. Gwen had half-expected for him to insist that they made their way to the Houses of Parliament to assist the MPs in escaping the chaos, but instead he merely suggested that they head down to the jetty. Cannock had managed to get the boat undocked and out onto the water, but it was easy for both of them to fly over the Thames and land neatly in the boat. It was so crammed with passengers that Gwen wondered if the Movers should remain in the air. But how long could they stay in the air with enemy Movers waiting for a chance to send them falling into the water?

The *Margareta* wasn't the only boat heading down to the sea. Hundreds of other boats were taking sail, fleeing the chaos gripping London town. Some of them had clearly been commandeered by rich folk with sense, others were crammed with passengers to the point where a single mistake might capsize the boat and drown everyone on board. Master Thomas snorted in disapproval as a richer man used a whip to discourage swimmers from climbing aboard his boat, before making a slight motion with his hands and hurling the offending man into the Thames. Gwen shook her head sadly as the fleet of boats picked up speed. An entire tide of humanity was fleeing, leaving the city behind. How many of them, she wondered, would return to find that their houses had been burned to the ground, if they ever returned at all. England wasn't France or Prussia, used to heavy population movements in times of war or unrest. There would be no provisions for the refugees downstream. Those who had friends and family living elsewhere could probably make their way there, but the ones who had lost everything? What would happen to them?

"Look," someone called. "It's the Navy!"

Gwen followed the pointing finger and nodded. A massive wooden-hulled ship of the line was sitting in the river, watching for...what? The Royal Navy could hardly bombard London into submission. Her father had once commented that the day of the wooden ships was almost over; some of the new developments in steam engines and ironclad hulls would make the wooden ships little more than expensive targets. And yet, the ship was dauntingly attractive, with the Union Jack flying from her stern. How could anything hope to defy the wooden walls that protected England and made her great? No nation could compete with the English at sea.

"Useless," Master Thomas said, bitterly. "The rebels aren't trying to get out to sea, are they?"

"No, sir," Cannock said, "but the scrum will be held if they try."

"One Blazer would be able to set that ship on fire," Gwen pointed out. "And then what would happen to the crew?"

Master Thomas said nothing. Instead, he floated into the air and drifted over towards the warship. Gwen hesitated, and then followed him, hearing the shouts of the refugees echoing in her ears. The vessel's commander, a Captain wearing a magnificent uniform, looked surprised to see Master Thomas, but was instantly respectful. He clearly knew just how much power Master Thomas had at his command, both direct and indirect. Besides, the Navy knew little of what was happening above them in London.

"You need to watch yourself," Master Thomas said, after a brief explanation. "I'm assigning a pair of Movers and Blazers to you – and a Talker to keep you in touch with us. God alone knows who's in charge at the moment."

The Captain tossed an odd glance at Gwen, and then nodded. Some sailors, Gwen recalled, thought that having a woman on board their ships would bring bad luck. Gwen suspected that this particular ship had already had its stroke of bad luck. Besides, there was no such thing as good or bad luck. The pieces fell wherever they chose.

"Understood, sir," the Captain said. "Where are you going?"

"The planned emergency refuge for the government is Hampton Court," Master Thomas said, slowly. "But that may be too close to London for safety. I've been trying to contact Talkers who should be with the government; Lord Liverpool should have been rushed out of the city as soon as the crisis began. If not Hampton Court, then Oxford..."

Gwen smiled to herself. King Charles had fled to Oxford after his disastrous attempt to capture his enemies in the Long Parliament. And that hadn't ended well for the King. Charles had lost his head, an ironic end for a man whose grandmother – Mary Queen of Scots – had met the same fate at the hands of her cousin Elizabeth. Who knew what would be going through Lord Liverpool's mind if he had to retrace the long-dead King's steps?

The thought reminded her about a different King. "Master Thomas," she said, "what about King George?"

Master Thomas sighed. "There's nothing we can do for him now," he said. "We'll just have to hope that he's safe."

Chapter Thirty-Six

We have men positioned at all of the planned points," Ruddy reported. "The soldiers are in position and ready to move."

Jack smiled. The confusion that had once overwhelmed military commanders – making them incapable of knowing what was happening outside their own positions – was a thing of the past, thanks to Talkers. He had enough Talkers scattered around London to keep the different units in contact, even though they weren't as capable as those working for the enemy. But then, the Government had always offered the best terms to Talkers. The British Empire never had enough of them to keep the different parts of the Empire in contact.

"Tell them that they can move in," he ordered. "I want the MPs alive if possible; the defenders are to be killed on the spot."

Ruddy quirked an eyebrow. "They won't surrender if they know that they will be killed after capture," he pointed out. "They need to think that there is a chance of life after the revolution."

"Traitors," Jack snarled. The dragoons had taken the King's Shilling, joining the army instead of the underground. They had helped to crush dissent and rebellion in the past. Why should the rebels show them any mercy? They certainly hadn't shown any to *their* victims. "Why should we offer them a chance at life?"

"Because it's a great deal easier to govern if you convince people that they have a future," Ruddy said, mildly. "If they have nothing to lose, they'll dig in and fight to the death."

Jack frowned as the sound of explosions echoed in the distance. London, perversely for the capital of the greatest empire the world had ever seen, was barely defended. The Trained Bands had never been fully trusted by Charles II and his successors, while the regiments had either been tied down or eliminated during their march into the poorer parts of the city. The security of London rested in the hands of the Royal Navy – and the Navy's Marines didn't have the manpower to secure London. They'd planned for an invasion from France or Spain. Large-scale unrest and a planned revolution had never been considered. And yet, what men *were* trying to defend the established order were holding firm. They might just hold out long enough to break the revolution.

"Very well," he said, quietly. "Tell them that we will accept surrender – but make damn sure that they can't change their minds once they're safe. We can shift them to one of the prisons and make sure that they stay out of temptation's way."

"Yes, sir," Ruddy said. He nodded to his Talker, a young girl who looked barely old enough to walk the streets. She would never have been accepted by the Royal College. "I'll see to it personally."

Jack nodded and launched himself into the air. The Houses of Parliament and St. James' Palace were hardly armed fortresses. Smoke was drifting up from where a bomb or a shell had landed near to the House of Lords. Jack wouldn't mourn any of the lords if they were killed in the fighting, but it was extremely difficult to force a surrender if you killed the only people who *could* surrender. In times of war or unrest, the MPs would probably have planned to make their way to the Tower of London, which was why Jack had assigned no less than three hundred men to seizing the tower. The Warders wouldn't be able to hold them back, not with much of their manpower sent to the slums. There would be nowhere for the MPs to hide.

The handful of guards – and a number of MPs who had military experience – were holding out as best as they could, but the outcome was inevitable. Jack had planned his assault carefully, sending in men from all directions while using Movers to land troops on the roof. The defenders had taken up positions to snipe at his men – some of the lords, excellent huntsmen, were proving to be alarmingly good snipers – but they didn't have the manpower to survive long enough to escape through the tunnels. Besides, Jack knew where the tunnels led, unless they'd been changed or expanded in the years since he'd abandoned Master Thomas. St. James' Palace was already under siege. A party of armed men were already on their way to the more clandestine exit on the other side of the Thames. There was a good chance that they might even take the King himself prisoner.

A bullet cracked out – and bounced off his magic. Jack allowed himself to float down towards the roof of the House of Commons, where a handful of MPs were still hiding from his men. Jack knocked them down with his magic and waited for his men to secure them, even though he wanted to blaze them down or throw them over the edge of the roof. The lords couldn't be faulted for being lords, but the commons – the MPs elected by the commoners who met the stringent property qualifications – should have stood up for the common herd. Some of them had, over the years, but most of the others were more interested in bettering themselves than in bettering their fellow man.

He followed his men through the door and down the stairs into the House of Commons. The building shook several times as the assault parties used explosives to bring down the outer doors, allowing them to storm the building. A handful of MPs and their assistants were cowering in one of the upper rooms, praying that rescue would come before they were captured or killed by the rebels. They had no time to react when Jack led his men into the room, had them searched roughly and then tied up on the floor. There would be time to work out who they'd captured – and what use could be made of them – once the fighting was over.

"Keep heading downwards and search the entire building," he ordered. "And watch out for hideouts."

It had been years since he'd stood in the Houses of Parliament, long before he'd left Master Thomas and joined the underground. The public were not allowed into the building, a measure that was supposed to be for the MPs protection, but was actually to prevent the public from seeing just how many backroom deals were made between the commons and the lords. What did the unease of one's constituents matter when there was a peerage to be had? Peers were not allowed to sit within the House of Commons, but far too many peers had risen up *from* the House of Commons. And peers didn't have to be elected.

He kicked down the door that lead into the Commons Chamber and marched inside. It was almost exactly as he remembered; two long rows of benches for the MPs, a large and ornate chair for the Speaker and a set of tables in the centre of the room. It was strange to reflect on how the home of the British Empire was probably the freest country in the world, but still kept most of its population in bondage. That would change, he promised himself, and the revolution would soon be exported to Europe. Jack had no illusions about *why* the French had supported him – unrest in Britain would make it harder for the British to prevent the French from realising their designs on the Ottoman Empire – but they were in for a nasty shock. The movement had been international for years. Jack would see the French peasants and the Russian serfs liberated in his lifetime.

The Speaker rose from his chair to challenge Jack, showing no small amount of bravery. Martin Pathway was old, old enough to remember the American Revolution and George III's slide into madness. He was an elderly man wearing a long white wig and his robes of office; by law and custom, the Speaker was meant to be politically neutral. Pathway had been no better than many of his predecessors; he'd taken bribes, allowed himself to be pressured and almost certainly promised a peerage if he didn't upset Lord Liverpool too much. Even if he retired without a peerage, he would have enough money to live a life of luxury.

"This place is untouchable," he said, harshly. His voice echoed oddly in the vast chamber, where MPs practiced their oratory and pledged themselves to support the government, rather than upholding the interests of the people. "You have..."

"You have sat too long for any good you have been doing," Jack said. Oliver Cromwell had said the same, back during the time when Parliament had run the country. Cromwell had had the perfect opportunity to rid Britain of hereditary peers and create a new republic, but he'd failed. Jack would not fail. "In the name of God, go!"

His men filed in behind him and took the MPs and their Speaker into custody. Some of them offered a violent protest, only to be slapped down into silence. One of the underground chambers was large enough to hold most of the prisoners and Jack ordered the MPs taken there and separated from their assistants. The assistants were traitors, just like the ones who had fought to defend the Houses of Parliament, but maybe they could be induced to switch sides. Or perhaps they were junior politicians serving the MPs in preparation for their own rise to Parliament.

Jack waited until the chamber was empty and then looked around, unsure of his own feelings. He'd won, he told himself. Whatever happened afterwards, the country would not forget the day that the people had risen up and cleared the Houses of Parliament of the corrupt men who had exploited them for their own purposes. And yet...he'd planned the rebellion for so long that he was unsure of what to do next. He'd won the city, perhaps the entire country – and now began the harder part of the task. The hard work of government lay ahead.

He walked through the connecting passage and into the House of Lords. Someone had turned it into a chamber for the dead, stacking up bodies like logs of wood. Jack recognised a couple of faces, including a Lord whose tastes in women matched those of the late unlamented Lord Fitzroy. No one would mourn him, particularly his children. A man with enough power and clients could even get away with incest. Jack had little faith in God – religion seemed only to keep the masses quiet, with rebellion termed a mortal sin – but there were times that he prayed that there was a God, and a Hell. Lord Fitzroy would be violated by devils for eternity.

Walking down the steps, he saw the prisoners lying on the ground. A handful had objected and had rapidly been knocked into silence. The Lords seemed shocked by the sudden change in their fortunes, although a handful looked as if they were trying to see how the situation could be turned to their advantage. A group of bishops had been gagged. Jack guessed that they'd been trying to uphold the dignity of the Church to men who had found themselves forced to give some of their hard-earned money to the Church, while their wives and families starved for lack of food, or froze for lack of heat. Jack recognised a handful of the noblemen and smiled at the fear in their eyes when they saw him. They all knew who he was and what he'd done when he'd been a rebel. What would he do now that he effectively ran the country?

Shaking his head, he walked back outside and lifted himself

into the air. The Tower of London was only a short flight away – and it had been taken by his men. A number of Wardens sat outside, their hands tied behind their backs; the dead had been piled up outside the castle and abandoned. Jack made a mental note to insure that the bodies were cremated before the end of the day. The fear and hatred of necromancy wouldn't change even if his government secured the entire empire without further ado.

Davy had set up his headquarters in one of the chart rooms that had once housed the most elaborate collection of maps in the British Empire. Mapping was an important skill, as Lord Nelson had amply demonstrated during the invasion of Cuba, thirty years ago. The thought made him smile. Lord Nelson hadn't been taken prisoner yet and part of him hoped that the naval hero was safe outside the city. He was a genuinely popular hero and holding him prisoner might swing public opinion against Jack's government. The same couldn't be said of Lady Emma, whom the country considered an embarrassment, or their lovechild. Horatia Nelson had married a clergyman and had little contact with her famous father.

"We have the city," Davy said, as Jack stopped on the other side of the table. A map of London had been spread out and Davy was marking it, aided by a small army of scribes and messengers. The scribe guilds loathed their lords and masters with just as much intensity as many of the other guilds and had been happy to pledge their support. Besides, the scribes had done good work in bringing reading and writing to the masses. "The last bodies of organised troops have been surrounded or destroyed."

Jack glanced down at the map. London was a vast sprawling metropolis, holding upwards of five *million* human beings. They'd risen up against the government – aided and abetted by Jack's men – but they'd all expect a new heaven and a new earth. Simply feeding so many mouths would be a daunting task; Jack had given priority to taking and securing the warehouses that held stored grain and other foodstuffs. Even so, London depended on vast amounts of food being brought into the city from the surrounding farms. Someone with a combination of intelligence and ruthlessness – Lord Mycroft, for one – could reduce London to starvation quite quickly.

"Good," he said. "Get organised patrols running through the entire city; I don't want anyone using the chaos as an opportunity to loot and rob their fellow citizens. And then start recruiting people for the army. We have enough weapons in the Tower to outfit a much larger force...what about defences?"

"Ruddy is already supervising the barricades," Davy informed him. "The walls of London won't offer much resistance if they bring the army..."

Jack nodded, sourly. London had never been heavily defended since the Restoration. It had always struck him as short-sighted, but maybe the authorities had had a point after all. Or maybe not; the French had persisted in their plans for invasion for the last hundred years and had never given up on the dream. If all the talk about new ironclads proved to be more than a fool's dream, the vast wooden ships of the Royal Navy would be rendered obsolete overnight. And then the French would have their long-awaited opportunity to land in Britain...

"Make sure that we have scouts out on all the approaches," he warned. Ruddy knew more about the military and Davy was a great organiser, but he still found it hard to relax and let them work their magic. The entire revolution rested on his shoulders. "They may try to bring in men from Scotland or even Ireland."

"There were reports of uprisings in Manchester and Liverpool," Davy said. "The toffees may have other problems then just London."

Jack shook his head. "London isn't just the capital – it's the seat of their power," he said. "As long as they're in exile from London, they look weak. They have to come and smash us first."

He shrugged. The Irish had risen up before, but had then lost their chance to become an independent nation because they'd started to fight each other, allowing the English a chance to rebuild and reassert their control over Ireland. But it also served as a reserve for the British Army, with several regiments based permanently on the Emerald Isle. Public opinion was strongly against a standing army, yet it was also in favour of keeping the Irish firmly in their place. It was a delicate balancing act; Lord Stafford was far from the only politician whose career had run aground on Ireland.

"Do you have the lists of prisoners?" He asked. "How many of the bastards do we have alive?"

Davy's smile widened. "We have one very special prisoner," he said. "We caught him before he could make it to Hampton Court. And I believe that he's looking forward to talking with you."

Jack lifted an eyebrow. He'd hoped – prayed – that they'd take one very specific nobleman, but his plans hadn't rested on it. "Good," he said. "Where is he?"

"We put him in the traitor's rooms," Davy said. "We would have put him in the cells upstairs, but no one had managed to repair them since you were last here."

"I'll speak with him now," Jack said. He glanced out of the window. The sun was setting, even though it barely felt like noon. Had it really taken hours to seize the city? "Keep me informed."

The Tower of London was far from an ordinary prison. Quite apart from rebels and traitors, it also housed noblemen who had been accused of vile crimes. They got quarters that were almost as well appointed as their private apartments in Pall Mall or their London mansions, for who knew if they would be convicted or not? The Warders would not wish to make a powerful enemy of a nobleman whose fate had yet to be determined. Queen Elizabeth had locked a number of powerful men in the Tower, and then released them as the fancy took her.

Jack passed the sentry on guard and – absurdly – knocked on the door before he pulled back the bars and walked into the room. The sole occupant looked up at him from an ornate couch, his face half-twisted in a smile.

"Good evening, Master Jackson," he said. He didn't sound particularly alarmed, or worried, even though he was very close to following Charles I to the headsman. "I wondered if I would see you again."

Jack swallowed. Old habits die hard. "Good evening, Your Majesty," he said. "I never doubted it."

Chapter Thirty-Seven

here were only two places in the British Empire where those who wanted a political career could be educated. The twin university towns of Oxford and Cambridge, between them, provided almost all of the graduates who took up positions in government, or within the vast civil service that actually made the country work. Those who went to either seat of learning made friends and contacts among their fellow students that would last for their entire lifetime, contacts that could be used to boost their career far higher than they might otherwise have risen. They joined the Old Boys Network at university and allowed it to dominate their entire lives.

Oxford, like Cambridge, was actually a network of universities and colleges, each one carefully ranked according to social standing and expense. Some of them were impregnable to anyone who wasn't born to an aristocratic family of long standing, even if they were wealthier than several peers put together. Others, more democratically, allowed wealth to guide them in the selection of their pupils. A handful of lucky boys won scholarships to Oxford or Cambridge, only to discover that their lack of wealth made them socially isolated. And the life of an outcast was barely worth living.

Gwen stood on the roof of Porterhouse College, staring down at the streets below. Porterhouse claimed to be one of the oldest colleges in England; it was certainly one of the most exclusive. David had told her that Porterhouse offered little more than a remarkable dining experience – the King had granted them permission to eat swan in perpetuity, apparently – and enviable social cachet. But then David, who had been intended to go into business before making the shift to government, had spent his time at a separate part of Oxford University. Porterhouse's reputation might be ill-deserved.

Or maybe not, she thought, as she caught sight of a group of students trying to climb over the rear wall. They were not supposed to be out after dark, according to the Senior Tutor, and anyone caught trying to slip in through the main gate could be assured of a few uncomfortable days after meeting their tutor in the morning. The back wall – topped with spikes and patrolled by the fearsome-looking gatekeeper – provided the kind of challenge that Porterhouse's ethos upheld. Those who managed to slip back into the building without being caught were destined for great things. The group she was watching looked too drunk to make it over the wall without some help from a magician. They'd probably gone out in the afternoon, spent the evening drinking and whoring, and then discovered that night had fallen while they'd been having fun. God alone knew what happened to those who stayed out all night, but Gwen doubted that it would be pleasant.

She'd never been to Oxford – or Cambridge – herself, of course. Women were not supposed to study at universities and Lady Mary had flatly refused to even allow Gwen to attend the few speeches and lectures that had been open to female attendees. What few women *did* get to attend the universities were isolated, barred from many of the more important lectures and persistently accused of lesbianism. David had openly admitted that he hadn't learned much at Oxford, but he *had* made contacts that had helped the family business. Gwen couldn't help, but wonder how different her life would have been if she'd been allowed to study at university herself.

The Royal College *had* established smaller training centres for magicians in both of the university towns. Gwen knew that she might be able to spend time there, although Master Thomas seemed to want to keep her in London. It wasn't too hard to understand why; there was only one other Master Magician in the service of the Crown and other magicians couldn't teach her how to use her powers in unison. She shook her head as a cold breeze drifted across the rooftop, a mocking reminder that winter was on its way. Down below, the night watch were closing in on the drunken students, preparing to drag them around to the gate and report their names to the gatekeeper. Gwen felt little sympathy for them. They had a whole wealth of knowledge – Oxford's collection of libraries were famed throughout the land – and yet they chose to spend their time tossing back beer and singing out of tune. A snatch of song reached her ears and she blushed. She wasn't supposed to know that such songs even existed, let alone what their words actually meant.

A footstep behind her caught her attention. "Begging your pardon," a female voice said, "but Master Thomas requests the pleasure of your company in the tutor's study."

Gwen turned. An elderly woman stood there, one of the women who changed beds, cleaned the building and generally looked after the male students. Gwen had been surprised to discover that none of the maids looked young or attractive, but it made a certain kind of sense. Young men, away from home for the first time in their lives, chased every woman they saw, with little concern for the social niceties. Hiring elderly women to work inside the university probably helped avoid the kind of scandals that resulted in unexplained pregnancies and dismissals.

"Thank you," she said, finally. She was ruefully aware that she was the youngest woman in the building. Some of the students had already tried to invite her into their beds, only to retreat in confusion when Gwen had used her magic to pick them up, hold them upside down and then let go. No one had been seriously harmed, but they'd given her a wide berth since then. "I'm on my way."

The interior of Porterhouse, according to the Master of the College, had been constructed in the years before Henry VIII had separated the English Church from the Vatican. It had once served to educate priests before the building had been taken by the Crown and then handed over to one of the King's more scholarly friends. Gwen wasn't sure how much of the story to believe – one of the tutors had claimed that the building dated all the way back to 1200 – but it hardly mattered. The ornate stone corridors and carefully designed rooms for young students appealed to her, unlike the students themselves. They all looked as if the only thing keeping them from obesity was the heavy exercise they did every morning. What Porterhouse lacked in academic excellence was compensated for by its remarkable sporting record. It was a rare year when Porterhouse didn't dominate the sporting field in Oxford.

There were two soldiers on guard outside the heavy wooden door leading into the tutor's study. They looked Gwen over carefully before standing aside and allowing her to walk into the study. Lord Mycroft, Lord Liverpool and Master Thomas were inside, seated in front of a roaring fire. From what Gwen had heard, much of the government had been dispersed or captured during the uprising. Lord Mycroft's escape had been just as hair-raising as their own. If his brother hadn't come to his rescue, Lord Mycroft would probably have joined many others in the Tower of London. Lord Liverpool, thankfully, had been on a visit to Cardiff when the rebellion had begun. His escort had managed to get him to Oxford before Cardiff was affected by the growing chaos.

Gwen found herself wondering, as she took the seat Lord Mycroft indicated for her, what had happened to the rest of the magicians. They'd had to leave most of them with the Royal Navy, but surely there were others. But Master Thomas – a far more skilled Talker than herself – had kept what he'd heard to himself. Gwen had been left with her imagination – and she'd been able to imagine all kinds of disasters. What if Jack had more magicians than the British Government? What if...

She looked down at her hands, wincing inwardly. Lucy's power had healed her, something she'd never told Master Thomas. What if she told him now? And yet...what would happen if the Royal College realised that Healers did exist? They would go looking for Lucy and put her into the farms. And then...she stared down at the fire, cursing her own ambition. She'd wanted to be important and develop her magic, hadn't she? And she'd gotten exactly what she'd wanted.

"The news is not good," Lord Mycroft said. "We have lost all control of London. What few troops were able to get out of the city have reported that many of the soldiers we sent into the poorer parts of London have been killed. The rebels have taken the Tower of London; the Warder, for whatever reason, was unable to blow the armoury before the rebels captured it. They now have access to one of the largest stockpiles of weapons in the country."

He scowled at Master Thomas, who said nothing. "There

have been smaller uprisings in a dozen other cities," he added. "The farmers are uneasy and may be on the brink of revolt themselves. Rumour has it that the Irish are planning a new rebellion. So far, no word has leaked out in America or Australia, but we expect that there will be more unrest once they realise that London has been lost to us. We must act fast."

Master Thomas frowned. "We would appear to have few options," he pointed out. "If we call up the militias, we might just discover that we are reinforcing the rebels. The militias have never been comfortable serving in a repressing role, have they?"

Lord Liverpool tapped the table. "This isn't the time for arguments," he said. "We can debate the true cause of these...uprisings later. The priority now is to recover London before the country comes apart."

"And to recover the King," Lord Mycroft said.

Gwen stared at him. "The King has been captured?"

"We must assume so," Lord Liverpool said. The Prime Minister, the man who had effectively sidelined King George, sounded bitter. His career was over, even if London was recovered quickly and without major damage. No one would ever trust or respect him again, not like they'd trusted Pitt the Elder or Pitt the Younger. "He certainly never made it to Hampton Court."

"He may be dead," Lord Mycroft pointed out. His beady eyes narrowed. "Should we not be honest here? We used the King to absorb much of the bad feeling generated by our...reforms of the British establishment. The rebels may have determined to kill him if he ever fell into their hands. Their hatred for him is unmatched."

Gwen shivered. One of the books she'd skimmed through ever since they'd fled London and reached Oxford had talked about the Tsar of Russia. The Tsar had created a myth that he loved his population and would help them, if he ever knew about their suffering. But he was surrounded by evil noblemen who ensured that the Father-Tsar never knew about their crimes against the serfs. The writer had concluded by noting that if the perception that the Tsar cared ever slipped, it would be the end of Russia. None of the serfs in the field had any loyalty to their lords and masters. Why should they feel loyalty to men who treated them as beasts of burden?

It was an ancient problem. Republican Rome had never managed to solve it; those who *had* tried to improve the lives of the poor and hopeless had come to sudden and violent ends. The Rome of Augustus had tried to impose some small manner of social reform, but it had never been enough. How could one balance the interests of noblemen with those of the poor? Gwen knew how David ran the family business; if he paid more in wages, the profits for expansion would go down. And who knew what would happen when more businesses started constructing airships? There was already more competition on the routes between England and France than anyone had expected, back when airships had first been proposed.

"Master Jackson would understand the value of holding the King as a hostage," Master Thomas said, sharply. "He wouldn't have killed him."

He didn't sound confident, Gwen realised. Jack was mad, after all; his madness gave him vision, but it also weakened his plans. He had staked everything on his demented plan to rescue the prisoners in the Tower. A single mistake would have ruined everything.

"Maybe he is no longer in command," Lord Liverpool said. "Uprisings have always lost control over their people..."

Lord Mycroft shrugged. "We must proceed under the assumption that the King is dead, long live the King," he said. "We cannot allow fear of his death to hold us back."

He looked down at the map. "Right now, we have only a few thousand soldiers in all of Britain," he added. "They're mostly Highlanders; capable enough in the field, but less capable in fighting within a city. We do have regiments in Ireland to call upon, yet it will take several weeks before we can move them over to England – and that assumes that Ireland will remain quiet. I doubt we will be so lucky."

"No," Master Thomas agreed. "The Irish will start an uprising the moment they see our troops depart – if they even wait that long."

Lord Liverpool shook his head. "If we lose control of parts of Ireland, we can regain it once we have secured England," he said, flatly. "The Irishmen always turn on each other as soon as they drive the English out – or sometimes they don't even manage to do that before they start killing their fellow Irishmen."

There was a knock on the door, which opened a moment later, revealing the Duke of India. Lord Liverpool rose to his feet and shook hands with the Duke, who took a seat next to Gwen. The commander-in-chief of the British Army looked tired and worn; Gwen realised, suddenly, that he had to have been targeted by the rebels when they rose up in London. He'd escaped, somehow, but was that actually a good sign? The Duke of India was known to be utterly inflexible, a reactionary to the core.

"I've been talking to Lord Waxhaw," the Duke of India said, without preamble. "He feels that we can pull four of the regiments out of Ireland, but that will not be enough to recover London. We need to consider other options."

Lord Liverpool looked shaken. "But the regiments...four regiments are nearly twenty thousand men," he said. "Surely that will be enough to retake London."

The Duke of India didn't mince his words. "I was in France during the uprisings that formed the Paris Commune," he said. "The French Army was gutted by the fighting that allowed King Louis to recover Paris – and Paris itself was devastated. We cannot assume that the rebels will surrender when they see us coming – and fighting in cities is always costly, even when the defenders are untrained rebels. And *that* assumes that the soldiers will stay loyal. Very few of my men signed up to fight their fellow countrymen."

There was a long pause. The Duke's bluff manner – and his well-known competence in military affairs – contrasted sharply with Lord Liverpool's gloom. He wouldn't have told them that their plans couldn't work, Gwen knew, unless the situation truly *was* hopeless. Jack had caught them in a neat trap; the government could negotiate and make concessions, or it would have to expend much of the British Army recovering London. And the devastation left afterwards, whoever won, would be hideously expensive to rebuild.

And it wouldn't stop there. There would be rebellions in Ireland, America, India, Australia and maybe even South Africa. The government would have to fight a massive war on several fronts at once, even if the French or Russians didn't take the opportunity to knife the British in the back. Jack's plan might be more cunning than she'd assumed; if the British Empire faced so many different problems, it might shatter. And then...who knew what would replace it?

"I think we must start bringing the regiments over anyway," Lord Liverpool said, finally. "Please see to it. Master Thomas..."

"No," Master Thomas said, flatly. "You don't know what you're asking."

"There's no other choice," Lord Liverpool said. "One final throw of the dice."

Gwen glanced from him to Master Thomas, puzzled. "Is power really worth the price?" Master Thomas asked. "Do you know what this will do to us, even if we win?"

Lord Liverpool's gaze was unflinching. "I know the price," he said. "You know that there is no choice."

"No choice?" Gwen repeated. "No choice, but to do what?"

The Duke of India, surprisingly, answered. "A long-held contingency plan," he said. He sounded...appalled. "Prime Minister..."

"The decision is made," Lord Liverpool said. "Master Thomas?"

Master Thomas hesitated, and then nodded. "Very well," he said. "I hope you can sleep at night afterwards."

With that, he got up and stalked out of the room. Gwen hesitated, and then followed her tutor, keeping a distance. Master Thomas had sounded angry – and disgusted. Gwen was unsure what to feel, but if it worried the Duke of India, it worried her too. Master Thomas walked up to the roof, ignoring the small number of students and staff he encountered along the way, and stepped out into the darkness. Gwen was on the roof just in time to see him leap into the air and head towards London. Even for a skilled magician, it would be a very long flight.

For a long moment, she waited on the roof, unsure of what to do. No one had given her any orders, yet she had a feeling that Master Thomas would have wanted her to stay in Oxford, out of immediate danger. And yet...

She leapt into the air and followed Master Thomas, holding well back from her tutor. The darkness enveloped her as she rose into the sky, following him towards London. They would be almost invisible from the ground.

Wherever he was going, whatever he was doing, she wanted to know what it was.

She was sure that it was nothing good.

Chapter Thirty-Eight

 suppose you wouldn't," the King said. "You never doubted anything."

"Your government is at an end," Jack said, ignoring the gibe. He was finally in a position to dictate terms to the King, the Monarch of Great Britain and her Empire. "Your people have risen up and overthrown you. Your aristocrats will no longer exploit the common people for their advantage, while leaving their victims scrabbling in the dirt..."

The King smiled. "You mean like you acted, before you discovered that your life was a lie?"

Jack's eyes flashed fire. "I could kill you right now," he snapped. Lightning danced over his hands. "I could behead you and stick your head on a pike in front of the tower."

"Of course you could," the King said. He didn't seem worried by the threat. "And someone in the Line of Succession would be acclaimed King and the country would go on. These aren't the days when losing a monarch meant the end of everything. The government will carry on without me."

Jack had to smile. "And that prospect doesn't bother you?"

For a moment, he saw tiredness in the King's face. "While my father was alive, I woke up every day unsure if I was Prince Regent or not," he said. "He had days when he was the man I remember from my childhood and days when his mind was clearly gone, when he wanted me to marry a rosebush or to form a marriage alliance with the Tsar in Russia. The pressure of the Throne destroyed my father's life. If I had my life all over again, I'd want to be someone happy and distant and *small*."

"Really?" Jack asked. "I think you'll find that happiness

and powerlessness don't go together in the modern world."

"Maybe not," the King agreed. "Lord Owen...I want to be like him. Spend my days happily pottering through libraries, researching ancient history while allowing the world to pass me by. You thought of me as an absolute ruler, but in truth I have less choice than you might think. I didn't choose my wife..."

"You settled for abandoning her instead," Jack pointed out, tartly. "How many mistresses have you had?"

"Too many and too few," the King said. He looked up at Jack, sharply. "And how do you explain the women in the farms you...mated with while you worked for the Crown?"

Jack winced, inwardly. "I had sex with them, yes," he confessed. "I didn't know what they were or what I was..."

The King snorted. "Of course you knew what they were," he said. "They were women who were helpless to resist you, who simply couldn't say no. You have no sense of natural justice at all; your revolution is built on a lie. You're the man who couldn't face up to what he was without allowing it to warp him into a monster. Do you even know the names of the men and women who died on the airship you brought down in the Thames?"

"There's no such thing as natural justice," Jack said, quietly. The King was right, no matter how much he wanted to deny it. "There's only what we make for ourselves."

"And you have made a new world for yourself," the King said. "What will you do with it, I wonder?"

He smiled. "You've taken the city," he added, "but you will find governing to be much harder than you think. What will you do for money if you abolish half the taxes, or if you force the businesses to pay better wages instead of using the profits to pay the government, or if you abandon the sugar colonies in the Caribbean? Who will feed the country if you abandon the new farming technology in England? What will you do when the colonies start revolting? And who will serve in the Royal Navy if you remove the country's natural leaders?"

"We will find answers to those problems," Jack said, mildly.

The King snorted, louder. "People have been trying to find solutions to those problems since the days of Alexander the Great," he said. "There are countless texts on the subject of what makes a good monarch, or an ideal system of government. No one has ever produced a permanent solution – and no one ever will. Whatever system you devise, there will always be winners and losers.

"You rail against the rich aristocrats who patronise the poor," he added. "But if you take away their wealth and distribute it to the population, who will have enough money to invest in railways and shipping – even airships? Who will *want* to invest when there are no profits to be had? What will you do then?"

He looked up. "I'll tell you what you'll do then," he said. "You'll break your own principles and do whatever it takes to rebuild Britain's power. You'll force the colonies to submit rather than granting them any independence. You won't free the slaves..."

"I will," Jack said. "Slavery is a great evil..."

"Would the slaves in America be better off without their chains?" The King asked. "And what would you say to those who own the slaves? Will you pay them for their human property or will you force them to let the slaves go without compensation? And if you do, what will you do when they produce a revolt against you?"

The King chuckled. "Do you see why I was content to leave the government to Lord Liverpool and his Cabinet?" He asked. "I was King – and I could do nothing without risking the collapse of the entire system. Perhaps you'll do better than me, perhaps not...I'll wish you good luck. You're going to need it."

Jack's eyes narrowed. "And what would you say if I told you that you were going to be executed on the morrow?"

"I trust that you would allow me a parson so I could make my peace with God," the King said. The tiredness had crept back into his voice. "If the sacrifice of a monarch is required for peace in my country, I am willing to serve."

"I don't believe you," Jack said, flatly.

"You're in charge now," the King said. "You can believe what you like."

Jack scowled at him, resisting the temptation to ram his fist into the King's chest. "Your men have deserted you," he said. "Your Butler escaped into London and hasn't been seen since."

"Edmund has always looked after himself first," the King

said. He didn't sound worried or concerned. "You'll probably find him in one of the pie-shops, eating a pie and plotting his escape. He always thought of me as an idiot, even when I sought to patronise the latest works of English scholarship. I don't suppose I can blame him. I've certainly spent enough time pretending to be nothing more than an idle pleasure-seeker."

"Instead of doing your job as King," Jack hissed.

"The job is impossible, as you will soon find out for yourself," George IV said. He smiled. "Do you want to know what my father told me, during one of his lucid moments?" Jack cocked an eyebrow. "He asked me what right we had to be Kings – and then he answered the question. We had the right because we *were* Kings; like it or not, there was no one else on the Throne. We had to play the role because there was no one else in our shoes."

He shrugged. "And now you're in charge, of London at least," he said. "Best of luck, Master Jackson. You're going to need it."

Jack studied him for a long moment, and then turned and walked out of the door, closing it firmly behind him. He wasn't sure what he had expected when he met the King for the first time in five years; a man who gloated over what had happened to the poor during his reign, or a man who begged and pleaded for a mercy he knew would never come? Jack hadn't expected to see a tired monarch, resigned to his fate. And yet he was right about one thing; there was always another monarch. Charles I had been beheaded – and instantly succeeded by Charles II, who had eventually returned to England and reclaimed the Throne. The government – whatever was left of it – wouldn't give up just because Jack held the King in his clutches.

Olivia met him as he came down the stairs and into the map room. "There was a runner from Pall Mall," she said. "Lord Blackburn has not been taken into custody."

Jack nodded, unsurprised. Lord Blackburn had always been good at looking after his own skin. A quick change of clothes, a pause long enough to scoop up everything valuable in his apartment and then he'd be out into the city, heading towards Oxford or Cambridge or wherever Lord Liverpool had fled since the uprising had begun. Besides, a Charmer was hardly as dangerous as Master Thomas. He might be caught on the streets and lynched before his magic had a chance to work on his attackers.

"There are a lot of angry people out there," she added. "They want to loot and burn the noble mansions."

"Leave them covered," Jack said. He couldn't blame the poor and downtrodden for wanting to destroy houses that would never be open to them, but they needed the aristocrats alive and – more importantly – the wealth stored within those houses. "If anyone shows too much enthusiasm, we'll move them to the barricades."

The air in the map room was calmer than it had been earlier, with Davy and Ruddy directing their troops with the aid of several Talkers and a small army of messengers. Jack nodded to them as he glanced at the map, noting the system of barricades that were already taking shape within the city. If – when – the Army came to disperse the rabble, they wouldn't find it a particularly easy task. There were even mines being floated down the Thames to make life interesting for the warships gathered where the Thames merged into the sea.

He shook his head, exhausted. They would only have a few days to train most of the new recruits in using their weapons and other basic combat techniques. And then...who knew what would happen when the Army attacked the city? Davy's figures suggested that they had about thirty thousand men, which seemed a vast number until one realised that they had to be armed, trained, and then deployed in a ring around the city. Smaller units would have to be kept in reserve; without Talkers, the task would have been nearly impossible. Jack didn't know how Wolfe or Amherst or even Cromwell had coped in the days before Talkers. Coordinating a military force, even one on the defensive, would have been far harder.

"We seem to be in charge of the city," Davy said. He looked tired, Jack noted. Davy had never been a particularly inspiring leader, but he was a genius at organisation and managing large numbers of people. He'd been a foreman in a factory before his brother had been badly injured in an industrial accident that had cost him the use of his legs. The factory owner had tossed him out onto the streets – and Davy had left the following day, vowing revenge. "We've moved most of the toffees into our safekeeping here and fed them on gruel. Some of them had the nerve to complain."

Jack smiled. Gruel was either unpleasant or tasteless – and cheap, cheap enough to be fed to workhouse children or factory drudges. It provided basic nourishment, but little more besides. The rich population of London would never have had to taste it until now. Maybe it would give them a new sympathy for the poor.

"We've also been distributing food to the new volunteers," Davy added. "Many of them are happy to work with us for food and drink, thankfully. I've put the ones who we can't arm yet on clearing up the bodies and moving them to the crematorium. Thousands of people died in the fighting, Jack..."

"Thousands more will die when the Army comes for us," Jack said. He scowled down at the map. "Have we heard anything from the Government?"

"They're in Oxford, apparently," Ruddy said. "One of our agents flashed us a message; there's an entire regiment in the city, providing security for the government. There won't be an uprising in Oxford, I fear."

He hesitated. Jack recognised the signs of a man with bad news. "The Duke of India escaped," Ruddy added. "I believe that he will have made it to Oxford."

Jack swore. The Duke of India was not much liked by anyone – particularly his men – but they respected him and trusted him not to get them killed for nothing. His presence outside London would be a major rallying point for the government – and no one doubted his competence. He'd unite what forces had escaped London with newcomers from Ireland and then bring them back to the rebel-held city. The street-fighting in Paris had been ghastly and hundreds of thousands had died. God alone knew what would happen when the British Army attempted to secure London, except that it was going to be bloody. Jack and his followers had nowhere to go.

"The assassins misfired, then," Jack said. He'd taken the risk of assigning their best Blazer and Mover team to the task of assassinating the Duke, but the Duke had earned his honours in combat. And magic didn't make a person invincible. He should have left the attack on Parliament to Davy and Ruddy, while taking care of the Duke himself. Jack shook his head, dismissing the irritating thought. Hindsight was always perfectly clear. "We'll have to see if we can get a team up to Oxford and cut off the government's head."

Ruddy snorted. "I'm afraid not," he said. He tapped the map. "We've been sending scouts out of the city. The remaining Dragoons have been operating in flying patrols around the outskirts, intimidating the farmers and blocking our routes out of the city. We could probably scatter them if we marched our army out of the city, but that would only disperse our force – unless we head for Oxford now."

Jack hesitated. He knew the strengths – and limitations – of the force he'd built in secret. The men weren't ready to face a stronger enemy and the Duke Of India would have at least one regiment on hand to defend Oxford. At best, the rebels would have to take a staunchly defended city. And if that misfired...they'd be intercepted outside Oxford by a regiment with much better training and experience. It would take time to train up the volunteers, time he suspected he wouldn't have. They would have to hope that they could break the Duke's army when it returned to London.

"We'll consider it in the morning," he said. He yawned, suddenly. "Make sure that the Talkers are replaced before they get too tired to function, and then have someone wake me when the sun starts to rise. Get your own replacements here and then get some sleep yourself..."

Walking out of the door and heading up towards one of the cells, he was surprised to run right into Olivia.. The girl was sitting halfway up the stairs, her hands clasping her legs. She looked...distracted, almost as if her mind was elsewhere. Jack placed his hand on her shoulder and she jumped, surprised.

"Oliver," he said, using her male name, "what's wrong?"

"I don't know," Olivia admitted. She rubbed the side of her head, frustrated. "I just feel...wrong."

Jack leaned down to peer into her eyes. Sometimes, when a person was hit on the head, their thoughts started to wander. But Olivia's eyes were clear blue, as always. And who would have struck her? The rebels held the Tower of London. Who would have risked hitting Jack's personal messenger? Even if someone had seen through her male guise, they'd have to be insane to risk irritating a Master Magician.

"Get some sleep," he said, finally. It wasn't much, but short of asking Lucy to leave the wounded and check Olivia personally, there wasn't much else he could do. Perhaps it was tiredness; Olivia had been awake since dawn, before the world had turned upside down. "I'll see you in the morning."

He helped Olivia up the stairs, opened one of the unlocked cells and random and was relieved to discover that it was empty. Jack broke the lock, just in case, and waved Olivia towards the bed. She hesitated, perhaps fearing that he was going to insist on joining her, before Jack closed the door, leaving her alone. He walked down the corridor to the next cell, opened the door and staggered over towards the bed. There would be enough time to sleep, he told himself firmly, before something happened that required his attention.

The bed was soft and warm. Jack closed his eyes; instantly, he felt his mind begin to wander. He'd never been as capable with the Sight as Master Thomas, but he could visualise the Tower of London, despite the magic woven into its stone. Nothing seemed to be amiss...but now that he was alone, something felt *wrong*. It hovered on the edge of his mind, taunting him. Something was wrong. Olivia had sensed it and now Jack understood. It was a nagging presence, something that could be ignored, but never pushed away.

Puzzled, Jack felt sleep overcoming him. His last thought was a memory. They'd never identified Olivia's magic, despite running all the basic tests. Perhaps she had a new, undiscovered talent, much like Lucy was a Healer. Or maybe her talent wasn't new at all, but something old and very rare. Maybe she was a Master, the second female Master known to exist. Or maybe...

He was asleep before the thought took him any further.

Chapter Thirty-Nine

ondon was wreathed in shadow, almost invisible against the gloom.

Gwen felt exhaustion tugging at her breast as she flew onwards. Before the uprising, she'd seen London as a city of lights, illuminated by the glow of streetlights and noble mansions. Now, London seemed almost dark, with only a handful of lights glimmering out in the darkness. She could see a couple of fires from where she knew noble mansions to be, roaring up into the dark skies. It reminded her that her family was missing, lost somewhere in London or perhaps among the crowds of refugees that had fled the city. If she went to Pall Mall to look, would she find her brother – or would there be victorious rebels, laughing as they destroyed the buildings?

Master Thomas was still ahead of her. She couldn't understand how he managed to keep flying, not when it had taken almost all of her energy to remain in the air. He was older than her, yet he'd been a practicing magician for almost all of his adult life. Maybe he knew tricks to conserve magic while flying, tricks unknown to his young apprentice. Gwen's entire body was burning, as if she was running out of magic. She found herself hacking and coughing as she started to descend, against her will. The magic that was holding her up in the air was starting to fade away...she barely had a moment to react before the ground seemed a great deal closer. Gwen grabbed for her remaining magic, no longer caring if she lost Master Thomas, and slowed her fall as much as she could. It was still jarring when the ground came up and hit her.

She found herself lying on the grass, one hand in a cold pond. The shock of impact had stunned her and she took several minutes to pull herself together enough to lift her hand out of the water. Something had been nibbling at her fingers; London had been indulging a craze for fish-keeping over the last few years and everyone who was anyone – or thought that they were anyone – had installed a fishpond. Some of the fish were very rare, brought in from the colonies; Lady Mary had been surprisingly proud of her fishpond. She hadn't done any of the work of actually building it, of course.

A hand fell on her shoulder and Gwen started. She hadn't sensed anyone nearby, but she'd been so focused on her flight that she'd neglected her other senses. Her mind swam dizzily the moment she reached for her magic and she realised, grimly, that she was almost helpless. She could do nothing more than lie on the grass like a ragdoll...

"You are a very lucky girl," Master Thomas said, from out of the darkness. Gwen almost sagged in relief. Her mind had been pointing out that whoever had found her might have dark intentions. "And you're also a very naughty one. You should have stayed in Oxford."

A light glimmered in front of her as Master Thomas knelt down beside her, heedless of the wet grass against his expensive suit. "I couldn't push myself that far when I was your age," he said. "But then...what kind of magician would I be if I hadn't known that I was being followed?"

Gwen tried to speak, but her body was completely drained. "I knew almost from the moment you took flight," Master Thomas said. "I should have ordered you back home, but I was curious to see how long you could stay in the air...it was a mistake. You're completely drained, on the verge of losing everything. And I don't have time to stay with you."

He reached into his belt and produced a small gourd. Gwen felt him reaching under her and turning her over, so she lay on her back staring up at the night sky. Master Thomas knelt in front of her again and placed the gourd against her lips. Something – water, but like no water she'd ever tasted – fell into her mouth and down her throat. There was a moment of nothingness...and then she felt a sudden flash of energy. She found herself sucking desperately on the gourd, like a baby at her mother's breast, and the flashes of energy grew stronger and stronger. A moment later, she sat upright, staring down at herself. The energy burned through her body, washing away the tiredness that had rendered her helpless. She felt almost as if she could fly around the entire world.

"What...?" Her mouth felt as if she hadn't spoken in years. She swallowed hard and tried again. "What was that?"

Master Thomas frowned. "Back when we were collecting legends of magic to study, we came across a legend of a druid who could brew a potion that gave the drinker superhuman strength," he said. "It was nonsense, of course, but it gave Doctor Norwell an idea. What if an Infuser were to infuse magic into a liquid, which could then be drunk by another magician? In theory, the second magician should be able to draw on the first's magic."

He shrugged. "It didn't work the first few times we tried it, until Master Luke tried it – and it worked, for him. We kept experimenting and eventually we discovered that it took both Infusing and Changing to make a magical potion – and combining the two talents could only be done by a Master. Some of our attempts to produce potion with a team of magicians failed spectacularly. In the end, we just kept it to ourselves. I don't think I ever told Master Jackson about the trick. I produce some potion every week and draw on it when I need extra power..."

Gwen looked up at him. "I feel great," she said. "Where..."

"I should thrash you," Master Thomas snapped. "Do you have any idea just how close you came to death tonight? What would have happened if your powers had failed while you were high in the sky? You'd have fallen to your death. What would have happened if someone had stumbled across you while you were helpless? You'd have had your throat cut – if you were lucky. I ought to send you back to Oxford to stay out of danger until this is all over..."

"I'm sorry," Gwen said, contritely. She meant it too. It hadn't occurred to her that she would be putting her life in so much danger, let alone delaying Master Thomas from completing his mission. Her body felt strange; parts of her seemed to be bursting with energy, other parts felt almost dead, on the verge of collapse. It struck her that she might be safer finding a quiet place to sleep and resting, except London was held by the rebels. What would Jack do if he found her alone and helpless?

"How many times have I told you that magic is useless without discipline?" Master Thomas raged. "You need to learn to *think* before you act. Right now, some Charmer with a good grasp of their talent is going to be able to twist you into his servant, just because you never think about what you're doing. If you'd been born a man, I would thrash you right here and now."

Gwen bowed her head, a confusing mixture of emotions flowing through her. She'd risked her own life and, as the only other loyal Master, the future of the Sorcerers Corps. If he wanted to thrash her...part of her wanted to run, because the prospect was terrifying, and part of her felt as if she deserved punishment. Lady Mary had never punished her, at least not physically. Her mother's tantrums had lost their power to affect Gwen long ago.

"Turn around," Master Thomas ordered. Gwen obeyed, feeling oddly vulnerable. She was his student, his apprentice – and she was supposed to obey him. Her father had put her into his care. "Bend over."

Gwen had no time to react before he slapped his cane against her bottom. There was a moment of nothing – and then the pain hit, a searing line of fire across her rear end. She yelped in pain, jumping forward and rubbing at her behind. The pain refused to fade, no matter how many mental disciplines she tried to use. It hurt, badly...what if he wanted to do it again? Or cane her bare bottom? Or...she tried not to think about it. The pain seemed to suck away all her thoughts.

Master Thomas shook his head, resignedly. "You may as well come with me," he said, slowly. Gwen, who had been expecting another stroke, started in surprise. "I may need your help. But if you disobey me once more..."

He left the threat hanging in the air as he turned back towards the south. A moment later, he leapt into the air and flew away. Gwen followed him, rather shakily. Her magic felt wrong, somehow, as if it was catching and then falling away from her. But it wasn't her magic, she realised slowly; she was drawing on magic Master Thomas had stored for himself. No wonder it felt odd, or so she told herself. Or maybe it was her own confusion. Master Thomas had been right. She had come close to killing herself because of her own curiosity.

She heard shouts from below and glanced down, sharply. A mob was chasing a man who was running as fast as he could, but he couldn't outrun the angry crowd. They caught him, dragged him to the nearest streetlamp, and produced a rope. Gwen had only a moment to realise what they had in mind before they strung him up and jeered as he choked to death. There was nothing she could do to save him, leaving her wondering who he had been before he met his end. An aristocrat? A factory owner? A loan shark? There was no way to know. He might even have been someone unpopular, perhaps a Jew, no longer protected by the forces of law and order. The working class hated the Jews, just as much as they hated the Irish and the black slaves who worked on plantations in the Americas. Jack would have been smart enough to realise that such small hatreds were only used to distract them from their true enemy. How many others wouldn't be able to see anything that wasn't in front of their noses?

Parts of London seemed almost deserted, even the docks. They were normally busy at all times of the day, but now...only a handful of men were working with the boats docked in the Thames. The warships to the east would be blocking all travel in and out of London, at least until Jack went downriver to deal with them personally. She half-expected Master Thomas to meet up with a boat and its crew, but instead he flew onwards to Soho. It had been a poor part of the city before an epidemic had swept through the area, killing hundreds of helpless men and women. Doctor Norwell had used it as an example of the good magic could do; magicians had discovered that Cholera was caused by tiny creatures living in water, as opposed to 'bad air', one of the theories that had rendered it impossible to stamp out the epidemic. Soho was still almost deserted, even with so many people desperate for a roof over their heads. It had a very bad reputation. The Rookery, she suspected, wasn't half as fearsome as a place infected by something that killed everyone it touched.

The stench reached up towards her as Master Thomas touched the ground. She gagged, despite herself. Breathing through her mouth seemed difficult, but every breath she took through her nose made her feel queasy. It was easy to understand why so many people had believed in 'bad air' – the stench seemed to be almost a living thing. The ruined buildings, deserted apart from animal life, seemed to belong to another world. Jack's words echoed in her mind and she shivered. If she'd lived in such hopelessness, she would do whatever it took to get out – even whoring, selling her body to strangers.

"Be careful where you put your feet," Master Thomas said. "The paving here is very thin; they used to collect night soil below us. The Gong Farmers would come every so often and drain it, taking the night soil out of the cities and using it on farms. After they discovered that night soil often helped epidemics to spread, they just abandoned the cesspools under London. They should have burned this part of the city to the ground, but...they had their reasons for leaving it alone. No one in their right mind would come here."

Gwen started as a dark shape flashed across the road. It was a dog, but not of a breed she recognised. It was larger than any dog she'd seen before, eying her with a gaze that suggested that it was very far from tame. Without a human presence, the animals in Soho had reverted to the wild; dogs and cats had gone feral, hunting down rats and weaker dogs to feed themselves. A string of spiders made her jump as Master Thomas's light illuminated the gap between two of the smaller buildings. They'd built up the webbing over years, she realised, out of reach of dogs and cats alike. Indeed, maybe a weaker dog or cat would be caught in the webbing. A rat seemed to have been caught by the spiders down towards the paving. They were swarming over the corpse...what did spiders do to their prey? Gwen couldn't remember. Some of the spiders were larger than her hand, scuttling over the ground with deadly intent. Gwen shivered and turned away. Master Thomas was right. This part of London should have been fed to the flames.

Another dog appeared in front of them as they reached a set of buildings. They looked as decayed and abandoned as the other slums, but there was something about them that caught Gwen's attention. She studied it thoughtfully, trying to understand, yet the nagging thought at the back of her mind refused to come into the open. The dog sat up and paced forwards, disturbingly human eyes locked on their faces. Master Thomas stopped and held out his hand, allowing the dog to sniff it sharply. There was a long pause and then the dog sat back on its haunches. Its face twisted and warped into the face of a man, almost doglike in its intensity. Gwen stumbled backwards, but Master Thomas caught her arm.

"It has been so long," the dog-man said. "I thought that it would never end."

Gwen spoke before she could stop herself. "You live here, among the monsters?"

The dog-man looked at her, inquisitively. "My apprentice," Master Thomas said, sharply. "She is welcome in this place."

"No one is welcome in this place," the dog-man said. His voice was deep, almost a growl. Gwen saw his tongue as his mouth opened and blinked in disbelief. It was far longer than the average human tongue. "I have lived here for many years. I find the solitude reassuring. The other dogs know that I am not one of them and give me my privacy. One day I shall die here, alone, mourned by none."

Master Thomas shrugged. "You chose it," he said. "You could have gone elsewhere."

"True," the dog-man agreed. "I hope you know what you are doing, Master Thomas. Some things are best left buried."

His face twisted and warped, falling back to the doggish form. He stood up on all four legs, winked at Gwen with one canine eye, and started to walk off into the shadows. Gwen felt sick, a strange combination of fear and pity overcoming her. A man who was half-dog, just like the werewolves who worked for Scotland Yard...but really, was there any better guard for a building in a place where few humans would dare to tread? It struck her, suddenly, that he might even have a doggy family...the thought was sickening, so sickening that she tried to push it out of her head. How could anyone live like that?

"He was never quite sane when we found him," Master Thomas said, answering her unspoken question. "There was a report of a werewolf haunting the backstreets of London. We hunted him down and found him; God only knows what happened to his family, or even if he *had* a family. He was happier as a dog than a man, for sure. Eventually, we asked him to serve as a guard here – and he took us up on it. All he ever wanted was to be left alone."

His lips thinned as he used his magic to open the building. Gwen stared in puzzlement, and then understood; only a magician could open the doors, perhaps only a Master. There was magic infused into the walls, she realised; it would be very difficult to break them down, even with explosives. Someone had gone to a lot of trouble to prevent people from breaking in– or, a part of her mind whispered, to prevent something from breaking *out*. But what could be hidden inside the building and remain dangerous for so long?

"There's always a price," Master Thomas said, more to himself than to Gwen. "There's always a price for whatever you want to do. And even stability comes with a price."

Gwen recoiled. The stench pouring out of the building was unbearable. It was *wrong*, something that shouldn't exist; she staggered backwards, hearing the buzzing of angry flies in her ears. Master Thomas seemed unmoved, or perhaps he knew how to use his magic to shield himself from the stink. The feral dogs, she realised suddenly, were howling. Something was *very* badly wrong...

And then the first creature stepped into view.

"No," Gwen said. She couldn't believe her eyes. "No..."

"There is no choice," Master Thomas said. "There is always a price for stability."

Chapter Forty

o," Gwen said, again. All fear of punishment had been driven from her mind. "You can't..."

The undead revenant advanced forward, step by step. It had once been human, but there was nothing left of humanity in this rotting corpse. The stench rolled forward, forcing her back; Master Thomas remained unaffected. Its greying skin seemed almost to be falling off its bones; it staggered slightly and flakes of dead flesh dropped to the ground. Yellow eyes, utterly inhuman, fixed on Gwen's face and refused to move. The revenant seemed to pause, almost as if it was listening for something, and then it started forward again. Gwen had to fight down an urge to run, or to hide. This couldn't be happening.

A second revenant appeared, followed by a third. It had once been female, Gwen could tell; one breast was dangling towards the ground, hanging by a piece of torn skin. She could see bones poking out from the dead flesh, somehow holding the monster together. The lead revenant opened its mouth – it lolled open, almost like a tired dog's mouth might – and moaned. Almost as one, the other revenants echoed the moan. Their dead gazes were fixed on Gwen's face. She could sense the magic holding them upright now, a magic that buzzed and crackled around Master Thomas. He was no necromancer...but he had the talent, just like he had all of the other talents. But to use necromancy – even to be a pure necromancer – was death, Gwen knew; Master Thomas was *responsible* for hunting down necromancers. The mere possession of the talent was an automatic death sentence.

There hadn't been many books on necromancy in Cavendish Hall, almost as if researchers were frightened to write down what they knew. The revenants were slow, but incredibly deadly. They couldn't be frightened; they had to be destroyed. Each revenant would keep moving as long as it could, no matter what happened to the body. Pain didn't stop them; the only thing that *did* stop them was fire. Their bodies had to be incinerated to stop them in their tracks. And that required magic, or a flamethrower.

Their real threat wasn't in their shambling forms, all the books had asserted. They spread the necromantic plague. A human who was bitten by one of the revenants would fall ill quickly and die within a few days – and rise from the dead as one of the undead monsters. Some people had thought that revenants were miracles, back when the first necromancer had inadvertently awakened the dead; they'd learned quickly that nothing of the former living personality remained. The only thing that drove the revenants was a desire for living human flesh. They would happily eat their former friends and family, using their flesh to sustain their existence. Even being close to a swarm of revenants was dangerous. Some people had tried eating their flesh once and caught the plague.

And a single revenant was stupid, the books had said; it was quite easy to stop, provided that one had the right tools. But a mob of revenants shared a communal intelligence. They were hardly as intelligent as a human, thankfully, yet they definitely showed signs of being able to hunt down humans through actual tactics, rather than just shambling after the nearest human. No one really understood *how* they tracked down the living, but they did – nowhere was truly safe from a mass of revenants. The book's writer had noted that revenants could bring down trees, dumping any human who climbed up the tree to escape the mob into their midst. A small army of them would be utterly lethal. And extremely difficult to stop.

"They thought that necromancy could be used as a weapon at one time," Master Thomas said. "The French had managed to slip an army into Louisiana and it was feared that they would be able to land on our shores. I was asked to develop necromancy as a weapon; eventually, I created these storage bunkers. The revenants have no need to fear cold; indeed, it preserves their dead flesh. As long as they remained inside these buildings, they were inert – and they were guarded, just in case."

Gwen stared at him, wildly. "Master…you can't unleash

them on London."

Master Thomas sounded almost reasonable. "You heard Lord Liverpool," he said, quietly. "The longer the rebellion holds London, the weaker the Empire becomes. And how long will it be before we find ourselves confronted with more rebellions than we can put down? We have to stamp this rebellion out before…"

"By turning London into a necropolis?" Gwen demanded. "There are hundreds of thousands of innocent civilians in this city!"

"I know," Master Thomas said. He sounded…regretful. "Many of them are no doubt loyal to the British Crown. But we cannot take the risk of the rebellion spreading, Gwen. We have to do whatever it takes to stop it."

"If you do this," Gwen said, "the world will never forgive you."

She shuddered as the revenants continued to inch forward, drawn to their living flesh. They'd be deadly, all right. London would have to be burned to the ground to stop them – and the rebels couldn't do that, not without destroying themselves in the process. The revenants would be almost unstoppable. She'd sworn an oath to the King, she'd accepted service with the Crown, but…this wasn't right. And there was the prospect of her family being caught up in the mass slaughter. The thought of David or Laura rising again as revenants…

"The world will not care," Master Thomas predicted. "The world cares nothing for common decency. Do you not see how absurd society is? The same men who will be shocked to hear a swearword used in front of a lady – a *lady* – will think nothing of going to a whorehouse and satisfying their lusts on a common whore. Lord Liverpool knows that the only way to deal with this threat is to act decisively – and to hell with our posterity. What would posterity say if we lost the Empire because of our scruples?"

He fixed his gaze on her. "It's time for you to go back to Oxford," he said. "And you will say nothing about this to anyone you meet."

"No," Gwen said, flatly. She pulled herself to her full height, trying to ignore the shambling mass of revenants. They kept pressing forward…how many, she asked herself desperately, had been crammed into the building? Revenants didn't need to eat, or sleep; they certainly didn't object to living amidst vast numbers of their fellows. There could be hundreds, or thousands, within London, hidden from the public's view. "I won't allow you to do this."

"You swore an oath," Master Thomas said. He didn't sound angry, just...tired. "I know what you're feeling. Once upon a time, I would have shared your feeling."

Gwen tried to reach out to him. "But...what happened to you?"

"I learned that the world doesn't care," Master Thomas said. "There is no point in clinging to the moral high ground if you lose everything that matters to you. The rebellion will be destroyed, Gwen. It's only a matter of time."

"No," Gwen said, again. She couldn't destroy them all, not on her own. But she knew who could help her – and who needed to be aware of the threat. Perhaps the revenants could be destroyed before they escaped Soho and entered the populated parts of London. "I won't let you do this."

She stepped backwards and launched herself into the air. Master Thomas looked after her, seemingly confused. Gwen herself wasn't sure of what she was doing, but she couldn't stay near the shambling monsters any longer. Their very presence was making her feel sick. The sky seemed to welcome her...and then her magic seemed to twist against her, despite her best efforts. It wasn't like having a Mover try to knock her out of the sky; it was more like...her own power was no longer obeying her will. She floated down towards the ground and fell to her knees the moment she touched down. Her body was simply refusing to do as she demanded.

"I won't permit you to change this," Master Thomas said. He still sounded more tired than angry. What was he *doing* to her? Gwen had thought she was capable, but Master Thomas had been practicing magic for nearly seventy years. He knew things she couldn't even begin to imagine. Even Lord Blackburn, the most powerful Charmer in Britain, couldn't control someone directly. Charm had its limits. "I've worked too hard for too long to allow you to change anything."

He seemed to be speaking more to himself than to Gwen. "I told myself that I would be able to lay down my burden," he said. "I was the last Master until he appeared – and I thought I could retire and devote my life to study. And then he turned on me and fled into the underworld, threatening to tear down everything I had built. I pinned my hopes on you. You at least should have known how lucky you were. Your excellent mind would be utterly wasted without magic."

Gwen struggled against his control, but it was impossible to break free. She couldn't even *feel* his control; her body simply refused to obey her. What was he *doing*? Her mind ran in circles, gibbering on the edge of panic. No one could control another person directly, no one.

"And now you turn on me too," Master Thomas said. He was walking closer, followed by his small army of revenants. Gwen could see them even from her kneeling posture. They looked...hungry, their expressionless faces fixed in a horrifying grimace. No living human could ever hope to have such a dead face. How many had he stored in the warehouse? "I should have known better. I don't get to rest, ever. I'll die the Royal Sorcerer..."

He stopped, right in front of Gwen. It took everything she had to lift her eyes to meet his gaze. He looked...determined. It was more frightening than anything else, even the lust she'd seen in the eyes of the first man she'd killed. Master Thomas intended to do something horrific to her, she was certain, something that would change her forever. And yet – no matter how she struggled, her body refused to move more than a few inches. Even breathing was difficult.

"No," Master Thomas said. "I'll change you into someone like me. Someone who can always make the hard choices and do the hard things, whatever the cost; someone who can take up my burden and replace me when I die. I wish you'd been more like me naturally, but it seems that I alone can handle the burden without breaking or embracing madness."

Gwen managed to speak, somehow. "You have to stop this," she said. Her lips felt icy cold, as if they were frozen solid. Speaking was a struggle. "You'll destroy everything the Empire stands for..."

"No," Master Thomas said. "I will ensure that the Empire stands for all time."

Something clicked in Gwen's mind. Master Thomas was a Master Magician. He could *combine* the talents. He'd told her as much long before she'd drunk his magic potion and used his magic to reinvigorate herself. And a Talker could send messages to another Talker or read a mundane person's mind...and a Charmer could influence defenceless listeners. What would happen if someone combined the two abilities into one? They'd have the power to control a person directly, without having to Charm them into submission. No ordinary magician could do it, but a Master...somehow, understanding what was happening to her made it easy to see it happening. Master Thomas had slipped right through her mental shields and grasped her mind with his powers. And it had never occurred to her that he could do more than send messages to Talkers.

His voice was whispering insidiously at the back of her mind, fiendishly difficult to separate from her own innermost thoughts and feelings. Why bother fighting? It was hopeless; Master Thomas was so much stronger than she was – she couldn't hope to win. And he wasn't going to hurt her, not really. He was merely going to make her better, more capable of doing her job. She should submit to him, accept his love and his judgement. He meant her no harm. And he knew better than her. And he knew better than her. And he knew better than her...

Gwen gritted her teeth. She'd felt Lord Blackburn's influence before, but even then she'd been able to sense that it was an unwanted intrusion in her mind. Master Thomas's whisperings were partly of her own creation, she realised, springing from the part of her mind that believed that the struggle was hopeless. They were putting forward reasons to surrender, reasons woven into her thoughts so perfectly that it was impossible to recognise them as anything other than part of her. No wonder so many Talkers went insane under the bombardment of outside thoughts. Reading minds was hardly an enviable skill when the Talker was unable to block the inrushing thoughts in any way. They'd go mad inside their own skulls. Even the women at the farm might have been unable to block out other thoughts.

It was so hard to focus, but she saw the revenants and her mind cleared, for a few seconds. Carefully, she began to concentrate on pulling her shields back together. His grip was easy to sense now, but blocking it was incredibly difficult. Her very perception of his grip helped to weaken her defences, for it seemed impossible to keep him out. She recovered a little control – a very little control – and tried to move backwards, but it was useless. It wasn't enough to break free of him completely.

Desperately, she reached out with her magic, unsure of quite what she was hoping to achieve. Master Thomas had combined two of his powers; Gwen, she was sure, could do the same with a little practice. Somehow, she combined Moving and Infusing, pushing a little magic into the pavement behind her former tutor. Master Thomas had no time to react before an explosion knocked him forward, slamming him right into Gwen. Gwen cried out as he knocked her to the pavement, but managed to wriggle out from under him before he grabbed back control of her mind. Now he was distracted, she managed to raise the strongest mental shields she could and slam them firmly in place. Master Thomas was bleeding, she noted absently, but he didn't seem badly wounded. He was pulling himself to his feet and reaching for her...

Gwen launched herself into the air again, splitting her attention between her desperate flight and her mental shields. She felt Master Thomas reach for her, only to be deflected away from her mind. The sensation gave her a boost of confidence and she flew faster, bracing herself for what she knew was coming. He could still disrupt her flight and send her hurtling down towards the cold streets, far below. Nothing materialised to stop her. For whatever reason of his own, he'd allowed her to fly free. Gwen hoped that meant that he'd repented of his dark intentions, but she suspected that she knew better. Master Thomas still needed someone to take his place and he'd need her alive so he could twist her into his ideal replacement. She wondered if he would give chase, but he seemed to be staying with the revenants. That made sense, she told herself firmly; necromancers had to stay near their creations, if only to ensure that they didn't go rogue and start hunting down random humans.

But wasn't that what Master Thomas wanted?

The thought was a bitter one, but it had to be faced. As far as Lord Liverpool and the Duke of India had known, there were no loyalists left within London. The soldiers on the streets had been hunted down and killed, even if they had killed ten rebels for each dead soldier. Those who could flee would have already done so; those who hadn't escaped in time would have been made prisoners. And the King himself was a prisoner. There was little to lose, from a strictly pragmatic viewpoint, from allowing the revenants to roam free. The only people who would be caught and eaten – and then left to reanimate and rise from the dead – would be rebels.

She shuddered as she hurled herself towards the Houses of Parliament. She couldn't let it happen, whatever the cost. No one would believe that the timing of the outbreak was a coincidence. Everyone in the British Empire would know that the Government had authorised the use of revenants to crush the rebel forces. And the rest of the world would be horrified. If the British Government was prepared to use revenants against its own people, it wouldn't hesitate to use them against other countries. The thought of a vast horde of revenants making their way across France, systematically killing and reanimating the French population, was terrifying. No one would be able to destroy millions of revenants as they marched across the Earth. The entire world would go to war against Britain first, joined by mutinies and uprisings right across the Empire. She couldn't let it happen.

But she had no idea where to go…

The Houses of Parliament were always illuminated, until the rebels had risen and blood had run red in the streets. Gwen hovered above darkened buildings, part of her mind mourning the damage, the remainder trying to deduce where the rebel leadership would have made their headquarters after taking the city. She caught sight of a patrol on the ground and dropped down low. Who knew? Maybe Jack would have given orders to take her alive.

And if not, she promised herself, she would force them to take her to Jack.

He was the only one who could help her save London.

Chapter Forty-One

ack!"

Jack opened his eyes, reaching for his magic before remembering where he was and why. Yesterday, they'd taken the city – and he had slept in the Tower of London of his own free will. He pulled himself upright, cursing his decision to sleep in his clothes, and stumbled towards the door. Lucy was standing just outside, her long red hair trailing down her dress. She looked just as tired as Jack felt. He felt as if he hadn't slept at all.

"Yes," he said, groggily. Something felt *wrong*, right on the edge of his mind. It refused to sharpen, no matter how hard he concentrated. "Have they attacked the city?"

"It's Olivia," Lucy said. She didn't sound happy; she sounded worried. "She's not well at all. Something's wrong with her magic."

Jack allowed her to urge him down the corridor and into Olivia's cell. The young girl hadn't undressed before trying to sleep, but she looked worse than Jack felt. She'd stained the bed with vomit and she was shaking, helplessly. Jack placed one hand on her forehead and swore. Olivia was fever-hot, her eyes bright and helpless. He'd never seen anything like it, but it reminded him of some of the horror stories told about diseases from Africa. But Olivia had never been outside London in her entire life, apart from their short trip up the Thames.

"Her magic is twitching," Lucy said. The Healer sounded helpless, almost beaten. "I've tried to heal her, but it seems to resist my power. And I don't have much left after…"

Jack nodded. Lucy had been healing the wounded after they'd taken the Tower of London. Jack had prepared plenty

345

of food and drink for her, but using so much magic had left her drained and worn. It was possible to burn out a magical talent through overuse, Jack knew, and he assumed that Healing was no different. Lucy really needed rest before the dawn rose and the Duke of India started his counterattack. He'd proven himself master of the bold stroke in India; who knew, perhaps he felt that he had enough men to strike at London without waiting for the regiments from Ireland.

"I don't know," he admitted. He knew more than anyone else in the underground about magic, thanks to Master Thomas and Doctor Norwell. The French had paid a steep price for much of his hard-won knowledge, but there had been nothing in his lessons about the healing talent, or whatever talent Olivia possessed. Jack scowled in frustration, even as he helped Olivia to her feet. They'd have to put her in a clean room and hope that her condition improved. "I've never seen anything like this."

Lucy nodded and took Olivia from him. The street urchin was badly ill, so badly that she'd cuddled up to Jack despite her lingering fears of his intentions. Lucy would make sure that she had some broth to drink and perhaps some boiled water, but there was little else she could do, even with her talent. They just didn't know enough about the healing talent to know what it could or could not do. Jack silently promised himself that he'd talk Lucy into undergoing a full series of tests once the revolution was over and they had won. If they could find a way to test for more Healers, it would revolutionise the world.

There was a sharp knock on the door and Jack looked up, to see Ruddy standing in the gap. He hadn't gone to bed at all, despite Jack's orders. He'd insisted that someone had to remain awake to monitor the city and ensure that the rebels didn't turn to looting.

"You're going to have to come downstairs," he said. "You won't believe who's just arrived, asking for you."

Jack frowned. "A messenger from the government, perhaps?"

"No," Ruddy said. "Master Thomas's young pupil herself."

**

346

In the end, it had been easier than Gwen had expected. The moment she'd shown herself to the patrol, they'd demanded to know who she was and what she wanted. They'd known that they couldn't beat a magician, so they'd been very relieved to discover that Gwen only wanted them to take her to Jack. After some debate, they'd escorted her to the Tower of London, fingering their weapons in a vain attempt to intimidate her. The swords and pikes they carried would be intimidating enough to the average person but after seeing the revenants, Gwen was less impressed by their weapons. Even if they were armed with rifles or the first generation of automatic weapons, the revenants would still march through them, leaving their soulless bodies to rise from the dead.

She'd never actually been to the Tower of London and she'd been amused to discover that the rebels hadn't actually destroyed half of the fortifications, as some of their number had planned to do five years ago. Instead, it had been turned into a command post, with runners – and a handful of Talkers – sending messages all over the city. Gwen was sure that other Talkers were trying to eavesdrop on rebel mental communication, but God alone knew how much luck they were having. Irene had told her that trying to listen in to a mental conversation was harder than it sounded, particularly if the two holding the conversation wanted to keep it to themselves.

They'd asked her to wait in a small room and Gwen had obeyed. There was little in the room, apart from a handful of tapestries that looked as if they were a few hundred years old. The Tower of London had been in existence for nearly a thousand years, Gwen recalled. It had never really stopped being the ultimate guarantee of London's security, despite the invention of cannons – and, later, the discovery of magic. The building would have been near-impregnable in the days of swords and shields. Even a disciplined Roman legion would have had trouble storming the Tower.

"Lady Gwen," a voice said, from behind her. Gwen turned to see Jack standing there. He was alone, carrying no weapon – but then, he didn't need anything overt to be dangerous. Like Master Thomas, he had far more experience with his powers than Gwen herself. During their last encounter, she suspected, he had carefully refrained from pushing her too hard. He'd wanted to lure her into a trap, not kill her outright. "You're a strange messenger from the government."

Gwen sagged. She hadn't slept and the magic potion's effects were wearing off. Everything was catching up with her. "Lord Liverpool doesn't know I'm here," she admitted. She wondered what the Prime Minister was thinking. Had he even realised that Gwen had left Oxford? "I didn't come at anyone's request."

Jack frowned, puzzled. "Really?"

"Really," Gwen said, too tired to be offended. "Listen."

She ran through the entire story, from the conference at Oxford to escaping Master Thomas – and the horde of revenants the government had been preserving for a rainy day. Jack listened in growing horror, something she found oddly reassuring. The revolutionary hadn't seen fit to create his own army of revenants and send them out against the government. And Master Thomas...

"I don't understand," she confessed after she finished the story. "What's got into him?"

"He was always willing to do whatever it took to safeguard the status quo," Jack said, although he sounded deeply shocked. But then, the laws against necromancy had been on the books almost since necromancy had been discovered. The entire country would rise up in horror when they learned what the government had done in their name. "And he was always too impressed by authority figures."

He scowled, pacing the room. "And you're sure that the army can't mount an attack on London?"

"They won't *have* to mount an attack on London," Gwen said. Waiting in the antechamber had given her time to think. "The revenants will destroy your forces and consume most of the witnesses. And then the soldiers will move in, destroy most of the revenants, and blame the outbreak on you. Anyone who could tell differently will either be consumed by the undead or killed in the flames."

Jack nodded. "Lord Mycroft would not approve," he said, slowly. "I sense the hand of Lord Blackburn in this, somewhere."

"He wasn't at the conference," Gwen said. It struck her as an odd thing to worry about when a horde of undead revenants were slowly spreading out from Soho. London's sprawling urban areas would turn into charnel houses as they consumed living flesh and grew stronger and more dangerous. And if Master Thomas was directing them, they would be heading straight for the centre of organised resistance. "It was Lord Liverpool who ordered it."

"Lord Blackburn vanished when we took London," Jack said. He shrugged, drolly. "He's probably still running. Do you think he'll stop to catch his breath in France, Russia, or China?"

Gwen glared at him. "Were you not listening?" She demanded, angrily. "There is a horde of undead monsters heading towards you and you're cracking bad jokes!"

Jack smiled. "Any rational assessment of the odds would say that our revolution was doomed to failure," he said. "Jokes are the one thing that keeps us going."

He stopped pacing before Gwen could give in to the temptation to slap him, hard. "I have to talk to my allies," he said. "I'd like you to wait here for us."

Gwen turned, angrily. "And how many people will die while you debate what to do?"

"Too many," Jack said, gravely. "I'll be back as soon as I can."

***

The antechamber had been designed to allow a number of people to listen to conversations within the chamber without revealing their presence. Ruddy and Davy had taken two of the listening holes, at Jack's suggestion; Lucy had taken the third. They met him outside as soon as he closed the door behind him, their faces twisted with horror. There was no nightmare more feared than the revenants, not after the outbreaks that had been quelled with so many dead – and then reanimated by a necromancer's will. Jack had studied what little material there was on the undead back at Cavendish Hall, but most of it had been speculation.

Necromancy didn't seem to obey the normal laws of magic – but then, there were plenty of question marks over just what the normal laws of magic actually *were*. The commonly accepted theory was that the undead somehow consumed life energy from their victims, using it to keep their dead bodies animated by their living will. As their brains were effectively ruined by death, the undead were unable to manifest anything that reassembled human intelligence, or anything much more than a desire to feed and survive. Perhaps their damaged brains also allowed them a form of telepathy, for they *were* more dangerous in large numbers. And when a necromancer was directing them with his will...

The story was unbelievable, but Jack was inclined to believe it for that reason alone. He *knew* Master Thomas – and he knew many of the personalities who ran the British Empire. Some would recoil in horror, but Lord Liverpool, who had used military force to crush a dozen riots and uprisings, wouldn't hesitate for a second if it meant securing London without any further fighting. Indeed, the whole plan had a sort of horrific logic; London's crowded slums would be burned to the ground, allowing long-held plans to rebuild the heart of the British Empire into a new Rome to be turned into reality. As long as they didn't lose control of the undead, it was almost perfect...

...But what if they *did* lose control of the undead?

The largest outbreak of the necromantic plague had been on Cuba, a dependency of the British Empire since it had been taken from the Spanish in 1801. Thousands of negro slaves had been infected, slowly dying and rising from the dead. They'd been a nightmarish foe for British Redcoats and North American Rangers, but they'd eventually been defeated – even though parts of Cuba were no longer fit for human habitation. London – even after the fighting – had around three to four million humans living within its boundaries. How intelligent would the undead be if they had that many within their ranks? It was quite possible that the madness Master Thomas had unleashed would spread out of control.

"That can't be true," Lucy said, sharply. "The bitch is lying through her teeth."

Jack frowned. "If she was lying," he said, "I think she would have chosen a more credible lie."

Davy snorted. "The toffees have always seen us as stupid, grubbing in the dirt," he said. "They might have sent her here and told her to lie."

Jack shook his head. "It has the ring of truth," he said. It would be nice to have a lie-detecting talent, but – apart from mind-reading Talkers – no such talent had ever been proven to exist. Or...maybe it *could* work, between two Masters. He could ask Gwen to Talk to him and see if it felt truthful or not. "Master Thomas would do *anything* to maintain the status quo. I think she's telling the truth."

"But they have laws against necromancy," Ruddy pointed out. "They hung a young girl four years ago on the mere *suspicion* of necromancy."

"There are laws against rebellion and revolution too," Jack countered. "I didn't notice an angel manifesting outside the Old Bailey to force us to go back to slaving in the fields for our lords and masters."

Lucy's scowl deepened. "Joke all you want," she snapped, tartly, "but I don't believe it. They probably want her to distract us long enough to ram a whole army up our behinds and sodomise us..."

"There happen to be laws against that too," Jack commented. Davy laughed, earning himself a furious glare from Lucy. Ruddy merely looked aloof from the debate. "If there really is a horde of undead revenants coming to kill us, it will soon become obvious."

He looked over at Ruddy. "Is there any sign that the Duke of India intends to mount a counterattack?"

"Nothing so far," Ruddy said. "I'd say that it would take the Duke at least a week to get organised, even without the forces from Ireland, but he's a past master at turning his forces around and launching a counterattack on the enemy. His career in India suggests that he won't leave us alone any longer than he has to..."

He scowled. "And most of our scouts are very new to the job," he added. "The Hustlers might manage to get past them and into the barricades without any of the scouts realising that they were there. And the Duke would know precisely how to take advantage of it."

Jack held up one hand. "We're going to assume that the threat is real," he said. "I want you to send messengers to the reserve forces; I want barricades set up around Soho, now. Anyone within the area is to be forced to strip down so they can be checked for bites...no, have dogs sniff them instead. The dogs won't be able to stand anyone who has been bitten and it'll save them freezing off their dongles in the cold night air."

"Yes, sir," Ruddy said. "And what should we do if we sight the undead?"

Jack scowled. The undead weren't tough, in a conventional

sense, but they were fiendishly difficult to kill. Beheading one wouldn't kill it; the body would just thrash around on the ground, flailing out at anyone unlucky enough to be caught in its arms. The only sure way was fire...and that could only be applied over a limited area.

"Cut them down *thoroughly*," he said, finally. "Tell the men to make sure that they hack each undead down and make damn sure they can't get up again. I want their legs and arms severed from their bodies; behead them too if you can. Distribute swords and axes to the reserves; they'll work better than guns against the undead."

He hesitated. "And remember to warn them to do the same to anyone who has been bitten," he added. "There's no cure for the necromantic plague."

"You're taking a hell of a chance," Davy observed, finally. "What if she's lying and she just wants us to look in the wrong direction?"

"Then the men on the barricades hold the Duke of India long enough for us to get reserves up to push him back." Jack said, tightly. The rebellion had around forty thousand men now, mainly new recruits. It sounded like a large number, larger than the armies that had conquered India for the British Empire, but it was tiny compared to the scale of the problem. London was a vast city and holding a set of barricades around the entire edge of the metropolis would spread his men thin. "I don't think we can afford to assume that she's lying."

Lucy made a face, but said nothing. Jack didn't know why she was acting oddly; she'd *healed* Lady Gwen, back when Jack had first tried to convince her that he was doing the right thing. The world had turned upside down since then – they'd won a city, but now they were on the verge of defeat. Jack rubbed the side of his head, cursing his tiredness. He needed rest, yet he had to go out with his men. They would need a magician or two to cover them if they did run into the undead...

He strode back into the antechamber and found Gwen waiting for him. She looked tired, almost vulnerable, yet there was a determination in her eye that rivalled that of many an older and wiser man. Gwen wouldn't give up, Jack realised; she would be true to herself even if the man she'd trusted as a tutor had betrayed his own ideals.

"We're going down to Soho," he said. He held out a hand;

Gwen, after a moment's hesitation, took it. "If you're right about what our old tutor is doing, we'll meet him there."

Gwen looked...nervous. "He's crafty," she warned. "He knows more about our powers than we do."

"That's fine," Jack assured her, affecting a confidence he didn't feel. Master Thomas was a formidable foe – and he had an entire army of the undead to support him. If nothing else, perhaps they could delay him long enough to evacuate the area. "I know a few tricks myself. Some of them will be new to our old friend."

Chapter Forty-Two

here was something in the air.

Gwen could feel it, right on the edge of her awareness. Ahead of her, dawn was slowly glimmering into existence, casting an eerie light over London. Few would see London from a hundred yards in the air, even from an airship. A handful of smoke plumes rose into the sky, but London seemed almost to be dead. It wasn't a thought that brought her much cheer.

She turned her head and saw Jack looking at her. He looked just as concerned as her, yet...there was something else there. A hint of respect, even admiration, coming from a man who had turned the world upside down. Gwen had never been admired for herself before; she'd been admired for her beauty and for her family linage, but no one had ever admired Gwen for herself. She blushed, despite herself, feeling emotions she'd thought that she would never feel. Girls whispered about love when their parents weren't listening, talking about feelings they had for men – men whom they would never be allowed to marry. Even Gwen had heard such talk among the maids...but she'd never thought that it would happen to her.

Jack winked at her...and dipped suddenly, flying down between the buildings. Gwen followed him instinctively, realising that he was daring her to catch him. His prowess was remarkable, almost as if he had spent years flying under his own power, forcing Gwen to learn quickly to keep up with him. He *had* planned to speak to her alone, the last time she'd chased him; he could have outrun her with ease. The thought was not a pleasant one, but she told herself that she should be grateful. How would she have known who to contact when Master Thomas unleashed his secret weapon without that earlier meeting?

The buildings spun past her with terrifying speed. Down below, men, women and children stared up at the two magicians, even as they scrambled to put some distance between themselves and the oncoming revenants. Gwen could sense them almost as soon as she remembered their existence, a lurking presence ahead of them, polluting the aether with their vile stench. Her head swam and she nearly dived into the street, before catching herself. It took all of her discipline to keep their whispers out of her mind.

Jack landed on a rooftop and peered towards Soho, his face grim and bitter. He could sense them too, Gwen realised; if he'd doubted her, he no longer believed – or hoped – that she had been lying. She landed next to him and caught her breath. Flying was truly the greatest of all the talents – and Jack had pushed her into developing it far further than she had believed possible. She was suddenly very aware of his presence as he caught her arm and pulled her back from the rooftop edge. His touch felt wonderful against her skin and she blushed, again. There was no time to explore her new feelings, or worry about introducing him to Lady Mary…

She laughed, despite herself. The odds of surviving the dawn – let alone the rest of the day – were not high. And she was worrying about introducing Jack to her mother? He might not share her feelings, or he might not want to spend time with her afterwards, or…there were too many possibilities. She tried to lock her feelings away inside her mind and concentrate on the growing presence. They weren't far from the growing horde.

"I can feel them," Jack said. His face was twisted in disgust. "I never…I have never sensed anything like them before, not ever."

"I know," Gwen said. There was nothing else to say. She would have given anything to have been wrong, even though Jack and Lucy and the rest of his band would have denounced her as a lying aristocrat. There were shouts and screams in the distance, growing louder. Soho might be largely isolated from the rest of London and left to rot, but there were hundreds of ramshackle buildings surrounding the area. The revenants would make quick work of the sleepers before they awoke, she suspected. Even if the alarm was raised, few would know how to fight the undead. "I'm sorry."

"Me too," Jack admitted. He reached out for her and pulled her into an embrace. Somehow – and Gwen was never sure how – their lips met. The kiss seemed to last for hours. "I wish…"

Jack let go of her and stepped back towards the edge. "Come with me or stay here," he said, slowly. "I have to speak to my men."

He jumped into the air and lowered himself towards the ground. A barricade was being built at the end of the street, composed of wooden furniture, blocks of stone and everything else that could be rounded up on short notice. The rebels looked disorganised, but their commanders seemed to know what they were doing and there was no disagreement. They could all smell the growing stench from Soho. It was utterly *wrong*, the stench of the grave yet animated by a hideous power. The law was right, Gwen decided; necromancy was utterly beyond redemption.

Jack turned to her as the rebels picked up their weapons and prepared for their stand. "I'm going to start burning them as soon as they come into view," he said. "I suggest you do the same. That should force Master Thomas to show himself – or let us burn his army to ashes before they can grow out of control."

Gwen nodded, tightly. The last time she had faced Master Thomas, she had barely escaped with her life – and she suspected that she'd been *allowed* to escape. Master Thomas had had plans for his successor, plans that required her to be alive. But this time…whatever else happened, the government would want no witnesses alive who could swear to the origin of the necromantic plague.

The breeze shifted and the stench grew stronger. A moment later, the first of the revenants stumbled into view. It had been a child before it had been bitten and forced to rise from the dead, still wearing the rags of a street urchin. Gwen, who had discovered that most street urchins were lucky to have any kind of roof over their heads, wasn't too surprised. They'd probably colonised the outer edges of Soho and become the first victims when the revenants started their shambling expansion. She drew in a breath as the second revenant appeared, followed rapidly by dozens more. Eerie inhuman eyes – some dangling from eyestalks – fixed on the barricades. No, she realised, it was an illusion. The revenants didn't seem to be looking at the living defenders, but they could still sense them. It was indisputable that they had some way of navigating the living world. Maybe they could smell the living. Gwen was uneasily aware that she hadn't had a bath for nearly two full days.

She jumped as the dogs started to bark, the sound blurring together into a single deafening howl of grief. Some of them struggled to pull free of their handlers, trying to flee the undead horde advancing towards them. Others whined and tried to burrow into the mass of humans, seeking safety among their masters. Their growing panic was contagious; Jack barked orders, moving from place to place to reassure his followers. Gwen was mildly impressed, even though she didn't blame the rebels for being on the verge of panic. Revenants didn't just kill their victims; they brought a fate worse than death. There were churchmen who claimed that to be bitten by a revenant was to lose one's soul.

Jack lifted one hand, almost casually, and a burst of flame flared into life. It roared out towards the advancing horde, which marched right into the fire without hesitating. Their undead skin blackened and then caught alight, sending the lead revenants to the knees as their legs collapsed. They kept trying to crawl forward until the fire destroyed their ability to move at all. Gwen pinched her nose – the stench was growing worse by the second – and created her own wall of flames. The revenants simply kept coming, even as they burned to ashes. She allowed herself a moment to believe that they could stop the horde, but it was self-delusion. The shambling creatures kept pushing forwards, the lead ones shielding their followers from the worst of the fire. They'd made a terrible mistake, she realised suddenly; the burning creatures would spread the fire to the barricade. The fire would rapidly spread out of control.

"Tricky," Jack agreed. He narrowed his eyes and concentrated. A wave of magic scythed forward, pushing the revenants back as if they were caught up in a gust of wind. The flames raged onwards, destroying hundreds of undead bodies, but there were always more behind the burning corpses. Gwen added her magic to Jack's, yet it wasn't enough to hold them back forever. And some of the burning undead – having been thrown against the buildings – had set fire to the surrounding street. The barricade might become useless even before the revenants reached their prey.

Gwen scowled and picked up a small cobblestone. Infusing it with magic, she hurled it into the mass of revenants. It exploded, blowing dozens of them into dead shreds of flesh. Jack laughed and copied her tactic, hurling dozens of stones of his own with terrific force. Not all of them had been infused with unstable magic, but it hardly mattered. Breaking the bones of revenants would make it much harder for them to shamble forward – and yet still they kept coming. A flaming monster crashed against the barricade and clutched onto the wooden structure with an inhumanly strong grip. It was rapidly dispatched by one of Jack's men, but the damage had already been done. The flames that had been consuming the revenant had spread to the barricade. It was coming apart right in front of the defenders.

"Fall back," Jack ordered. Gwen hadn't heard the instructions he'd given to his subordinates, but it was clear that he'd expected to lose the barricade. "Swordsmen forward; cripple the bastards. Everyone else to the next barricade!"

The swordsmen moved forward, carrying swords that would have been the envy of a Roman legion – and completely outmatched against a modern army with rifles and cannon. They were hellishly brave, Gwen realised, as they started to slash out at the oncoming revenants, cutting off their heads and arms in smooth motions. Physical wounds didn't bother the undead – if they felt pain, no one had ever proved it – but they could be crippled, forced to slow down or even stop. The swordsmen were quicker than their foes; they leapt in, slashed out and then leapt back before the moaning creatures could grab them with their rotting hands. Some of the swordsmen weren't quick enough; Gwen saw a man caught by one of the revenants, his throat bitten by the monster and his living blood spilling over the cobblestones. He fell, his wound already taking on the chilling dead greyness of the undead. Gwen summoned her power and incinerated his body. There was nothing else she could do for him.

Another swordsmen fell to the ground, where he was swarmed by three revenants. He'd concentrated on dealing with those facing him and ignored the one crawling forward towards him, using its hands to pull itself across the cobblestones. It had been so badly wounded that, as a man, he would have had no hope of survival, but the dark power animating its rotting flesh hadn't cared, as long as there was a chance of biting into human flesh. Jack yanked the swordsman out with his magic, but it was already too late. The revenants had killed him – and damaged his body so badly that there was a good chance he wouldn't reanimate as one of the revenants. Jack incinerated him anyway, just to be sure.

The heat from the fires was growing stronger. Gwen watched as slums burst into flames, fires that posed a danger to the living and undead alike. They'd been emptied long ago, she told herself, and hoped that she was right. Anyone trapped inside would burn to death a long time before they could be rescued. The fires might well start destroying the barricades, unless it could be brought under control. But instead, Jack seemed to be using his powers to pick up blazing pieces of wood and throwing them into Soho. Gwen was puzzled at first, and then she realised that Jack intended to incinerate the entire district. If there were other revenants hidden within the abandoned buildings, they'd be destroyed before Master Thomas or a necromancer could reanimate them.

"We're going to have to fall back," Jack said, catching her arm. "We can't stand here."

Gwen looked around, puzzled – and then horrified. Most of the swordsmen had fallen or were in retreat, leaving the advancing waves of revenants unimpeded. Jack summoned fire again and blazed it across their legs, sending many of them tumbling down into the ashes, but there seemed to be no limit to their numbers. Gwen wondered if Master Thomas had visited a graveyard and reanimated every rotting corpse in their coffins. It sounded absurd, yet…she had no idea if it was even possible. The books she'd read had been long on warnings about the evils and dangers of necromancy, but there had been very little hard information. There was a slight shortage of necromancers willing to share their illicit knowledge with the Royal College, knowing that they would be executed after they had been drained of all of their dangerously-won insight.

She nodded, allowing him to pull her into retreat. She tripped over something – a dead body – and hit the ground, just in time for one of the shambling monsters to reach for her. Absolute panic overcame her, only for a second, and flames blazed up all around her body, just before she hurled herself into the air. She had a nightmarish glimpse of a dead face as she rocketed into the sky, undead hands reaching for her. The flames seemed to be pushing her upwards; for the first time, she could look down on London as dawn rose over the city. She could hear the sound of battle all around the city, leaving her to wonder, once again, just how many revenants had been raised from the dead. And how many of those who had tried to stop them would have been bitten and turned into the undead themselves?

She dropped down next to Jack, who looked over at her grimly. The force they'd had on the first barricade seemed to have been reduced sharply; it tore at her that she hadn't even seen those men fall. Their bodies would have been destroyed by their fellows or started the process that led to their reanimation. She hoped it was the former; behind them, where she had launched herself into the air, the undead were crawling over the bodies of the recently living, heading towards the next barricade. Surely, she told herself, they had to run out of bodies sooner or later. How many had died in Soho?

But the area had been contaminated by disease long before necromancy had been anything other than a legend, she reminded herself. There could be hundreds of thousands of bodies under the city, just waiting for their chance to reanimate and go forth to prey on the living. They were the ultimate soldiers, in a sense; they not only felt no pain, but they were utterly expendable. Their lives – their undead lives – could be thrown away at will. She had a vision of shambling armies laying siege to castles, scrambling over their own fallen to finally climb over the walls and attack the living within.

"It doesn't sound good," Jack admitted. Gwen realised that he'd been listening to some of the rebel Talkers. "They've broken through the entire first ring of barricades and they're advancing on the second – some of them have even burst out of the sewers and attacked us from the rear. Master Thomas knows what he's doing, all right."

Gwen nodded, wearily. She hadn't had any proper sleep – and the effects of Master Thomas's magic potion seemed to have faded away completely. Her body, she realised dully, was on the brink of shutting down. She accepted a mug of wine and several cakes gratefully, realising that the rebels were taking a few seconds to fortify themselves before the battle resumed. The shambling horde of the undead seemed to be pausing, almost. They almost seemed to be stumbling aimlessly, as if they'd lost the force that was guiding them. Gwen realised that Master Thomas had perhaps overreached himself. No wonder their tactics were so basic; the person directing them had to concentrate on several different fronts at once. She *knew* she was right. And yet...something wasn't right.

Sure, part of her mind muttered. *You're fighting beside rebels against the government to which you swore an oath, trying to stop undead monsters unleashed by a man who is sworn to prevent such monsters ever menacing England ever again...of course something isn't right, idiot!*

Jack looked down at her, his face tired and streaked with sweat. Gwen reached out and took his hand in hers, grateful for the human contact. Jack smiled at her, despite his tiredness, and Gwen felt her heart flutter. Her heart was meant to pump blood around her body, all of the autonomy textbooks had stated. They had never mentioned the feelings of...desire, of love, of...everything. Her heart seemed to be pounding like a drum.

And then everything changed.

She looked up as a figure dropped down from high above, wearing a long black cloak that seemed to swirl around him. The tip of his cane rapped out as it tapped against the cobblestones. Master Thomas had arrived.

Gwen drew in a breath. This was not going to be easy.

Chapter Forty-Three

ack let go of Gwen's hand, staring at his old tutor.

Master Thomas had seemed ageless; he'd seemed a man who had carried the weight of the world on his shoulders for over thirty years and somehow refused to allow it to wear on him. He had lacked a peer since the other two Masters had died; Jack knew that his tutor had hoped that Jack would grow to take their place. But now...Master Thomas looked old, old and tired. The only thing holding him upright was his sheer will to live and succeed.

Jack took one breath, and then another. He had no illusions about the difficulty of facing, and beating, his old tutor, even with Gwen by his side. Master Thomas had had more years than both of his opponents combined studying – and practicing – magic. He'd very likely forgotten more than they'd ever learned; no, Jack reminded himself, Master Thomas forgot nothing. He looked upon his old tutor and remembered the days when he'd learned magic, before he'd learned the truth behind his origins. Master Thomas had taught him purpose – and how to fix his mind on a goal and to work out how to achieve his aims. Jack knew that his rebellion would not have succeeded without those lessons...

...And he'd loved the old man. Jack's real father would never be known, unless the farms had kept records of which man had impregnated which woman. There was a very strong possibility that Master Thomas might *be* his father, although Jack privately doubted it. Master Thomas might have been old, but he was still a virile man; if Masters beget Masters, there would be far more Master Magicians in the Royal Sorcerers Corps. His adopted father – the man he had thought was his real father until the day he'd discovered the truth – hadn't really shaped Jack's development. It had been Master Thomas who had taught him, disciplined him and – eventually – made him a man. Betraying Master Thomas had hurt more than being forced to flee Britain for France.

Master Thomas was wearing his black suit and top hat, leaning on his silver-topped cane. Jack wasn't blind to the message Master Thomas was sending, even as he allowed himself to hope that Master Thomas was as tired as Gwen and himself. He represented authority and order, the authority of the British Empire; the Empire that ruled more than a quarter of the world. And Master Thomas, the man who had played a major role in building that Empire, would uphold it with his last breath. Whatever he might have thought – about the farms, about the wars of conquest, about the transportation of anyone who dared to object to the Empire's dictates – he would keep it to himself. He was the Empire's man.

Gwen spoke first, despite the exhaustion that Jack could hear in her voice. "Master," she said, her voice almost breaking, "this is wrong."

Master Thomas ignored her, his gaze fixed firmly on Jack. It had been the first time they'd seen each other for five years, apart from their brief encounter weeks ago at the ball, where Jack had been trying to escape. Master Thomas had taught him…and even though Jack had developed some tricks of his own, there was no way of knowing just how much Master Thomas knew. Combining Talking and Charming…Jack had never thought of that, not in the five years he'd spent experimenting and teaching in France. And he'd refused to even *think* about necromancy. There were some things that were best left in Pandora's Box.

What else did Master Thomas know?

"She's right," Jack said. He pulled himself to his full height and stared down at his former tutor. "Master…you cannot allow this to go on."

"You betrayed me," Master Thomas said. His voice was almost a whisper. Controlling – or at least reanimating – so many revenants had drained his magic to the limit, yet he was still dangerous. Jack tightened his mental shields, watching carefully for any attempt to influence or destroy his mind. The most dangerous assassins in Britain's service – all officially denied by the government, of course – were Movers with very weak powers. But they didn't need to be strong to move a handful of cells around in a person's brain, bringing on instant death. "I had thought you dead."

"I don't die," Jack said. Magic didn't make one invincible, but he believed – completely – that he wouldn't die until he had served his purpose. It was one of the reasons he'd risked his insane attack on the Tower of London. "And I had thought that you were a better man than this."

He indicated the revenants, lurking behind his former tutor. The other rebels were pulling back, either unwilling to face the Royal Sorcerer or attempting to take advantage of the delay to establish other defence lines further into London. Now the threat had been proved real, Davy would be able to move troops from the city defences to Soho in hopes of stopping the infection before it ran out of control.

"This is madness," he said. "Even if you win, you'll blight the British Empire for the rest of time."

Master Thomas stared at him. "The Empire has been the greatest force for good in the world since the end of the Roman Empire," he said. "I will not allow the Empire to rot away from within, to lose sight of its true nature, to weaken itself to the point where a horde of mangy barbarians can topple the Empire. I will do whatever it takes to end this quickly."

"Even necromancy?" Gwen asked. Jack risked a glance at her. The girl was breathing heavily, clearly exhausted. They'd both been using their magic furiously, burning through the revenants before they could reach the barricades. "How many people in this city are innocents, caught up in the desperate struggle to survive?"

"It always starts like that," Master Thomas said. "The people with high ideals and lofty plans come forth and give the poor their bread and circuses. It isn't more than a few decades until the poor riot when they are refused their surplus, even through the state is bankrupting itself trying to provide for their care and feeding. And then the state spends itself into collapse and shatters."

"You don't see the poor," Jack said, quietly. "I have seen men forced onto the streets because they are crippled, crippled in factory accidents that would be avoidable if the factory owners spent a little more of their profits on safety. I have seen women forced into prostitution because it is the only way they can pay the bills and feed their children. I have watched children grow up on the streets, watching people who have so much while they have so little – and I have seen those children hang for stealing a crust of bread. And they were the lucky ones. Some of those children are used for sexual gratification by their lords and masters. I killed Lord Fitzroy for what he was doing to the children."

His gaze sharpened. "You speak as if the poor *choose* to be poor," he said. "You speak as though hard work would earn them a palace, with enough food to feed their families and education that will allow them to rise to the very highest levels of society. But it won't; each child born into a poor family finds that the odds are already stacked against him. They are forced onto the streets or into workhouses – or into the arms of thieves who use them to steal from the rich, or those who merely earn a few coins every day. There is no hope – why should they not rebel against you and your masters? *What do they have to lose?*"

"They could go to the Americas, or South Africa," Master Thomas pointed out, mildly. "There are still vast lands awaiting settlement in the American West, or deep in the heart of Africa."

Jack snorted. "Very few poor families could scrape together the money to emigrate," he said. "They have to place themselves in the hands of richer men, who treat them as slaves or worse. How many of them ever earn the forty acres and a mule promised by the emigration companies?"

He sighed. "The world is stacked against them," he said. "Drink is freely available on the street, leading to violence as men drown their sorrows and become drunkards, drinking themselves to death. There is no hope, Master Thomas; tell me – *what do they have to lose?*"

Master Thomas took a step forward, and another, lifting his cane almost as if it were a shield, or a sword. "The rebels always think that the problems can be solved easily," he said, softly. "And yet...if you took the total wealth of the British Empire and shared it out among its population, how much would they each receive? And *tell me*; how long would it be before gambling and indulgence had recreated the pattern of rich and poor?"

He shook his head. "I always thought well of you, Jackson," he said. "Give up now and you won't be harmed."

Jack felt something twisting and dying inside his soul. He'd hoped that Master Thomas would understand, but instead...his former tutor had drawn heavily on his magic, using a talent few understood and even fewer possessed. Necromancy placed great strain on the mind, according to some of the experts...could it be that Master Thomas was on the edge of madness? Or had he already stepped over the edge?

"I always respected you," Jack said, quietly. "I'm sorry."

Master Thomas lifted his stick, and then brought it down suddenly in a slashing motion. Jack jumped aside as...*something* flashed through the air, right where he'd been standing. He heard a scream from behind him and cursed. Master Thomas had revealed another trick, one that might be deadlier than mental control or magic potion to enhance one's endurance. Jack brought his own magic up around him, shielding his body from a second burst of magic, and then launched a counterattack. A beam of light lanced from his fingers, only to dissipate harmlessly in front of its target. Jack smiled, inwardly. Master Thomas would hardly be challenged by such a direct attack, but perhaps he'd be distracted...

He reached out with his magic, picking up chunks of debris from the remains of the first barricade. Launching a second pulse of magic right at Master Thomas, he pulled the debris forward and hurled it towards his target's back. Master Thomas leapt upwards sharply, dodging the debris with ease. Years of practice had given him what amounted to a set of eyes in the back of his head. It was literally impossible to sneak up on him. Master Thomas landed on a rooftop, ignoring the flames licking their way around the building, and raised his stick, pointing it right at Jack's chest. A blast of magic struck him before he could dodge, hurling him back into a second barrage. It was followed by a hail of debris...

Master Thomas leapt into the air as Gwen fired a long burst of magic into the roof, just under his feet. Jack grinned as he deflected the raining debris; he'd almost forgotten that Gwen was present. And she'd pulled a sly trick on Master Thomas; he could counter a burst of magic aimed at him, but with the rooftop disintegrating under her magic he might well be hurled into the flames. Instead, he landed on the cobblestones and launched his own burst of magic at Jack.

Seconds before the beam reached his shields, it split up into a dozen smaller beams, each one coming at Jack from a separate direction. Jack was impressed – he hadn't known that anyone, even an experienced Blazer, could do that – and had only seconds to react. He threw himself out of the way, finding some cover against a stone wall, just as the beams of light twisted and came right at him. His shields absorbed them as Gwen threw her own bursts of magic at Master Thomas. Their tutor said a word Jack was surprised to discover he even knew and waved a hand at Gwen. She was hurled backwards and pressed against the cobblestones.

Jack reacted instantly. Focusing his own magic, he launched it right towards Master Thomas. His shields held it, but Jack was already infusing magic into a set of broken cobblestones. They exploded all around Master Thomas, forcing him to stagger backwards. Gwen was bleeding from her nose and mouth, but she was alive. Jack stared up at Master Thomas, realising that his old tutor – the man he had once admired – had lost all trace of sanity. His attack on Gwen had been murderous. It would have killed her if Jack hadn't saved her life.

Cursing, he allowed his magic to pick up debris and throw it at Master Thomas. None of it would get through his defences, but it would keep him occupied, just for a handful of seconds. Jack used them to reach out to the revenants and pick them up, throwing them after the debris. A single bite would prove as fatal to a necromancer, he assumed, as it would to a mundane human. Master Thomas wouldn't know any better, if only because there had been a shortage of volunteers to test such dangerous theories. No one had ever survived a bite from one of the undead. The lucky ones lost conscious quickly, sparing them the torment of feeling their body dying around them. Master Thomas lashed out, shattering the undead bodies and scattering pieces of flesh and bone everywhere, almost as if he was on the verge of panic. Jack grinned, despite himself and closed in. Perhaps there was a chance...

...But no. Master Thomas kept moving, jumping backwards and launching bursts of magic of his own. More subtle attacks followed, some chillingly effective, others easy to sense, but harder to deflect. Jack hadn't realised just how much Master Thomas had learned over the years, even though he'd been the sole practicing Master for nearly twenty years. Master Saul and Master Luke had died quickly, fighting the French and Spanish – at least according to one version of the tale. No one was quite sure what had actually happened to them. Grimly, Jack wondered if Master Thomas had killed them – but no, that couldn't be possible. Master Saul and Master Luke were as highborn as any grand society dame could hope for. They wouldn't have sided with the poor and the downtrodden.

The ground seemed to explode around him as magic flared up everywhere. It was an Infuser's trick, one mastered by a magician who shared all of the talents. Jack was bitterly impressed even as he was hurled into the air, his magic protecting him from the worst of the shock. Master Thomas's magic reached out to disrupt the magic keeping him airborne and he fell, only to be caught by Gwen's magic before he hit the ground. Gwen might have been unpractised compared to either of the men, but she was strong. Jack felt an odd sensation that he realised, after a moment, was regret. They'd been born on wrong sides of the social divide. Who knew which way Gwen would jump after the fight was over, assuming that they both survived?

"You cannot win this fight," Master Thomas informed them. Jack realised that he might well be right. He hadn't limited himself to infusing magic into water, but also into his clothing and the rings he wore on his fingers. If Master Thomas had spent an hour or so every day infusing magic into a ring, being careful to ensure that the magic remained stable and wasn't on the verge of blowing up, he would soon have a stockpile of magic that would allow him to keep fighting, hours after the other two had collapsed from exhaustion. "Give up. You'll receive a fair trial."

Jack laughed, suddenly very aware of the pain in his body. Master Magicians could take a great deal of damage – he suspected that they were using magic to heal themselves, without being consciously aware of what they were doing – but he was rapidly reaching his limits. And Gwen had never pushed herself so hard in all of her life. Strong as she was, she wouldn't be able to remain on her feet much longer. But he wouldn't consider retreat, or surrender. It would be the ultimate betrayal of the people whose cause he'd made his own.

"I don't think we will receive anything in your kingdom of the dead," he said. It hurt to speak. He could taste blood in his mouth, always a bad sign. "What do you think your masters will command you to do once they realise how many revenants you can control at once?"

He laughed and coughed. Red flecks were spewed out of his mouth and he wiped them away with his sleeve. "I'm sure that the undead will give their masters much less trouble," he said. "None of that irritating lust for freedom. No bad habits like drinking and whoring and cheap nasty-smelling tobacco. Just obedience – everything they want in a single necropolis, a city of the dead. What's a little matter like a law against necromancy when it's so *useful*?"

Master Thomas glared at him, his face twisted with anger. Jack sensed his magic building up, reaching out to strike Jack down. He saw the rising sun behind his old teacher and almost smiled. The pain in his chest told him that he would never live to see another sunrise, even if the fight ended before Master Thomas could kill him and put an end to the revolution.

He felt hands on his shoulder as he staggered backwards. Gwen had caught him just before he fell, holding him upright. A strange feeling flowed through him, almost as if Gwen was sharing some of her energy with Jack...he realised, with a sudden chuckle, just what she was doing. She was Healing him!

"I'm sorry, Gwen," he whispered. It still hurt to talk. "I'm so sorry."

Gathering all of his remaining magic, he hurled himself out of her arms and right at Master Thomas. His magic cancelled Master Thomas's magic and they crashed together, the force of the impact knocking Master Thomas over backwards. He'd be healed in seconds, Jack knew, but it was just long enough. He pushed his hands against Master Thomas's face – trying to forget the times they'd had before he'd fled to France – and infused magic into his skull. It destabilised seconds later.

The world vanished in a blinding flash.

Chapter Forty-Four

wen lifted her hand to shield her eyes. When the flash had faded, two dead bodies hit the ground, both horrifically charred. She stumbled forward, despite the pain that was demanding immediate attention. Master Thomas's head had almost disintegrated, leaving a headless corpse. Jack had fewer obvious signs of death, but she didn't have to feel for a pulse to know that he was gone. She felt hot tears dripping from her eyes. He couldn't be dead...

But he was.

She stumbled backwards, unable to look at the corpse any longer. The flames seemed to be dying down without magic fuelling them, although they were still burning through the unclean slums. Gwen barely noticed the heat, or the sun rising in the distance; the two most important people in her life were dead, right in front of her. She was the sole survivor of a battle without precedent in the history of magic. Somehow, the thought failed to cheer her. There was truly nothing so dark as a battle won – apart from a battle lost. And there was still the army outside the city...London might fall yet.

A moan caught her attention and she glanced up, sharply. The revenants had remained still during the battle between the three magicians, but they were slowly shuffling back into life. A new intelligence seemed to flicker between them, the silent whispers Gwen could hear at the back of her mind growing louder and more focused. Understanding came a second later as the moan spread from revenant to revenant until they were all moaning, the sound blurring into an eerie dirge for their lost humanity. It tore at Gwen's mind, even as she stumbled to her feet and backed away from the ranks of the undead. They'd been held back by Master Thomas, who had used them merely to challenge the barricades. Without his directing mind, they would start rampaging completely out of control. The moan changed, blending into an atonal sound, as the massed ranks started to advance, their rotting hands raised as if they intended to tear the life out of Gwen's body. She summoned up what remained of her magic and tried to push them back, but her magic only held them for a second before they pushed forward, remorselessly.

There was no choice. She turned and ran towards the third barricade, convinced that the next second would be her last as the revenants brought her down and drained their blood to fuel their undead rampage. It struck her, suddenly, how powerless mundane people must feel, without magic to protect them or to help them to heal from serious injuries. The barricade was ramshackle compared to the first two, assembled using scraps of debris and whatever furniture could be dragged from the nearby slums. Gwen told herself that the rebels behind it, holding their swords uncertainly, would be able to hold the line, but she had her doubts. The advancing horde would have all of the advantages of the undead, without any of the disadvantages that came from being bound to a single necromancer's will. She scrambled over the barricade and dropped down to the pavement beyond, her gaze meeting that of the rebels. They didn't look confident either, but they did look determined. If the revenants broke out of Soho, their families would be next to be eaten and left to reanimate on their own.

Gwen caught sight of the bodies she'd left behind. Both of them had died through magic, rather than through being bitten; it was possible, she told herself, that they wouldn't reanimate. If not…she didn't know if she could kill either of them a second time, even if they didn't have their powers. No one knew if a revenant who had been a magician while still alive would keep their powers even after they joined the ranks of the undead. It didn't seem likely, but…she smiled, despite herself. They might find out today if they were unlucky.

"Burn them," one of the rebels – the one called Davy – urged. "They'll break through the barricade in no time."

Gwen shook her head, tiredly. "I don't have enough magic left," she admitted. Her head was fuzzy, as if she'd pushed herself too far. Too much magic used too quickly could be fatal, she knew; it would be the height of irony if she'd lost her powers permanently, while trying to stop Master Thomas, the man who had taught her how to use and control her abilities. "We have to stop them with swords."

Davy nodded, a hint of bitterness in his eyes, and passed her a short sword. It was surprisingly heavy in Gwen's hands and her exhaustion didn't help, but she held it up anyway. The blade glittered as it reflected the light of the rising sun, reminding her of the tales of King Arthur and his magical sword. Maybe an Infuser or a Changer could create a sword that could cut through anything...she shook her head, dismissing the thought. The odds were good that she wouldn't live long enough to find out. She could hear the moaning getting closer as the revenants approached, their dead faces seeming to stare at the living, taunting them with their fate. *We are the risen dead,* they seemed to say; *we will destroy you, the living. You will not stand against us.*

A hand caught hers and she turned to see a short man holding a set of pistols and an oversized rifle. "You can't add anything here, lass," he said. "Go back to the medical station and..."

The moan suddenly grew louder, almost overpowering. Gwen staggered, feeling an impact both on a physical level and inside her soul. It felt dirty, as if her body had been stripped naked and displayed to an army of leering men. *She* felt dirty. The revenants were the products of magical corruption and they would spread their corruption to all of humanity – unless they were destroyed first. But Gwen, despite her limited knowledge of infantry tactics, could see that they were playing it smarter. Revenants were climbing up on rooftops and heading down the side streets, rather than merely charging the barricades. Maybe there were enough revenants, she wondered, to create a genuine intelligence. Or maybe she was merely trying to put a face on the ranks of the undead.

They scared her, at a very fundamental level. A human opponent – even one like Master Thomas, or Jack – was understandable. She could have understood what drove a thief, or a murderer, or even a soldier fighting for an enemy nation. But the revenants were a faceless mass of the undead, with only one goal; they wanted to destroy humanity and create their own race in the ruins. There was no way of bargaining with such a foe, no way of convincing them that they couldn't hope to win; the choice was between victory or total, final, defeat. And the undead felt no pain. Nothing could deter them. They would keep coming until they were exterminated.

"I told you to go," the man snapped. "Now!"

Gwen barely heard him. The whispers were growing louder, and darker. Necromancy...necromancy was control over the dead. Necromancers could raise the dead, or they could summon the ghosts of the slain – or so she had been given to understand. Necromancy had never been studied properly, not like some of the other talent; after all, anyone who discovered that they had necromantic powers would be well-advised not to tell anyone.

Master Thomas hadn't been a necromancer; he'd been a Master. He'd had all of the talents – including, one assumed, necromancy. And if he had those talents, logically Gwen had them too. But she didn't know how to use it. Necromancy didn't seem to be related to any of the other talents, or perhaps young magicians had always assumed that to be true. Carefully, she tried to reach out with her mind, but the revenants ignored her. The flickering, almost demonic entity she could hear wasn't responding to her pleas. For all she knew, necromancy didn't work like that – or perhaps she wasn't strong enough to make them respond to her.

She heard a shriek and glanced up, horrified. Someone had torched the leading revenants with burning oil, but they hadn't burned them to ashes. The revenants were still walking forward, dozens of mobile fires spreading chaos and panic everywhere. They'd collapse soon, Gwen hoped, but by then they would have destroyed all semblance of order. She tried to reach out with her mind again, yet nothing happened. Her head swam as she struggled to force her magic to work. She hadn't slept in far too long. The urge to just sit down and close her eyes was almost overwhelming.

Instead, she allowed the man to push her back down the streets. Hundreds of thousands of citizens were fleeing their homes, heading for the outskirts of London. Maybe they'd be safe out in the countryside, if they ever got that far. The Duke of India was out there somewhere, along with whatever magicians could be scraped up from the Sorcerers Corps.

Gwen considered trying to send for them, but her Talking had never been powerful enough to reach very far – and besides, the army might not be able to get into London in time to help.

"Lady Gwen!"

Gwen spun as she heard her voice being called. She saw Lucy, the Healer, standing there waving at Gwen frantically. The rebels had set up a makeshift hospital in what had once been a shop, laying out their wounded to receive medical care. Lucy hadn't healed them all, Gwen saw, although she couldn't disagree with the logic. There was only so much magic in any magician, even a dedicated magician with only one talent. Lucy passed Gwen a flask of water and Gwen drank it gratefully. It wasn't supercharged with magic, not like Master Thomas's magic potion, but it was refreshing. Her stomach growled, reminding her that she hadn't eaten in far too long. The rebels had probably set up a small pile of food for their soldiers, but it had been stripped bare – if it had ever existed at all. London consumed a vast amount of food every day. Perhaps the Duke of India would try to starve Londoners into submission rather than try to take the city by force.

Her head spun as she heard the whispers of the dead, right on the edge of her mind. They were getting louder, which suggested that the revenants were getting closer – and more numerous. How many of the rebels had been bitten, she asked herself; it was clear that some of the wounded had been bitten and well on the way to death and rebirth, despite Lucy's powers. Someone would have to slit their throats and burn their bodies before they returned to life and joined the ranks of the undead.

A scream split the air, from behind a curtain. Gwen walked over to the curtain and pulled it aside, ignoring Lucy's half-hearted attempt to stop her. A small boy – barely ten years old, if that – lay on a blanket, twisting and turning as if he was being slowly killed by a horrible wasting disease. His face was pale, but Gwen didn't think that he'd been bitten. The symptoms reminded her of something, but what?

"She's been like this for hours," Lucy said. She? Gwen looked at the boy again; now Lucy had pointed it out, it was clear that the person she'd thought was a boy was actually a girl, dressed in male clothing. Perhaps, like Gwen had once or twice, she'd enjoyed dressing as a man because of the freedom it brought. No one tried to talk down to a man, but when talking to a woman a man would often be condescending towards her, even if she were his social superior. "I haven't been able to do anything for her."

The girl shuddered, her entire body twisting so violently that Gwen feared – for a moment – that she was on the verge of snapping her own spine. Her clothes were stained with sweat and even blood, dripping from scratches on her hands and face. Someone had been beating her...no, she'd done it to herself. Her fingernails were coated with her own blood. If someone hadn't restrained her, she might have torn out her own eyes.

"I can hear them," the girl whispered. Her voice sounded as if she was on the verge of blacking out. It would be difficult to move her unless she was tied down securely or knocked out. Her face twisted, as if she'd just swallowed something awful. "I can hear the voices. My parents are calling to me."

Gwen knelt down beside the girl, one hand touching her forehead. The girl – her name, according to Lucy, was Olivia – didn't seem to be feverish. Her forehead was damp and cold. Crusted blood started to fall from her nose, a symptom Gwen recalled from reading some of the early records written by Master Saul. Master Thomas's peer had been a long-winded bore to rival Doctor Norwell, judging by his writings; he wouldn't take a paragraph to write something if he could cover it thoroughly in an entire chapter. And yet...

The first Talkers showed symptoms very quickly, Master Saul had written. *Blood dripped from their noses, ears and even their mouths. They who failed to control their magic soon found that it overwhelmed them, leaving us with no choice, but to place them in a bedlam for their own safety...*

But Olivia couldn't be a Talker, Gwen realised. The rebels had had other Talkers – and they'd had Jack, a Master. They would have recognised another Talker and ensured that she was trained to control her powers before she grew into them properly, before they had a chance to overwhelm her mind. And that meant...there were two possibilities. Olivia had a new talent, one that hadn't been recorded by the Royal College, or she had a very rare talent – a very rare and dangerous talent.

"They're calling to me," Olivia whispered. "I need to go to

them."

"She's delusional," Lucy said, grimly. Gwen had sensed that Lucy didn't seem to like her for some reason, but that dislike had clearly been forgotten in the struggle to save Olivia's life. "It happens when someone is on the verge of death and they can't afford the drugs…"

"No," Gwen said. She wasn't sure if she was right – and she would be doing Olivia no favours if she was right – but there was no other choice. London would become a city of the dead – a necropolis – by the end of the day, unless they could stop the revenants. "Olivia…I need you to listen to me."

The girl shivered again, blood dripping from her nose and down onto her blanket. "You can hear the dead," Gwen said, and prayed that she was right. A necromancer – one without any other talents – would be far stronger at necromancy than a Master. "You have to tell them to stop."

Olivia's eyes opened wide. They were old eyes for such a young girl, eyes that had seen everything on the streets, where she'd done whatever she had to do to survive. Gwen's heart went out to her, even as she pulled Olivia to her breast, preparing to use her mercilessly. If they survived the day, she promised herself, she would ensure that Olivia had a new life and a chance to blossom in safety. Gwen had a small inheritance of her own, even if the Royal College refused to pay her wages. And there was always her brother.

A deafening crash announced the arrival of the revenants. The door didn't hold them, not when the room stank of dying humans. Gwen looked up as the screams began, seeing a revenant stumbling towards her. Its lifeless eyes held hers; desperately, Gwen fumbled for what was left of her magic. Maybe she could push it back hard enough to get Olivia and Lucy out of the room. But nothing happened. Her head felt as if she'd banged it hard against the wall. She hadn't felt worse since the day she'd fallen out of a tree as a six-year-old girl, the day she'd come into her magic.

She held Olivia to her, praying inwardly for success. "Tell them to stop," she repeated. "Focus on the creature and tell it to stop…"

She sensed the magic a second before it flared into existence. Olivia screamed out loud as the revenant froze, and then collapsed to the ground. But there were still screams from outside…

"Tell them all to stop," Gwen said. She was pushing Olivia right to the edge, but there was no other choice. The ruthless part of her mind understood that one small girl's life was a small price to pay for saving London. The rest of her was horrified at her callousness. But she was the Royal Sorceress now, the only one who could save the city. Maybe Master Thomas had felt the same, years ago. "Tell them to stop."

The screams from outside started to fade. Lucy stood up and walked towards the remains of the door. "They're all lying on the ground," she said, her voice quiet, yet awed. "They've stopped!"

"Get parties working on burning them," Gwen ordered.

She'd expected resistance, but Lucy nodded and headed out of the door. Gwen looked down at Olivia, who had stumbled into a faint, and shook her head. The law was clear; necromancers were to be executed. There was no right of appeal.

Gwen shook her head. The law was wrong. And besides, they had to convince the government and the rebels to come to terms. If they had to go through it all again, the next bout of civil unrest would be worse.

Picking up the girl's light form, she walked out of the makeshift hospital and waved to one of the horse-drawn carriages. It would only be a short ride to the Tower of London – and then she could talk to the one man who might be able to make a difference. And, for that matter, the one man who could issue a pardon for a necromancer.

And she would do whatever it took to ensure that that pardon was issued, and honoured.

Chapter Forty-Five

would very much like to know," Lord Liverpool said, "precisely why you feel that you can…dictate to us in this manner."

Gwen sighed. It had taken a week to convince the Prime Minister to agree to the meeting. A week, during which London had burned the bodies of the revenants and their honoured dead, side by side. She'd expected Lord Blackburn to be attending the meeting, dripping poison into their ears, but it seemed that Lord Blackburn had decided to take a short holiday overseas. Someone would have to take the blame for the whole crisis – and the British aristocracy, ruthlessly pragmatic when pushed to the wall, had already decided who was going to be publicly accused. The decision to put troops on the streets on London was placed firmly on Lord Blackburn's shoulders.

"She has the support of the King," a new voice said. The Prime Minister stumbled to his feet as George IV, King of Britain and Emperor of the British Empire, walked into the room. He was wearing his finest robes, decorated with symbols that dated all the way back to the first monarchs of England. "We have lost all confidence in your government, Liverpool."

Lord Liverpool stared at him. Gwen felt a flicker of sympathy, which died when she remembered how many thousands of people had died over the last two weeks. Lord Liverpool had guided the British Empire through the unrest that had threatened its stability, but even he couldn't stand openly against the King. George IV's public loss of faith in the Prime Minister would force him to stand for re-election, but his party would almost certainly drop him like a hot coal.

"You mishandled this crisis very badly," the King said. His

voice was calm, but there was absolutely no give in it at all. "You helped create the conditions for revolution by allowing many of your supporters to exploit those without the money or connections to defend themselves. You put troops on the streets in a highly volatile situation – and then failed to back up those troops when you lost control of the streets. And finally, you unleashed necromancy on British citizens. Do you really feel that Parliament will stand for that?"

Lord Mycroft coughed, heaving his enormous bulk around to face the King. "Your Majesty," he said, "I was under the impression that a French necromancer was responsible for the plague of undead."

They exchanged long looks. Gwen had wanted to publicly blame Lord Liverpool for sending Master Thomas to reanimate the government's secret weapon, but the King had talked her out of it. Parliament – and the British population – would convulse if the full truth ever got out, forcing Lord Liverpool to spend all of his political capital to avoid impeachment. The agreement they'd made would blame everything on the French, giving the country something to unite around – and in return, Lord Liverpool would retire quietly and gracefully. Enough people knew the truth to ensure that he could never return to politics.

"It does sound like something the French would do," the King agreed, quietly. "They sent a monkey to spy on Hartlepool after all. I'm sure that a necromancer would be well within their powers. They'll deny everything, of course."

They would, Gwen knew, and they wouldn't be believed. Fear of France was one of the few things that united all Englishmen behind their government. It would provide a face-saving excuse for the government to make concessions and the rebels to accept them, ending the uprising without further bloodshed. Gwen had quietly promised herself that she would ensure that all of the promises were upheld. She was indispensable as long as there were no other Masters, giving her tremendous influence. And Master Thomas, for reasons known only to him, had left her most of his possessions in his will. She was also suddenly one of the richest people, male or female, in the British Empire.

Lord Liverpool looked at Gwen for a long moment, as if he couldn't believe how much she'd changed. Neither could

Gwen, to be honest. "These…concessions you wish us to make," he said, finally, "will upset many people. I would go so far as to say that they will upset everyone."

"Good," the King said. "It will please no one, but they can accept it. And I will spend the rest of my reign ensuring that they are honoured."

There was a pause. Some of the concessions weren't too onerous. Universal suffrage; men and women of all social classes would get the vote, by secret ballot. A minimum wage for workers and manager liability for any accidents within their factories that could have been avoided; strict laws on the use of child labour; universal education, better medical care…the British Empire could survive making such changes. Besides, in the long run, Lord Mycroft had already determined that they would benefit the British Empire. Few doubted his word.

But others would be a struggle. The rebels wanted a universal right to bear arms, pointing out that successive governments had disarmed the population and then forced them to accept wildly unpopular policies. There would be no regular army units within the cities; instead, the Trained Bands would be resurrected and actually trained. The police would operate under strict laws that would prevent them from abusing their position, or accepting bribes. And there would be government-funded emigration, allowing anyone who wanted to settle elsewhere to migrate without indebting his entire family for life. Lord Liverpool would burn up the rest of his political capital forcing Parliament to accept them, something that would render him ineffective if he did somehow manage to remain in politics.

Gwen told herself that Jack would have understood, but in truth she wasn't too sure. Officially, Jack and Master Thomas had died heroically, fighting the revenants. Far too many people had watched the fight for the truth to be completely buried, but few people would want to believe the truth. It was far better for the country to believe that the ultimate defender of the old order and the man who had brought hope to the poor had died together, united in a common cause. Or so she'd been told, by none other than Lord Mycroft. She could only hope that he was right.

The King rose to his feet and smiled down at his servants. "I shall be returning to Windsor Castle this evening," he said.

Windsor Castle was currently being defended by a unit of rebel troops, taking the place of the King's normal bodyguards. The Prime Minister wouldn't be blind to the significance of the King's unspoken statement – or, for that matter, the difficulties of disarming the rebels after London was back in government hands. "I will expect to see a signed treaty by then so I may take it to London myself."

He left the chamber, not looking back.

Lord Mycroft chuckled, harshly. "I wonder what we have unleashed on the world, Madam Sorceress," he said. It was the official title for Royal Sorcerer, adapted for a Sorceress. Gwen still found it strange to be addressed in such a manner. "You have shaken the entire country. What will you do next?"

"Go to Cavendish Hall," Gwen said. "I have work to do there."

***

Most of Cavendish Hall was still intact, despite the rebel bombardment and the fire that had scorched part of the interior. Gwen had managed to assert her authority to convince many of the staff to return, along with hiring a number of builders to start repairs. No one had quibbled too loudly. The death of Master Thomas and the rise of an undead army had shocked them and most of the magicians had accepted Gwen's authority without demur. A handful hadn't and had complained to Lord Mycroft, only to be told that they could either accept Gwen or hand in their resignations. Most of them had chosen to stay, although she suspected that some of them were just waiting for her to make a mistake. Or, perhaps, for another Master to appear.

Master Thomas's rooms should have been hers, but she had been unable to bear the thought of moving into them. The staff sealed them up, after Gwen had carefully removed every book and paper and transferred them to her own rooms. She would have to go through them all carefully, paper by paper, looking for whatever secrets Master Thomas might have taken to the grave. And if she failed to find his notes, she would have to discover the techniques herself. She stared down at a logbook that dated all the way back to the foundation of the Royal College and shook her head. It had to be read, but not today. And maybe not by her.

A knock on the door brought her back to herself. She wiped her eyes and used magic to unlock the door, allowing Doctor Norwell to enter. The theoretical magician, barred by long custom from claiming any real authority within Cavendish Hall, looked concerned. Gwen was unlikely to forget his role in planning and supervising the farms – and, as a mundane human, he was expendable. Lord Mycroft wouldn't even raise an eyebrow if Gwen told him to leave the Hall and never return.

"I have the logbooks you requested," Doctor Norwell said, after taking the seat Gwen had indicated was for him. She'd have to set up a proper office, she told herself firmly, although that was hardly a priority right now. There were hundreds of matters that had to be attended to before she could deal with her own comfort. "Everything from the first year to...the end of the program."

Gwen nodded, slowly. "Good," she said. "And the farms themselves?"

Doctor Norwell looked pained. "My Lady, with all due respect..."

"The farms were a crime against humanity," Gwen said, flatly. She would never forget the image of Lord Blackburn having sexual congress with a woman who hadn't wanted to be there. "I want the entire program shut down. The children are to be allowed to grow up on their own, without pressure."

"Yes, My Lady," Doctor Norwell said, tightly. "I will see to it personally."

Gwen had no intention of budging on that particular matter. Besides, the papers she'd seen had confirmed that around half of the children were born without any magic at all. They tended to be removed from the program by the time they reached their late teens. At least they'd been given a small lump sum from the government. She shuddered to think what would have happened if they'd just been turned onto the streets.

"And after that, I want the records sealed," Gwen added. He shrank under her gaze. "No one is to even know that the program existed."

She watched Doctor Norwell leave the room and shook her head as soon as he had closed the door behind him. It wasn't something she wanted to think about, but someone would have to make sure that the theoretical magicians never tried to reopen the program. Perhaps there was a compromise, perhaps paying mothers to have children with the right fathers...she shook her head again. The entire concept was sickening.

Twenty minutes later, there was a second knock on the door. This time, it opened to reveal Lombardi and a rather nervous Lucy. Gwen had assigned Lombardi to look after Lucy, counting on his shy manner to reassure the Healer. Lucy would have felt out of place in Cavendish Hall, even without having to face the attentions of a great many theoretical magicians who wanted to study a Healer. Lombardi had strict orders to ensure that they didn't overwhelm her while they tried to work out how to look for other Healers. Besides, Lucy's existence had given Gwen another tool for convincing the government to make peace with the rebels. A Healing talent would work to the government's advantage.

"This place is a nightmare," Lucy said, as Lombardi closed the door. "I don't know how you coped with them poking and prodding you while they tried to find out how you made magic work."

"I wasn't unique," Gwen pointed out. There had been four other Masters; it struck her, suddenly, that she *was* unique. The farm program had only produced one Master in its entire existence. Doctor Norwell insisted that more research would allow them to grow Masters without having to rely on random (and unknown) factors. Gwen had shut the program down instead. "I'm sorry about it, you know."

"I understand," Lucy said, without bitterness. She sat down and dismissed Lombardi with a toss of her head. "I want to talk about another friend of ours."

Gwen nodded. "She should be safe," she said. The King had signed a pardon for Olivia the day after she'd stopped the undead army in its tracks. Lord Blackburn – if he'd still been in Britain – would probably have quibbled over its legality. Someone smarter, with an eye to the long-term issues, would know better. Raising the question of the King's right to grant a pardon would eventually call into question the legitimacy of the government itself. Besides, having at least one tame necromancer in the Sorcerers Corps might come in handy. The French or the Russians might eventually develop a necromancer of their own.

"Good," Lucy said. "And I want to make a point clear of my own. I intend to use my powers to help people who need it, rich and poor alike. I'm going to donate at least half of my time to healing the poor. I want you to make certain that any other Healers we discover do the same. You have that power now, according to Bruno. Will you do it?"

Master Thomas would probably have hesitated, Gwen knew, or tried to strike a bargain. Doctor Norwell would certainly have asked Lucy to have children in the hopes of producing more Healers. But Gwen didn't hesitate. It was the right thing to do – and it might teach the magicians that the poor were still human.

"I will see to it," Gwen promised. The clock on her desk chimed and she scowled at it. She didn't want to go to her next appointment, but it had to be done. "Take care of yourself, all right? We need you."

***

By law, any family proceedings involving the nobility had to be conducted with the presence of a registry officer. Births, deaths, weddings...they all had to be recorded, scribbled down in the blue ink that denoted nobility. Gwen had seen it all as a waste of time before she'd become a magician; now, with the gaze of hindsight, she realised that it allowed the government a chance to track bloodlines that had produced magical children. And, just to give the program some cover, to ensure that lines of succession and inheritance were firmly delineated before the wrong person died. It was always useful to know who was going to inherit.

She stepped down from the carriage – no magic here, not in front of her parents – and helped Olivia down after her. Lady Mary frowned as soon as she saw the child, although she had the sense to keep her comments to herself. Adoption was rare among the nobility, where the family bloodlines had to be kept in the open, but it did happen. It had even been known to happen retroactively. But for someone of Gwen's age to adopt a child...

Gwen's lips twitched, imagining what High Society's grand dames would have to say when they heard the news. No one in living memory had ever adopted a child from the streets, certainly not a girl who had spent most of her life dressed as a boy, pick-pocketing just to remain alive. But Gwen was the Royal Sorceress, a position that came with a title, and the heir of Master Thomas, who had had a title and fortune of his own. They would never be able to shun Gwen's adopted daughter, at least not publicly. What they said in private would never have to come to Olivia's ears.

But she hadn't adopted Olivia just to upset High Society. The public had been told that a French-born male necromancer had raised the dead in London, intent on destroying the trust that made Britain function. Enough people, however, knew the truth to make Olivia's position a little unsure. Some of them might decide that the risks of having a living necromancer outweighed the benefits. But they would never be able to execute Gwen's adopted daughter without bringing down the wrath of High Society on their heads. No one would stand for such an act. It was the best protection Gwen could give the young necromancer, and what – she was sure – Jack would have wanted.

"Olivia," she said, quietly. The girl looked up at her, shyly. "This is your grandmother and grandfather. And" –she nodded towards a carriage, where David was helping Laura to clamber out – "that is your uncle and aunt. Welcome to the family."

After the ceremony, Lady Mary managed to draw her aside, just for a moment.

"Gwen," she said, sharply. "What *were* you thinking? What about the family name?"

Gwen smiled. "What about it?" She asked. "You don't think that my daughter is worthy to bear our name?"

Lady Mary snorted and stalked off, doubtless to inflict her presence on some unsuspecting footman or housemaid. Gwen watched her go, shaking her head sadly. Lady Mary would hate having a grandchild from such a disreputable background, yet she would never be able to say anything, not in public. And she would have to suffer the snide comments and glances from her fellow society butterflies. Her entire life was based on her position in society, and Gwen had weakened it...

And yet, she was the mother of the Royal Sorceress. No one would be able to shun her, or to refuse to invite her to parties. They would all have to be polite to her – Gwen too, if she saw fit to accept their invitations...

She smiled and winked at David. Her brother had understood, of course. His sister could lead her own life now, without having to worry about her mother's wants and desires. And she could be happy.

The future seemed bright and full of promise.

Epilogue

he streets of Cairo were stained with blood.

Five days ago, the Sultan of the Ottoman Empire had crossed into Egypt, intending to make the first state visit of an Ottoman Sultan to his vassal state in centuries. The Mamelukes, the hierarchy of military families that effectively ruled Egypt, had set out to challenge the Sultan as his army headed towards Cairo. They had no fear of Ottoman Power, not after they had contemptuously repulsed every half-hearted Janissary advance directed from Istanbul. The Sultan would be repulsed, perhaps even taken prisoner. And then who knew where their ambitions would lead them?

They had led them to death. Four days ago, the two armies had met – and the Mamelukes had been smashed. Barely one in a thousand survived, and only then because the Sultan wanted them to escape to spread the word. The green-coated army that he had created was invincible and the Mamelukes, who hadn't changed their tactics or organisation in decades, were powerless to stop the Sultan from entering his city. A handful of powerful families fled in the night, others found themselves evicted from their palaces when the Sultan's men claimed them to billet their troops. No one argued twice. The grim-faced men holding rifles and long sharp swords were a silent promise of the Sultan's willingness to enforce his laws by force.

Three days ago, the Sultan had proclaimed his new order. The laws that had reformed the Ottoman Empire would be propagated in Egypt. Those who heard the pronouncements were shocked. The old ruling class was effectively disbanded and slavery was abolished, while the taxes that had crushed Egypt's merchants were lifted – and the repression of the Jews and Christians was at an end. Henceforth, they would enjoy the same civil rights as their Muslim brothers. A number of street thugs – well used to beating Jews and molesting their womenfolk, for everyone knew that Jewish women were whores – had tried that very evening to sport with the Jews. The green-clad soldiers had beaten them, killed several, and marched their prisoners off to the vast pens that were already being erected outside the city.

The word spread rapidly. In the mosques, the sheikhs and imams worked to raise the anger of the crowd. The day after the beatings saw vast mobs rising up in Cairo, intent on tearing the Sultan and his army limb from limb. Even the Mamelukes had feared the wrath of the crowd; now, with their holy men in the lead, the crowds advanced towards the soldiers. And a special detachment of men – half carrying clubs and shields, the other half carrying whips – advanced to meet them. They had trained hard to deal with rioters. The riot came to a bloody end only a few minutes after the crowd had slammed into the soldiers and had been stopped cold. Hundreds died in the crush; others tried to flee, only to discover that the soldiers were blocking most of the escape routes. The crowd's dominance of the city was brought to an end in blood and pain.

Those that survived were marched out to the holding pens, where their first task was to dig a mass grave for their comrades who hadn't survived the riot. The Sultan had abolished slavery, but there were still vast projects to be undertaken in the empire and he had plans for the rioters. Five years spent helping to dig a canal between the Mediterranean and the Red Sea would teach them their true place in the Ottoman Empire. Egypt's long period of *de facto* independence had come to an end.

Henry Blackburn, still a Lord in the privacy of his own mind, smiled darkly as he saw the crosses outside the Viceroy's palace. The religious leaders of Cairo, the ones who had directed the crowd to its bloody meeting with the Sultan's men, had been crucified, a clear symbol of the Sultan's determination to prove that he was in charge. They would be replaced, his guide had assured him, by religious leaders trained in Istanbul itself, ones trusted to ensure that the Sultan's laws were respected. That, he told himself firmly, was the way to deal with the rabble. None of the coddling that had forced him to flee London; nothing, but brutal punishment. He had little time for Turks and less still for Islam, but perhaps there was something England could learn from their customs.

The new Sultan frowned on the ornate rituals favoured by his predecessors. After a quick search – his pistol and sword were confiscated – Henry found himself being lead into the Viceroy's former throne room. The Ottoman Empire's Viceroy had been powerless; the Mamelukes had kept all the power concentrated in their own hands, even as they swore loyalty to Istanbul. Now...the man standing in the centre of the chamber, surrounded by his green-clad soldiers, was the absolute master of Egypt. Resistance would be crushed mercilessly.

Henry stopped and bowed, using the moment to study the Sultan. He was shorter than Henry had expected from the tales that had been told of his deeds, with bright, almost hypnotic eyes. Rumour attributed all kinds of powers to this man, but even if he didn't have magic, he was clearly a man to be reckoned with. He'd risen from a humble Corsican Janissary to absolute control of the Ottoman Empire. Who else could claim such a climb to power?

"Your Excellency," he said. For once, he found himself tongue-tied. Charm wouldn't work on the Sultan – and would almost certainly lead to his death. England would probably be quietly relieved if the Sultan ever informed them that he'd had one of their people executed. It certainly wouldn't lead to war. "Thank you for granting me this audience."

The Sultan smiled – and in his smile, Henry saw boundless ambition. Who knew how far he could go? The Barbary States, still reeling from the thrashing Lord Nelson had handed out to them, would be easy prey. Or there would be the advance northwards against Austria, or Russia...or Persia. And if the Ottomans crushed the Persians, they'd have a gateway to British India.

"You are welcome," the Sultan said, quietly. His English was perfect, without even a trace of an accent. "And why do you wish to seek asylum with us?"

Henry bowed his head. He hated being a supplicant – let alone having his life depend on someone else – but there was no choice. Remaining in exile would be nothing, apart from a slow death.

"That is a long story, Your Excellency," he said, finally. They could help each other, one to build the greatest empire the world had ever known, the other to return home and extract revenge for his humiliation. "It will take some time to explain."

The Sultan's smile widened. "We have all the time in the world," he said. "Why don't you begin?"

The End

The Royal Sorceress Will Return In:

The Great Game

Elsewhen Press

a small independent publisher specialising in Speculative Fiction

Visit the Elsewhen Press website at elsewhen.co.uk for the latest information on all of our titles, authors and events; to read our blog; find out where to buy our books and ebooks; or to place an order.

Elsewhen Press

a small independent publisher specialising in Speculative Fiction

[Re]Awakenings

AN ANTHOLOGY OF NEW SPECULATIVE FICTION

※ ALISON BUCK ※ NEIL FAARID ※ GINGERLILY ※

※ ROBIN MORAN ※ PR POPE ※ ALEXANDER SKYE ※

※ PETER WOLFE ※

[Re]Awakenings are the starting points for life-changing experiences; a new plane of existence, an alternate reality or cyber-reality. This genre-spanning anthology of new speculative fiction explores that theme with a spectrum of tales, from science fiction to fantasy to paranormal; in styles from clinically serious to joyfully silly. As you read through them all, and you must read all of them, you will discover along the way that stereo-typical distinctions between the genres within speculative fiction are often arbitrary and unhelpful. You will be taken on an emotional journey through a galaxy of sparkling fiction; you will laugh, you will cry; you will consider timeless truths and contemplate eternal questions.

All of life is within these pages, from birth to death (and in some cases beyond). In all of these stories, most of them specifically written for this anthology, the short story format has been used to great effect. If you haven't already heard of some of these authors, you soon will as they are undoubtedly destined to become future stars in the speculative fiction firmament. Remember, you read them here first!

[Re]Awakenings is a collection of short stories from exciting new voices in UK speculative fiction, compiled by guest editor PR Pope. It contains the following stories: Alison Buck: *Dreamers; Intervention; Mirror mirror; Podcast*. Neil Faarid: *The Adventures of Kit Brennan: Kidnapped!* Gingerlily: *The Dragon and the Rose*. Robin Moran: *The Merry Maiden Wails*. PR Pope: *Afterlife; Courtesy Bodies; On the Game*. Alexander Skye: *BlueWinter; Dreaming Mars; Exploring the Heavens; Worth it*. Peter Wolfe: *If you go into the woods today…*

ISBN: 9781908168108 (epub, kindle)
ISBN: 9781908168009 (288pp paperback)

For more information visit bit.ly/ReAwakenings

Visit the Elsewhen Press website at elsewhen.co.uk for the latest information on all of our titles, authors and events; to read our blog; find out where to buy our books and ebooks; or to place an order.

Elsewhen Press

a small independent publisher specialising in Speculative Fiction

ENTANGLEMENT
DOUGLAS THOMPSON

FINALLY, TRAVEL TO THE STARS IS HERE

In 2180, travel to neighbouring star systems has been mastered thanks to quantum teleportation using the 'entanglement' of sub-atomic matter; astronauts on earth can be duplicated on a remote world once the dupliport chamber has arrived there. In this way a variety of worlds can be explored, but what humanity discovers is both surprising and disturbing, enlightening and shocking. Each alternative to mankind that the astronauts find, sheds light on human shortcomings and potential while offering fresh perspectives of life on Earth. Meanwhile, at home, the lives of the astronauts and those in charge of the missions will never be the same again.

Best described as philosophical science fiction, *Entanglement* explores our assumptions about such constants as death, birth, sex and conflict, as the characters in the story explore distant worlds and the intelligent life that lives there. It is simultaneously a novel and a series of short stories: multiple worlds, each explored in a separate chapter, a separate story; every one another step on mankind's journey outwards to the stars and inwards to our own psyche. Yet the whole is much greater than the sum of the parts; the synergy of the episodes results in an overarching story arc that ultimately tells us more about ourselves than about the rest of the universe.

Douglas Thompson's short stories have appeared in a wide range of magazines and anthologies. He won the Grolsch/Herald Question of Style Award in 1989 and second prize in the Neil Gunn Writing Competition in 2007. His first book, *Ultrameta*, published in 2009, was nominated for the Edge Hill Prize, and shortlisted for the BFS Best Newcomer Award. *Entanglement* is his fifth novel.

ISBN: 9781908168153 (epub, kindle)
ISBN: 9781908168054 (336pp paperback)

For more information visit bit.ly/EntanglementBook

Visit the Elsewhen Press website at elsewhen.co.uk for the latest information on all of our titles, authors and events; to read our blog; find out where to buy our books and ebooks; or to place an order.

Elsewhen Press

a small independent publisher specialising in Speculative Fiction

Queens of Antares

Bloodline returned

VOLUME 1 OF THE BLOODLINE TRILOGY

PR POPE

What would you do if you found out your dotty old Gran wasn't from Surrey after all, but from a planet six hundred light years away across the galaxy? Not only that, but she's really an exiled Princess from a Royal family that has been virtually wiped out by a tyrannical usurper. Would you believe it?

That's the question being asked by Caroline, Alex and Emily Wright, after moving in with Gran when their Father loses his job.

But you might find it easier to believe, if you were actually standing on that self-same planet looking into a sky with two suns.

That's the situation in which Caroline, Alex and Emily find themselves when they accidentally get transported across the galaxy.

Would you join the fight for freedom against the tyrant, if that was the only way to get back home to Earth?

You now understand the dilemma facing Caroline, Alex and Emily.

What would you do?

Queens of Antares: Bloodline is a new trilogy for readers of all ages from 10 to 100. Already compared to CS Lewis and CJ Cherryh, PR Pope weaves an enchanting tale around three young people who are accidentally transported from their mundane lives to a new world, where they must find the strength to lead a revolution in order to make their way home. On the way they discover who they really are, where they belong and the enduring power of a bloodline.

ISBN: 9781908168115 (epub, kindle)
ISBN: 9781908168016 (224pp paperback)

For more information visit www.queensofantares.co.uk

Visit the Elsewhen Press website at elsewhen.co.uk for the latest information on all of our titles, authors and events; to read our blog; find out where to buy our books and ebooks; or to place an order.

Elsewhen Press

a small independent publisher specialising in Speculative Fiction

BLUE FRIDAY
MIKE FRENCH

In the Britain of 2034 overtime for married couples is banned, there is enforced viewing of family television (much of it repeats of old shows from the sixties and seventies), monitored family meal-times and a coming of age where twenty-five year-olds are automatically assigned a spouse by the state computer if they have failed to marry. Only the Overtime Underground network resists.

Dystopian science fiction, *Blue Friday* tells of a future where many live in fear of the Family Protection Agency, a special police division enforcing the strict legislation that has been introduced to protect the family unit. Combining dark humour with a vision of the future that inverts the classic dystopian nightmare, this latest novel from Mike French follows in the tradition of great Speculative Fiction satirists such as Jonathan Swift. Thoughtful, while at the same time prompting a wry smile in the reader, it reverses the usual perception of a future regime driven by productivity and industrial output at the expense of family, demonstrating that the converse may be no better.

Mike French is the owner and senior editor of the prestigious literary magazine, *The View From Here*. Mike's debut novel, *The Ascent of Isaac Steward* was published in 2011 and nominated for The Galaxy National Book Awards. *Blue Friday* is his second novel. He currently lives in Luton with his wife, three children and a growing number of pets.

ISBN: 9781908168177 (epub, kindle)
ISBN: 9781908168078 (192pp paperback) November 2012

Visit the Elsewhen Press website at elsewhen.co.uk for the latest information on all of our titles, authors and events; to read our blog; find out where to buy our books and ebooks; or to place an order.

About the author

hristopher Nuttall has been planning sci-fi books since he learned to read. Born and raised in Edinburgh, Chris created an alternate history website and eventually graduated to writing full-sized novels. Studying history independently allowed him to develop worlds that hung together and provided a base for storytelling. After graduating from university, Chris started writing full-time. As an indie author, he has published five novels (so far) through Amazon Kindle Direct Publishing. The Royal Sorceress is his first novel to be professionally published. Chris is currently living in Borneo with his wife, muse, and critic Aisha.